G000134859

FATAL BETRAYAL

Off The Grid: FBI Series

BARBARA FREETHY

Fog City Publishing

PRAISE FOR BARBARA FREETHY

"Barbara Freethy's suspense novels are explosively good!" — *New York Times bestselling author Toni Anderson.*

"A fabulous, page-turning combination of romance and intrigue. Fans of Nora Roberts and Elizabeth Lowell will love this book." — *NYT Bestselling Author Kristin Hannah on Golden Lies*

"Powerful and absorbing...sheer hold-your-breath suspense." — *NYT Bestselling Author Karen Robards on Don't Say A Word*

"Barbara Freethy delivers riveting, plot-twisting suspense and a deeply emotional story. Every book is a thrilling ride." *USA Today Bestselling Author Rachel Grant*

"Freethy is at the top of her form. Fans of Nora Roberts will find a similar tone here, framed in Freethy's own spare, elegant style." — *Contra Costa Times on Summer Secrets*

"Freethy hits the ground running as she kicks off another winning romantic suspense series...Freethy is at her prime with a superb combo of engaging characters and gripping plot." — *Publishers' Weekly on Silent Run*

"PERILOUS TRUST is a non-stop thriller that seamlessly melds jaw-dropping suspense with sizzling romance, and I was riveted from the first page to the last...Readers will be breathless in anticipation as this fast-paced and enthralling love story evolves and goes in unforeseeable directions." — *USA Today HEA Blog*

PRAISE FOR BARBARA FREETHY

"Barbara Freethy is a master storyteller with a gift for spinning tales about ordinary people in extraordinary situations and drawing readers into their lives." — *Romance Reviews Today*

"Freethy (Silent Fall) has a gift for creating complex, appealing characters and emotionally involving, often suspenseful, sometimes magical stories."— *Library Journal on Suddenly One Summer*

"If you love nail-biting suspense and heartbreaking emotion, Silent Run belongs on the top of your to-be-bought list. I could not turn the pages fast enough."— *NYT Bestselling Author Mariah Stewart*

"Hooked me from the start and kept me turning pages throughout all the twists and turns. Silent Run is powerful romantic intrigue at its best."— *NYT Bestselling Author JoAnn Ross*

"An absorbing story of two people determined to unravel the secrets, betrayals, and questions about their past. The story builds to an explosive conclusion that will leave readers eagerly awaiting Barbara Freethy's next book."—*NYT Bestselling Author Carla Neggars on Don't Say A Word*

"A page-turner that engages your mind while it tugs at your heartstrings ... DON'T SAY A WORD had made me a Barbara Freethy fan for life!" —*NYT Bestselling Author Diane Chamberlain*

"*On Shadow Beach* teems with action, drama and compelling situations... a fast-paced page-turner." —*BookPage*

ALSO BY BARBARA FREETHY

Off the Grid: FBI Series

PERILOUS TRUST

RECKLESS WHISPER

DESPERATE PLAY

ELUSIVE PROMISE

DANGEROUS CHOICE

RUTHLESS CROSS

CRITICAL DOUBT

FEARLESS PURSUIT

DARING DECEPTION

RISKY BARGAIN

PERFECT TARGET

FATAL BETRAYAL

Lightning Strikes Trilogy

BEAUTIFUL STORM

LIGHTNING LINGERS

SUMMER RAIN

Mystery Thriller Standalones

ALL THE PRETTY PEOPLE

LAST ONE TO KNOW

For a complete list of books, visit Barbara's website at
www.barbarafreethy.com

FATAL BETRAYAL

© Copyright 2023 Barbara Freethy
All Rights Reserved

No part of this book may be used or reproduced in any manner whatsoever
without written permission except in the case of brief quotations embodied in
critical articles and reviews.

This is a work of fiction. Names, characters, places, and incidents are products of
the author's imagination or are used fictitiously. Any resemblance to actual
events, locales, organizations or persons, living or dead, is entirely coincidental.

For more information on Barbara Freethy's books, visit her website:
www.barbarafreethy.com

PROLOGUE

EIGHTEEN YEARS EARLIER....

Fourteen-year-old Andi Hart hopped off her bike as she and Cooper Bradford reached the top of the hill. Her heart was pumping, and she was sweating in her shorts and tank top. It was almost ten o'clock at night, and it was still seventy-five degrees in Beachwood Canyon, a hilly neighborhood just below the infamous Hollywood sign. The streets were steep and curvy, with single homes tucked in between thick trees.

The moon was full tonight, giving them plenty of light, which should make their job easier. They walked their bikes behind the big oak tree across the street from where their principal, Donald Jenkins, lived. Mr. Jenkins was a married man whose wife and baby had gone to Texas for the week to visit his wife's mother.

Andi probably shouldn't know that, but she'd made it her business to know everything about the man who had gotten her favorite teacher suspended two days ago. She couldn't just stand by and do nothing when someone she liked was in trouble.

"This is stupid," Cooper declared.

She turned her head and frowned at his look of annoyance. She'd been seeing that look a lot on his face. In the past year, he'd grown three inches, his blond hair had gotten longer, and his teenage body was filling out in a way that made her feel a little uncomfortable around him. They'd been best friends since they were eight, but lately Cooper seemed to find her irritating and she sometimes felt that way about him, too.

"It's not stupid," she said. "It's going to happen. We just have to wait."

"You don't know if anything is going to happen, and even if you're right, even if Mr. Jenkins is banging his wife's best friend, what are we going to do about it?"

"We're going to use it as leverage to get him to bring Ms. Taylor back. He only suspended her because she made us read a book he doesn't like."

Cooper gave her a long-suffering look. "You are not going to blackmail our principal, Andi. You'll get thrown out of school. You'll get us both expelled. And I don't think our parents are going to be happy about that."

"He won't know it's us. We'll just take some photos and send them to Mr. Jenkins anonymously. We don't have to do anything else. He won't want his wife to know. He'll cave," she said confidently. But Cooper's doubts were giving her some doubts as well. She didn't want to get expelled, although that might actually get her parents to pay some attention to her.

Cooper sat down on the curb, stretching out his long legs. "You know you don't have to make up shit just to get out of the house, Andi. There doesn't have to be a big mystery to solve. You could have just said you wanted to go for a ride, so you didn't have to hear your parents fight."

"I'm not making this up. I heard Ms. Taylor talking to her friend on the phone about how Mr. Jenkins had a lot of nerve trying to act like he was so ethical when it was clear he was cheating on his wife."

"Then maybe she should be trying to blackmail him instead

of us," Cooper said, always practical. "What are your parents fighting about tonight?"

She hated that he knew her so well. "Who knows?" She sat down on the curb next to him. "I don't like listening to them. It makes me want to throw up."

"Do you think they're going to get a divorce?"

Her stomach churned at that thought. She didn't want her parents to split up, but a part of her thought they might all be happier if they did. "I don't know. I don't want to talk about it. Look, Mr. Jenkins turned a light on upstairs, and the curtains are open."

"There aren't any cars around. I don't think anyone else is there," Cooper said. "This is a bad plan, Andi."

"You don't have to stay."

"Yes, I do," he said, meeting her gaze. "I always do."

An odd little flutter ran through her. She didn't understand it. She didn't want anything to change between them, but it seemed to be happening anyway. Although, he did keep coming out with her, even if he spent a lot of time telling her how dumb her ideas were. Maybe they were stupid. Maybe she was just looking for a distraction, something else to think about, some problem she could actually fix.

The lights in the house they were watching suddenly went out.

"That's it," Cooper said. "Nothing is going to happen tonight. Nothing that we can see, anyway."

"Maybe not," she said wearily. Now, she'd have to go home and hope that the fight was over. She reluctantly got to her feet and got on her bike.

As they headed back down the windy hilly streets that led to their houses, which were directly across the street from each other, the wind blew her brown-haired ponytail back and she felt the coolest she'd been all day.

She loved being out at night. In the dark shadows, she felt free. Of course, her parents didn't know she was out. They thought she was in her room, and they'd be too busy fighting to notice she was gone.

She remembered when her mom and dad used to creep into her room after she'd gone to bed. They'd tuck her in, kiss her forehead, and whisper that they loved her. She'd always pretended to be asleep because she liked the feeling of their love. And when they were gone, she'd sneak her book out and read by flashlight until she couldn't keep her eyes open. But they hadn't come into her room in a long time.

Her anger and sadness sent her flying down the hill, even faster than she usually liked to ride. She was almost at the bottom of the hill when a car sped through the intersection, and she slammed on the brakes, stopping so fast she almost landed in the bushes of the house on the corner.

Cooper caught up to her a second later. "What's wrong with you?" he asked. "Why are you riding so fast?"

"It was a hill. Did you see that car that almost hit me? I think it was your brother's car."

"I saw a car; it wasn't my brother's. He's at a concert with Will. He probably won't be back until midnight. I can't wait until I'm eighteen and don't have to be back in the house by eleven on weekends."

She thought he was lucky his parents cared enough to give him a curfew, but he wouldn't appreciate that. Instead, she said, "I'd like to go to a concert. My mom says I'm too young." She let out a sigh. "I'm so tired of being too young."

He laughed. "You'll get there."

"Hey, you're only six months older than me," she reminded him.

"Yeah, and I've already been to a concert," he bragged.

She rolled her eyes. "Only because you have an older brother. I had to be an only child."

"Sometimes, I wouldn't mind being an only. Monica is a pest," he said, referring to his younger sister. "And Kyle—well, he's Kyle."

She nodded. His older brother definitely had some issues, but he wasn't a bad kid, just a little weird. She was about to get back on her bike when sirens pierced the air. A moment later, two police cars raced past them, coming to a screeching halt at a house around the corner.

"What's that about?" she asked. "Let's check it out."

"Andi, wait," Cooper said.

But she was already on her bike, riding around the corner and down the block. Five houses in, she saw the cars had stopped in front of the Montgomery's house. Mrs. Montgomery was in the yard. She was crying and the nanny, Gemma, had her arm around her while Mr. Montgomery talked to the police.

Another police car pulled up as neighbors came out of their houses, including their friend TJ Lassiter, who lived next door to the Montgomery's home. The red-haired, freckle-faced kid saw them on the sidewalk and came over.

"Do you know what's going on?" she asked.

"I heard Mrs. Montgomery yelling that Hannah is missing," TJ said. "They were all running around the yard. Mr. Montgomery pounded on my door. Scared the shit out of me. I didn't know what was going on. I let him in our side gate and went in the yard with him to look for her, but I didn't see her. She's a baby. How could she have run away?"

"She's not a baby; she's two," Andi said, her heart pounding against her chest at the thought of Hannah being missing. She'd babysat Hannah last weekend, and she was a sweet little girl with blonde hair, blue eyes, and a big smile. How could she be gone?

"She must have gotten out of her crib," TJ said. He paused. "Hey, there's Will." He waved to his older brother, who was walking down the street.

"What's happened?" Will asked.

"Hannah is missing."

"Like she's lost?" Will drawled. As he moved closer, Andi wrinkled her nose. He smelled like weed. Actually, both he and

TJ smelled like that, which was becoming more and more the norm with those two.

"Like someone took her," TJ said.

"We don't know what happened," Cooper interjected. "I'm sure she's somewhere. She's just hiding."

"Hannah loves to play hide-and-seek," she said, having first-hand knowledge of Hannah's love of the game on the times she'd babysat for her when the nanny had the night off. "That has to be it. They'll find her soon."

As they all turned toward the scene, she reached for Cooper and grabbed his hand. For a second, she thought he might pull away, and then he tightened his fingers around hers.

"It's going to be okay," he told her.

She really wanted to believe him.

CHAPTER ONE

PRESENT DAY...

Andi Hart woke up in a sweat, rolling over in bed as the morning light streamed through her window Tuesday morning. She hated when Cooper and Hannah invaded her dreams, because all their lives had changed forever on that summer night. She should have stopped reliving that horrific event by now, but the memories always came back. She knew why they had returned now, because today was her official first day back in Los Angeles after a very long absence.

She drew in a breath and slowly blew it out, trying to calm her still-racing heart. As she glanced at the clock, she realized it was almost nine, and her never-ending nightmare had made her late for work. Scrambling out of bed, she hurried into the bathroom, taking the fastest shower of her life. She hated to be late under any circumstance, but today was especially bad. She was starting her new job as an agent on Flynn MacKenzie's FBI task force.

It didn't matter that Flynn had told her not to come in early, knowing she was taking a late-night flight back from New York and hadn't even had a chance to fully move into her new apartment, but she hadn't wanted to take him up on that offer. At this point, she had no choice.

After throwing on gray slacks, a blouse, and a black blazer, she pulled her brown hair into a ponytail and dashed down the stairs. While her apartment was still basically empty, awaiting a bigger furniture delivery, she had picked up a coffeemaker when she'd gotten the keys two weeks ago, knowing that a bed and coffee were the two things she couldn't live without.

Thankfully, the coffeemaker had made her desperately needed morning dose of caffeine on schedule. Grabbing her keys, she raced out the door and headed to her new office. She'd been reading about Flynn and his team's exploits the past few years and was more than a little impressed, but not really surprised. She'd met Flynn on her first day at Quantico and many other members of his team had come from their class. It was difficult to believe that had been seven years ago.

Back then, she'd been a twenty-five-year-old kid, one of the youngest trainees in the class. She'd been incredibly green, but her ambition and drive had gotten her through the academy and into some great jobs since then. She'd worked her way through field offices around the country, specializing in kidnappings, with a focus on children. Flynn had asked her several times to join his team, but when his kidnapping specialist Bree Adams had gone on an extended maternity leave, he'd become even more persuasive. Lured by the idea of having more autonomy on cases, she'd finally said yes.

She was excited to work with Flynn again. He'd managed to not only climb the organizational ladder in record time but had also been able to break away and create his own unit, a team that worked fast and often away from the layers of bureaucracy that could slow down an investigation. She didn't know how he'd gotten all that power, but she was looking forward to working with a unit that could move fast and under the radar.

Despite her excitement about the future, as she drove

through the streets of the beachside city of Santa Monica in LA county, her thoughts turned to the past. She'd never lived in this city, but it was only about thirty minutes away from where she'd grown up in Beachwood Canyon, in the Hollywood Hills. She'd been to Santa Monica many times, usually on her way to the famous pier and adjacent beach. But this mid-March day was partly cloudy and cool, and there was no beach traffic, just people trying to get to work and a few tourists.

She hadn't lived in LA since she was fourteen, and while she'd returned a few times over the years, it had been six years since her last very short visit, which had comprised a brief work meeting and a bittersweet reunion with her estranged father that had turned more bitter than sweet when she'd stumbled upon another one of his transgressions. That had been the last time they'd spoken. And she wasn't sure they'd ever talk again.

Frowning, she dragged her thoughts ruthlessly back to the present. There might be some personal ghosts in this city, but it was the real monsters she needed to catch and put away. She could build a life for herself in the present. Santa Monica wasn't Beachwood Canyon, and she wasn't a kid anymore. She was a federal agent, one who was very good at her job. That's what she would focus on, what she always focused on, and she was eager to get to work and drive all the shadowy memories of the past out of her head.

The task force offices were in a nondescript three-story building in Santa Monica with absolutely no signage. She parked in an empty spot and jumped on the elevator at half-past ten. The office suite was on the second floor. There was no reception, just two double doors leading into a large open space filled with desks, computers, and people at work. Several glass-walled offices and conference areas ran around the perimeter.

As she moved into the space, Flynn came out of the largest office to greet her with a big bear hug. With his blond surfer looks and big smile, Flynn had an instinct for charming and disarming. It was impossible to dislike him. Although, he didn't look much like a surfer today in his tan slacks and button-down shirt.

"You made it," Flynn said.

"I had hoped to be here earlier, but my flight was delayed, and I didn't get to my apartment until after two AM. It was a little difficult getting up this morning."

"You could have taken the day off," he said. "I told you that."

"I know. But I'm eager to get started. And I'm still waiting for most of my furniture and boxes to arrive anyway."

"Andi," a woman exclaimed. "You're here. I can hardly believe it."

She smiled as Savannah joined them. The former beauty queen was dressed down in dark jeans and a turquoise sweater that set off her blonde hair and light-green eyes. "It's true. How are you?"

"I'm good and slightly pregnant." Savannah put her hand on her belly. "Four months."

"Congratulations. That's wonderful."

"Thank you. I'm so glad Flynn finally talked you into joining us."

"She was a tough nut to crack," Flynn said. "I practically had to beg."

"It wasn't that bad," she said dryly. "But you did put the pressure on."

"I had to. With Bree out of commission for the next year, I need your expertise on my team. There have been a lot of changes around here the past year. Not only is Bree out, but Wyatt has also moved to Ohio. His wife, Avery, got a big job at NASA. Lucas is now heading up the office in Dallas, and Diego has gone international. Oh, and Savannah will be on desk duty for a while."

"Everyone is making changes."

"But we still have a good team," Flynn said. "And you're not the only new hire. Here's one more now."

She turned her head to see Nick Caruso heading toward

them. Nick had also been in their class and was a darkly handsome man with jet-black hair and brown eyes. He wore dark jeans and a polo shirt under a lightweight bomber jacket.

"Hello Andi, Flynn, Savannah," Nick said. "Looks like I finally made it to the big leagues."

Despite his words, she knew Nick did not lack confidence in any area. He was incredibly smart, insightful, and was exceptionally good at finding someone's weakness.

"Me, too," she said with a grin.

"Yeah, yeah," Flynn said with a wry smile. "You two don't have to butter me up. I only pick the best people, and you both have had many opportunities to join me before now. I'm just glad it finally happened. Elia Khan will also join us in a few weeks. As soon as she finishes up her work on an investigation in Miami."

"That's awesome," she said. "I haven't seen Elia in years."

"So, where do we start, boss?" Nick asked.

"I'm putting you with Caitlyn, Nick. She'll read you in on an ecoterrorism case we're developing. She should be here any second. In the meantime, grab some coffee and say hello to old friends."

"I could use some coffee," Nick said.

"The breakroom is out the door and down the hall to the left," Flynn said.

"We'll catch up later, Andi," Nick promised.

"I'm looking forward to it."

As Nick left, Flynn turned to her. "We've been working on a slowly developing trafficking case that I want you to weigh in on. Savannah will get you the pertinent information. It's early in the investigation. We're just starting to dig in."

"Great."

"I'll show you to your desk," Savannah said, as Flynn's admin told him he had a call.

Savannah led her to an empty desk by the window. "It's not an ocean view, but you'll get some sun."

"It's fine," she said, setting her bag on the desk. "I can work anywhere."

"Dana is the office admin. She ordered you some business cards for when you need to operate in an official capacity." Savannah motioned to the small box on the desk next to a mobile phone. "That's your new phone. Our team numbers are programmed in. I assume you're using your own weapon?"

"I am," she said, tapping the gun at her waist. "Do we work in teams, have partners, go solo?"

"All of the above. Depending on the case, you could be undercover on your own, working with a partner or part of a bigger team. In this unit, we check our egos at the door. Lead agents change on every case. Sometimes you're in charge, sometimes you're backup. We do what we need to do to get the job done. While we sometimes work with the LA office and share resources, we mostly work independently."

"How does that go?"

"Very well, because Damon and Flynn get along great."

She nodded. "I know they were always good friends when they weren't competing to be the best, but it's still hard for me to understand how Flynn could build this unit without oversight and with so much flexibility. How did he manage that?"

"Flynn has a way with people, especially the director, and this unit has proven itself to be extremely valuable, which has given us even more leeway." Savannah paused. "Why don't I grab the file on the investigation we're starting and meet you in the conference room in a few minutes?"

"Sounds good."

"That's going to have to wait," Flynn said, interrupting their conversation with a grim look on his face. "I need you, Andi."

"What's happened?"

"A six-month-old baby was kidnapped from her home this morning. Damon heard you were working for me now, and he wants you to run the case through our unit."

"All right." A surge of adrenaline ran through her, as it did at the start of every investigation. "Details?"

"Not many," Flynn replied. "Nanny was home with the baby while parents were at work. She went to check on the child, and she wasn't in the crib. Back door was open. No sign of forced entry. The alarm was off." Flynn paused. "I'll drive you to the house. Damon will meet us there. Savannah, can you set up a team here? We'll need security footage from the homes and businesses in the area. Address is 416 Manor Drive, Beverly Hills."

"There should be plenty of security systems in that expensive neighborhood," Savannah commented.

"Apparently, home security at this property wasn't operational, but hopefully someone else's camera caught something," Flynn said. "Let's get our forensics team out there as well."

"I'm on it," Savannah said.

"Ready to jump into the fire, Andi?" Flynn asked.

"Always. Let's go. She grabbed her new phone and put a few business cards into her pocket, leaving her bag behind. Then she followed Flynn down to the garage, her mind sprinting with the few details she'd been given. There was a ticking clock with kidnappings. Every single minute counted. She couldn't afford to waste even one.

As Flynn drove, Andi looked for information about the family on her phone. Neil Benedict, the father of the missing child, was a movie producer, following in the footsteps of his famous father, Robert Benedict, who had produced several blockbuster films in the seventies and eighties. While Neil hadn't reached the same superstar status, he had several successful films, including a documentary that had won an Emmy the previous year.

Neil had been married twice, having divorced his first wife of thirteen years, an actress by the name of Shana Grier, three years ago. He'd married his current wife, Claire, a children's casting agent, a year ago, and they'd had a baby named Elisa a few months later.

They were a very attractive family, she thought, feeling a pang of worry for the smiling infant with the curly blonde hair and big blue eyes captured in the photo taken and shared on social media on Valentine's Day. She made a mental note to look for more public shares that might have resulted in raising someone's interest in the child.

As she thought about what she learned, she had one big question. "I'm still not clear on why the LA office is handing this case to us," she said. "They have a dedicated team working on kidnappings in the county and far more resources. With the Benedict's stature in the community, there will be media interest, and usually that requires a formal FBI presence."

"Yes, you're right, but there are extenuating circumstances," Flynn said. "The father of the missing child, Neil Benedict, is currently making a docuseries on falsely accused and incarcerated individuals based on a book by the infamous forensic psychologist, Cooper Bradford."

She stiffened at the mention of Cooper's name, shocked to hear that her childhood friend had a connection to Neil Benedict. "Seriously?"

"Yes. In the pursuit of that project, Mr. Benedict and Dr. Bradford have had some awkward and confrontational conversations with several agents in the LA office, including one agent who was involved in a previous kidnapping case that had an unresolved outcome."

Her stomach flipped over. She knew exactly which case he was talking about.

"Damon doesn't want any accusations of bias," Flynn continued. "He wants us to take over the case, or, more specifically, you. He'll provide backup resources as needed. With your work in New York, you have a reputation for being one of the best in this area, so it will be a win-win for everyone."

"Got it," she said shortly, hoping that Neil's connection to Cooper wasn't going to bring her former best friend and now mortal enemy into her orbit. But all she could worry about now was the missing child. "Will we be working together on this? I didn't realize you were still so hands-on, Flynn."

"I love the field," he said with a smile. "You'll be lead. Damon and I will offer support and assure the Benedicts that no stone will be left unturned in getting their daughter back."

She smiled back at him. "I already like my new job. I'm in charge. You and Damon are backing me up. That's sweet. And definitely not the way it was at Quantico, when you two were battling it out as team leaders, and I was just one of the followers."

He laughed. "That was a long time ago. I'm very familiar with your work, Andi. You turned out to be exactly the kind of agent I knew you would be. By the way, your former boss gave you a raving recommendation with one caveat."

"I would have thought any recommendation Eric gave me would come with a caveat, probably something like: doesn't always play nice with others."

"Eric said you were smart and driven and you don't stop until you run out of road and then sometimes you make your own path."

"Which he didn't always appreciate."

"He mentioned he thought you'd do better with fewer people looking over your shoulder. So, take whatever space you need. I trust every agent implicitly and I expect them to use their unique, individual strengths to close out a case."

She realized now why everyone was so excited about working with Flynn. His words almost seemed too good to be true, but he seemed sincere, and it was exciting to work for someone who viewed her with a high level of respect.

They arrived at the family home a few minutes later, a palatial three-story residence in the very expensive neighborhood of Beverly Hills, which was home to many film and television stars, as well as industry executives.

There were two police cars out front and several black SUVs, probably belonging to Damon's team. The police had set up a loose perimeter around the house, and there were more than a few neighbors gathered on the sidewalk.

As her gaze landed on a couple of teenagers on bikes, she felt herself whisked back in time to that night eighteen years ago when she and Cooper had followed police cars to the Montgomery house to find out Hannah was missing. She had wanted so badly to help find that little girl that she'd become obsessed with the case. It had taken up every second of her consciousness for months. It had destroyed her friendship with Cooper and ultimately driven her to her current career.

Forcing herself to look away from the kids, she unfastened her seatbelt and got out of the car. When they moved deeper into the front yard, they were greeted by Damon Wolfe, someone she hadn't seen since Quantico, but his black hair and penetrating blue eyes were still the same.

"Andi," he said with a nod and a brief smile. "It's good to see you again. I'm glad you're here." He tipped his head to the gray-haired man standing next to him. "This is Detective Martinez from the LAPD. Agent Hart and Agent MacKenzie."

"What can you tell us, Detective?" she asked. The older detective had the weary eyes of a seasoned professional. Hopefully, he would be forthcoming with information and support. Her goal was to keep all agencies working together for the benefit of the missing child.

"Call came in at 9:45 a.m. from the nanny, Kristine Rozic," the detective answered. He consulted a small notebook in his hand. "Officers arrived within seven minutes. Mother arrived four minutes after that. Father came in at just after ten. No sign of forced entry. Back door of the house was open. Security camera on the front door didn't pick up any unusual activity. Alarm was off. Cameras at the back of the house were disabled and offline." He looked up from his notes. "Mr. Benedict said they had just finished a remodel addition at the back of the house and had yet to reinstall the cameras. I'll make our interviews available to you, but there isn't much more to report. Forensics hasn't picked up anything of note, but they're still working. Let us know how else we can help."

"Thank you."

As the detective moved away, she turned to Damon. "Does the family have any idea who might have taken their child?"

He shook his head. "They said they've had no problems, altercations, or threats from anyone in their personal or work lives."

"Ransom demand?"

"Not yet, but they are extremely wealthy, so my guess is it's coming."

"I want to talk to the parents and the nanny," she said.

"They're waiting inside," Damon replied. "I'm going to head back to the office. Keep me posted. This case will no doubt become very high profile as soon as the media gets wind of it. We need to move fast."

"Our favorite way to move," Flynn said.

When they entered the house, they were met by another patrol officer, who escorted them into the living room where a half-dozen people were gathered.

She spotted the parents immediately. Neil Benedict, a forty-three-year-old male with leading-man good looks, dark-brown hair and eyes, and a fit physique, stood by the fireplace talking to an older man with similar features. She guessed that was his father, Robert.

The mother, Claire Benedict, was sitting on the couch sobbing as she talked to an older woman, who was probably her mother-in-law. An older Hispanic woman and a young blonde were standing in another corner of the room, looking extremely uncomfortable. She was guessing one of them was the nanny.

As they moved into the room, Neil came forward to greet them.

"Mr. Benedict," she said. "I'm Agent Hart. This is Agent MacKenzie."

"Thank God you're here," he said fervently. "You have to

bring Elisa home. She's only six months old. She won't know where she is, where we are."

She could hear the panic in his voice. "I know you've told the police everything, but I need you to go through it once more for me. Can you do that?" she asked, wanting him to focus on facts and not fear.

He cleared his throat. "Of course."

"Why don't you start by introducing me to everyone else?" she suggested.

"My father, Robert Benedict, my mother, Julia, my wife, Claire." He tipped his head to the nearby women. "Our nanny, Kristine Rozic, and our housekeeper, Solange Guerrero."

"Let's all sit down," she said, as the group settled into the large seating area, Neil and his wife sat on the couch, along with his parents, with Kristine and Solange on a nearby loveseat while she took a seat in one of the armchairs. Flynn hovered nearby. She didn't know if Flynn wanted to observe her in action or was there to lend support, but she didn't care either way. Her only interest was in the facts of the case.

"Can you tell me what happened this morning?" she asked. "Let's start with you, Mr. Benedict." The nanny probably had the most information, but she wanted to hear from the parents first.

"I got up at six," Neil said. "When I left the bedroom, Claire was asleep, and Kristine was in the family room giving Elisa a bottle. I kissed Elisa on the forehead…" His voice broke and he drew in a big breath. "She gave me a sweet smile, and I told her I'd see her later. *God!* I have to see her again. I just have to."

At his words, Claire started to cry, and the two embraced.

She gave them a moment, then continued. "What time did you leave the house, Mr. Benedict?"

"About seven," Neil said, pulling himself together. "I went to the gym for an hour and then to my office."

"What about you, Mrs. Benedict? How did your morning go?"

"I woke up around seven thirty," Claire said, struggling to get the words out. "I got dressed, grabbed a coffee, and then I went into the yard where Kristine and Elisa were playing. They were sitting on a big blanket on the grass in the sunshine. Elisa loves to be outside. She was so happy."

"How long were you in the yard?"

"About ten minutes. I had a work meeting at nine, so I had to leave." Claire's face crumpled. "I don't think I told Elisa that I loved her."

She steeled herself against the heartbreaking note in Claire's voice. Her job was not to get emotional but to find the baby. She turned to Kristine, her gaze running over the young woman's pretty face. She was probably in her early twenties and looked teary and shocked, but she was holding it together. "When did you go back into the house?"

"I didn't look at the time," Kristine said, an accent in her voice that Andi couldn't quite place. "It was just after Claire left, so I think it was about eight-thirty. Elisa had been up since six, and she was getting cranky. I changed her diaper, read her a book and then I put her down for a nap around nine. She usually sleeps for about an hour in the morning."

"Where did you go after you put her in her crib?"

"I went to my room. I had the baby monitor on," she added defensively. "Everything was quiet. I didn't hear a thing. Elisa never cried or anything."

"What were you doing in your room?"

Kristine looked startled by her question. "Uh, I was watching a show on my tablet. But I didn't have my head-phones on. I would have heard Elisa if she cried, but she didn't cry."

"When did you check on her?"

"Around nine-thirty. I couldn't believe my eyes when she wasn't in the crib. I couldn't imagine what had happened to her."

"Where is your room in relationship to Elisa's room?"

"It's down the hall. There's a bathroom and a guestroom in between," Kristine answered.

"Do you remember closing the door to the backyard when you came inside?"

"I'm sure I did, but it was open when I ran downstairs."

"Why did you run downstairs? What did you think had happened?" she asked curiously.

"I thought Claire or Neil had come home and taken the baby downstairs or outside. But there was no one in the house or the yard. I called Neil and told him what happened and then I called the police. Everyone arrived within a few minutes." Kristine blew out a breath. "I don't know what happened. I can't believe she's gone."

There appeared to be genuine fear and emotion in Kristine's eyes, but it was interesting that she had called Neil before she'd contacted the police.

"You have to find her," Neil said. "It's almost noon. She's going to be hungry."

"And scared," Claire mumbled through more body-shaking sobs. She gave Andi a desperate look. "I have to get her back. I have to hold her in my arms again."

"I will do everything I can to find her." She paused, looking at Solange. "Were you in the house this morning, Ms. Guerrero? Do you live here as well?"

"I only stay here when I work late, a couple of times a year," Solange said. "I wasn't here last night or this morning. I got here right after the police did."

She stood up. "I'd like to see the baby's room and also your room, Ms. Rozic."

"I'll take you upstairs," Neil said.

Leaving Flynn with the rest of the family, she followed Neil up a grand staircase to the second floor. He pointed out the master bedroom, which was just across the hall from Elisa's room. As they stepped into the baby's room, she was impressed by how beautifully decorated it was. Everything was luxurious and very pink.

Along with the crib, there was a beautiful rocker in the

corner, a changing table, dresser, and walls filled with art and photographs. A mobile with circus animals hung over the crib. The windows were closed. There was a door to an adjacent bathroom and one to the hall. She checked out the bathroom, then asked Neil to show her Kristine's room.

It was at the end of the hall with the guestroom and bathroom in between, but still not that far from Elisa's room. The furnishings were comfortable but not over the top, a queen-size bed that was neatly made, a desk that held a laptop computer, and a matching dresser. A pair of running shoes were by the bed.

"The police already went through these rooms," Neil said. "I don't think they found anything."

"How long has Kristine worked for you?" she asked, turning to face him.

"Four months. We hired her when Elisa was two months old. She came highly recommended. She worked for a friend of mine before the family moved."

"Where is she from? I heard a slight accent."

"Croatia originally. But I believe she spent some time in Belarus before coming to the US for college."

"Where did she go to school?"

"She went to Long Beach State. She graduated three years ago and has been working as a nanny since then." He paused, his lips tightening. "You don't think she had something to do with this, do you? Kristine is a sweet girl, very good to Elisa. We've been happy with her work."

"I'm just asking questions. Kristine was the only one here, so her actions will be under a microscope. What about Solange? How long has she worked for you?"

"I've known Solange for ten years. She worked for me and my first wife for a long time. She actually stayed with Shana after we divorced, but last year she told me that she and Shana weren't getting along that well and asked if I would hire her, which I did. She's great. And she also helps with Elisa when Kristine has time off."

"Okay. Is there anyone you might suspect of doing this? Anyone who doesn't like you? Unusual visitors to the house? Threats?"

"No. Nothing. I've already gone over all of this with the police. We need to stop talking and start acting," he said in frustration.

"We're already acting. We're gathering security footage around the area, interviewing neighbors, and going over any forensic evidence that may have come to light during the initial search. We're going to do everything we can to bring your little girl home."

"They won't hurt her, right? This has to be about money." He ran a hand through his disheveled hair. "But no one has asked me for anything yet."

"That could still happen. If someone contacts you or your wife, they'll ask you not to talk to the police or to us, but you must tell us. You cannot handle this on your own," she said firmly. "I cannot emphasize that enough."

"I'll pay anything to get her back."

"I understand, but we want to act in a way that will bring her back. Money is your leverage. Don't give it up without talking to me. Do you understand? This is really important, Mr. Benedict."

"I get it."

"Good. One more thing. The press will start to hound you, too. They may set up camp in your front yard. The police will keep them away from your door, but you'll feel pressure to speak to them. Don't."

He stared back at her, his mouth twisting into a frown. "Why not? Maybe they can help find her. Why wouldn't we want as much publicity as we can get?"

"We'll handle the press. We'll use them the right way. But you and your wife and your family need to stay silent. The first twenty-four hours are critical. We don't want anyone to know what you're thinking, what you're feeling, what you want to say."

"That doesn't make sense. What harm is there in saying I want my daughter back? If it's because you think the ransom demand will go up, I don't care. I'll pay anything."

"It's not about that. We don't need to give the kidnapper any insight into the investigation. We will speak to the media when appropriate, not before." Talking parents out of speaking to the press was always one of her most difficult jobs, but she'd seen too many times the downside of a parent's desperate, panicked comments.

"I need to go back to my wife," Neil said, not making any promises, but she hoped that he'd heard her.

"Of course."

As they went down the stairs, she saw a tall man arguing with the police officer at the front door. He turned his head toward them, and her heart stopped.

She stumbled down the next step, grabbing on to the railing so she wouldn't fall. She couldn't believe what she was seeing. But it was him. The once dirty-blond hair was a light brown now, and his body had filled out to match his frame, but his eyes were just as green, just as sharp, just as surprised.

"It's okay," Neil told the police officer, moving ahead of her. "I asked Cooper to come."

Her blood thundered through her veins. She'd told herself a million times that coming back to LA didn't mean she would see Cooper again, but he was here. One of her ghosts had just come back to life.

CHAPTER TWO

"AGENT HART, this is Dr. Cooper Bradford, a forensic psychologist," Neil said when she managed to get down the final few stairs. "He's an expert on criminal behavior. I think he might be able to help us."

She stared at Cooper, knowing she was probably giving away far too much in her eyes, but she couldn't put on her usual professional mask. This man had once been her best friend in the world, the one who had known her better than anyone else. But that friendship had shattered eighteen years ago.

"We've met before," Cooper said shortly, his gaze running across her face, a much more guarded expression in his eyes.

"Yes," she agreed.

"Good," Neil said, completely oblivious to the undercurrents running between them. "I want you to work together."

"What?" she asked in shock.

"I'll do whatever I can to help," Cooper said. "I'm so sorry, Neil."

"It's a nightmare," Neil said. "My baby girl gets taken right out of her crib. Who does that? Who commits that kind of crime?"

Since Neil had addressed his question to Cooper, she was

curious to hear how he would answer. While she hadn't seen him since she was a teenager, she was familiar with his work.

Cooper had gotten a Ph.D. in criminal psychology and had written several bestselling books on falsely accused criminals and the biases inherent in profiling. He also had a hugely popular podcast and was a frequent guest on talk shows. But while the media and the public might like him, his words and actions had made him an enemy of law enforcement.

"Neil," his father interrupted, coming out of the living room. "We need you in here. Claire is hysterical."

"I'll be right there, Dad." He turned back to them. "Agent Hart, I want you to allow Cooper to work with you. He knows me. He knows Elisa. And he knows the problems that can arise in investigations. I don't want any of those problems, not with my daughter's life on the line. You two talk, work together," Neil said. "If that's an issue, tell your boss to talk to me." Neil gave her a pointed look that told her if she wanted to fight his request, he would fight back.

As Neil left them alone, she crossed her arms in front of her chest and gave Cooper a hard stare. "The last thing we are going to do is work together. You need to stay out of the way so we can bring Elisa home as quickly as possible."

"Same old Andi," he drawled. "You always liked to call the shots, but you're not in charge."

"I am in charge. This is my case."

"And Neil is a friend of mine who wants me involved. You heard what he had to say."

"Yes. He wants you to look over my shoulder to make sure I don't screw up. But you're going to get in the way, and I can't have that."

"It's not your choice."

She became acutely aware of the passing time and the curious interest from the nearby patrol officer. "I need to get back to the office."

"I'll go with you."

"No, you won't. This is a legal investigation, Cooper." As she finished speaking, Flynn came through the front door.

"Ready to go?" he asked.

"Yes."

"Hold on," Cooper said, a hard, determined note in his voice. "Neil asked me to help, and that's what I'm going to do, with or without your cooperation, Agent Hart."

Flynn's eyebrow shot up at Cooper's words. "Excuse me. Who are you?"

"Dr. Cooper Bradford. Mr. Benedict asked me to consult on the case. I have some experience with profiling and criminal behavior."

"Dr. Bradford," Flynn echoed. "I'm familiar with your work. You don't think much of the FBI, do you?"

"That's not important right now, Agent…" Cooper gave Flynn a questioning look.

"MacKenzie," Flynn supplied.

"My only goal is to find Elisa," Cooper said. "We don't have to be adversaries. We're on the same page. I can be a helpful liaison between your office and the family. They trust me. They know me. They want me involved. And I can't imagine why I would be anything but an asset to you."

Flynn turned to her. "What do you think? It's your call."

She debated her options. "Mr. Benedict made it clear that he wants Dr. Bradford to be his eyes and ears. I don't want to waste time arguing over this. If Dr. Bradford can help, then that's a win for everyone."

"All right," Flynn said. "Why don't you come to our office, Dr. Bradford? We'll go from there?"

"Good," Cooper said.

Since Cooper was clearly going to be involved, she needed to square things away with him before they went any further. "I'll ride with Dr. Bradford," she told Flynn. "I can fill him in on what we know so far."

"Then we'll regroup at the office."

She followed Flynn out of the house, with Cooper at her heels. As Flynn hopped into the SUV, she immediately regretted her decision to go with Cooper, but there was no way to avoid the inevitable awkward conversation that was coming.

They ducked under the police tape and walked down the block to Cooper's vehicle. As they walked past the neighbors, her gaze swept the crowd, looking for anyone who seemed out of place, or overly curious, but no one jumped out.

Cooper's car was a silver electric SUV, which clearly had cost some money. Apparently, writing books about tearing down law enforcement protocols was lucrative.

She got into the car, feeling irritated, angry, and nervous. She had a lot of reasons to dislike Cooper, but he had even more reasons to dislike her.

As he slid behind the wheel, she couldn't help taking a closer look at him. He'd filled out his long, lanky teenage frame, with broad shoulders and an athletic build. He was a man now—a very attractive man with brown hair and sharp green eyes that had always seen her a little too well. But his gaze now was more hardened than it had once been. He'd lived through a lot of years, a lot of pain. And there was a part of her that really wished she could have taken away some of that pain, but she was the last person who could do that.

"We need to talk," Cooper said, his assessing gaze meeting hers.

"We don't have time to rehash the past. There's a child missing."

"Exactly. We need to work together."

"We don't need to do that," she countered. "I'm an FBI agent. I'm trained in finding missing children, and I'm extremely good at it. You are a psychologist. You may have insight into why someone is a criminal, but you don't know how to catch them."

"How would you know what I know?"

"I've heard you talk on television. I've read articles about you. You believe that too many people are falsely accused. I understand why you've made that problem your mission in life. But today isn't about you or me or your brother. So, start the car, or I'm going to call for a ride and get back to the office."

Cooper's gaze drilled into hers. Then he started the car and pulled away from the curb. "Tell me what you know," he said.

She related the facts she'd been given, reaffirming the scene in her mind. The fact that the back door was open, and no cries had been heard over the baby monitor, bothered her the most, suggesting that either the nanny had let someone in or taken Elisa downstairs and handed her off to someone.

"What do you make of the missing cameras in the back?" Cooper asked.

"According to Neil, they were taken down during a remodel that lasted several weeks. Any number of people on the construction crew might have been aware of that. The nanny or the housekeeper could have tipped someone off as well."

"They would both be easy suspects."

She bristled at the suggestion that she was zeroing in on anyone because it was easy. "Everyone in that house is a suspect. This child was taken out of her crib. The kidnapper knew how to get into the house and how to get out without alerting anyone."

"But as you said, the house has recently been under construction. A lot of people might have known the layout of the interior."

"Exactly. Are you trying to make a point, Cooper?"

"Are you, Andi?" he countered. "I'm just talking."

"More like accusing. You don't trust me, but I'm good at what I do."

"I'm sure you are. You wanted to be an investigator since you were eight years old."

"But?"

He flung her a quick look as he stopped at a light. "I didn't say but."

"You didn't say it, but I heard it."

"Well, that's on you. Don't put words in my mouth."

"Let's get back to the case," she said, annoyed with herself for getting distracted by Cooper. "What is your relationship with the Benedicts? How long have you known them?"

"I met Neil about three years ago, but we started working together last year on a potential docuseries based on my books. We've been developing that project for a while now and are good friends."

"Did you know his first wife?"

"Yes. I met Neil and Shana right before they divorced. I actually pitched my project to both of them, but Neil was the one who later followed up about it."

"Was it an amicable divorce?"

"No. From what I understand, it was a nasty breakup. Neil said he'd stayed in the marriage far too long. Once he met Claire, he discovered what real love was. He adores Claire and calls her the love of his life. He was over the moon when they had Elisa. He has been incredibly happy the last few months."

"What do you think of Claire?"

"She's very sweet, kind, a little on the quiet side. She loves kids. She works as a children's casting agent."

"Does Claire love being a wife and mother?"

"She seems very devoted to Elisa, and she and Neil always seem to be happy."

"No one is always happy," she said cynically.

"That's true," he conceded.

"Have you ever spoken to the nanny, Kristine, or to Solange, the housekeeper?"

"A few times in passing. Neil has known Solange for years."

"He mentioned that. But Kristine is a newer employee. Neil said they got her from another family, friends of his who were moving out of town."

"The Weiselbergs—Theresa and Glen. Theresa worked for Neil as a production assistant at one time. They moved to New York." Cooper paused, then said, "What happens next? Since you're the expert, I assume you have a plan."

"I'm going to use every resource I have to find out who entered their house this morning and took Elisa. I have to believe that a camera somewhere caught something. Every house on that block had one. Beyond that, we work the case, investigate everyone tied to the family, and if there's a ransom demand, there will be more clues to follow."

"What if there is no security footage, no ransom?" He gave her a sharp look. "We both know some kids are never found."

"Right now, the only child I'm thinking about is Elisa," she said. But as Cooper got on the freeway, her mind went back to the first girl in her life who'd gone missing. Hannah had never been found. Eighteen years had passed, and there still wasn't an answer as to what had happened to her.

"I'm surprised you came back to LA," Cooper said a few moments later. "I heard you and your father stopped speaking years ago."

"Who did you hear that from—your parents?"

"No. They don't talk to your dad. Not that he's home a lot. They said he travels every other week. I ran into Mrs. Lassiter last week. She filled me in on all the gossip she thought I needed to hear. As much as I wanted to, I couldn't stop her from sharing."

"She always loved to gossip."

"She told me she sees your dad at the golf course, and he said you were never coming back."

"I'm sure you were happy to hear that."

"But he was wrong. Here you are. Why did you come back?"

At this moment, she wasn't even sure she could answer that question, because she was already regretting her decision. Finally, she said, "I had a job opportunity I wanted to pursue, and it was here in LA. I didn't think there would be any reason for any of us to run into each other."

"Life is funny, isn't it?" he mused.

She could have used a lot of other adjectives besides funny— like cruel or ironic.

"What happened with you and your dad?" Cooper asked.

"It doesn't matter."

"How's your mom?"

She shook her head. "I don't want to do this, Cooper. We're not old friends. We're not catching up."

"You're very defensive, Andi. Does that come from your guilt?"

"No. I have nothing to feel guilty about," she lied, thankful that they were nearing the office. She needed this ride to be over so she could bury herself in work. She just wished that work wasn't going to include Cooper, but she had a feeling he was going to be a thorn in her side for a while longer.

When they entered the office suite, Flynn was standing at one end of the room, in front of several large monitors and a dozen agents and analysts. Judging by the simmering energy in the room, she hoped they had a lead.

"What's happened?" she asked.

Flynn tipped his head to the video. "This vehicle was caught on camera at the corner, three houses down from the Benedict's at nine-thirty AM. The car is registered to Jillian Markham, who works as a production assistant for First Look Studios, which is housed in the same building as Neil Benedict's company. Unfortunately, we don't have any footage that captures the driver or the interior of the car."

"Can we pick up the car anywhere else?" she asked.

"Still checking traffic cams," Savannah answered. "But Ms. Markham has no record. She's single, twenty-seven years old, works in Beverly Hills, lives in Culver City."

"There's a good chance she knows Neil if she works in his building."

"She knows Neil," Cooper said, drawing all gazes to him.

"This is Dr. Bradford," Flynn said to the group. "He's consulting on the case at the request of the Benedict family."

She could see by the reactions in the room that most of them knew exactly who Cooper was and were not excited about working with him. But none of them had that choice.

"Tell us more," she said.

"Jillian Markham worked for Neil's production company but quit three months ago after complaining that she was being sexually harassed by his partner, Larry Friedman," Cooper said. "She told me that Neil refused to do anything about her issues with Larry."

"So, she doesn't like Neil, either," Andi said.

"She probably hates his partner even more," he countered.

"Does she like you?" she asked.

He shrugged. "We're friendly. We had several long lunches when we were working on my project before she quit. She might be more amenable to talking to you if I'm there."

"Then let's go." She looked to Flynn to see if he agreed, and he gave her a nod.

"We'll keep working on other leads," Flynn said. "Take one of our cars." He took some keys out of his pocket and tossed them to her. "Slot 26."

"Got it," she said, heading out of the conference room.

"I can drive," Cooper told her, as they got on the elevator.

"You're a consultant. I'm driving." She needed to get her power back, and getting behind the wheel was the first step.

CHAPTER THREE

COOPER DIDN'T CARE that Andi was driving. It gave him a chance to catch his breath, something he'd been trying to do since he'd walked into Neil's house and had seen her coming down the stairs. He had known she was an FBI agent but thought she was on the other side of the country. And that's where he wished she'd stayed. As far away from his life as she could be.

But she was closer to him than ever. Barely a foot separated them. He could smell the lavender of her perfume or her soap. It had been her favorite scent when she was thirteen, and, apparently, it still was. The ponytail was also familiar. She'd always worn her dark-brown hair pulled back off her face. Her brown eyes were as intense and determined as ever.

Other things, however, had changed about her. She wasn't a skinny, young teenager anymore, with braces on her teeth. She was a strikingly pretty woman, with curves in all the right places.

But he wasn't going to think about her body.

That reminder had a familiar ring to it. It was only in the last few months of their friendship that he'd become aware of her body. And it had put an awkwardness between them even before everything else had fallen apart. He'd gone from seeing her as his buddy, his friend, to a girl he wanted to kiss and that had shocked the hell out of him. He didn't think she'd realized the direction his mind was going. She'd been too focused on everything else in her life, too determined to find mysteries to solve, to even see that there was a mystery unfolding between the two of them.

In retrospect, that was probably a good thing. He'd never had to tell her how he felt, never had to ask her if she ever thought about him in the same way, because all conversations between them had ended a few days after Hannah Montgomery disappeared.

He wished they'd never gone out that summer night, never heard the sirens or seen the police cars racing to Hannah Montgomery's house, because that case had given Andi, who loved a mystery more than anything else in the world, the perfect puzzle to unravel. Unfortunately, she'd unraveled it in such a terrible way that she'd destroyed his family. He could never forgive her for that.

"You're staring," Andi said abruptly, giving him an irritated look.

"You did the same when I was driving," he countered.

"Well, it's weird to be sitting next to you."

"I couldn't agree more."

"Then let's talk about Jillian Markham," she said, clearly eager to change the subject.

That was fine with him. He needed to do everything he could to get Elisa back home and get Andi out of his life again. He didn't want to work with her any more than she wanted to work with him. But Neil was his friend, and he was in trouble, shattered, devastated. If Neil wanted him to help, then that's what he would do.

Clearing his throat, he said. "Jillian graduated from USC and used family connections to get into the production business. She told me she was hoping to become a producer at some point, that being an assistant wasn't much better than being an intern, which she had apparently done more than once in the past."

"What about the sexual harassment? Did she mention that to you?"

"Jillian told me about it the last time we spoke, which was probably a week before she quit. That was a couple of months ago. She said Larry was an asshole who'd been hitting on her for weeks, and that he wouldn't stop. Neil didn't believe her or was choosing to ignore her problem, because he needed Larry's connections for his business."

"Is that true? Did Larry bring valuable relationships to the company?"

"Yes. Larry is ten years older than Neil and has been around the business longer, so he has contacts that Neil doesn't have. Plus, Neil had had to rebuild after having to leave his first company when his marriage dissolved. Neil feels loyalty to Larry for joining him in his new venture and helping him restart his career." He thought for a moment about Jillian. "I'm sure Jillian dislikes Neil, but I can't see her kidnapping his child. Just because she was driving down his street and used to work for him means nothing. I would guess just about everyone in that neighborhood has a Hollywood connection."

"But she has a motive to want to hurt Neil, and she was on his block around the time Elisa went missing. She's the best lead we have."

His gut tightened, her words taking him back in time. "You thought my brother was a good lead, too. Just because a car that might have looked like his went down the street around the time Hannah was kidnapped. You still love to jump fast, don't you, Andi?"

"I don't think we should talk about what happened when we were kids. I wasn't leading that investigation. I told the police what I saw."

"That's not what you did," he countered, unable to stop himself from going back there, even though he probably should.

"You told the police you saw my brother's car. But you didn't know it was his. You even asked me if it was my brother's, and I told you it wasn't. But you still pointed the police in Kyle's direction."

Her profile hardened, but she kept her gaze on the traffic in front of them. "The police had other reasons to question your brother's whereabouts that night. We know Kyle left the concert early, and his story kept changing as to where he'd been, who he'd been with."

"He was an eighteen-year-old kid, who had some mental issues that made it difficult for him to defend himself. But he didn't commit that crime."

"And he wasn't charged for it."

"He was arrested. He was interrogated. He was held overnight in jail before the police decided they didn't have enough evidence to keep him longer. His name was given to the media. His life was ruined. Everyone thought he was a kidnapper, a child molester. And it wasn't just my brother the community went after; it was my entire family." He felt his rage return with each word that he spoke.

She turned in to the parking lot behind the building they were going to and pulled into a slot. As she pulled the key out of the ignition, she turned and faced him. "I'm sorry, Cooper. I'm sorry that you and Kyle and your family went through all that."

Disappointment and anger ran through him. "But you're still not willing to take responsibility for what you did."

"Like I said before, I just told the police what I thought I saw."

He shook his head. "You did a hell of a lot more than that. But forget it. You're never going to admit you were wrong."

She stared back at him with a mix of emotions in her gaze. "I was a kid, Cooper. I wanted to find Hannah. I loved that little girl. I thought I was helping."

"Did you know Kyle killed himself?" he asked abruptly.

She swallowed hard, then gave a quick nod. "I read about his suicide in one of the press articles about you and your books. I couldn't believe it. I felt bad for you and your family, especially your mom."

He stiffened against the sympathy in her gaze. "It was probably inevitable from the moment he was targeted for that kidnapping. Kyle spent the next ten years in unrelenting pain and the shame from being falsely accused, from people looking at him like a monster who had gotten away with murder. He couldn't stand it anymore. He didn't think it could get better."

Cooper felt a rush of pain run through him at the memory of that horrible day when his big brother had taken his own life. From that day on, Cooper had vowed to find some way to help someone else so that their family didn't have to go through what his family had gone through. That's what had taken him into forensic psychology, into working with the criminal system, writing books, and trying to help others who were innocent and incarcerated, their lives ruined by a false accusation.

"I'm sorry," Andi said again.

"Well, that doesn't mean much."

"I get that." She paused. "Look, we need to talk to Jillian, and we can't be arguing with each other, Cooper. If you're not up to this—"

"I'm up to it," he said, cutting her off. In fact, he already regretted telling her anything about his brother. He shouldn't have gone there, not now. They needed to find Elisa. "Let's go."

They got out of the car and entered the six-story building that showed a number of production and film-related companies on the listing of occupants. First Look Studios was on the second floor while Neil's company, Benedict and Friedman Productions, was on the sixth floor.

When they entered the lobby for First Look Studios, Andi flashed her badge to the receptionist, who gave them an alarmed look and asked them to wait before disappearing down the hall.

Andi tapped her foot impatiently. Even as a kid, she'd hated to wait. She'd been a whirlwind of energy and ideas. That hadn't changed.

The receptionist returned a moment later and said Jillian would be right out.

As they waited, he got a bad feeling. Jillian was taking a little too long. When he glanced back at the glass door leading into the office, he saw a flash of red. He dashed into the hall in time to see Jillian punch the elevator button in a frantic, desperate manner. Apparently, she'd found another way out of her office.

"Jillian," he said sharply, moving down the hall.

She gave him a startled look. "Cooper? What are you doing here?"

"I came to see you," he said, as Andi followed him down the hall. "This is Agent Hart."

"Where are you going, Ms. Markham?" Andi asked as the elevator doors opened.

"I have a meeting out of the office," Jillian said, as she jumped into the elevator. He moved fast enough to prevent the doors from closing. Then he and Andi stepped into the elevator with her. The doors had barely closed when Andi hit the emergency stop button, and the elevator jolted to a stop.

Jillian stumbled forward, bracing her hand against the wall, giving them both a shocked, scared look.

"Why did you do that?" she asked breathlessly.

"We need to talk to you," Andi replied in a hard voice. "The receptionist told you that, didn't she?"

"I'm sorry. I don't have time."

"Well, you'll make the time. A child's life depends on that."

Jillian's eyebrows shot up. "What—what are you talking about?"

"Elisa Benedict, the six-month-old daughter of Neil and Claire Benedict, was kidnapped this morning from her crib, and your car was on his block at around that time," Andi said.

"I—I don't know anything about that," Jillian said, shock in her voice.

He gave her a thoughtful look, measuring her reactions, weighing her sincerity. He'd spent the last ten years talking to criminals, which made him very aware that some people could lie convincingly, and others would capitulate as soon as it appeared they were going to get caught. He didn't know yet which category Jillian fell into.

"Why were you in that neighborhood?" Andi pressed.

Jillian licked her lips. Another nervous gesture. She seemed stunned by what she was being accused of, but also guilty of something.

"I was visiting a friend."

"On Neil's street?" he challenged. "What is the name of your friend?"

"Uh. Do I have to say?"

"Yes," Andi replied. "We need to find Elisa. Every second counts. If you know anything or saw someone, you need to tell me right now."

Jillian's gaze swung to him. "I don't know anything. I didn't see anything."

"Are you sure?" he challenged. "You drove right by Neil's house. Maybe there was a car out front, maybe someone walking nearby."

"I don't know. I wasn't paying attention. I was just driving, listening to music. I wasn't looking at his house or his neighborhood. I'm sorry. I swear I know nothing about Elisa getting kidnapped. I can't believe that happened. She's a sweet little baby. Neil and Claire must be devastated."

"They are," he said.

"We know you had a problem with Mr. Benedict," Andi told Jillian.

"My problem was with his partner, with Larry," Jillian corrected. "But I have a new job now, and I want to keep it. That's why I didn't want to speak to you in the office. I don't want them to think I'm in trouble. I wish I could help you, but I can't. I need to get to my meeting."

The phone in the elevator suddenly rang. Apparently,

someone in the building had noticed that the elevator had stopped.

Andi restarted the elevator. "What is the name of the friend you were visiting, Ms. Markham?"

"I don't want to talk to you," Jillian said. "I don't have to, do I? You're not arresting me or anything, are you?"

Andi gave Jillian a hard stare. "I can take you down to my office. I can make sure your new employer knows of my interest in you. I would suggest you cooperate."

The elevator hit the lobby floor, and the doors opened. They stepped out as a throng of people moved into the elevator. He thought Jillian might make a mad dash for the front door of the building, but she just moved to the side of the lobby, away from people getting on and off the elevators.

"Okay. I wasn't in the neighborhood to see Neil," Jillian said. "Larry Friedman's ex-wife, Michelle, lives three blocks from Neil. I went to see her, to ask her if she knew of any other women who had been harassed by her husband, because I knew I wasn't the first one. I also knew that Michelle had accused Larry of infidelity in her divorce papers."

"Did you speak to Michelle?" Andi asked. "Can she verify your story?"

"Yes. We spoke for twenty minutes and then I left. Are we done?"

"For now," Andi said. "But I want to show you something first." She pulled out her phone and opened an image, turning it around so Jillian could look at the picture of a smiling, happy Elisa. "This is whose life is at stake."

Jillian caught her breath and shook her head. "I hope she's all right. I really do. I don't like Neil, but I wouldn't wish this on him or anyone." Jillian turned and walked toward the lobby doors.

"Do you believe her?" he asked Andi.

"Let's see where she's going," Andi said as they followed Jillian.

When they left the building, they saw Jillian run down to the curb, her phone in her hand. A moment later, a rideshare car picked her up.

Andi jotted the license plate onto her phone.

"You're going to track her?" he asked in surprise.

"Absolutely."

"It sounds like she was at Michelle Friedman's house."

"That might be true, but she was lying about something. She tried to run away from us. That's not the sign of an innocent person." She punched in a number on her phone, then said, "Savannah, Jillian Markham was picked up by a rideshare in front of her office building a few minutes ago." Andi rattled off the name of the company, the license plate, and the address. "I need to know where she's going." Andi waited, once again tapping her foot impatiently on the sidewalk.

"This could be a waste of time," he told her. "There are several other people you should follow up on. Why are we spending so much time on this one woman?"

She put up a hand as she listened to the agent on the other end of the line. "Got it. Thanks." She ended the call. "Jillian was just dropped off at a café a few miles from here." She walked briskly toward the car. "I'd like to see who she's meeting."

"All right. But I'm going with you. You can consider me backup."

She gave him a bitter smile. "There's no way I would ever count on you to back me up."

His smile was just as bitter. "I'm still going with you."

"I don't have time to argue," she said, as they got in the car.

Within minutes, they were on their way to the Stella Café in Century City. They parked and then hurried into the restaurant. The café had a busy counter, with a line winding through the restaurant and most of the tables filled, but at a small table in the corner was Jillian Markham.

Andi stopped so short, he almost ran into her. Jillian wasn't alone. She was with Neil Benedict.

CHAPTER FOUR

ANDI WAS SHOCKED to see Neil with Jillian. After everything she'd heard about their relationship, she would have thought that Jillian would be the last person Neil would want to see. Unless this was about ransom…

Maybe Jillian was connected to the kidnapping, and Neil, like some other parents she'd worked with in the past, had taken matters into his own hands.

"Did you see that coming?" Cooper murmured in her ear.

She wished she could say she had, but he'd know that was a lie. "Let's see what these two are talking about," she said, striding forward.

Neil jumped to his feet as soon as he saw them approach. Jillian looked guilty and probably would have run again if she wasn't trapped between the table and the wall.

"What's going on?" Andi asked Neil. "What are you doing here, Mr. Benedict?"

"I came to talk to Jillian," he said. "Has something happened? Were you looking for me?"

"No. I wanted to see who Jillian was meeting. I'm surprised it's you. It's my understanding that the two of you don't like each other," she said. "So, why would you leave your terrified wife to meet with a woman who holds you responsible for not doing something about your partner harassing her?"

Neil's gaze turned wary. "How do you know about that?"

"Does Ms. Markham have something to do with your daughter's disappearance?" she asked.

"I just asked her that. She said no."

"And I'm not lying," Jillian put in. "I asked Neil to meet me early this morning, long before Elisa was taken and before you two showed up at my office." Her gaze moved to Neil. "Why didn't you text me and tell me you couldn't meet?"

"Because I wondered if you were involved," Neil returned.

Jillian appeared devastated by his words. "Neil. Come on. It's me. I would never do something like that."

"I don't know you anymore, Jillian. You're trying to destroy my company."

"I'm trying to make sure Larry can't hurt anyone else. You have been unwilling to act, so I wanted to tell you I'm tracking down former employees who had problems with Larry. This will go bad for him, Neil, and if you don't put some distance between yourself and Larry, you'll get caught up in it, too. There's still time for you to make it right, to confront him, to denounce his actions, to end your partnership with him."

Neil ran a hand through his hair. "I can't do this right now. All I can think about is Elisa." He looked back at Andi. "Why are you here again?"

"We followed Ms. Markham from her office."

"Why? Because of her accusations against Larry?"

She preferred not to give the family too much information, especially info that hadn't been vetted and put into context. But she also wanted to see how he would react, because there was a part of her that wasn't buying his story.

Why wouldn't he have texted Jillian and told her he couldn't meet because his daughter had been kidnapped? Dealing with his office problems should have been the last thing on his mind.

"Ms. Markham's car was spotted on your block this morning during the time in which Elisa disappeared," she said.

Surprise ran through his gaze, dropping his jaw. He looked at Jillian again. "Why were you at my house?"

"I wasn't at your house. I went to see Michelle."

"Why the hell would you do that?" He shook his head. "Never mind, I don't want to know. I don't care about any of that right now. I have to get back to Claire." His gaze returned to Andi. "I haven't heard anything from the kidnappers. It's been a couple of hours. What's taking so long?"

"I don't know. But you should go home and wait there."

"I'm doing that now." He gave Jillian a quick look and then headed out of the café.

"Are you following me?" Jillian asked. "Am I under surveillance or something?" She got to her feet. "I have to go back to work. Unless you're going to arrest me?"

"Not yet," she said.

Jillian shivered at her words and then walked away.

"You can still scare people," Cooper commented.

"Still? I don't think I was a scary kid."

"You definitely had some scary ideas. What do you think about Neil and Jillian meeting up?"

"I'm confused."

"Me, too," he muttered, a frown on his face.

Cooper had the puzzled look he'd always had when things didn't add up. Like her, once he started a puzzle, he didn't want to quit.

She pressed one hand to her head as a headache pressed at her temple. Things were moving fast, but she wasn't operating on a lot of sleep. "I need coffee."

"You look like you do," he commented, his sharp gaze sweeping her face.

She wondered what he saw when he looked at her, because every time she looked at him, she noticed something different, some detail that hadn't been there before, like the white scar that ran across the bridge of his nose.

"How did you get that scar on your nose?" she asked.

"Took a fastball to the face when I was a senior in high school."

"Oh, my God. That was your mother's worst nightmare every time you got on the mound."

"That was the worst injury I ever had. It was bad. There was a lot of blood."

Now she felt a queasiness to go along with her headache. "Let's get a coffee," she said, moving toward the end of the line. "I got off a plane late last night. I didn't get a lot of sleep."

"We should order something to eat as well. I'm guessing you didn't stop for breakfast this morning."

"I've never been a breakfast eater."

"No. Always too eager to start the day."

"More like eager to get out of the house when I was a kid," she said. "And we don't have time to eat."

"Do you have time to collapse?" he countered, with the old Cooper logic that she'd never been able to avoid.

She didn't want to admit he was right, but she needed energy and sustenance. "Maybe I will get one of those pre-made sandwiches," she conceded. "I can eat it in the car."

"Where were you flying in from last night?"

"New York. I had to wrap a few things up before making my move official."

"You've just come back to LA then?"

"Yes. I got my apartment last month, moved in a bed and shipped my car a few weeks ago, but the rest of my furniture is coming later this week." She realized she was rambling and giving him too much information. "Where do you live now?"

"Santa Monica."

Great. They were living in the same city. Just what she needed. "How long have you been in Santa Monica?" she asked, her gaze not meeting his. She didn't want to appear too curious about him, but she was.

"Three years. Moved around before that."

An awkward silence fell between them, and she was relieved when it was time to order.

"Let's sit down and eat," Cooper suggested, when they got their food and drinks. He moved toward an empty table and pulled out a chair. "Or are you going to be stubborn like you always were?"

She hesitated, but seeing the knowing look in his eyes, she decided to prove him wrong on at least one point. "Fine." She sat down across from him and took a swig of coffee, feeling immediately better. Then she unwrapped her sandwich. As she took a bite and looked across the table at him, she said. "This is so weird."

"You said that before."

"Because it still feels strange to be here with you. It's the same and yet really different, because we're not kids anymore."

"Nope," he muttered, his mouth full of a big bite of his chicken pesto sandwich. He swallowed, then said, "We're definitely not kids."

"I didn't think I would ever see you again, much less have to work with you."

"Can't say I saw this coming, either, Andi."

"I still don't understand why Neil thinks you should follow me around? Has he always been suspicious of law enforcement, or did that come from the time he's spent with you putting together your docuseries?"

"Our relationship has definitely changed some of his opinions about the criminal justice system, profiling, and how sometimes law enforcement gets it wrong. He wants to make sure that doesn't happen now. He's panicked, and he doesn't want to make a mistake."

"I understand that, but I'm not sure what you're going to be able to do, Cooper. I would have gotten the same information from Jillian, whether or not you were there."

"I don't know if that's true. And I told you why you needed to talk to her in the first place. Remember?"

She frowned as she munched on her sandwich. He had a point. She just didn't like it. "All right, you gave Jillian a motive. That was helpful. But now you're done."

"I'm just getting started. I'm part of Neil's circle. I'm on the inside. You need me."

"I don't need you, and the kidnapper may have nothing to do with Neil's circle."

"Really? You don't think whoever did this is connected to Neil?"

"I didn't say that." She paused. "But since we're on the topic of Neil, do you think he would have a motive to hire someone to kidnap his daughter?"

His gaze widened. "No. There's no way that happened."

"But he was here meeting with Jillian, someone who doesn't like him, and who was near his house this morning, when he should have been at home with his terrified wife. His actions today make little sense. He also told us he came here because he didn't know if Jillian had something to do with the kidnapping or not. It's as if he wanted to keep suspicion on her. And she was shocked when he said that. She looked betrayed."

Cooper frowned. "I think you're reading a lot into what he said and how she looked. But why don't I call Neil and ask him more about the meeting? If he doesn't know you're with me, he might be less guarded."

"All right. I'd be curious to see what he says. But not here. Let's go to the car."

They discarded their trash and headed back to the SUV.

"Put it on speaker," she told Cooper as he pulled out his phone. "After you ask him about Jillian, find out if he has any suspicions about the nanny that he didn't express to me."

Cooper gave her a smug look. "So I am proving to be useful. Anything else?"

"Don't tell him you're with me."

"I know what to do, Andi."

"But can you do it?" she challenged. "If Neil implicates himself, can you keep him talking? Or will you worry about him being falsely accused?"

His lips tightened at her words. "My only goal is to find Elisa. I'll do whatever that takes." He punched in a number and a moment later, Neil answered with a flurry of words.

"Do you know anything? Has the FBI gotten a lead on Elisa?" Neil asked.

"Not yet," Cooper replied.

"Are you still with Agent Hart?"

"No," Cooper lied. "Are you home?"

"Yes. And there's still no ransom demand. I'm going crazy. Claire can barely speak. This is my worst nightmare."

Every word that came out of Neil's mouth seemed genuine. She could hear his panic, his fear, but neither of those emotions matched his recent actions.

"What were you doing with Jillian?" Cooper asked.

"She texted me when I was at the gym this morning that she had to see me, that it was urgent, and I would regret it if I didn't come. After Elisa was taken, I had this terrible feeling that maybe Jillian was behind it. I had to meet her so I could find out. But you heard what she told me. She was shocked to hear about Elisa and denied having anything to do with it."

"Do you believe she was at Larry's ex-wife's house this morning?"

"I do. You heard her. Jillian is trying to gather a group of women together to take my company down because she has a grudge against Larry. But honestly, I don't know what she's capable of. She could be a pathological liar. Larry claims he did nothing to harass her." He blew out a breath. "What has the FBI come up with?"

"Not much," he said. "Is there anything else you can tell me? I'm trying to help, but they're not giving me a lot, and I need more information."

"I told you to stay close to them, Cooper. I need you to do that for me."

"I am. But they don't let me into every meeting. Tell me about Kristine. Where is she now? Has she told you anything else that she might not have told the police?"

"She went to get us some food a few minutes ago," Neil said. "She hasn't said anything beyond expressing how sorry she is that she didn't hear or see anything or check on Elisa earlier. She's feeling very guilty."

"What do you know about Kristine?" Cooper asked. "She's only been with you for a few months, right? Is it possible she's involved?"

"No way. She worked for the Weiselbergs for eight months. They thought she was terrific. They gave her a very strong recommendation. And we love her. She's great with Elisa. She's been with us since Elisa was two months old."

"Does Kristine have friends nearby? Does she have a boyfriend, someone she sees regularly?"

"She has friends she sees on her days off, but I've never met them. She's a sweet girl, kind of quiet. She doesn't talk that much to us."

"What about her family?"

"They're in Europe. She moved here on her own. Why does it matter? If Kristine was going to kidnap Elisa, why would she still be here?"

"She doesn't draw attention to herself if she stays put. But she could have let someone into the house. She was the only one there."

"She wouldn't have any reason to do that." Neil paused. "Unless you're suggesting she was bribed or something. But then, where's the ransom demand?"

"I don't know." Cooper frowned as there was a sudden

commotion in the background. "Neil?" When Neil didn't answer, he repeated his name. "Neil? What's going on?"

Andi tensed as she heard a female voice shrieking in the background.

"Oh, God," Neil said, coming back on the line. "Claire just realized that the kidnapper took some of Elisa's clothes from her closet and a couple of stuffed animals. Why would they do that? What does it mean?"

Andi's gut clenched at that piece of information.

"They're not going to bring her back, are they?" Neil asked, pain racking his voice.

"You don't know that," Cooper said forcefully.

"Neither do you," Neil retorted.

"It could be a good thing," Cooper said. "Whoever took her wants to have clothes to put her in. They're taking care of her. They wanted to make sure she had her toys."

Damn! Cooper was good, she thought. He was talking Neil off the ledge, and she couldn't help but remember that he'd done that for her a few times.

"You're right. They wouldn't have taken her clothes if they weren't going to take care of her," Neil said with relief.

"Exactly. Keep the faith."

"I'm trying, but Claire is on her way to a nervous breakdown. I called Dr. Mulders, but he's out of town. Maybe you could come back at some point and talk to her, or do you think it's better for you to stay with Agent Hart?"

"I'll make time to do both," Cooper said, ignoring her miming the word GO. "You haven't heard from anyone else, have you, Neil? You know you can't handle a ransom demand on your own, right? You need to loop in the FBI."

"I haven't heard from anyone. I can't imagine who would do this. Maybe it is Jillian. She hates me now. I can't think of anyone else who dislikes me, although maybe I'd have to put Shana in that category, too. They both think I'm oblivious to what's going on around me. Hell, maybe I am. Maybe I missed something important, and that's why Elisa is gone. This could be my fault."

"We don't know anything yet, so stop beating yourself up."

"I can't help it. I have this hole in my heart, and it's getting bigger with every minute that goes by. I never thought I could love anyone as much as I love her. It's overwhelming. I wish I could trade places with her. If I could, I would die for her."

She heard the fervent note in Neil's voice. It was hard to believe he was anything but a devastated father. On the other hand, while Neil had given Cooper a plausible reason for his meeting with Jillian, that didn't mean it was the whole truth. It also felt like Neil was trying to convince Cooper about the level of his pain.

"No one is going to die," Cooper told Neil. "Stay strong. I'll talk to you soon."

Cooper set down his phone, and they stared at each other for a couple of long seconds. "Something is off," he said.

She was surprised by his words, but she couldn't disagree. "I think so, too."

"He was trying too hard," Cooper added. "I need to go see him, to figure out what's off. That's where I have the most value right now. I can be with the family in a way that you can't."

"That's true." She felt a mix of emotions at his words. She should be relieved he was going to leave her alone, but for a few minutes it had felt like it used to, like they were friends, on the same page, embroiled in the same adventure. But this wasn't an adventure. It was a case—her case. "I'll take you back to your car."

"I don't want Neil to be involved in this," Cooper continued. "I've always thought Neil was a good guy. I can't imagine why he would kidnap his own daughter. It's not like he's going through a divorce. He and Claire are solid."

"You never know what's inside someone else's relationship."

"That's true. The clothes taken out of the closet, the toys… It feels like someone is planning on keeping Elisa for a while."

"Like you told him, the missing clothes are probably the best piece of news we could have gotten at this point. They might buy us some time."

"So, you think I'm right?" he quizzed.

She met his gaze. "About that—yes. But you're wrong about a lot of other things."

"But I'm right about that. Let's just leave it there. Have you ever seen a ransom demand come in days after the kidnapping?" Cooper asked, changing the subject.

"A few times."

"Why would someone wait?"

"The parents get more desperate with each passing day. They're easier to get to as time moves on and are willing to work outside of law enforcement because they don't think we can get their kid back. I had a ransom demand come in eight days after a kidnapping several years ago. The mother paid the ransom, and luckily, the child was left in a parking lot unharmed. We eventually found the perpetrators, one of whom was a coworker of one of the parents and knew they'd just inherited a great deal of money." She paused. "Because of the missing clothes and toys, I hope that the intent is not to hurt Elisa but to use her in some way—a bargaining chip for money or some other influence. This is Hollywood, after all."

"Right. But where's the demand if it's not about money?"

"That's why you need to make sure Neil isn't holding something back."

"What if it's about something worse?" Cooper asked. "Like human trafficking for illegal adoption? That theory was discussed when Hannah Montgomery disappeared."

"It's a possibility." She hoped that wasn't the case. Because if it were, Elisa could already be miles away.

CHAPTER FIVE

ANDI DROPPED Cooper off at his car and then went upstairs to the office at just before three. Flynn, Savannah, Nick, and Caitlyn were in the conference room.

"Nice to see you, Andi," Caitlyn said, getting up to give her a hug. The attractive brunette had been her roommate at Quantico, and at one time, they had been very close. But they'd lost touch over the years. She was happy they were reunited.

"We need to catch up, but it will have to wait."

"Unfortunately, yes," Caitlyn agreed.

"We're just about to do a recap," Flynn said. "Before we get started, how did it go with Jillian Markham?"

"She led me to Neil Benedict. That's who she met after she left us."

"I didn't expect you to say that," Flynn said, in surprise.

"Neil said Jillian asked him to meet earlier that morning. Because of the urgency of her request, he wondered if she'd had something to do with the kidnapping, so he went to see her. When we showed up, shortly after she'd told him she knew nothing about the kidnapping, he took off." She paused. "I think they were both only telling me part of the story."

"It's strange that Neil would meet with an ex-employee with his daughter missing," Savannah agreed.

"Maybe there's something more intimately personal between them," Caitlyn suggested.

"I was going to say the same thing," Nick interjected. "They could be having an affair."

"All possibilities," she said. "But we don't have any proof. Even if they are having an affair, it may not connect to Elisa's kidnapping."

"Where's your shadow, Dr. Bradford?" Flynn asked.

"He went back to the house to see if he can get any more information from Neil." She glanced at the digital screens at the far end of the room, featuring the key people in the case: Neil and Claire Benedict, Kristine Rozic, the nanny, and Solange Guerrero, the housekeeper. There was also a landscaping service run by Eduardo Jerome, and a construction company owned by Grant Petrie. "Anything new?" she asked.

"I've run financials," Savannah said. "Nothing out of line with anyone. No large cash deposits or withdrawals. Kristine has very little financial history. Her bank account was opened eighteen months ago. Most deposits have come from her last three employers: The Back Street Bar in Santa Monica, the Weiselberg family, and the Benedicts. There are some small cash deposits, but the most was for three hundred dollars."

"She has no other work history?" she asked in surprise. "Neil said she'd been a nanny since she graduated from Long Beach State three years ago."

"No," Savannah answered. "She came to the US from Belarus on a student visa when she was nineteen. She lived in an apartment in Long Beach for three years. She worked at the bar for six months, then moved on to the Weiselberg's where she worked for eight months, ending up at the Benedict's house for the last four months."

"We need to know more about her," she said, drumming her

fingers on the table. "What about college? She must have had transcripts, some way to pay for school. Where is her family?"

"I'm working on that," Savannah said. "Also, forensics came up with nothing in the baby's room, no prints that didn't belong there."

"I've been vetting Solange Guerrero," Caitlyn interjected. "I spoke to her by phone thirty minutes ago. She confirmed she has worked for Neil off and on for ten years. She has mostly been a live-out housekeeper, but after her husband died two years ago, she has occasionally stayed overnight if there's a party, or the nanny is out. She has four children ranging in age from twenty to twenty-seven. Her youngest kid, Daniel, has been in and out of rehab and was arrested for a DUI last year. He lives at home with Solange. He was enrolled at the community college last year but dropped out. He doesn't appear to have a job."

"Daniel probably knows the layout of the Benedict's house and possibly the morning routine," she said.

"Exactly," Caitlyn agreed. "But according to Solange, Daniel was in a boxing class at an LA gym this morning and was seen by many people. I confirmed that with the gym, although I haven't spoken to Daniel directly. He wasn't at home, and I haven't gotten a call back."

"Even if Daniel wasn't at the house, he could have been involved and made sure he had an alibi," she said. "Anything else?"

"I talked to Grant Petrie," Nick put in. "He owns the construction company that handled the Benedict's remodel. He stands by his crew, but he can't account for the whereabouts of every single person who had been in the house. He's going to send me a list, and I'll follow up."

"What about camera footage?" she asked. "How did someone get in and out of the property without anyone seeing them?"

"Best guess," Flynn said. "The perpetrator parked on the street behind the house. There's a narrow pathway through the trees. The house behind the Benedicts is up for sale and is currently unoccupied with no working cameras. We've been tracking cars on both streets, but there are dozens of vehicles and, aside from Jillian Markham, none belong to anyone who might have a connection to the Benedicts."

"Both Neil and Claire work," she said. "They're connected to many people in their respective businesses. We don't know where all the connections are." She paused, realizing she hadn't shared the most interesting bit of information. "When Cooper—Dr. Bradford—was on the phone with Neil, Claire discovered that some of Elisa's clothes and toys are missing."

Everyone around the table straightened at her words.

"Someone had time to pack a bag," Savannah murmured, a glint in her eyes.

"Yes. And they wanted Elisa to have some of her toys, probably to keep her happy."

"How could the nanny not have heard someone spending that much time in the kid's room?" Nick asked.

She wondered the same thing. "Good question. Kristine said she heard nothing on the baby monitor, but she could have been lying to protect herself. She could have been asleep, or the monitor was off, or she was part of it. But she's still at the house, acting as distraught and worried as Neil and Claire. I need to talk to her again. I'll go back to the Benedict's house now. And I'll also check out the bar where she used to work."

"What's the deal with that psychologist following you around?" Nick asked curiously.

"He's good friends with Neil Benedict. They're producing a docuseries based on Dr. Bradford's books."

"Which do not paint the Bureau in a good light," Savannah said. "I looked him up. What I found interesting is a blurb I read on a Hollywood gossip site that said the docuseries is on indefinite hold and that Neil's partner, Larry Friedman, was quoted as saying that they were no longer pursuing development of the project."

She started at that piece of information. "That's odd. Both

Neil and Cooper made it sound like they were still working together."

"My source was basically a gossip column," Savannah said with a shrug.

She nodded, her brain whirring with questions. Cooper had full access to the house. It didn't appear that they had any bad blood between them, and when they'd talked about Larry and his problems, Cooper had never mentioned an issue with Neil's partner. But she didn't like when things didn't add up.

She got to her feet. "I'll check in later. Keep digging. Let me know if you come up with anything else."

There were two news vans in front of the Benedict house when Cooper arrived. A female reporter shouted some questions to him, but he didn't bother to answer. When he entered the house, he felt a great weight of fear and unhappiness. It hung heavy in the air.

Neil was on a call with his brother, who lived in Australia, so his father, Robert Benedict, ushered him into the kitchen, where Claire was staring mindlessly at a full mug of tea in front of her. Her mother-in-law, Julia, was making some sort of soup at the stove.

As soon as they saw him, mixed emotions raced through their eyes, from hope to fear and everything in between.

"I know nothing," he said before they could ask, his words immediately erasing the hope from their eyes. "The FBI is working very hard to find Elisa. They have lots of people on the investigation and the most sophisticated research tools available." It felt strange to be praising the Bureau when he'd spent many years tearing the organization apart for their investigative tactics. But he had seen firsthand the focus they were putting on finding Elisa. And he wanted to make sure that the Benedicts could hang on to the hope that their daughter would be found.

This wasn't just a case to him. He and Neil had become good friends. He'd had dinner with Neil and Claire a dozen times. He'd even gone to Robert's birthday party a few months ago and celebrated with the whole family. It was difficult to see them so despairing. They were a great family. In some ways, spending time with them reminded him of his childhood, when his family had been whole, when things had been good, when being at home had felt safe and happy.

He hadn't felt like that in forever. But now the home was cold, the family shattered. Another kidnapping. Another missing child. He couldn't quite believe he'd ended up back in a place he'd been once before.

And with Andi, too. That was the most unbelievable part.

"It's been so long," Claire said, drawing his attention.

She looked ragged from crying for hours on end, and he wished he could say something to make her feel better. He saw the helpless expressions on Julia and Robert's faces. They wanted so badly to fix it, but they couldn't.

Claire kicked back her chair and stood up. "Come outside with me, Cooper."

"Sure," he said, surprised by the request.

He followed her through the house and into the backyard. His gaze swept the property, realizing that the back of the house wasn't as secure as he would have thought. There was a path behind the yard, through some vegetation, to the street behind them. There were also yards on both sides of the home. And no cameras. How the hell had Neil neglected that?

Actually, he could answer that question. Neil was a big-picture guy. He wasn't good at details. He also wasn't a worrier, not about things like personal property or safety. He worked behind the camera. He didn't feel like a celebrity. He probably didn't think he'd ever be a target.

"This was the last place I saw Elisa," Claire muttered, wrapping her arms around her thin body as the breeze blew through her blonde hair.

It wasn't a cold breeze; the temperature was still in the mid-sixties, but Claire looked like she was freezing. She also looked very alone.

"What should I do, Cooper?" she asked. "I don't know what to do, where to go. Should I get on TV and plead for the kidnapper to bring my child back? Should I stay silent, which is what Neil and the FBI want me to do? Should I get in my car and drive around the neighborhood? I feel so..." She shrugged, unable to complete the sentence. "I can't just sit here and wait when my child needs me. I miss her so much. I feel this aching pain deep in my gut. I keep thinking it's a bad dream, and I'm going to wake up, because the alternative is just horrific. I can't imagine losing my baby. I can't." She shook her head as more tears gathered in her eyes.

"You have to find a way to stop thinking about the worst outcome. Focus on Elisa coming home. She'll be happy to be back. She won't even know what happened."

"I want to believe that, but did Neil tell you that the kidnapper took some of her clothes?"

"That's a positive. It means they're taking care of her, and that's what you want."

"It's not what I want. I want her home. And I don't know how to stop thinking about the worst. I can't feel anything but fear. It's overwhelming."

He reached for her, but she flinched, and he dropped his hands. She didn't want comfort, not from him, probably not from anyone. She didn't want to wrap her arms around any person but her child.

"What's going on with Neil?" she suddenly asked, her gaze sharpening. "He left the house for an hour. He said he went to talk to the FBI. Is that true?"

He didn't want to lie for Neil. "He spoke to Agent Hart and me," he prevaricated.

"Why did you call him down there? Did it have to do with Jillian?"

"Why would you ask that?" he countered.

"Because she's been texting him all the time. She's trying to cause trouble for him and Larry. She said Larry was sexually harassing her."

"Do you think that's true?"

"Neil said Larry was just joking in a crude way. But I wouldn't bet against him being more harassing than joking."

"Did you tell Neil that?"

"He wouldn't discuss it with me. He's very loyal to Larry, because Larry helped him restart his business. Neil's ex-wife took a lot of their projects and clients, people that Neil had brought into the company. He had to start completely over, and Larry was there. He feels he owes him."

"I understand loyalty, but Neil also has an obligation to protect his employees."

"I told him that, too. He said he was handling it and not to worry about it. But Jillian started texting me last week. She sounded crazed and now I'm wondering if she had something to do with what happened. If she wants to hurt Neil, then she found the right way."

"It seems like her real vendetta is against Larry."

"That's true." She sighed. "I just can't imagine who else would want to hurt us. And then I think maybe it's a stranger, one of the construction guys, and that seems even worse. Because I don't want Elisa to be with anyone who might scare her." She bit down on her lip. "I feel like a spinning top, Cooper."

"Have you tried to rest, just lay down and close your eyes?"

"I'm afraid to close my eyes. I don't know what I'll see. Don't suggest a sedative. I have to be ready to go if Elisa needs me."

"You have to pace yourself, Claire. This may not be resolved tonight." He could see that she knew that. She just didn't want to admit it.

"Tell me how to do that."

"Keep breathing through the pain and hold on to hope. Don't

think about the worst outcome; think about the best. Envision that."

"I am trying, Cooper. I just wish I was stronger."

"You are strong. You're doing everything you need to do by letting law enforcement do their job."

"You never think they do the best job," she reminded him. "Look at all the cases in your books where the wrong people were arrested, where law enforcement screwed up. How can you trust them now?"

He thought about how best to answer that. "First of all, I don't think they never do the best job; I just think that sometimes they could do better."

"I don't want this to be one of those times."

He needed to tell her that the case was in excellent hands, that Andi was dedicated, determined, and smart. But he couldn't get those words out of his mouth because she'd messed up before. She'd turned the police in the wrong direction. She could be too impulsive, too reckless, too confident. Of course, she had been fourteen. She clearly had a lot more training now and years of experience.

Before he could come up with something to say, Neil joined them in the yard, and he was grateful for the interruption.

"Everything okay out here?" he asked, his gaze worried.

"Nothing will be okay until Elisa is home," Claire snapped. "Don't you get that, Neil?"

On that sharp note, she turned and walked back into the house.

"I can't seem to say the right thing." Neil ran a hand through his already tousled hair. "I just make her angry."

"She's hurting. Yelling at you probably releases a little tension."

"Which I'll gladly take," Neil said. "Whatever makes it easier for her. But I know nothing will be right until our daughter comes home. What are you doing here? I thought you were going to stick close to that FBI agent."

"She kicked me out for a while, but don't worry, I'll get back in. I wanted to check on you."

"Check on me or ask me more questions about Jillian?" Neil challenged, an edge to his voice.

"Maybe both," he said honestly. "It feels like you're holding something back, and I don't want Agent Hart to have a reason to focus on you, Neil. What aren't you telling me?"

Neil stared back at him for a long minute. "It's not relevant to anything."

His heart sank. That wasn't what he wanted to hear. "What's not relevant?"

Neil looked over his shoulder to make sure they were alone. Then he said, "Jillian and I had one drunken night over a year ago, but it meant nothing."

"Does Claire know?"

"Of course not."

"What does Jillian want from you now?"

"She told me if I won't get rid of Larry and tell the world he's a predator, she'll tell Claire that I cheated on her."

He'd finally gotten to the truth. "She's blackmailing you. When did it start?"

"Last week. Before that, she was pressing me to end my partnership with Larry, but then she took it up a notch."

"You have to tell the FBI about her threats."

"I don't have any proof, nothing in writing. And if I tell Agent Hart, Claire will find out. Jillian didn't kidnap Elisa. She wouldn't have done that."

"Would you have thought she was a blackmailer before last week?" he challenged. "Are you sure you know what she's capable of? Kidnapping Elisa might be a desperate act, but she sounds desperate."

"She wouldn't have kidnapped Elisa," Neil said stubbornly.

"Okay. Let me ask you something else. Is there a reason you're protecting Larry?"

"I don't have any proof Larry did anything wrong. He says he never harassed Jillian. Larry has been extremely loyal and helpful to me. I'm not going to end our partnership on a he-said, she-said situation."

"You need to give this information to the FBI, Neil."

"I can't do that. I told you why."

"Jillian was on this block this morning, Neil."

"To talk to Michelle."

"I'm betting she's also been in this house, right?"

"Yes," Neil admitted.

"Jillian knows the layout of your home. She knows where you and Claire are in the morning. And she has a powerful motive to hurt you. You need to stop downplaying the situation. It's bigger than you think it is."

Neil stared back at him. "If Claire finds out I cheated on her now, she'll completely fall apart."

"I don't think the FBI is going to give Claire that information unless it's absolutely necessary. But they need to know." He saw the hesitation in Neil's eyes, and he didn't understand it. "This is about your daughter. Whatever happens to you and Claire's relationship is secondary."

Neil drew in a breath and let it out. "You're right. You can tell Agent Hart. Just remind her that Claire is fragile right now."

"I will. Is Kristine here? I'd like to talk to her."

"She went for a run. She's a big runner. She can do ten miles in a day. She'll probably be back in a few hours." Neil paused as his father came into the yard.

"Agent Hart is here and so is Larry," Robert said. "They didn't appear to come together, but they showed up at the same time. Agent Hart went upstairs to talk to Claire. Larry is in the study. Do you want me to tell him to go?"

"No. I'll see him." Neil paused. "Could you check on Claire for me, Cooper? I don't want Agent Hart upsetting her."

"Sure," he said, following Neil into the house.

He went upstairs, hearing the women in Elisa's room. They were talking about Elisa, and Andi had a compassionate note in her voice as she asked about the baby. He decided to leave them alone for the moment, so he moved down the hall to Kristine's room, curious to look around. The police and FBI forensic teams had already been through the room and found nothing, but maybe he could get a clue about her personality, her interests. The truth was in the details.

He found an unexpected and unwelcome smile lifting his lips as he could hear Andi telling him that very thing whenever they were going on some crazy hunt for clues to solve a mystery that was usually only happening in her head. Although, sometimes, she had been on to something. Sometimes, she had made a difference.

He frowned, not wanting to remember the good times. None of those times outweighed what she'd done. They'd been best friends, and she'd betrayed him in pursuit of glory at being seen as a good detective.

He shook his head, his lips tightening. He needed to get his head out of the past and into the present. He quietly opened a few dresser drawers, finding that Kristine was very neat, and did not have an overly large number of clothes. There was a desk with one middle drawer that held pens, notepads, and a few blank envelopes. He saw nothing personal, no bills, no letters, no photos.

"What are you doing?" Andi asked.

He whirled around, surprised to see her in the doorway. "Just looking around."

"And…"

"It's what's not here that's interesting. There's nothing personal. It's like a hotel room."

Andi's gaze swept the room. "I thought that when I came in here earlier, that it was cold and sterile."

"Did Claire tell you anything? I heard you talking. I didn't want to interrupt."

"She had little to say. She's sitting in a rocking chair, holding Elisa's stuffed rabbit. I asked her a few questions, but I didn't get far. She's very distressed." Andi paused. "She seems irritated with Neil."

"It's not uncommon to express fear through anger at the person closest to you."

"Thank you, Dr. Bradford, for that insightful observation."

"You're welcome," he said, ignoring her sarcasm. "I was in the yard with Claire earlier, and I noticed that the back of the property is very open. I assume you checked cameras on the street behind the house?"

"Of course, but nothing of interest was captured on any of the home security systems. The house directly behind this one is for sale, and no one is living there, so their cameras weren't activated."

"That's convenient."

She nodded. "It's probably how the kidnapper got away. Unfortunately, they managed to stay out of sight."

He sighed. "So, what are you going to do now?"

"Check out the bar where Kristine worked before she became a nanny."

"I'll go with you."

"I thought you were going to stay close to the Benedicts."

"I've spoken to both of them. I think they need a breather from me."

"Well, that sounds about right," she said dryly.

"I set you up for that one, didn't I?"

"Like blowing up a balloon and handing me a dart," she replied with the sassy smile he'd once been completely fascinated by. But that wasn't going to happen again. "Let's get out of here. I'll drive," she added.

"I figured."

"And on the way, you can tell me why you've been lying to me."

He stiffened. "What the hell are you talking about?"

"Not here," she said, as she headed out of the room.

CHAPTER SIX

WHEN THEY LEFT THE HOUSE, the vans were still outside. One reporter was recording a piece from the sidewalk. They stayed out of the shot as they moved to Andi's vehicle, which was parked down the street.

As he got into the car, he said, "You haven't changed at all, Andi. You still love to be dramatic. But I have not lied to you, so I don't know why you would say that I did."

She fastened her seatbelt and shot him a pointed look. "You told me you and Neil are developing a docuseries, but there's an online story that says Larry called off the deal."

"He didn't call it off; it's on hold." He frowned, realizing the implication of her words. "Are you suggesting that I have a motive to hurt Neil? I'm a kidnapper now?"

"I didn't say that. But you didn't tell me the docuseries wasn't happening, and neither did Neil. I can't help but wonder why."

"Because nothing has been officially decided," he replied. "Larry thought we should take a narrower approach. He wanted to focus on a few individuals who were falsely convicted, while I wanted to look at the entire criminal justice system: institutional bias, profiling, public defenders, and overeager, politically motivated law enforcement and prosecutors."

"So, you're going to correct and improve the criminal justice system all on your own through a docuseries. That would be quite a feat."

"I'm just putting a spotlight on issues that need to be looked at," he said evenly. "And individuals and organizations who want to do the right thing shouldn't be afraid of that light."

"I'm not afraid of it."

"Some of your colleagues are."

"And some of them think you're trying to make a buck off the hard work of public servants."

"Is that what you think?" he asked curiously, telling himself he shouldn't care what she thought.

"Honestly, I don't know. It's been a long time since I knew who you were."

Her answer was surprisingly candid. "I feel the same way about you, Andi. But I see signs of that stubborn, determined kid I knew in the way you operate now. Plus, there's the ponytail," he added with a smile. "I always wondered why you didn't just cut your hair when you were so annoyed with it getting in your face."

"My mom wouldn't let me cut it. Her mother always made her have short hair, and she hated it, so she loved looking at my long hair."

"Do you ever wear it down?"

"Why are we talking about my hair, Cooper?"

He laughed. "Hell, if I know. Another thing that feels familiar. Our conversations used to get off track all the time. That was mostly on you. Your brain would jump from one thing to the next, so fast it was hard to keep up."

"I've always had a lot of thoughts running through my head, too many sometimes," she admitted.

As their gazes met, he felt a connection to her that was still strong after everything that had happened. But he needed to focus on the case and nothing else. "I didn't lie to you, Andi. I didn't believe the status of my project with Neil was relevant."

"Well, I don't want to get blindsided."

He smiled at the irony. "Yeah. That's not a good feeling. Speaking of being blindsided..."

"Please don't bring up the past, Cooper."

"I wasn't going to. Neil told me something you need to know."

She'd started the engine, but at his words, she turned it off and faced him. "What?"

"He and Jillian had a fling about a year ago. Since he's refused to end his partnership with Larry or support her claims, she's decided to blackmail him. If he doesn't get rid of Larry and out him for his predatory behavior, she's going to tell Claire about the affair."

Her brown eyes widened with his words. "Unbelievable. How could he keep that from us? He just gave Jillian an even bigger motive."

"That's what I told him. He's requested that you don't share the information with Claire."

"Well, I can't make that promise, but it's not a conversation at the top of my list." She shook her head. "I knew he and Jillian were lying about something."

"He doesn't believe Jillian took Elisa."

"I don't have any confidence in what Neil believes. We'll go by Jillian's office on the way to the bar."

He checked his watch. "It's after five. I doubt she'll be there."

"Can you call her? Do you have her number, or do you need it?"

He took out his phone. "I have it." He made the call. The phone rang four times, then went to voicemail. "She's not answering."

"Try the office number," Andi said, texting him the number.

He got a different voicemail saying the offices were closed. "Strike two."

"Then we'll try her at home. Savannah sent me the home addresses of all of our persons of interest." She ran through her phone, then put the address into the GPS. Restarting the engine, she sped away from the house with a heavy foot on the gas.

"You drive like you used to ride your bike," he commented. "Fast, purposeful, and maybe on the edge of recklessness. You used to fly down hills. I almost expected to see you take off one day."

"I am not a reckless driver, but I enjoy speed," she admitted.

"Who taught you how to drive? Your mom?"

"One of her boyfriends. He took me out a few times, but I pretty much taught myself."

He was torn between wanting to know more about her life after she'd moved away and wanting to keep some walls up between them. Because he couldn't let the good memories overcome the bad ones, which had been really terrible.

So, he looked out the window and watched the scenery passing by, trying not to think about the girl she'd once been or the woman she was now.

Andi didn't know what Cooper was thinking about, but his words had taken her back in time. She could still picture herself flying down the hills of their neighborhood on her bike. She hadn't been afraid of falling; she'd been too interested in escaping, in giving herself a rush that would make her happy for at least a few minutes. Unfortunately, the high had never lasted. Eventually, she had to get off her bike and go home.

As the traffic in front of her increased, she hit the brake, realizing she was going a little too fast, and she didn't want to make Cooper right about her being reckless. She didn't want to make him right about anything.

Although, she silently admitted to herself that he had been more helpful than she had expected. He'd gotten Neil to admit to an affair with Jillian, which was huge. Whether it turned out to be a factor in Elisa's kidnapping, she didn't know, but it was the best lead she'd gotten.

They arrived at Jillian's apartment building a few moments later. It was in a modest neighborhood of apartment buildings in Culver City. Jillian's apartment was on the second floor of a building called The Palms. After ringing the bell, a redheaded woman answered the door.

"I'm Agent Hart with the FBI," she said. "I'm looking for Jillian Markham. Does she live here?"

"She left about fifteen minutes ago," the woman replied, a worried light in her eyes. "What's going on?"

"What's your name?" she asked, ignoring the woman's question.

"Tamara Kinzie," she replied.

"How long have you known Jillian?"

"Not long. I moved in here a couple of weeks ago. A friend of a friend told me she was looking for a roommate."

"Did she say anything to you about a missing child or about Neil Benedict?" she asked.

"Nothing about a kid," Tamara said. "But she rants about Neil and his douchebag partner, Larry, all the time. She's kind of obsessed with how awful they are. I told her she's just going to drive herself crazy trying to get justice for sexual harassment in Hollywood. It's all over this town. But she can't let it go. I think something else must have happened that she didn't tell me about."

"Like what?"

"I don't know. I just get the feeling her anger comes from more than harassment, like maybe someone went further than that. But she didn't tell me anything."

"Where did she go?" Cooper cut in. "Did she drive off in her own car?"

"No. I think she got a ride with someone. Not sure if it was a rideshare or a friend." Tamara paused. "She took an overnight bag with her. I think she might be gone for a few days."

She felt a wave of disappointment that they'd missed Jillian. She could be anywhere by now, and it didn't sound like she was coming back soon. "Do you mind if we come inside and look in her room?"

"Uh, I guess not," Tamara said, allowing them to enter the apartment.

The living room was messy, with fashion magazines and empty coffee cups piled up on the coffee table in front of a worn couch that had been made more comfortable with a bunch of colorful pillows. Tamara pointed them to the first room off the hallway.

Jillian's room was also cluttered with clothes on the bed and on the floor. Judging by the empty hangers in her closet and a couple of opened drawers, it looked like she'd packed in a hurry.

On the desk, she found a pile of scripts, some with comments, some that looked unread, but it was the file with Larry's name on it that drew her attention. "Look at this," she murmured.

Cooper peered over her shoulder at a list of women's names with notes jotted next to them, where they worked, when they met Larry, what they'd said about him. It was pretty damning for Larry, with specific dates, locations, and descriptions of far more than sexual harassment.

"She's definitely building a case against Larry," Cooper muttered.

"Looks like a solid one. But we're not working that case. Where is Neil in all this? Where is Elisa?"

Cooper opened the drawers in the nightstand next to the bed. "Whoa," he said. "I don't need to be looking at this."

She saw an array of female masturbation tools in the drawer before Cooper slammed it shut with an awkward grimace. She bit back a smile. "It's perfectly natural," she said. "We need to find Jillian and bring her in."

"It sounds like she might be hard to find."

"In the meantime, let's check out her car."

As they walked out of the apartment, she handed Tamara her card. "If you hear from Jillian or she comes back, call me right away. Where is her car parked?"

"It's in number three, the silver Toyota," Tamara said as she pushed them out the door and quickly closed it.

They found Jillian's car in her spot. It was locked. Peering inside, Andi didn't see any evidence that a child had been inside in the vehicle, but it was doubtful that Jillian would have left that kind of evidence behind.

"Looks like we're out of options," Cooper said. "Jillian isn't here. Her car is locked. What's next?"

"I'll let my team know about Jillian's affair with Neil and her blackmail strategy. That should be enough to bring her in if we can find her. I'll also get someone out here to check her car for forensic evidence."

As they left the garage, she pulled out her phone and called Savannah as she walked back to her car, filling her in on the pertinent details. When that was done, she said, "Let's check out the bar where Kristine worked, and then I'll need to get back to the office."

"All right." As she drove away from the building, Cooper added, "It's strange how fast things can change, isn't it? I woke up this morning, thinking I wanted to get in a workout, prep for my next podcast, do some research, maybe get a haircut."

"Sounds like an exciting day," she said dryly.

"And now I'm helping you—someone I never thought I'd see again—chase down a kidnapper. It's surreal. But maybe not as much for you."

"Not as much," she agreed. "I'm used to days ending completely differently from how they started."

"What did you think you were going to be doing today?"

"Beginning a new job, reconnecting with old friends. I'm working with many people I met when I started at the FBI. We were in the same class at Quantico."

"That's cool. You've all kept in touch."

"Off and on through the years."

"I've been meaning to ask you, why aren't you working out of the LA office?"

"I'm part of a special unit run by Agent MacKenzie."

His brows drew together in confusion. "But why did your unit take the case? More specifically, you?"

"I'm good at my job."

He frowned. "That still doesn't explain why the LA office, which has a team of agents that works on kidnapping cases, isn't taking the lead. I know a lot about that team, because your old friend is still there. And we've had a few conversations."

"Agent Burnett was never my friend," she snapped. "He was just the agent assigned to find Hannah. He questioned me like he questioned dozens of people, including you."

"Wait a second. I know why you're in charge," Cooper said. "This is about Neil and me and the questions we asked Burnett and his coworkers a few months back."

"Questions or accusations?" she asked, sending him a quick look. "Did you get into it with Agent Burnett about your brother?"

"I might have had a few questions for him about his relentless focus on Kyle," Cooper conceded.

"A few questions?" she asked doubtfully. "What really happened?"

"Burnett got hostile and defensive. Started yelling at me to back off. He said he wasn't going to cooperate with any hit job on the bureau and threw Neil and me out of the building."

"Then you just answered your own question as to why my unit is involved," she said. "Damon—Agent Wolfe—the head of the office didn't want there to be any hint of bias or lack of cooperation in getting Neil's daughter back. But my team is just as good, if not better, than Burnett and the other agents. You don't have to worry about that. You don't need to get Neil worked up about the fact that this investigation is being run through a special task force."

Cooper didn't say anything right away, making her worry that he was going to muck things up by causing a problem where there didn't need to be one.

"I'm not worried," he said finally. "I'm actually happy. I wouldn't want Agent Burnett anywhere near this case."

He probably wasn't too happy to have her as his only alternative, but he left it at that.

"Good," she said, relieved to have one less problem to deal with.

"Have you ever spoken to Agent Burnett about Hannah's case since you joined the FBI?" Cooper asked.

"Yes. I looked at the file about a minute after I became an agent, but I didn't talk to him for another six or seven months after that. He was hard to get a hold of, but we were finally able to have a conversation about it."

"What did he say?"

"That the case still haunts him."

"Does he think Hannah is alive?"

"He wouldn't go that far, but he had hope that she was."

"Maybe the case haunts him, because he did a shitty job."

"He investigated other people, Cooper. Their interviews were in the file. It wasn't all about Kyle."

"It was mostly about him. But, of course, you'd be on Burnett's side."

"I'm on Hannah's side. I was always on her side," she said forcefully. "I actually do think Burnett could have done a better job, but it was eighteen years ago. He didn't have the resources then that we have now. But…"

"But?" Cooper pressed.

"I'd rather not say. I'm afraid you'll quote me in your next book."

"This is off the record. I want to know what you think."

"No, you don't. You just want me to agree with you, to say you're right."

"Well, that too," he admitted. "But whatever you have to say, finish saying it. I won't quote you. I swear." A half-smile followed his words.

A reluctant smile lifted her lips, too. They had sworn a lot to each other when they were kids. "Well, if you swear…"

"I do."

"I believe Agent Burnett could have dug deeper, pushed harder for a longer period of time. His investigation ended quickly. He told me he was working a lot of cases back then, and he was just one person. They didn't have the manpower they have now."

"Sounds like an excuse."

"Maybe, but even if he had tried harder, pushed longer, dug deeper, he still might not have found Hannah. Some kids are never found. I wish that wasn't true, but it is." She paused. "I'm sure there are families who feel like I've let them down. Sometimes, I feel that way myself. I wish I could bring every child home, but it doesn't always work out that way."

"I know," he said, a somber note in his voice.

"That said, I'm not giving up on finding Elisa," she told him. "We're just at the beginning. There's no reason to lose hope. And I won't stop looking for her. You can believe that or not."

"Do you swear?"

She looked over at him again, seeing a gleam of humor in his eyes. "I swear."

"Then I believe you."

CHAPTER SEVEN

ANDI'S BREATH of relief surprised Cooper. He wouldn't have thought she'd care one bit about what he thought, but apparently, she did. Maybe it wasn't that shocking, because she'd always desperately needed to be good at what she did, to feel like she was succeeding at whatever she was trying to accomplish.

He wondered how she dealt with the kids who didn't come home, the failures she'd alluded to. He couldn't imagine they would be anything but crushing for her.

The traffic thickened in front of them, and she tapped the brakes. "It's going to take forever to go a few miles," she muttered.

"No more speed for you," he said lightly.

"I need the speed for more than me," she returned. "Every second counts in a kidnapping case."

"How do you handle it?" he asked curiously. "When a child doesn't come home. What do you do to handle disappointment, the failure?"

"Well, I don't talk to psychologists," she said tersely.

"Why not? Are you against therapy?"

"I just don't think it works for me."

"How would you know if you've never tried it?"

"I tried it. My mom made me go to a therapist after the divorce, when she moved me to Chicago and wanted me to be super happy about all the changes in my life. It didn't help at all. The woman was a hundred years old, and we couldn't connect on any level. She kept telling me I needed to exercise more, like she thought I could outrun my problems."

"You didn't go to the right person."

"Probably not, but I don't know who would have been that person."

"Someone you would respect. You never had much tolerance for people you didn't respect."

"Does anyone?" she challenged. "Tolerating idiots is a waste of time."

He laughed. "Not everyone is an idiot who thinks differently than you."

"I know that, but this woman was just phoning it in. She wasn't even trying. That's what I really respect, Cooper—effort. It's not intelligence or what job title someone has or how much money they make, it's how hard they try, the energy they bring to whatever they're doing. I don't think that's too much to ask for."

"No, it's not," he admitted.

"Do you see patients? It doesn't seem like you have the time or the focus for that."

"I was part of a clinical practice the first two years of my career, but I was more interested in other things."

"Like books and podcasts and docuseries."

"Yes," he said unapologetically. "I felt like those pursuits would help me make a bigger impact on changes I feel are important in the study of criminal behavior and the justice system. I don't treat patients, but I have talked to hundreds of people in the last several years. I get my hands dirty. I hear it all, the good, the bad, the horrific, and the unimaginable."

She shot him a questioning look. "And how do you handle all that?"

"I actually run and work out a lot," he said with a smile. "Exercise is good for mental health. But I also have gotten better at compartmentalizing, at seeing the whole of a person, not just the worst part or the best part of them."

"You always tried to do that. But not everyone who says they are innocent is innocent."

"I'm not stupid, Andi. I'm very aware of the ability some people have to lie very well. But there are also people who have paid a terrible price for someone else's mistake. And if I don't help right that wrong when I see it, then what's the point of all the knowledge I've gained?"

"Helping those people is not a bad thing, but you still won't get Kyle back."

Her words hit a nerve. "I know that. But someone else will get their Kyle back."

"That's true," she said, sighing as the traffic in front of them stopped once more. "Do you think you would have become a psychologist if Hannah hadn't been kidnapped, if Kyle hadn't been accused?"

"No. I would have tried to be a professional baseball player."

She smiled. "You were a great pitcher. What was that pitch you used to throw that everyone raved about?"

"The submarine."

"That's right. It's like you were throwing sidearm or under-arm. Your mom thought you were going to break your arm. But your dad said it was your secret weapon."

He frowned. "How do you know that?"

She gave him an astonished look. "How do I know that? I sat with your parents at every game you pitched for like four years."

"You didn't come to that many games."

"Yes, I did. I used to freeze in the stands when you played at Hillside. How can you not remember that?"

Because he hadn't wanted to remember any of the good parts of their childhood friendship. "Well, I probably would have wrecked my arm with that pitch if I'd kept going," he said. "And it usually only worked the first time through the lineup. Then the batters would figure it out."

"Did you play throughout college?"

"I quit after high school graduation. It was too hard to focus on baseball. It didn't seem important enough. What about you? Did you go out for the school paper when you moved to Chicago? Were you the first reporter on every scene?"

"No."

He was surprised. "Really? But you wanted to be a journalist back then. It was all you talked about."

"Things were different after I moved and changed schools. I didn't fit in. I didn't have any friends, and I didn't know what I wanted to do, so I didn't do a lot."

"That's not the Andi I remember."

"You weren't the only one who had a rough time after the kidnapping, and then, with the divorce, I had a lot of other stuff to deal with. It was hard not to have anyone to talk to."

His heart squeezed in an unfamiliar way. He didn't want to feel sorry for her. Even if she'd stayed, he wouldn't have talked to her again after what she'd done to Kyle. But knowing her as well as he'd known her, he felt a rush of sympathy for the girl who'd always wanted her parents to love her more than they hated each other.

"Thank goodness we're finally moving," Andi said.

He was relieved as they sped up. They were getting a little too close, and he couldn't let that happen.

Ten minutes later, they parked on a side street and walked down an alley to the Back Street Bar. It was six-thirty and getting darker by the minute; the sun having slipped past the horizon a half hour ago. As they walked down the alley, there were all kinds of delicious smells coming from nearby restaurants.

"We should make some time to eat," he murmured.

"First, we work," she told him.

He smiled to himself once more. So many things about Andi had changed and yet so many had stayed the same. When she was on a mission, she was all in. Food and everything else could wait.

The bar was crowded when they walked inside. The clientele felt like an after-work group with twenty- and thirty-year-olds filling the tables and barstools."

"Nicer than I expected from the name," Andi said.

"I was thinking the same thing. So, Kristine worked here?"

"Apparently, before she became a nanny. Hopefully, someone will remember her and be able to tell us more about her."

"You'll have to wade through the line to talk to the bartenders," he said. "Maybe we should get a table and see if a server can give us information."

"All right."

As he turned around to find an empty table, his jaw dropped in shock at the man suddenly facing him. He hadn't seen that red hair and freckled face in at least a decade. "TJ Lassiter?" he murmured.

"Cooper Bradford," TJ said, surprise reflected in his gaze. His eyes widened. "And Andi Hart? What is going on? You're here together?"

"Hi, TJ," Andi said. "Long time, no see."

TJ's engaging brown gaze ran up and down Andi's pretty form, and Cooper frowned at the look in his eyes.

"Well, you certainly grew up," TJ said.

"So did you," Andi said.

"You look good," TJ added with an approving smile. "Doesn't she look good, Coop?"

Andi did look good. He just hadn't wanted to tell her that or spend time thinking about it.

"I thought you were living on the East Coast, Andi," TJ continued.

"I just moved back."

"Really? And you and Cooper are hanging out now?"

He could see the question mark in TJ's eyes, and so could Andi. Everyone in their neighborhood had witnessed the collapse of their friendship and the break between their families.

"Just having a drink," Andi said lightly.

"Can I join you?" TJ asked. "My girlfriend is coming, but she's not here yet."

Andi hesitated, clearly not wanting to waste time on TJ but also not wanting to say no. "Sure. Why don't you guys grab a table, and I'll get us drinks?" she offered.

"Beer works for me," TJ said.

"Same," he said, knowing she'd use the opportunity to talk to the bartender so they wouldn't waste time chatting to TJ.

They found a table in the back corner and sat down. He and TJ had been good friends growing up, at least until the kidnapping. He'd spent hours playing video games in TJ's garage with him and his older brother, Will. But that relationship, like all of his friendships, had changed when Kyle was brought in for questioning. There had been so many rumors and awful stories about his family that he'd barely made it through school each day.

Because Will and Kyle had been together earlier on the night that Hannah had disappeared, Will's comments about Kyle picking a fight with him and leaving early, had also helped put the spotlight on Kyle, putting a wall between his family and the Lassiter's. That wall had crumbled over time. His mom and TJ's mother, Kim, had eventually started talking again, and they'd become even closer after Kyle's suicide, and then again when TJ's father died.

But he'd never had much to do with TJ or Will after high school, and he was fine with that. He'd gone away to college in San Francisco, wanting to leave his past as far behind him as he could. Eventually, he'd made his way back to LA, but by then everyone he had known was gone or had moved on.

TJ scooped up a handful of nuts from a bowl in the middle of the table and popped them into his mouth. "I guess you're famous now, Cooper."

He shrugged. "I wouldn't say that."

"My mom sends me articles about you all the time," TJ said. "It's good what you're doing to help people falsely convicted. Kyle would be proud of you."

"Thanks," he said shortly.

"For the record, I never thought Kyle did it. I did wonder about Mr. Montgomery, though. I used to see people coming down the side yard between our houses late at night, and I'd hear him talking to them. I thought he was buying drugs. But I guess the police couldn't find anything."

He remembered TJ suggesting that years ago, but as TJ had said, nothing had come of it. Just another lead that had never been investigated.

He cleared his throat, not wanting to talk about the past. "What are you up to these days?"

"I'm working as a sound engineer. I have my own music studio. My mom found me this great space in Culver City. It's small, and I don't have a ton of business, but I make enough to keep the lights on, and I'm doing what I love."

"You loved music, surfing, and smoking weed," he added with a smile.

TJ grinned back at him. "Still love all three. Named my business Wave Studios."

"Very appropriate."

TJ looked around and then leaned forward. "So, dude, seriously, what's with you and Andi hanging out together? And man, she is much hotter than she used to be, don't you think?"

"She's okay. We just ran into each other." He didn't want to get caught up in why he and Andi were together. "So, you said you're meeting your girlfriend?"

"Naomi. And there she is now." He waved to a very thin and attractive Asian woman wearing a clingy short dress.

Naomi gave him a curious look as she came over. "Hello."

"Babe," TJ said, waving his hand toward Cooper. "I want you to meet an old friend of mine, Cooper Bradford. He grew up a few blocks from me. My girlfriend Naomi Chu."

"Nice to meet you, Naomi."

"We've actually met before, Dr. Bradford," she said with a gleam in her brown eyes.

"We have?" he asked with surprise.

Before she could reply, Andi returned to the table with a pitcher of beer and four glasses.

TJ introduced Andi to Naomi and then started filling their glasses. As he did so, he said, "I had no idea you knew Coop, Naomi."

"Wait, you two know each other?" Andi asked.

"Naomi said we met somewhere," he replied.

"But he doesn't remember me," Naomi said with a smile. "And I'm not surprised. We were at Covington Studios where I work. I was at your pitch meeting with Neil and Larry last year."

"Oh, I'm sorry. I don't remember meeting you."

"We didn't actually speak. I'm a lowly assistant. I was getting coffee for the group, but I was in and out of the room," Naomi said. "I keep telling myself that being in the room is just the first step, but I've been on that step a little too long. Anyway, I thought your project sounded interesting. I was surprised when Larry pulled it. I thought our VP was very interested."

He frowned. That wasn't what Neil had told him had happened with Covington Studios. He was wondering if he knew the real story. After Elisa came home, he needed to find out what had actually gone down with their pitch.

"You're going to be running that room one of these days, babe," TJ told Naomi. "You're the smartest woman I've ever met and the hottest," he said, giving her another kiss. "Sorry, guys, I can't help myself."

"It's nice to see you happy," he said.

"The happiest I've ever been," TJ said. "Ever since I met this woman, I can't stop smiling."

"Oh, please," Naomi said. "You had plenty of other women wanting to make you smile. I had to get in line."

"None like you."

Andi cleared her throat, and he sensed she was getting a little uncomfortable and impatient with the love talk and the PDA going on at the table. "Do you know Neil and Larry well?" she asked Naomi.

"I actually worked for Neil when he was running his company with his ex-wife Shana. That was six or seven years ago. I thought he was very good at picking the right material to produce. But there was a lot of tension between him and his wife, and they didn't have enough job potential for me, so I left." She paused, her smile fading. "I heard a rumor on my way over here that something happened to Neil's daughter, that she was kidnapped."

"Whoa," TJ said. "Seriously?" His gaze swung to Cooper's. "Did you know that?"

"Yes."

"Have you spoken to Neil?" Naomi asked.

"I have. He's very upset and worried."

TJ shook his head in bewilderment. "That's terrible. I hope his kid comes home, but we know that doesn't always happen…" His voice trailed away, and his gaze sharpened as it moved from him to Andi. "Wait a second. Aren't you in the FBI, Andi? Is that why you're here? Are you trying to find Neil's kid? Are you and Cooper solving another mystery together?"

"My team is working on the case," Andi said. "Cooper and I ran into each other at Neil's house, and we decided to catch up."

"But you hate each other," TJ said in bemusement.

"Not anymore," Andi said. "How's your family?"

"My dad passed away a couple of years ago. Will is a real estate agent now. He was working with my dad, but now he's running the company and very full of himself. I don't see much of him, which is fine with both of us."

"And your mom?"

"Busy. She's still working at the travel agency. She's running some tours to Europe, which is fun for her to actually get out of the office and see some of the places she sends people to." TJ paused. "I was just telling Coop that I have a music studio now, making my music and engineering others."

"That's great. You were always so talented, TJ. I remember when you and Tim Waters had that band in the eighth grade with Heather and Rocco."

TJ grinned. "That lasted about five minutes. But I actually recorded with Heather the other day. She's releasing her music online, and it's doing well. What's it like being an FBI agent? Do you have a gun? Do you have it with you now?"

"It's an exciting and rewarding job," she said.

"You always wanted to be a detective. When we were kids, you were constantly trying to solve mysteries."

"They were mostly just games back then."

"Until they weren't." TJ turned to Naomi. "I told you about that kid who lived next door to me who got kidnapped. Well, Andi and Cooper were on the street that night. They were the first at the scene."

"We were just riding our bikes," Cooper interjected. "We weren't looking for trouble."

"It's sad that little girl never came home," Naomi said.

"It was awful," TJ said with a hard glint in his eyes. "I used to play with her sometimes. She was always so happy. I still can't believe someone took her and no one ever figured out who." He looked back at Andi. "I hope this other kid is found. Do you have any leads?"

"We're talking to a lot of people," Andi replied. "Naomi, do you know Jillian Markham, by any chance?"

"I've met her a few times. She used to work for Neil, but she had a problem with his partner, Larry Friedman. That surprised me, because I always thought Larry was a good guy, not a creep like so many producers in Hollywood," Naomi added.

"She said Larry sexually harassed her," Cooper interjected.

"I heard that," Naomi admitted.

"That bothers me," he continued. "I don't want to work with a company that's not protecting their employees." He didn't want to throw Neil under the bus, but he did want more information from Naomi.

"Well, I don't know what happened. I like to believe women when they make these claims, but Jillian seemed like the kind of person who would lie to get ahead. Why are you asking about her? Is she a suspect?"

"We're investigating everyone tied to Mr. Benedict and his family," Andi answered.

"You sound so formal, Andi," TJ put in. "Hard to believe you're the same girl who used to shoot spit wads at me through a straw."

Andi laughed. "That was you, TJ, not me."

"That's not the way I remember it." TJ's expression shifted. "I've missed you guys. We ran around for so many years together, and then everyone was gone. That kidnapping changed so many lives."

"I would have been gone even if that hadn't happened," Andi said.

"Right. Your parents' divorce. That sucked."

"Yes, it did," Andi said.

"My mom still sees your dad quite often, either in the neighborhood or at the golf club. I think she said he got remarried, but then divorced again and now has a girlfriend."

"Yes," Andi said with a sigh. "My father is not someone who should ever be married. He doesn't believe in monogamy. Hopefully, no other woman will be fooled into thinking he does. Anyway..." She finished her beer, then gave him a look, "We should get going, Cooper."

"Okay," he said, as they stood up. "It was nice to meet you, Naomi, and to see you again, TJ."

"Let's meet up again sometime. Why don't you give me your number, Coop?" TJ took out his phone.

He hesitated, not sure he wanted to get back into the old crowd, but TJ would probably never call him anyway, so he gave him his number. And then he and Andi walked out of the bar.

They paused in the alley just outside. "That was crazy running into TJ," he said. "But do you really want to leave? I know you came here to get information on Kristine."

"I talked to a bartender," she replied. "He confirmed that Kristine worked there. She didn't socialize and was kind of quiet. He said she wasn't a good fit for the bar business. She left after a few months."

"That describes the Kristine I know."

"He also said she's still part of a run club that meets at the bar on Thursday nights. He saw her about two weeks ago and said she seemed happier than she used to."

"Thursday is a long time to wait to get more information on her from the run club."

"Well, if we don't have anything else before then, we can check it out," she said. "I have to say I didn't think LA was going to feel like such a small town. I didn't think I'd run into anyone I knew. First you, then TJ. And Naomi knows Neil, Larry, and Jillian."

"Well, they're all in the same business, so that's not that surprising."

"I guess not. Are you really going to call TJ?"

"No. And I don't think he'll call me. People say they want to get together again and then it doesn't happen, which is fine. I don't need to hang with TJ."

"You used to like him."

"I don't dislike him now. He's just not a part of my life anymore, and that's fine."

"I get it. Anyway, I need to get back to the office."

He nodded as they started walking down the alley. "What's next?"

"I don't know. I need to regroup."

As they walked out of the alley and crossed the street, a car came screaming around the corner, bearing straight toward Andi, who was slightly in front of him. He grabbed her arm and pulled her back, shoving her behind a row of trash bins as he dove on top of her.

CHAPTER EIGHT

THE VEHICLE HIT one of the cans, knocking it over with a loud crash, and then the car sped away. Cooper's heart jumped against his chest as he looked down at Andi's shocked brown eyes. He couldn't believe how close they'd come to being run over. "Are you all right?"

"I—I think so," she said breathlessly. "Are you?"

"Yes," he said, suddenly becoming aware of her soft body beneath his, which seemed more dangerous than the speeding car. He rolled to the side, then helped her to her feet. They ran toward the street, but the car was long gone.

"Did you see what kind of car it was?" she asked.

He shook his head. "I was blinded by the headlights."

"Me, too."

"He drove straight toward us, Andi. It was deliberate."

"Maybe it wasn't," she said, her voice uncertain. "He came around the corner so fast he might not have seen us." She tucked a loose strand of hair behind her ear. "I should have been paying better attention. I got distracted talking to you about the past, and I can't be distracted on the job. That's why you and I should not be working together."

"Your distraction wasn't my fault." He didn't like the way she was reframing the situation. "Instead of blaming me, you should thank me for saving your life."

Her eyes suddenly blazed with fire. "I'm not blaming you. But you didn't save my life. You just gave me a shove."

"Which got you out of the way." He felt a driving need to keep the anger between them, because whatever else was brewing was a lot more terrifying.

"You are so annoying. You always have to be right," she complained.

"Me? I'm not the one who always has to be right. That's you."

She blew out a frustrated breath. "I need to get back to work."

"This wasn't an accident," he said again.

"You don't know that."

"My gut says someone was waiting for us."

"Well, your gut is trained in psychology. Mine is trained in investigation."

"Then you should investigate."

"I intend to do just that. I need to go back to the office and see if we can find the car on any traffic cams in this area. I'll drive you back to the Benedict's house, so you can get your car."

"I'll call a rideshare," he said. "You need to go to work. And I need to…get the hell away from you for a while."

"It doesn't have to be a while. You should step away completely, Cooper. If this wasn't an accident, then it's not the end; it's the beginning."

"I'm not stepping away. I'm just taking a break."

He pulled out his phone. She took a few steps, then turned back to him.

"Thanks," she said.

Their gazes met and clung together for a long couple of seconds. A lot of emotions flew between them. Neither one of them had ever been good at backing down, being wrong, or apologizing, but he could see the truth in her eyes, and his tension eased. "You're welcome."

"You might not believe this, but I don't want you to get hurt,

Cooper. So go home. Support Neil with your friendship and let me do my job. Can you do that?"

"I can do that tonight. But tomorrow, I'm back with you. That's what Neil wants, and it's what I want. And, by the way, I can take care of myself." He paused. "Give me your number."

She hesitated, then rattled off her number.

He sent her a text to confirm. "I'll talk to you tomorrow, if not before."

———

Andi drove back to the office Tuesday night, her mind whirring with questions, her emotions all over the place. She was glad that Cooper had wanted a break from her because she desperately needed a break from him.

He had saved her life when, as recently as twenty-four hours ago, she would have said he'd be the first one to push her in front of a speeding car, not save her from getting hit. And when he'd landed on top of her, when their bodies had gotten tangled up, with adrenaline surging through her veins, she'd felt a physical attraction to him that was completely unexpected.

It was why she'd felt the need to yell at him, to make sure they both remembered that they didn't like each other, that they weren't best friends like they'd once been; they were mortal enemies.

She suspected he'd felt the same need, maybe even more strongly than she had, because he blamed the devastation of his brother's life, his family unit, on her. Maybe he was pissed at himself for shoving her out of the way.

But, of course, he wouldn't do anything else. Cooper always had a tremendously strong sense of right and wrong. When she was a kid, she liked to push boundaries, sometimes rationalizing that the end justified the means. Cooper had been the one to hold her back from going too far.

Conversely, she'd sometimes pushed him to go further than he wanted to. That had made them a good team for a long time.

Now they were a team again, but not voluntarily. They'd been forced together by a kidnapping, by a desperate father. Which only reminded her that she was wasting time thinking about Cooper when she needed to focus on what had just happened and why.

If it was deliberate, if the driver had been waiting for her and wanted to take her out or scare her in some way, then she was making someone nervous. That meant she was closer than she thought to a lead. But who was the lead? She'd talked to everyone attached to Neil's household and spoken to Jillian twice. That didn't narrow anything down. She needed more help, and the sooner she got it, the better.

When she arrived at the office, she found most of the agents had gone home, with the exception of Savannah and Nick, who were still working on the investigation. She filled them in on the near miss at the bar, as well as what she'd learned about Kristine and Jillian since her last check-in.

The three of them spent another thirty minutes trying to find traffic cam video from the area around the bar. Unfortunately, since she hadn't gotten a good look at the car, they didn't have much to go on.

"Maybe it was just a reckless driver," Savannah said when they ran out of steam.

"It's a possibility," she conceded.

"But you don't believe that." Nick gave her an assessing look.

"It felt deliberate. But I can't imagine who would come after me from this case. Our investigation has barely started. I'm not close to finding Elisa or who kidnapped her."

"Maybe closer than you think," Savannah said. "Jillian Markham is looking more and more guilty by the minute. She was near the Benedict's house this morning around the time of the kidnapping. She ran away from you, had a secret meeting with Neil, where she apparently wanted to blackmail him, and then packed a bag and hightailed it out of town. Her roommate talked to you. Maybe she's involved, too. She could have told Jillian that you were closing in on her."

Savannah made a good case. "Jillian is the best lead we have," she agreed. "We need to find her."

"Another person that needs to be located is Daniel Guerrero, Solange's son," Nick said. "He's not returning calls. And his mother claims she hasn't seen him all day."

She sat back in her chair, feeling suddenly exhausted. Her lack of sleep was catching up to her.

"You look beat, Andi," Savannah said. "You should go home."

"There's a child missing."

"It's always hard to call it a day when that's in play, but there's not much else we can do tonight. I need to head out in a few minutes as well."

"Of course," she said, realizing it was past eight. "You should have left earlier. You don't need to be pulling long days."

"I'm fine, but I do occasionally need to see my husband," Savannah said with a smile.

"That's why I stay single," Nick said. "I don't have to worry about getting home to anyone."

"I don't think that's why you stay single," Andi said dryly. "You prefer the many over the one."

Nick laughed. "You don't think I've changed in the seven years since we last saw each other?"

"Have you?" she countered.

"Maybe a little," he replied, an odd shadow entering his gaze.

"Where are you living now?"

"About six blocks from here. What about you?"

"Two and a half miles away. So, neither one of us has much of a commute. Where do you live, Savannah?"

"Ryker and I have a house in Pacific Palisades. We decided we don't need to be as close to our offices as we used to be." Savannah stood up. "I want to have you both over when this is all over. We'll barbecue by the pool."

"Barbecue by the pool," Nick mimicked. "You sound very LA, Savannah."

"Well, that's where I live now," she said with an unapologetic smile. "I'll see you both tomorrow. Don't stay here all night. You'll have more energy for tomorrow."

"Goodnight," she said. As Savannah left, she turned back to Nick. "I appreciate your help today."

"Well, apparently, that's what we do here," Nick replied. "It's all-hands-on deck for whatever is the hot case. That's going to take a little getting used to."

"I agree. I'm used to a more formal hierarchy of power, but Flynn jumps right in with everyone else." She gave him a knowing look. "Are you already tired of being at a desk after one day?"

"Surprisingly, no. I've been working undercover a lot the last several years, living under another name, pretending to like things I hate and hate things I love. It's refreshing to just be myself and do my job with a little distance between me and the criminals."

There was an undertone to his words that made her curious about his last assignment. It sounded like he needed to find his feet again. Before she could ask any questions, her phone buzzed. The call was from the LA office. "This must be Damon," she said.

"Take it," Nick said with a nod. "I'm going to make some coffee."

"Make enough for two," she said, then took the call. "Agent Hart."

"This is Agent Burnett," a man said.

Her heart skipped a beat. "Agent Burnett. What can I do for you?"

"I understand you're working in LA now."

"Yes, I am."

"And you've taken the lead on the Benedict case."

"I have."

"Well, I might have some information that will be helpful to you. Why don't we meet tomorrow morning and discuss it? It won't take long. I can meet you for breakfast at Chicky's Pancake House. It's near your office."

She was surprised and felt a little uncomfortable agreeing to his invitation. Why was he getting involved in a case that had been taken out of his office and given to her? She didn't understand the local politics yet, so she decided to say yes and then speak to Flynn. "All right. What time?"

"Eight. And let's keep this between you and me for the moment."

"Why the secrecy?" she asked.

"I'll tell you tomorrow."

He clicked off before she could ask him any more questions.

"Everything okay?" Nick asked as he walked back to her desk with two coffees in his hand. He set one down in front of her. "I need to catch up with Damon one of these days."

"That wasn't Damon. It was another agent, Jim Burnett. He works kidnappings. We actually met a long time ago when I was a kid, and he was investigating the disappearance of a child on my block."

"I remember you talking about that at Quantico, how that kidnapping was why you became an agent." Nick paused, giving her a quizzical look. "But I thought we had this case, that Damon didn't want his agents working on it because of some possible perceived conflict of interest."

"That's what Flynn told me, but Agent Burnett said he has information and wants to talk to me tomorrow away from the office. In fact, he'd like me to keep the whole thing private, which, of course, I'm not doing, since I just told you about it."

Nick gave her a thoughtful look. "What do you think that's about?"

"I don't know. Flynn told me that Burnett and some of the agents on that team had a run-in with Neil Benedict and Cooper Bradford over a docuseries they're doing and that's why we're running things and not them. I guess I'll just meet him and see what he has to say."

"This guy must be a well-seasoned agent if he was working kidnappings when you were a kid."

"It was eighteen years ago. He was thirty-four at the time, fifty-two now."

"As a veteran agent with a ton of experience on what's going to be a high-profile case, I bet he's angry that Damon took him off the investigation. Maybe he wants to prove he would have been the better pick. Or he genuinely wants to help you solve the case."

"That about covers all the options," she said dryly.

Nick shrugged, giving her a light smile. "I've never been good at office politics. That was one perk of working out of the office."

"I'm sure you ran into politics and power plays in the criminal organizations you infiltrated."

"That's true. But those plays usually ended with someone dying, not getting a promotion."

"Well, I'm not going to worry about Burnett. I'll find out how he feels tomorrow. In the meantime, I'm going to do more research on all the players in the Benedict circle. I need to know a lot more a lot faster."

"Let's get to it," Nick said. "I have nothing else to do tonight."

She didn't either, and she'd rather work than go home and think about why she was suddenly feeling attracted to Cooper when he was the last person on earth she should want.

CHAPTER NINE

COOPER DIDN'T GET much sleep and woke up Wednesday morning at six with a kink in his neck and a bad attitude. His dreams had been all over the place. He'd thought about Elisa, Hannah, his brother, Kyle, and, of course, Andi.

He had liked it better when he knew exactly how he felt about her, when everything was black and white, no gray areas. But a lot of gray had come into play yesterday.

He'd saved Andi's life or at least he'd prevented her from getting hurt, but that hadn't bothered him as much as the way he'd felt when they were tangled up in each other, when her body had been beneath his, when her face, her mouth, had been so close... He shook his head, hoping to drive that disturbing thought out of his mind. He needed to remember who she was—and that was someone who had betrayed him. She'd broken their friendship. She'd done something she couldn't take back. His brother had died, in part because of her actions.

Needing to get away from his thoughts, he opted for a run instead of a shower. Six miles and an hour later, he ended up at the bakery in Santa Monica where his younger sister worked.

Monica looked a lot like his mom with blonde hair and hazel eyes, while he resembled his dad with brown hair and green eyes. Kyle had been a mix of both their parents. Monica took one look at him, then poured him a cup of coffee and put an apple-filled pastry on a plate.

"You look like you could use some caffeine and some sugar," she said.

"Is that a polite way of saying I look like shit?" he asked dryly.

"Yes, because I've matured over the years."

He couldn't argue with that. His baby sister was twenty-seven years old now and an assistant manager at this bakery. Monica was also becoming an excellent pastry chef.

As another clerk took over the register, Monica followed him to a table and sat down.

"What's going on?" she asked, her gaze intent on his face.

"Not much."

"Liar. You rarely show up here without something on your mind."

"That's not true. I come in all the time," he argued.

"And there's usually something you want to talk about, so talk."

"You're busy," he stalled, knowing she was right. He did want to talk, and while he could talk to Monica about anything, he didn't think anything included Andi.

Monica was five years younger than him and had only been nine when Hannah was kidnapped, when Andi had turned on the family. She might not have understood everything that had gone on between them, but she'd been around for the aftermath.

"Carey can handle the counter." Monica pulled the band out of her hair and shook out her blonde waves. It's not that crowded today. I can take a few minutes. What's bothering you?"

"Neil Benedict's daughter was kidnapped yesterday."

"Oh, my God. I had no idea. And you just said nothing much was going on. What happened? Isn't his daughter a baby?"

"Yes. Elisa is six months old. She was taken from her bedroom, from her crib."

"Oh, man. This must be bringing back some bad memories for you, Cooper."

"It is," he admitted.

"Well, hopefully, the outcome is better than what we saw with Hannah. I still can't believe that no one has ever found her." She paused, her gaze narrowing on his face. "And now I know why you look like you haven't slept. Hopefully, the caffeine and sugar will help."

He gave her a weak smile as he sipped his coffee. "It can't hurt."

"Is there something else? Because it feels like there's something else on your mind."

"Andi is back in LA. She's an FBI agent now, and she's working on this kidnapping case."

Monica's eyes widened in shock. "Your Andi?"

A strange tingle ran down his spine at her words. "She's not my Andi," he snapped. "And what other Andi would I be talking about?"

"Sorry. Did you see her?"

"I spent half the day with her yesterday. Neil asked me to make sure the FBI isn't going down the wrong road with their investigation, which means I have to follow Andi around."

"And she's okay with that?"

"Apparently, the FBI will play along up to a point, just to keep everyone happy and keep the focus on finding Elisa."

"This is crazy. What's Andi like now?"

He didn't know how to answer that question. "I don't know. Different—kind of the same," he said with a vague shrug.

"That doesn't tell me much."

"She's Andi—dogged, determined, and tough. I don't doubt that she wants to find Neil's kid more than she wants to take her next breath. She can't stand a question that she can't answer, a puzzle that she can't solve. But I hate the fact that she's the one on this case, with my friend's daughter's life on the line."

"Do you think she's going to make another big mistake, like

she did with Kyle? Or are you just unhappy that you have to spend time with her?"

He considered her questions. It would be easier to say he thought she might make a mistake, but that wasn't the truth, and he didn't like to lie, especially to himself. "It's mostly that I don't want to spend time with her, but the flip side is that I can keep an eye on her actions."

"What do you think so far?"

"That she's doing what she needs to do."

"I'm not surprised she became an agent. Playing detective was her favorite game—yours, too. Sometimes, you two even let me play, although not that often. And I always had to be the lookout."

"That was an important job."

She rolled her eyes. "It was a job to keep me out of the way." She paused. "Did you know she was an agent before yesterday?"

"Yes. But I thought she was working on the East Coast. Apparently, she just moved back this week."

"For good?"

"It sounded that way."

"So, you spent half the day with her, and you didn't kill her? How is that possible?"

"Not entirely sure," he admitted.

"Did you talk about the past?"

"A little. She said she was sorry about Kyle's death. But I don't believe she takes responsibility for the things she said that got Kyle arrested. She still doesn't believe she did anything wrong."

Monica stared back at him. "I know that you've hated Andi for a long time, but I sometimes wonder—"

"There's no wondering," he interrupted with annoyance. "I know what she did. She betrayed me."

"She was fourteen years old. She said what she saw, and she was wrong. But I don't think she tried to get Kyle into trouble."

"You don't know what she did," he said, shaking his head. "You were too young."

"I wasn't too young to know that Kyle had issues, Cooper. He didn't always act appropriately, and it wasn't just Andi's comments that put attention on him."

"It doesn't matter anymore. I don't want to talk about that."

She gave him a sharp look. "Then you must have come here to talk about Andi."

He ran a hand through his hair. "How did you get to be so smart?"

"It runs in the family. You're incredibly smart, too, but when it comes to Andi, you're blinded by emotion. I'm not saying she didn't stir up problems for us. She did. I just don't know if everything that happened to Kyle is all on her. You should get to know her again. Maybe you could be friends."

"I don't want to be her friend," he said immediately.

"Maybe you want to be more. And that's what really bothers you."

"Well, I think we're done talking about Andi," he said, disliking the new gleam in her eyes.

"I just hit a nerve."

"No, you didn't. And after Elisa is found, I don't see any reason why Andi and I should ever see each other again."

"It's weird that a kidnapping would bring you back together. You've come full circle."

"This one will end differently. Elisa will come home, and someone will pay for what they did. That someone will be the actual kidnapper, not just the most likely suspect who looks good on paper. That's what I'm going to make sure happens."

"I hope that is what happens. I better get back to work," she added as a group of teens came into the bakery. She pulled her hair back into a loose bun on top of her head and gave him a smile. "You'll know the right thing to do when you have to make a choice."

"That's a lot of confidence you have in me."

"Because I know who you are, Cooper, and I've watched you my whole life. On another note, tomorrow is going to be a rough day. You should stop by Mom's."

"I will," he said, knowing that tomorrow was the anniversary of his brother's death. It wasn't a day they wanted to remember, but one none of them could forget.

———

Andi got to Chicky's Pancake House a little before eight on Wednesday morning and grabbed a table. The restaurant was busy, and the plates going by made her stomach rumble, especially the ones with large stacks of pancakes topped with strawberries and blueberries. But she started by ordering coffee. She didn't want to be digging into a big breakfast when Agent Burnett arrived. Maybe once they were done talking, she'd order something.

She was going to need to fuel up for what would probably be another grueling day after what had been another short night of sleep. She'd thought she'd exhausted herself by researching the Benedicts and everyone around them until well after midnight, but as soon as she'd gone home, gotten into bed, and closed her eyes, Cooper had popped back into her brain. He was so confusing, hating her one minute, saving her life the next. She didn't like feeling off-balance, out of control, and that was the way he was making her feel.

But she couldn't worry about their relationship. She had a job to do, a child to find, and while she didn't have a concrete lead to pursue, she did have a long list of people she needed to talk to. She would start on that list as soon as she found out what Agent Burnett wanted with her.

A moment later, Burnett walked through the door. She'd last seen him six years ago. She'd thought he'd aged then, because in her mind he'd been a tall, stern, dark-haired man with a ruthless glint in his eyes. But he'd started to gray the last time she'd seen him, and now his hair was completely silver and much thinner. He'd gained some weight around his waistline, and his step wasn't purposeful but more of a weary shuffle.

She knew he was fifty-two years old, because she'd done some research on him when she'd first joined the Bureau, wanting to know more about the man who had both inspired her to join the FBI and had also taken what she'd told him too far and allowed the media and community to go after Kyle when they had no evidence to actually charge him with a crime. That hadn't been clear to her when she was fourteen, but it had become crystal clear after she'd become an agent.

Their last conversation had been somewhat confrontational, as he'd gotten defensive about her questions regarding Hannah's kidnapping, which was now a very cold case.

He pulled out the chair across from her and sat down, waiting to speak until after the server poured him a cup of coffee and gave him a menu.

When they were alone, he said, "I was surprised to hear you joined MacKenzie's unit."

"I just started yesterday," she replied.

"That's what Damon said when he took away what should have been my case." His dark eyes seemed to get colder.

"What can I do for you?" she asked, wanting him to get to the point.

"Well, I'm confused about one thing. I'm off the Benedict case because I had a run-in with Mr. Benedict and his sidekick, your old friend Cooper Bradford. But you, the girl who helped us arrest Bradford's brother, is fine to work on the investigation. Help me understand that."

"I don't know anything about the case politics. I did hear you had a run-in with Cooper and Neil Benedict."

"It was a difference of opinion, but I always do my job."

"You should take up your concerns with Damon. I'm only interested in finding the missing child. That's what I do now, what I've been doing for the past seven years."

"Seven years is nothing to the twenty-four years I've put in. You don't come close to my level of experience."

"I can't argue with that," she said evenly. "But I'm good at what I do."

"So am I," he returned. "You didn't answer my question."

"What was the question?"

"Does Damon know you and Bradford have a past?"

"It hasn't come up, but it's not a secret," she replied.

"Then you won't care if I tell Damon about it."

"Do whatever you want. But please don't tell me this is why you dragged me down here in the middle of an active investigation."

His jaw stiffened. "That's not why I asked you to meet. I have information that might be helpful."

"And now you want to help me?"

"Of course. As you said, there's a child's life on the line."

"Then let's talk about what you know," she said, still suspecting he had a hidden agenda.

He took a moment to lift his coffee mug to his lips and take a sip. Then he said, "Claire Benedict was treated for postpartum depression."

She had to admit he'd surprised her. "How do you know that?"

"I have a source. Mrs. Benedict saw Dr. Stefan Mulders for three months after her baby was born. She stopped seeing him a few weeks ago."

"Maybe she felt better."

"Or she was still struggling and did something to get rid of her kid," he countered.

"Who was your source?"

"I can't say, but the information is solid."

"I'll look into it. Was there anything else?"

"I can be helpful to you, Andi," he said. "I have a lot of connections in circles that include the Benedicts. I've been living in LA a long time. If you keep me updated on the situation, I might be able to provide some contacts for you."

"I appreciate that," she said.

"I hope you do. I also hope you don't believe that I botched the case involving your neighbor."

She wasn't about to go down that road now. "I don't want to get into all that. It happened a long time ago."

"Yes, it did, but it still feels like yesterday to me. It must be the same for you, too."

"It is," she admitted. "Especially now that I'm back in Los Angeles."

"I did everything I could to bring that little girl home. And Bradford's brother was a legitimate suspect. You were right to point him out."

"But he didn't do it, and whoever did, got away with it." She paused. "I still have hope that one day that person will pay, that Hannah will get justice."

"The case has never been closed. So that's still possible."

"I hope so. Thanks for the information."

"Like I said, I can be an excellent ally if you keep me in the loop."

She didn't comment on his statement. If she needed his help, she'd ask for it, but she was still suspicious of his motives. And she wasn't completely sure if he was trying to help her or send her in the wrong direction because he was angry she'd gotten the case. But she would talk to Claire about what he'd told her and go from there.

"How is it dealing with Bradford again?" he asked. "He was furious with you."

"A lot of years have passed since then."

"So you're friends now?"

"That's probably a stretch." She paused, knowing she shouldn't go back into the past, but she couldn't stop herself. "The Bradford family suffered a lot because of Kyle's arrest, and

I've wondered why you made it so public. Kyle was basically paraded in front of the community as the kidnapper."

"That's not what happened. I didn't treat Kyle any differently than any other suspect. The kids in the neighborhood talked to the press, not me."

"You did make a statement confirming that he was being investigated."

"I don't recall that. But it's possible I confirmed we were talking to him along with other suspects. You know how the media is. You have to give them something."

"I've never put that big of a target on a person of interest when there was so little evidence."

He bristled at her words. "That's not true. You've been in the press. I've seen some of your interviews. You've had to talk about suspects. And you know that no matter how good we are, sometimes we just can't bring a missing person home. That's a sad and harsh truth." He took an angry breath. "Your old friend, Bradford, needs someone to blame for his brother's death, and I'm a good target. Not just me, the entire team of agents that worked on that case. He's trying to destroy your fellow agents. I hope you don't forget that when you're talking to him. You can't trust him. You can't trust anything he says."

She couldn't tell him he was wrong, because he was the best target Cooper had besides herself. But there was something really uncomfortable about their entire conversation, and she was beginning to better understand why Damon had given her the case.

"Can I buy you breakfast?" Burnett asked.

She was still hungry, but she was eager to get to the Benedict's house, and she really didn't want to spend any more time with Agent Burnett. "I had coffee. That's all I need."

"Keep in touch."

She gave him a brief smile as she got to her feet. "Thanks for your help."

As she headed out of the restaurant, she got a call from Flynn.

"The media is hounding us for an update. We're setting up a press conference for eleven o'clock this morning. I'd love to have something definitive to say."

"I would love that, too, but we have next to nothing." She felt like a failure having to admit that. "The press conference could be helpful in increasing public awareness of the case and generating more leads. Have you spoken to Neil Benedict? Does the family want to make a statement?"

"I haven't spoken to him yet, but I'd prefer if they didn't make a statement. I'd like to keep this short and simple with just you and Damon at the microphone."

"Damon, not you?" she asked.

"It's less complicated if Damon looks like he's running things."

She was a little surprised that Flynn was so willing to stay in the shadows. On the other hand, that's where he'd always operated best. "All right. I'll go to the Benedict's house now and let them know that we'll be making a statement and hopefully talk them out of trying to be involved, too."

CHAPTER TEN

WHEN SHE ARRIVED at the Benedict home a little before nine, the media presence was heavy. The police had provided an officer to control the crowd, but as she walked past the caution tape, she was thrown numerous questions, none of which she answered.

Another officer let her into the house, and she found three members of the Benedict household gathered in the living room: Neil and his parents were having an intense and somewhat heated conversation when she entered. There was no sign of Claire, Kristine, or Solange.

"Agent Hart, I'm glad you're here," Neil said, getting up from the couch. "I want to make a statement. I want to ask for the public's help in finding my daughter."

"We're going to hold a press conference today at eleven," she said. "It will be at the LA office, and the director, Damon Wolfe, and myself will be making a statement and answering questions."

"Okay. So, Claire and I can speak as well."

"We talked yesterday about why that wasn't a good idea."

"It wasn't a good idea when we were waiting for a ransom demand, but that never came, and my little girl has been gone for twenty-four hours. We need everyone to start looking for her."

"I understand your desperation and your fear," she told him. "I would want to do the same thing, but it's better if you don't go on camera."

"Why?"

"You'll give too much away."

"Give what away? I don't know anything."

"Exactly. But the kidnapper doesn't know that. It's best if he or she doesn't have any idea how close or how far away we are to finding them."

"Are we close or are we far away?" he challenged.

"We're working hard to find Elisa."

He gave her a hard look. "You better not be trying to cover your ass in some way."

"Keeping you away from the press is about Elisa and nothing else," she returned.

"Where's Cooper? Why isn't he with you? I want him involved. I thought I made that clear."

"I haven't spoken to him yet today, but I will," she promised, wondering why Cooper hadn't reached out, but she was happy not to have to deal with him just yet. "Right now, I'd like to speak to Claire."

"Why?"

"Because I need to talk to her," she said. "Where is she?"

"She's upstairs in Elisa's room. She can't seem to leave it." Neil paused. "She didn't sleep at all last night. She's having a very difficult time."

"You both are," she said with compassion in her gaze.

"I just want to bring my child home."

"That's what we're going to do," she said. Then she left the living room and moved up the stairs.

Claire was in Elisa's room as Neil had predicted. She was sitting in a rocking chair, holding a stuffed rabbit to her chest, her face pale, her eyes and nose red from crying. She looked exhausted, like a shell of a woman.

"Claire," she said gently.

Claire started, her gaze swinging to Andi's. "Did you find her?"

"Not yet. I need to ask you a few questions. They're personal, and I wish I didn't have to ask, but I do."

"What?" Claire asked, confusion in her gaze.

"Have you been treated for postpartum depression?"

Claire's eyes widened. "Yes. Why?"

"How long were you in treatment?"

"A couple of months. But it went away. I got better." Realization entered her gaze. "You don't think I had something to do with this, do you?" She put a hand to her mouth. "My God! You think I hurt my daughter, and I'm trying to cover it up by pretending she's been kidnapped." Claire jumped to her feet, almost knocking Andi over. "How could you believe such a terrible thing? I love my daughter. I just had trouble feeling like myself." She shook her head in confusion. "I got better," she repeated.

"I believe you," she said. "And I don't think you hurt Elisa. I just need to know everything about everyone in Elisa's life and that includes you. Who treated you?"

"Dr. Mulders—Stefan Mulders. He'll tell you I snapped out of it a couple of months ago. It didn't last that long. And I'm a good mother. I swear I am."

She didn't want to believe that Claire had anything to do with Elisa's disappearance, but years of experience had taught her to investigate every clue, not just the ones that led her in a direction she wanted to go. "I'm glad you're feeling better. It must have been difficult to go through that."

"It was unexpected. I always wanted to be a mother. I thought it would be the happiest time of my life. I felt confused and numb, but I worked through it. Dr. Mulders said it's not uncommon. Lots of women suffer from postpartum depression."

"That's true."

"Neil had to help more during the early days, and then we got Kristine, who was wonderful with Elisa and with me. I don't think Elisa suffered because of my depression. I never wanted to hurt her. I just felt off, like I had no energy. I couldn't find any joy. And then, after talking to Dr. Mulders, the joy came back. I love being a mother now. I feel so empty with her gone. It's like there's a hole in my heart." She paused. "Do you have children?"

"No."

"Then you probably can't imagine how this feels."

"I can't," she agreed. "Can you tell me any more about Kristine? I haven't found much information on her. Does she have friends? A boyfriend? A relative in town? Has she talked about anyone in her social circle with you?"

Claire gave her a troubled look. "Kristine wouldn't hurt Elisa."

"That wasn't my question."

"She has a friend named Lindsay. I think she used to work with her somewhere before she became a nanny."

"What do you know about Lindsay?"

"You should just ask Kristine about her."

"I will, but what has she told you?"

"Not much. I think they run in a club together. Kristine doesn't really share her personal life. Neil and I try to respect her privacy."

"All right. Is Kristine here now?"

"I don't know. Probably. I haven't been downstairs."

"I'll go look for her."

"If you want me to take a lie detector test or something, I will. I love my daughter so much."

"I understand. Thank you for being honest with me. I hope we'll have good news soon."

When she left the baby's room, she headed down the hall to Kristine's bedroom. The door was open, the room was empty, and the bed was made. It looked exactly as it had yesterday, which made her wonder if Kristine had slept at the house. In fact, she wondered when anyone had last seen her.

She left the room and moved quickly down the stairs to find Neil. He was in the entryway, and he wasn't alone. Cooper was with him.

Her heart skipped a little beat as Cooper looked up and met her gaze, and something inexplicable passed between them. But she didn't have time to think about the weird tingle running down her spine.

"Where's Kristine?" she said, when she hit the last step.

Neil looked taken aback at her question. "She's around somewhere."

"Is she? When is the last time you saw her?"

Neil thought for a moment. "It was last night. She went out for a run around eight."

"When did she come home?"

"I didn't see her come back, but that's not unusual. I'm sure she didn't want to intrude on the family."

"How was she acting yesterday?"

"She was quiet and worried, feeling very guilty. She kept apologizing, telling me she was sorry. She tried to be helpful; she went to the store and picked up food. She tidied up the kitchen. I think she helped my mom make dinner, not that anyone felt like eating." He ran a hand through his hair. "She was being normal. Why?"

"I don't think she's here, Neil. And I'm concerned that no one seems to know much about her life outside this house. Claire mentioned a friend named Lindsay. Have you heard Kristine talk about her?"

"They run together."

Another mention of the running reminded her that the bartender had told her Kristine belonged to a run club that met there on Thursday night. But she needed to talk to Kristine before another day passed. "Is there anyone else Kristine has talked about?"

Neil frowned as he thought for a moment. "I guess we didn't really talk about her life much."

"Do you know how the Weiselbergs met her?" she asked.

"It was through another nanny at the park by their house. They tried her out for a few days and loved her. They gave her a strong recommendation. I assumed they vetted her before they hired her."

That might have been the wrong assumption. "Do you remember the other nanny's name?"

"No. I can call Glen and ask him."

"That would be helpful."

"I can't believe Kristine would be involved. Why would she be?" When Andi didn't answer right away, he turned to Cooper. "What do you think?"

"That people can be motivated to do things if the price is right. Does Kristine have family back home that she sends money to? Parents, siblings?"

"She did say her father died when she was young, and her mother raised her alone. I got the feeling they weren't close. Her mother didn't want her to move to the US. They haven't talked in a few years. I believe she was an only child. We paid her very well. She never asked for an advance on her paycheck or anything like that. She had free room and board here, so it was a great deal. It's not like she was desperate for cash or anything. And she lived a quiet life." He shook his head. "She's an obvious suspect. I understand that, but it doesn't make sense. It doesn't feel right."

"Well, I'd like to talk to her further, so I'd like you to call her and find out when she's coming back," Andi said.

Neil took out his phone and did as she requested, but Kristine didn't answer.

"Leave her a message to get in touch as soon as possible," she instructed.

"I'm sure she'll call me back," he said after he finished leaving the message. "She loves this job. She told me many, many times that she feels lucky to have found us. She adores children and being a nanny is the best thing she's ever done. I really don't want her to be involved in this. If I put my daughter's kidnapper in her bedroom, I don't think I can live with myself."

"One step at a time. We just want to talk to Kristine, to know more about her. We'll see where it goes from there."

He let out a heavy sigh. "I don't think I can stand not seeing Elisa for another day, much less another night."

"Hopefully, it won't come to that. I need to get to the press conference. I'll check in with you after that."

"Where's the conference at?" Cooper asked.

"The LA office."

"I'll see you there," he said.

She wasn't thrilled to hear that, but she was happy that he didn't want to go with her now. She needed to get ready for a multitude of questions that she wouldn't be able to answer, and she didn't need Cooper to distract her.

"Kristine didn't do this," Neil told Cooper. "Agent Hart is going down the wrong lane. It's more likely a stranger did this, someone from the construction company or something."

Cooper was a little surprised that Neil was so strong in his defense of Kristine. He'd only known her for four months. That wasn't a long time. And she had been the last one to see Elisa. Where was Neil's anger at the nanny? It seemed odd that he had heard none of that. After Neil's earlier confession about sleeping with Jillian, he really hoped that there was nothing going on between him and Kristine.

"How can you be so sure about Kristine?" he asked.

"Because I know her. She has a good heart. She's a kind person. She's not Hollywood. She's not materialistic and obsessed with fashion or style or social media. She's just a sweet, young woman. And she loved Elisa." He stopped abruptly. "God!

I'm talking in past tense. I don't want to do that. Kristine loves Elisa, and she wouldn't hurt her."

"Do you know where she is right now?"

"I don't. But it's not like she's missing. She was around all day yesterday."

"Well, as soon as you hear from her, you need to make sure she comes back and talks to the FBI. Her absence creates a void that will fuel speculation. The best way for her to protect herself is to be completely forthcoming."

"I don't think she's done anything to the contrary. She answered every question that was asked of her. They're circling back to her because they don't have anyone else. It just frustrates me because I want them to find the person who did this so we can get our daughter back."

"And no one has reached out to you privately, right?"

A flash of anger ran through Neil's eyes. "No. I haven't talked to anyone. And I'm still considering whether I want to speak to the media, even though Agent Hart strongly advised against it."

He didn't think it was a good idea, either. Neil wasn't disciplined enough to follow a script, and who knew what he'd say or how he'd say it? "Just give the FBI some more time," he said. "Let's see how the press conference plays out. Maybe it will generate new leads." As he finished speaking, Claire came down the stairs, tears dripping from her eyes. It was difficult to believe she had any left.

"Claire," Neil said with concern. "What's wrong now?"

"They think I did it," she said. "The FBI. Agent Hart knows about my postpartum depression. Did you tell her?"

"Of course not. And you don't have that anymore," Neil said, giving Claire a hug.

"I told her I didn't. I said I love my daughter. I never wanted to hurt her."

Neil turned to him with fury in his gaze. "Did you tell Agent Hart about Claire's issues?"

"No. I didn't even think about it, and Agent Hart never asked me about it."

"What the hell is she doing? We need another agent in charge. I have to call someone."

"Hold on," he said. "Let me talk to Agent Hart and find out what she's thinking."

"I need someone else," Neil said in frustration. "You were so right about inept investigators."

He hated having his words taken out of context. But that wasn't important now. "Look, if Agent Hart knows, then everyone in the Bureau knows, so there's no point in trying to get her off the case. I suspect she's just checking every possibility. I doubt that this will be an issue."

"It better not be."

"I love Elisa," Claire repeated.

"I know," he said. "Have you slept at all, Claire?"

"I can't close my eyes."

"You need to try. Maybe take a light sedative. Do you have something like that?"

Claire shrugged. "I don't know."

"I called Dr. Mulders' office, but he was out," Neil said. "He's going to call back as soon as he returns."

"I don't want to take anything," Claire said. "I need to be alert in case Elisa needs me."

"You need to rest so that you will have all your energy available when she's home," he told Claire. "Let Neil take you upstairs. Lay down for a while. See if you can get a little sleep."

"He's right, Claire," Neil said.

"Okay," she said wearily. "But you'll keep on them, Cooper?"

"I will. I'll go to the press conference now." As Neil took his wife upstairs, Cooper left the house. The news vans were mostly gone, probably heading downtown to the press conference. That was good. He didn't want Neil or Claire walking out of the house in panicked, edge of a breakdown mode. Hopefully, Claire could sleep and get herself a little more together.

He hopped into his car and started the engine. As he drove, he wondered why Andi had gone to Claire about the postpartum depression and where she'd heard about it. He actually hadn't even thought about bringing it up, because Claire had been fine the last few months, and he didn't believe it was an issue. But he could see why Andi had to ask her about it. He just wished she'd talked to him first. Maybe he could have smoothed the waters.

Even as that thought crossed his mind, he could hear Andi's voice in his head telling him that the investigation wasn't about making Neil and Claire comfortable. It was about finding Elisa, and she couldn't leave any stone unturned. She'd probably say that with a pointed look, because he was the one who said the investigators in Hannah's case didn't dig into every clue.

On the other hand, like the agents on Hannah's investigation, Andi had zeroed in on the close family circle and not on the broader pool of suspects. To be fair, she had to start somewhere. Frowning, he wondered why he felt the sudden need to be fair, because this wasn't about Andi's feelings, either.

He also wondered if he should have told Neil he had a past with Andi. In the beginning, he'd thought the case would be over before the sun went down, but as it went on, as Neil questioned Andi's actions, he was starting to feel like he should have been up-front from the start. Not that their past relationship was getting in the way. He was probably getting better information than he would have if they hadn't known each other before.

At this point, he didn't want to muddy the waters. Neil didn't need anything else to worry about, but what he did need was a strong liaison with the FBI, and that was him. So, he'd keep going and hope that together he and Andi would be able to do what they couldn't do before—bring a missing child home.

CHAPTER ELEVEN

ANDI KNEW the media was frustrated with their press conference. They had very few facts to relate and couldn't confirm any of the speculative suggestions from the reporters. Damon had spoken first, then introduced her to field questions. They'd done well in portraying a unified front, but they couldn't give the answers everyone wanted to hear, and she was thankful when it was over. She had never wanted to be the face of the FBI, but in her line of work, she'd found herself at far more podiums than she would have liked.

"That wasn't worth much," Damon muttered as they stepped away from the microphones. "But necessary. Hopefully, it brings in some new leads."

"I hope so," she said fervently, as Flynn joined them.

"I need to talk to you and Flynn for a few moments," Damon added. "Let's go to my office."

He led them out of the room, down a back hallway and up a flight of stairs to his office. There was a woman sitting outside who handed Damon a note as he paused at her desk.

Damon told her to give them a few minutes and then led them into a large room with floor-to-ceiling windows and a view of the park across the street. It was an impressive office for an impressive job, and she couldn't help thinking that both of these men, who had stood out at Quantico as natural-born leaders had definitely fulfilled the promise she'd seen then.

But she didn't like the way they were looking at her now, with a mix of questions and doubt.

"What's going on?" she asked.

"Why didn't you tell us you were friends with Dr. Bradford when you were kids, that you were the one who pointed law enforcement at his brother?" Damon asked.

"Oh, right. To be honest, I was thrown when he showed up, and then I didn't want to waste time getting into all that when a child's life was on the line. It's not a factor in anything."

"Of course, it's a factor," Damon said. "I gave you and Flynn this case, not realizing that Bradford has a grudge against you. I wanted to get away from politics and a conflict of interest, which was why I handed off this investigation in the first place."

She suddenly realized why Damon was coming down on her. Agent Burnett had told him he'd made a huge mistake by benching him and picking her to lead the investigation.

"There's no conflict of interest," she argued. "Cooper—Dr. Bradford—and I are fine dealing with each other."

"Is that true?" Flynn asked. "Because I remember you telling us about the kidnapping case that inspired you to join the Bureau and how you learned that the investigation doesn't always go where you want it to go. You pointed a finger at Bradford's brother, right? The one who was falsely accused, who started Bradford on his mission in life to prevent that from happening to anyone else."

"All that is true," she said. "But Cooper and I were fourteen when that happened. It was eighteen years ago. We've grown up. Our only goal is to find Elisa. We are not in conflict over that. And we can work together as the Benedict family wants us to do. There's really nothing to worry about. I'm sorry I didn't say something earlier. Everything was happening fast, and it didn't feel like a problem to me then. It feels like even less of one now.

Cooper has insight into the family and access that we don't have, and I have the investigative experience required to solve this case. We're a good team." She couldn't quite believe she was fighting to work with Cooper, but it was the best solution at this point. "Also," she added. "The person Cooper has the most problems with is Agent Burnett. I was a kid who said something about his brother. Burnett is the one who went after him."

"All right," Damon said. "Keep going and bring that kid home."

"That's what I intend to do. Is that it?"

"That's it," Flynn said. "I'm going to talk to Damon, so I'll catch up with you later."

As she walked out of the office, she really hoped her omission about her relationship with Cooper wasn't going to diminish Flynn or Damon's trust in her, because her new job wasn't going to work without trust. But all she could do now was her best. The rest would follow, or it wouldn't. She couldn't worry about any of that now.

She left the office and headed downstairs to the lobby. When she got there, she saw Cooper waiting by the front door.

"Did you catch any of the conference?" she asked, motioning for him to follow her outside.

"I didn't catch the beginning. Did you talk about Claire's postpartum depression?"

She started at his sharp question. Acutely aware that there were too many people in earshot, she led him across the street to the park. "Claire told you about our conversation."

"Yes. Neil is furious. Claire is a hysterical mess. You leave behind a rough wake, Andi."

"I had to ask her about it, Cooper. In fact, you should have told me she suffered from postpartum, since it sounds like you're not surprised."

"I knew about it, but this was months ago. It didn't even cross my mind that it could be a factor, and I don't believe it is." He paused for a moment. "Neil wants you off the case."

"Well, that's not his call," she said sharply. "I'm doing everything I can to find his daughter, and if that makes him or his wife uncomfortable, so be it. I'm not trying to upset them, but I'm not going to ignore a fact that could be relevant in finding Elisa. I'm working for her, not for them."

She was surprised when he nodded in agreement.

"I get that," he said.

"You do?"

"Yes."

They stared at each other for a long minute, each weighing the other's words. "Okay, then," she said.

"Do you really think it's relevant?" he asked.

"Probably not," she admitted. "But I needed to hear what she had to say about it."

"How did you find out? Not many people know."

"I had a source that I can't disclose."

"Interesting. A source that you can't talk about. I have to admit I'm curious about who that could be."

"Then you'll have to be curious." She pulled her phone out of her pocket. She'd turned it off during the press conference, and now there were several text messages. She read through them with a growing sense of excitement.

"Something has happened," Cooper said. "What?"

"My team found the car that almost ran us over last night. It belongs to Enrique Flores, the owner of The Fourth Street Garage, the gym where Daniel Guerrero, Solange's son, was working out the morning of the kidnapping. That doesn't sound like a coincidence."

"No, it doesn't."

She texted Nick that she would head over to the gym now. "I need to get to the gym."

"I'm going with you."

"Fine. My car is nearby. Where's yours?"

"Two blocks away in a parking garage, so you can drive."

"I was planning on it."

As they walked to her car, he said, "Has someone from your team spoken to Mr. Flores?"

"Not yet. Someone spoke to a staffer yesterday to confirm Daniel's alibi, but with this new piece of information, I'm curious to know what Daniel's relationship is with Enrique Flores." She shot Cooper a look as she started the engine. "Did you get anything else from Neil this morning?"

"No. Neil is frustrated and worried. I tried to calm him down, and I assured him you were doing your due diligence by investigating everyone."

She was surprised he could get those words out. "Did you tell him you and I knew each other when we were kids?" she asked.

"I did not. But it occurred to me today that I should have. What about you? Did you tell your team?"

"I just did. I should have done it from the beginning. They're hoping our past won't present a conflict for the case. Will it?"

"Not on my end."

"Because Damon will assign someone else to the case if you and I are going to be a problem."

"Someone like Agent Burnett?"

"Maybe."

"Well, he's the last person I'd like to see in charge. You're the lesser evil."

She sighed. "Well, I guess that's better than being the greater evil."

"That didn't come out right. The point is, I think you'll do a better job than Burnett, and I'll be there to help. We're on the same page where Elisa is concerned."

"That's what I told my boss." She pulled into traffic, working her way toward the freeway.

"Did you learn anything else last night after you went back to the office?" Cooper asked.

"I learned a lot about the Benedict's—Neil and his business dealings, his ex-wife, Shana, his partner Larry Friedman and his ex-wife, Michele, but it was all public information, nothing deep.

There was a lot less information on Kristine or Solange and her family."

"I asked Neil more about Kristine after you left. He's surprisingly defensive of her."

At the odd note in his voice, she asked, "What are you thinking?"

"Nothing really."

"Come on, Cooper. I won't hold you to it, and I can probably guess just by the way you said it."

"Fine. I'm hoping that they didn't have a relationship that wasn't strictly employer and employee."

"Do you think he would have told you if they had an affair?"

"Neil told me about Jillian, so maybe. But he didn't say that. He just kept reiterating that she was a wonderful young woman who wasn't into material things or social media. He felt like she was loving and kind and down to earth. It was all very glowing. He doesn't have one iota of doubt about her, which seems a little…"

"Surprising," she finished. "Considering that Kristine was the last person to see Elisa. And she's not at the house. Nor is she answering her phone."

"He's not that concerned. He said she was around all day yesterday and was willing to answer questions."

"You're right. She was willing; she just had little to say."

"Maybe she just has a really boring life outside of her job as a nanny. She didn't grow up in this country. She may not have many friends."

"Well, I hope she shows up before her absence makes her more of a suspect."

They arrived at the gym a little past twelve, and the fitness center was busy with the lunchtime crowd. After asking for Enrique at the front desk, they were waved into the manager's office where they found an older Hispanic man working on his computer. He had dark hair and eyes and wore a pair of reading glasses. He looked up at them with a distracted expression.

"Yes?" he asked.

"Are you Enrique Flores?"

"I am. Who are you?"

"Agent Hart from the FBI," she said. "I have a few questions for you."

"About Daniel Guerrero? I already told the FBI that Daniel was working out in the gym yesterday morning," he said, as he took off his reading glasses. "I don't have any other information."

"Where were you last night around 7 p.m.?" she asked.

"Me?" he asked in surprise. "Why are you asking me that?"

"Because your car was involved in a hit and run."

"I wasn't driving my car last night. My wife picked me up at six and we went to dinner at Moreno's."

"Who else would have had access to your vehicle?"

At her question, Enrique frowned. "I keep my keys in a drawer at the front counter. The car is used for pickups and deliveries. Sometimes someone gives a kid a ride home. It's not uncommon for someone else to be driving my car."

"Was the car here when you left?"

"Yes."

"I'm going to need a list of everyone who was working here last night."

"Tyler Holmes and Jamal Norlani were working the counter." He got on his computer. "Grant was running a class from 6:30-7:30. Caroline did a spin class at six and Kerry was teaching yoga at eight."

"Are any of those individuals here now?"

"Jamal," he said, getting to his feet. He walked out of the office, and they followed him back to the counter where a muscled, stocky male in his early twenties was folding hand towels.

"Jamal, did someone use my car last night around six thirty or seven?" Enrique asked.

Jamal's gaze wavered at the question as it moved from Enrique to her and Cooper. "Uh, I don't know."

"Well, you need to think harder," Enrique said sharply. "Because the car was involved in a hit and run, and I need to know who was driving it."

"A hit and run? I don't think that happened."

"Jamal, I'm an FBI agent," she interrupted. "This is serious. If you or someone else was driving the car, you need to come clean now."

"I wasn't driving the car."

"Then give us another name," she said.

Jamal hesitated, then said. "It was Tyler. A friend of his needed a ride home. He was gone about an hour and then he brought the car back. He didn't say he got in an accident."

"Do you know who Tyler drove home?"

"I didn't see who it was."

"When will Tyler be in? Does he work today?"

"He'll be here at five tonight," Jamal said. "He has classes until then. He goes to SMCC."

"Is Tyler friends with Daniel Guerrero?" she asked, hoping to find some connection between the car, the bar, and the deliberate run-down.

"He knows Daniel. We all do."

"Was Daniel here last night?"

"I don't know. He was here in the morning. I'm not sure if he came back."

"Look it up," Enrique told Jamal.

Jamal stepped up to the computer, punched in a few keys and then said. "Daniel checked in around five. I don't know when he left."

Finally, they were getting somewhere. "What can you tell me about Daniel?" she asked. "Did you talk to him yesterday? What kind of mood was he in? Does he have a lot of friends here?"

"I don't really know. He started boxing a few months ago. He's been a regular since then. He talks to Tyler more than me. I didn't notice his mood. I don't pay that much attention." Jamal paused as two women came into the gym and swiped their cards.

Enrique turned to her. "Are we done?"

"For the moment," she said. "But we need to talk to Tyler. Can you give me his contact information?"

Enrique tipped his head at Jamal once more, who then rattled off Tyler's phone number and address.

"Thanks," she said, then she headed out the door.

When they got into the car, she called Tyler, but his phone went to voicemail.

"Jamal could have tipped him off that you'd be calling," Cooper said as he fastened his seatbelt.

"Could have sent him a text the second we walked out the door," she agreed, meeting his gaze.

"Do you want to go to his house?"

"At some point, but I think it's time to talk to Solange again. Maybe we'll get lucky, and Daniel will be there, too."

"I haven't seen a lot of good luck so far," Cooper said dryly.

"Hopefully, that will change. I think Daniel was in the car with Tyler, because I don't see why this other kid goes after us."

"I'm not sure why Daniel would go after us. It would have been a reckless move, and it didn't result in anything more than drawing our attention."

"He could have hit us. Taking me out of the investigation could make a difference. Although someone else would take it over."

"Maybe not someone as good as you," he said. "But you're not out, thanks to my quick moves."

"How long are you going to hold that over me?"

"Probably a very long time."

CHAPTER TWELVE

AFTER PUTTING Solange's address into the GPS, she pulled out of the parking lot. "What do you know about Solange and her family?" Andi asked.

"She makes great enchiladas and tamales. She's been working for Neil for ten years and has always been a hard worker." He paused. "I was actually surprised when she stayed with Neil's ex-wife Shana for a while after the divorce. Solange always seemed closer to Nick. But once Claire was pregnant, Solange thought Neil would need help with the baby, and he was thrilled to have her back."

"It's interesting that she returned when the baby was born."

"Is it? It makes total sense to me. She thought he needed more help than Shana, and she was right. From what Neil told me, Solange was a godsend when Claire was struggling with depression. She moved in for a month before they found Kristine. Solange loves that little girl."

"Have you ever talked to Daniel?"

"Once or twice. He never had much to say, but sullen and distant describes a lot of boys his age."

"That's true. I remember thinking that you'd gotten a little weird the last few months we were hanging out. You didn't have as much to say as you used to. It felt like things were changing even before Hannah disappeared."

"Maybe they were," he muttered. "You were changing, too."

She was afraid to ask what he meant by that and also sorry she'd brought their past back up. A phone buzzed from inside her bag—her personal phone. Her work phone was on the console between them.

She pulled out her personal phone and saw her father's name flash across the screen. She sent the call to voicemail and dropped the phone back in her bag. A moment later, it buzzed again. She ignored it. The third time it buzzed, Cooper shot her a questioning look.

"Someone is eager to talk to you," he said. "If that has to do with Elisa—"

"It doesn't. It's my father."

"Oh." He said nothing else for a minute, and she hoped he would drop it, but it was Cooper, so, of course, he didn't. "Why don't you want to talk to him?" he asked.

"I'm on a case."

"That's not the reason. What happened between you?"

"It's none of your business," she said, as she heard the ding of a text message.

"Looks like he's trying to get a hold of you another way."

At the next light, she took out her phone again and read the text: *I know you're in LA. We need to talk. Please call me back.* She shook her head in disgust. It was just like her dad to believe she'd drop everything to speak to him.

"Everything okay?" Cooper asked.

She set down her phone shook her head. "Nothing has been okay with me and my dad since I was a little girl. He found out I'm in LA. He wants to see me."

"What happened after the divorce? Did you continue spending time with him? I know you moved away, but I thought you'd come back in the summers."

"I'm sure you were relieved I didn't," she said sharply.

"So you didn't see your father at all?"

"I told him I didn't want to be at our old house, so he rented a house on the beach in San Diego for two weeks, and I visited him there. He was barely around except for dinner. I didn't realize he was turning our beach vacation into an opportunity to schmooze with some clients in that area. The next year I saw him for Christmas in Aspen for a week. Same thing there. Then he got married, and I guess he thought he needed to look like a better father, so the next few vacations were slightly better. Then he and his new wife started fighting, and I felt like I was back where I'd been. By then I was in college, so we stopped forcing time together."

"You said you haven't seen him in six years. What happened six years ago? You would have been twenty-six then."

"I really don't want to talk about my father."

"Just tell me what happened."

She sighed, knowing that Cooper could be as persistent as she was when it came to getting a question answered. "I was in LA for a work trip, and I agreed to meet him for dinner. He wanted me to get to know his new girlfriend, who was twenty-five years old, a year younger than me. But he showed up late for dinner, because he got tied up having sex with a paralegal in his office."

"He told you that?"

"Oh, no. He said he had a meeting. But halfway into dessert, his paralegal showed up at the restaurant and said exactly what had happened. All hell broke loose. My dad had lied to two more women, both of whom seemed to have feelings for him, and I just couldn't stand it anymore. I told him we were done, and I left. I haven't talked to him since."

"Sorry," he said, sympathy in his voice.

She shrugged. "I don't need a father."

"What happened with your mother? Did she remarry?"

"Five years ago. Greg is a decent guy. He's very different from my father, very quiet, kind of meek. They don't fight. It's all very calm. In fact, they do yoga together. I guess that's what she needed—some peace."

"I'm glad she found happiness."

"Me, too. Once she met Greg, she finally stopped ranting about how horrible my father was, how much he'd hurt her. She started looking forward instead of back."

"Why do you think your dad wants to see you now?"

"I have no idea, and I don't really care. He was a terrible father, husband, and family man. He's narcissistic and cold, and sometimes I worry that..." Her voice fell away as she realized how much she was revealing to Cooper.

"Worry about what?" Cooper prodded, sending her a sharp, questioning look.

"This isn't a session. I'm not laying on your couch."

"No one lies on the couch. What do you worry about?"

"That I might be a little too much like him," she said finally.

"No way. You're nothing like him."

She appreciated the defense, but argued, "You don't know me anymore, Cooper."

"Then tell me why you think you might be like him."

"I have tunnel vision on the job. I lose track of time. I work all night long when I have to. I'm not good at relationships. I don't trust anyone. And love...that seems like a bad idea. Sometimes I think I'm dead inside." When Cooper didn't say anything, she gave him a quick look. "Forget I said all that. I don't know why I did. But you always had a way of getting things out of me."

"Only because I was willing to listen when you wanted to talk," he said quietly. "I don't believe you're dead inside. I think you probably care too much. You want to fix everything that's broken, but you can't."

"I do like to fix things," she conceded.

"Then why don't you want to fix your relationship with your father?"

She thought about that for a moment. "I don't think he deserves it."

"He didn't cheat on you, Andi."

"It felt like he did. My mom cried on my shoulder so many times. She told me all the ways he'd hurt her. She wanted me to hate him, and I did. But there was a part of me that wanted him to show me he was better than I thought he was. Every time I gave him the chance to do that, he failed."

"Does that mean you're done? No more chances?"

"I don't know," she said with a sigh. "I'll probably have to talk to him at some point."

"Or not. You don't have to forgive him, Andi. But if hating him hurts you, then he's winning."

She frowned at his far too insightful words. "I don't need you to analyze me, Cooper."

"It's what I do. I can't help it," he said with a small smile.

"Let's talk about you," she said, eager to change the subject. "Are your parents still together? Are they happy in their marriage? What's going on with your sister? She must be all grown up now."

"Monica is twenty-seven years old. She manages a bakery and is perfecting her baking skills."

"Twenty-seven? I remember her at nine. She was a sweetheart, and she always liked to hang out in the kitchen and bake with your mom, so her job makes sense. Is she married?"

"Very single. My parents are still together. They seem happy enough. They've been through a lot together, that's for sure."

"Your mom was always so friendly to me, so welcoming. I loved being at your house for dinner. It was much more fun than mine. Your dad would tease your mom, and she'd turn red and laugh. It felt like there was a lot of love between them."

"There still is, but they both wrestle with a lot of guilt about Kyle."

"Do they still live in your old house?"

"They do. They should have moved away years ago, but my mom loves that house, and even when the neighborhood turned against us, she refused to move. She wanted to hold her head high and prove to everyone that they were wrong about Kyle. I'm not sure she ever achieved that, but she gave it a hell of a try." He paused. "Kyle killed himself in that house. Did you know that?"

She shook her head. "I didn't. I'm sorry, Cooper."

"My dad found him. My mom was out to lunch when it happened. My father blames himself for not realizing that Kyle was in a bad place. But Kyle had actually been doing better right before that day. Maybe he'd decided he was ready to move on, to let go, and that eased the pressure that was always inside him. We'll never know. He didn't leave a note."

Her heart went out to Cooper and his family and also to Kyle. He'd been a little odd, but he'd never been mean to her, and she knew he'd struggled to fit in, to find his way in the world. At some point, it had just gotten to be too much for him. Maybe that wouldn't have happened if she hadn't seen his car or pointed him out to the police. Or maybe it would have. She'd never know that, either.

Her work phone rang, and she picked it up. "Hi, Savannah. Have we gotten any leads from the press conference?"

"Yes. A lot. We're going through them. Some of them seem worthless, but that's par for the course. We did, however, get an interesting anonymous tip that Shana Grier, Neil's ex-wife, was extremely angry that Neil had a baby with Claire. Apparently, he'd refused to have a child with her. That was one reason they divorced. Then a few months later, Claire turns up pregnant. I put in a call to Ms. Grier," Savannah continued. "Her assistant told me she was out of the office until three."

Andi checked her watch. It was a little before one, so she had some time before Shana would be back. "I'll go to her office then. Text me the details."

"Will do. How did your meeting with Flores go?"

"One of his staffers, Tyler Holmes was driving Flores's car. Tyler is a friend of Daniel's, or at least knows him. But he's in class right now and won't be back at the gym until tonight. I'm going to head over to Solange's house shortly and see if she's heard from her son."

"I just spoke to her again," Savannah said. "She says Daniel left last night and hasn't come back since then."

"He didn't sleep there?"

"Mrs. Guerrero said no, but maybe you can get more out of her. I stressed that Daniel needs to get in touch with us as soon as possible."

"Okay, thanks for the heads up. Let me know if you get anything else."

"Will do."

She had a feeling the trip to see Solange was going to be a waste of time, but she didn't have a better idea, and maybe she could get more from the woman in person. Or maybe Cooper would be able to do that, since he knew her, and she might consider him to be more of an ally than an adversary.

"News?" Cooper asked as she ended the call.

"A tipster suggested Shana Grier was extremely upset with Neil for having a baby with Claire when he wouldn't have one with her. What do you know about that?"

"Neil told me he never wanted kids until he met Claire, so I can't say the tipster is wrong, but I don't see Shana kidnapping Neil's kid."

"It's a long shot, but I'll talk to her later today. She's out until three." She paused. "I suppose you know Shana, too?"

"Not well, but we've met."

"Does she dislike you as much as she hates Neil? If so, maybe you should sit out that meeting?"

"She doesn't dislike me at all. She was the first person to read my books. She actually talked to me before Neil did, but when they divorced, he got my project in whatever settlement they made." He pulled his phone out of his pocket to read a text. "Damn," he muttered.

"What's wrong?" she asked quickly. "Is that Neil?"

"No, it's my sister, Monica. My mom called in a panic. Dad

isn't doing well. Tomorrow is a bad anniversary. She wants us to come over."

She saw the pain in his eyes and realized the anniversary had to do with Kyle's suicide. "I'm sorry."

Cooper looked around. "I know you want to get to the Guer- rero house, but do you think you could drop me off? We're closer to my parents' house than to where I left my car. I can get a ride back with Monica, but it would be faster to just go from here."

"Of course," she said, as she changed lanes and directions. She didn't resent him wanting to get to his parents if there was some sort of emotional crisis going on, but she was unnerved by the idea of going back to her old neighborhood. There were so many memories there, so many *bad* memories. But she was just going to drop him off and leave. She could handle that. As she glanced over at Cooper, she saw the hard line of his profile. "Are you okay?"

"No. I wish I knew how to help my dad. But nothing I say eases his guilt. It has sunk down deep into his bones, into his soul."

"I don't think you can talk someone out of that kind of guilt," she said quietly.

"I know, but I still can't stop myself from trying. Kyle had problems, but he wasn't a bad person. His brain just didn't work like everyone else's." He cleared his throat. "It will be ten years ago, tomorrow, that he took his life, but it feels like yesterday."

Ten years, she thought. Cooper would have been twenty-two, and Kyle, twenty-five. And Monica was probably seventeen at the time.

Kyle's suicide was no doubt the motivation behind Cooper's books, his desire to help free falsely convicted criminals, to go after the criminal justice system. Cooper wanted to do anything and everything he could to make sense of what had happened and try to stop it from happening to someone else's family.

She didn't believe Kyle had killed himself just because he'd been a person of interest in Hannah's kidnapping. By the time he committed suicide, eight years had passed since Hannah disappeared. The spotlight had long since faded. Kyle had had other problems, as Cooper had said.

But maybe she was just trying to let herself off the hook, because she hadn't ever needed Cooper to make her feel guilty, she'd seen what had happened to Kyle and Cooper's whole family when the police and FBI zeroed in on him. She'd wondered even then if maybe she'd made a mistake, but she couldn't talk to Cooper. He'd cut her off. His anger had been beyond anything she'd ever seen from him, and she'd been defensive, because she didn't want to be wrong.

As she got closer to their old neighborhood, her nerves tightened, and she braked hard at the stop sign by Hannah's house, her mind going back to that hot summer night, to her and Cooper riding their bikes to this very corner, hearing the police sirens, seeing the neighbors coming out on their porches wondering what was wrong.

She drew in a shaky breath. It felt like it was yesterday.

Cooper shot her a piercing look. "Are you all right?"

"I'm fine," she said automatically, but she didn't feel fine. She felt sick to her stomach.

"You've never come by here, have you? You only visited your dad at other locations. So, this is the first time since you left that you've been on this street."

"That's right, and I don't plan to stay long."

She turned the corner ready to slow down just enough for Cooper to jump out of the car. She wasn't going to look at her old house. But when she pulled up in front of his home, his sister and mom were standing on the sidewalk, and her queasy feeling got worse.

"You might have to stay for a minute," Cooper told her.

"Oh, God," she muttered. "Do they hate me as much as you do?"

"Looks like you're about to find out."

CHAPTER THIRTEEN

ANDI DIDN'T WANT to talk to Cooper's mom Joanne, or his sister Monica. But Cooper was already getting out of the car and both women were looking at her with varying degrees of surprise on their faces. She couldn't just drive away. She had to face whatever was about to come her way. Unfastening her seatbelt, she stepped out of the vehicle, walking around the car to join them on the sidewalk.

She told herself she was an adult now, a federal agent, but looking into Joanne's warm hazel eyes, she felt like she was a little girl again.

"Andi," Joanne said, opening her arms.

She was shocked by Joanne's response. She hesitated, then moved in for a hug. Joanne felt thin and more fragile than she used to. But she was still a good hugger. She still made Andi feel warmth and comfort.

As they broke apart, Joanne's gaze swept across her face. "My goodness. You're beautiful, Andi."

She flushed at Joanne's words, acutely aware of Monica and Cooper watching their interaction. "I'm sorry to hear that Doug isn't feeling well," she said, referring to Cooper's father.

"And I'm sorry I overreacted." Joanne said. "Doug is all right. I thought he wasn't talking to me, and it scared me, because he used to do that right after Kyle passed away. It would take him days to get out of a depression so deep he couldn't speak. But he had his earplugs in, and he just wasn't hearing me. I panicked too quickly. With the anniversary tomorrow, I assumed the worst."

"Well, I'm glad he's okay," Cooper said. "That's all that matters."

"He actually seems surprisingly okay," Joanne said. "Doug told me that I need to stop worrying about him, that he's handling things. And I should believe what he says. Anyway, since you're all here, come in and say hello. But don't tell him I called you." She paused. "You can say that Andi wanted to say hi."

Cooper gave his mother an incredulous look. "You think Dad will believe that?"

"Well, you are with her." Joanne gave her son a puzzled look. "Why are you and Andi together? I never thought I would see the two of you in the same space again."

"Andi is an FBI agent. She's investigating the kidnapping of Neil's daughter, Elisa," Cooper said shortly. "Neil asked me to consult on the case."

"Oh, I heard about that on the news this morning. I hope that little girl is all right," Joanne said, fresh worry in her eyes.

"We don't know anything yet," Cooper replied.

Joanne turned to Andi. "I have to say I'm not at all surprised you ended up as an FBI agent. Your father actually mentioned that to me a few years ago."

"I wasn't surprised, either," Monica put in. "You loved to play detective, Andi. You and Cooper used to make me answer the pretend phone for your fake detective agency."

She couldn't help but smile at the reminder. "You were good at that."

"And you were always trying to keep the teachers and the school on their toes," Joanne added. "Your mom used to worry that you would get yourself in trouble."

"I think my mother was more worried about her own problems than what I was doing at school," she said dryly.

"How is your mom?"

"She's good. She remarried and lives in Chicago."

"I heard your father is going to sell his house after all these years," Joanne said.

Now, she was the one who was surprised. "I hadn't heard that."

"Yes. He's been talking to Kim's son, Will, about listing the house."

"Well, it's probably past time for him to leave this neighborhood. I never really understood why he wanted to keep the house anyway."

"You haven't spoken to him then?"

"Not in a long time."

Joanne nodded, understanding in her eyes. "I can still hear the bitter note in your voice, Andi. Your dad broke your heart and your trust a long time ago."

"Yes, he did."

"Well, please come in. Just for a few moments," Joanne pleaded. "It will be a wonderful distraction for Doug and for me." Joanne didn't wait for them to answer, just headed toward the house.

Monica shrugged. "Are you really going to say no to anything she wants this week, Cooper?" she challenged and then moved up the path.

"Doesn't your dad hate me?" she asked Cooper. "Is this a setup? Am I going to step inside, and you'll all finally have a chance to rip me apart?"

"Do you think my family would do that to you? My mom just gave you a hug."

"Which made little sense to me. You've made it clear that you blame me for what happened to Kyle. Do they feel differently?"

He hesitated, then nodded. "Yes, they feel differently. They don't hold you responsible, Andi."

She was seriously shocked. "They don't?"

"Mom said you were just a kid. They were angrier with the police and the FBI than with you."

"But now I'm FBI. So that still makes me the enemy."

He shrugged. "You don't have to come in, Andi. It's up to you. You can drive away right now."

She looked from him to the house that had once been her safe haven. She'd always felt comfortable in Cooper's house, far more comfortable than she'd felt in her own home.

Joanne stepped back onto the porch and motioned them to come inside. "Come in, Cooper and Andi. I won't take no for an answer."

She couldn't ignore the plea in Joanne's voice. "I guess I'm going inside."

"I guess we both are."

When she stepped into the home, she was assailed with memories, but none stronger than the smell of something sugary and delicious. Joanne and Monica had often been baking when she'd come over, and there was usually some tasty hot treat waiting for her.

She stiffened as Cooper's father came down the hall. He had white hair now instead of brown, but otherwise he was an older version of Cooper, same green eyes, same long, lanky body. When his gaze landed on her, his eyes widened in surprise.

"I can't believe it. Is that Andi Hart?" he asked.

"It's me," she said, thinking Doug had aged more than Joanne had in the time since she'd last seen both of them. She didn't know if that was because he was a few years older than Joanne or because Kyle's suicide had just ravaged him.

"How are you?" he asked.

"I'm doing well. I just moved back to LA."

"That's great. I heard you're working with the FBI."

"Yes," she said warily.

"Do you like it? Are you good at it?" he asked in his usual pragmatic, no-nonsense manner. Cooper's dad had always had a way of breaking complicated issues into simple ideas.

"I do like it, and I am good at it. I have to say that this house smells exactly the way I remember it," she added, wanting to change the subject. "What did you bake today?"

"Oatmeal raisin cookies," Joanne said. "I leave the fancy stuff for Monica, now that she's a pastry chef."

"I'm still learning," Monica said with a self-deprecating smile. "But I'm getting better each day."

"Oatmeal raisin is my favorite kind of cookie," Cooper said.

His mother laughed. "Like I don't know that. You and Kyle used to fight each other for the last cookie." She stopped abruptly, her smile dimming.

"Well, can I have one?" Cooper asked.

"Only if you stay for lunch. I made chicken salad. There's plenty for all of you. I always make a big batch. What do you say?"

Cooper's gaze moved to hers. "Your call, Andi."

She hesitated. She wanted to talk to Solange and Daniel, but she was hungry. And she couldn't get to Shana Grier until after three, so she did have time for lunch if she wanted to take it. But things were going to get awkward at some point. How could they not? On the other hand, some food might help fuel new ideas, which she desperately needed.

"Lunch sounds good," she said belatedly, realizing they were still waiting for an answer.

"Perfect. It will be ready in a few minutes," Joanne said.

"I'll help you get it together, Mom," Monica said, following her mom into the kitchen.

"I'll meet you at the table," Doug said, disappearing into his study.

"And then there were two," she said lightly. She wrapped her arms around her. "This is weird, Cooper."

"Very," he agreed.

She lowered her voice. "Is your dad okay? He disappeared pretty quick."

"I'm guessing he's watching the end of the Dodgers' game. They're playing in New York today."

She smiled. Doug had taken her and Cooper to a couple of games at Dodger Stadium. Kyle had never been interested in baseball, but Cooper was, of course, a great player. Monica had refused to tag along, announcing that she'd watched Cooper play enough games; she didn't want to watch anyone else. So, Doug had taken the two of them and bought them Dodger dogs and cotton candy.

"Are you still a Dodger fan?" she asked Cooper.

"Can't be anything else in this town. What about you?"

"I have paid little attention to baseball in a long time." She paused. "Is your room still your room?"

"Not really."

"Let's see," she said, moving toward the stairs. Every step felt like she was going back in time. She was running up the stairs with Cooper to play a game or plot some mystery out on the floor of his bedroom.

When she reached the second-floor landing, she pushed open the door to his room. It was more the same than he'd admitted. Sure, a few things had changed, like the comforter and pillows on the bed were much more adult, and Cooper's posters of baseball players and rock stars were gone from the walls. But there were still books in the bookcase from his youth, including a stack of yearbooks.

"You still have the yearbooks," she said, grabbing the top one off the shelf and sitting down on the bed to open it. "Freshman year. I must have signed this."

Cooper pulled out the chair by his old desk and sat down across from her. "You wrote a Dr. Seuss quote."

She laughed. "I forgot about that." She found it on the first page of signatures and read it aloud. "Be who you are and say what you feel, because those who mind don't matter and those who matter don't mind."

"It was your favorite saying. You thought it excused everything you did that annoyed people, because you were just being yourself."

"I was an obnoxious kid, wasn't I?"

Cooper grinned in a way that she hadn't seen in a long time, because he was giving her an actual genuine smile.

"You were…you," he replied. "You said what you thought even when most people didn't want to hear it. You barreled ahead, past every *don't-go-past-this-point* sign. You stood up for people you didn't think had a loud enough voice. And you always expected success, even when the odds were long. That just made you more determined."

"So, a little obnoxious," she murmured.

"Along with pushy and bossy. You'd get stuck on something, and you'd just gnaw on it like a dog with a bone."

"Okay, now you're getting carried away. It's not like you were Mr. Perfect."

"Well, I wasn't obnoxious," he said with a laugh.

"No. You were annoyingly smart, often right when I didn't want you to be, and way too logical when I was brimming over with righteous indignation. But you also had a way with people. You knew how to make friends better than I did. When we got to high school, many people liked you, especially girls. You were hanging out with the popular kids; I was not. But that's when you started getting weird."

"How so?"

"I don't know. You just didn't act the way you used to. It's like I said before, you got sullen and quiet. And sometimes you gave me a funny look." She paused as his expression now reminded her of that funny look. An odd tingle ran down her spine as she realized now what she hadn't seen at fourteen. Cooper wasn't staring at her like he was mad at her, he was looking at her like he was attracted to her and didn't want to be.

"You just got it, didn't you?" he asked, meeting her gaze. "I can see it in your big brown eyes. It finally clicked in."

"You liked me?" she asked, surprised by that thought. "In a more than best buddy kind of way?"

"Yes, and it was confusing. I didn't know what to do about it. You were my best friend since we were eight, and then suddenly you were a girl. I didn't want to lose you as a friend. But I also didn't like when you started talking about other guys, especially Jeremy." He curled his lip in disgust.

"What was wrong with Jeremy?"

"He was a jerk—stupid, arrogant, full of himself."

"You just described every guy in our freshman class, including yourself." She shrugged. "Jeremy never looked twice at me anyway. He was too caught up in that slut, Kendall Richmond."

"Kendall wasn't a slut; she was just friendly."

"Oh, come on, Cooper. She had sex under the bleachers with Timothy Harding after a football game."

His jaw dropped. "No way. You never told me that."

"I think I found out about it after we weren't talking anymore."

"Oh, right."

Silence fell between them. "I missed you after it all went bad," she said. "It was hard to see your eyes burn with anger when you looked at me. I missed my best friend. It was almost a relief when my mom made us move. But it was sad, too." She swallowed a knot of emotion. "I can't believe your parents don't hate me."

"Like I said, they didn't blame you as much as law enforcement."

"But their opinion didn't change your mind."

"Because I was with you that night. I saw what you saw, and I told you the car you saw wasn't my brother's. But you wouldn't listen. It felt like you wanted it to be true, so you could take it to the police, so you could work with the cops, be a detective. It's like you wanted to find your way into a real investigation."

She couldn't believe that's the way Cooper had seen her actions. "I didn't make it up, Cooper. I thought that was his car that I saw. And I was ahead of you. I had a better view of it."

"It didn't stop with the car. You started talking to other people in the neighborhood, and you got some girls to say they saw Kyle hanging around the park one day when Hannah was there with her nanny."

"I didn't get them to say that," she corrected. "I overheard them talking, and I just asked if they'd told the police."

"Well, it just snowballed from there. Kyle was taken in for questioning. Everyone thought he did it. People would call him names like child molester, kidnapper, and murderer. Our cars and our house got egged. And it didn't just end with Kyle. I got a lot of hate, too."

She felt bad about all that. Things should never have gone so far in that direction, especially since Kyle was never charged for the crime.

"There were no other suspects but Kyle," Cooper continued. "He was found guilty in the court of public opinion based on absolutely nothing."

"There were other persons of interest. They also thought Mr. Montgomery might have had something to do with it, too," she reminded him.

"I don't remember people hounding him the way they did Kyle. Maybe there was some suspicion, but he also got a hell of a lot of sympathy."

"You're right. Kyle's reputation was smeared," she admitted.

"And my brother couldn't handle it. He had difficulties relating to people even before that. He had trouble making friends, communicating. You knew all that."

"I think I know more of it now than I did then," she defended.

"Come on, Andi. You knew."

"I felt horrible about what happened to Kyle and to your family. I didn't know any of that was going to happen. I wanted to find Hannah; it wasn't just a game, Cooper. I babysat that little girl. I could hear her laugh in my head. I could see her smile. I wanted to bring her back. But I couldn't. And in the end, I just drove my best friend away."

"Would you change anything if you could go back and do it again?"

She thought about his question for a long minute. "I can't go back, and I can't change it, so whatever I say doesn't matter. I did what I did, and you did what you did. We both thought we were right, and apparently we still do."

They were interrupted by the sound of his mother calling them down to lunch. That put a small smile back on her face. "How many times did your mom call us down for a meal?" she asked.

"Too many to count."

"We have a lot of history together, Cooper. Not all of it was bad. From the age of eight to fourteen, we were cool. You were a great friend. And your parents were the best role models I had."

"My mom always liked you. She told me once you were like a little bird struggling to fly. You were flapping your wings as hard as you could, but you weren't ready to soar, and it was making you crazy."

"That describes how I felt back then. I wanted to leave the nest because it didn't feel safe. I didn't feel loved. I was trapped in a war between two people who were obsessed with destroying the other. When I came over here, it was a different world. There were warm cookies, siblings, and lots of laughter. There were parents who asked about your day, so much so you were often annoyed by their questions. But I loved when your mom asked me stuff, because my parents rarely knew what I was working on." She drew in a breath and stood up. "We should go downstairs."

"We should. Before my mom thinks something is going on up

here that she needs to interrupt," he said dryly, as he got to his feet. "You might have been oblivious to my changing feelings about you, but didn't you ever wonder why my mother was suddenly bringing in my laundry and leaving the door open every time you came over? I swear she had a radar for whenever I was thinking about kissing you. Suddenly, she'd show up."

She stared at him in astonishment. "It never crossed my mind that you wanted to kiss me or that your mom was worried about that happening."

"You were great at observing everyone else but yourself and your best friend."

"Apparently, so. But the whole boy-girl thing also made me nervous. I tried not to think about it much. I'd pretend to have crushes on someone just to be in the conversation, but most of the crushes weren't even true."

"I didn't know that." He gave her a thoughtful look. "What would you have done if I had suddenly made a move on you?" he asked curiously, moving closer to her. "Do you think you would have slugged me or kissed me back?"

The air was suddenly charged between them. They weren't kids anymore. And she was definitely not oblivious to how attractive he was. Her palms started to sweat unexpectedly.

What would it be like to kiss Cooper?

It suddenly seemed like a very tantalizing question.

His gaze darkened as the silence between them grew tense.

She could feel the pull between them. Her gaze came to rest on his full, sexy lips.

And then the door swung open, and they both jumped.

Joanne appeared, giving them a questioning look.

"Everything all right in here?" she asked.

She smiled to herself as the tension between them vanished with that question. Cooper rolled his eyes, then said, "It's fine, Mom. We were just coming down."

"Well, hurry up," she returned, heading back into the hall.

"See. Every single time," he said with a sigh.

She laughed. "You move too slow, Cooper." She ran down the stairs, giving him time to think about that. She didn't know what she would have done if he'd tried to kiss her when they were fourteen. She also wasn't sure what she would have done thirty seconds ago.

CHAPTER FOURTEEN

LUNCH WAS BITTERSWEET. Joanne and Doug were as nice to her as they'd always been, especially Joanne, who kept up a steady stream of conversation, asking her about her mom and stepfather, and then talking about the trip to Rome she and Doug had taken a few months earlier. Joanne urged Doug to join in with his favorite memories, which he did with slightly less enthusiasm than his wife. It felt like there was a weight on Doug's shoulders, probably because of Kyle and the impending anniversary of his death.

Monica seemed quieter than she used to be, her gaze speculative as it moved between her and Cooper, clearly trying to figure out what their relationship was now. She silently wished Monica good luck on that, because she couldn't figure out what they were to each other.

Sometimes, it felt like they could be friends, but then the past always came back—the pain, the betrayal, and so much anger…

She couldn't imagine that they could ever get beyond all that.

As they finished with lunch, the topic came back around to her and her work as an FBI agent.

"I know you can't tell us anything, but are you hopeful that you can find Neil's little girl?" Joanne asked.

"I try to never lose hope." It wasn't a very good answer, but it was all she had.

"I don't know how anyone can be hopeful," Monica said. "So many people never come home, like Hannah Montgomery." Her words brought the mood down even lower. "I can't help thinking about her with another little girl missing from her bedroom. Every kid should be safe in their house. I remember how scared I felt going to sleep after Hannah was kidnapped. I was terrified someone was going to sneak into my room and steal me, too."

She could relate to that. She'd checked her windows every night after Hannah was taken. "Fortunately, it doesn't happen that often, that a child is taken from her home," she said. "It's shocking and terrifying when it does. But I'm doing everything I can to find Elisa."

"There's just not much to go on," Cooper put in. "We need something to break, someone to have seen something."

His frustration matched her own. "There's someone out there who knows something," she said. "We just have to find that person."

Doug cleared his throat. "I'm going to see what happened with the end of my ballgame." He got to his feet. "It was nice to catch up, Andi. Glad you're doing well. Say hello to your mom, won't you?"

"Of course. It was good to see you, too."

"I shouldn't have talked about the kidnapping," Monica said, regret in her eyes. "It made Dad think about what happened to Kyle when Hannah disappeared, and how that sent his life into a spiral. I should have kept my mouth shut."

Monica's words sent a cloud of pain through Joanne's eyes, and Cooper's mother's gaze was no longer as warm as it had been. Just like with Cooper, things went along fine for a while and then everyone remembered the role she'd played in the destruction of their family.

"I should get back to work," she said.

"Now, now, don't run off," Joanne said. "You haven't had your cookies yet, Andi. Let me get them."

As Joanne got up to get dessert, the doorbell rang.

"I'll get that," Monica said, eager to leave the table.

Andi looked at Cooper, who was sitting across from her. "I've gotten great at clearing a room."

"You had help from the cookies and the doorbell."

"And the reminder of what happened to Kyle."

"That, too," he admitted.

"Your mom is wonderful. I don't think I've ever known anyone as generous as she is." She felt an odd moisture gather in her eyes, and she blinked it away. She didn't get emotional. She didn't cry—ever. But she felt like tears were not that far away, and that was a shocking feeling.

Cooper gave her a funny look. "Andi? What's going on?"

Before she could answer, she heard voices getting louder. She looked to the doorway as Monica entered with an older woman, a woman she hadn't seen in a very long time. It was Kim Lassiter —TJ's mother. Kim was a curvy, short blond, now in her early sixties, wearing a white blazer over a sunny yellow dress that was as bright as her smile. Kim looked great, but there was a tightness to her face that suggested she'd had some work done. She certainly hadn't allowed herself to age as naturally as Joanne had.

"Hello, Andi," Kim said. "TJ said he saw you last night, and that you were with Cooper. That floored me. But here you are again."

"It's nice to see you, Mrs. Lassiter."

Kim waved her hand at her. "Oh, you're all grown up now, Andi. You can call me Kim. I saw your dad a few weeks ago. He really misses you. I hope you'll spend some time with him."

"We'll see."

"Your father told me you're very busy with your job."

She couldn't imagine how her father would know if she was busy or not. Despite his recent calls today, he had never tried that hard to see her. It was a little baffling that he was doing so now.

"Kim," Joanne said, as she returned to the table with a plate of cookies that she'd apparently warmed up. "Are you hungry? I have some chicken salad and cookies."

"I wouldn't mind a cookie. You are the best baker I know." Kim took the seat that Doug had vacated. "Is Doug around? I've been thinking about you all this week. I just wanted to stop in and say hello, ask if you need anything. I know this is a hard time for you."

"That's very kind of you," Joanne said, as she sat down. "We're fine. It's always a hard week, but we get through it, because we don't have a choice."

"I still remember when our boys used to hang out in my basement playing video games together. Will and Kyle and TJ and Cooper. It's hard to believe Kyle is gone. It was such a tragedy. Kyle was always kind to the younger kids, too. One time, when TJ was little, his bike broke down several blocks away, and Kyle walked him home to make sure he was safe. Kyle would have never hurt little Hannah, not in a million years."

"Kyle loved younger kids," Joanne said, nodding her head in agreement. "They were easier for him to deal with. They didn't have expectations. They didn't judge his behavior like kids his age did. Thank you for sharing that, Kim."

"I'm not sure if it helps or if it hurts to hear the memories."

"It helps more than anything," Joanne said.

"I hope so. Hannah has been on my mind all day since I heard about that other little girl going missing this morning. It brought back sad memories for me. So many days passed when I'd look at the yard between our two houses and wonder if someone had crept through there and taken Hannah out of her bed. I didn't sleep well for months after that. I kept checking on my kids every night."

"We all did that," Joanne said solemnly. "It was a difficult time."

"It was." Kim's gaze swung back to Andi. "Are you working on that case with the FBI?"

"I am."

"Well, that makes me feel better. I know how determined you are, Andi." Kim paused. "You were so caught up in Hannah's case, did you ever look it up when you started working for the FBI?"

"I did," she admitted, feeling the heat of everyone's gaze on her now. "I went through all the reports. I even talked to the agent who ran the investigation to see if he had any new thoughts about it, but he told me he'd hit dead ends everywhere he turned."

"I doubt he made many turns," Cooper said, bitter anger in his voice.

She wasn't going to defend Agent Burnett. "I may take another look at that case, see if there are any parallels to the current one."

"Do you think there's a connection?" Monica asked in surprise. "So many years apart?"

"I don't know. But both kids were taken out of their homes with no sign of a forced entry." She got to her feet. "I should get back to work."

"Your father is very proud of you. I hope you know that," Kim said, as she rose. "He's not a man who's good at expressing his feelings, but when he talked to me about your job, he was beaming with pride."

She found that ridiculously hard to believe, but she wasn't going to argue with Kim.

"I should go, too," Kim added. "And Cooper, TJ said he'd love to get drinks with you sometime and reconnect. I know you split apart in high school when everything was going on, but you were so tight when you were little kids. I hope you can find that friendship again."

"It would be great to spend more time with TJ. His girlfriend seemed very nice," Cooper said.

"Yes. Naomi is lovely, although I think she may be a bit more ambitious than my son, who I love dearly. But the only thing TJ has ever cared about is music, and it's hard to make money at that."

"Well, money isn't everything," Joanne said. "As long as your kids are happy, that's all that matters."

Kim's expression softened in sympathy. "You're so right, and I'm very lucky to have my boys. They kept me going after Steve died."

"I was sorry to hear about your husband's death," Andi said. "I still remember when Steve used to be the grill master for our Fourth of July parties."

"He always loved to grill," Kim said. "Although Steve was never willing to accept that some people just don't like their meat bloody rare. I'd make him throw my steak back on the grill every single time. But men can be stubborn, especially with barbecue." She ended her words with a shrill little laugh that rang a bell in Andi's brain. But she didn't know why.

As Monica, Kim, and Cooper walked out of the dining room, she lingered behind to give Joanne a hug. "Thanks for lunch and for not hating me."

"Oh, Andi, I couldn't hate you." Compassion filled Joanne's eyes. "And as much as Cooper wants to hate you, I don't believe he does."

"He seems to go back and forth. He forgets he hates me and then he suddenly remembers. I'm so sorry about Kyle and whatever part I played in what happened to him."

Joanne took her hands and gave them a squeeze. "You were a young teenager who was just trying to help. The police and the FBI went in on Kyle because he was an easy target. They gave him up to the press, and public sentiment was damning. It hurt Kyle a lot. It hurt all of us. But we got through it, and I know you were going through your own hard times then, too. You were looking for a distraction."

"Yes. I wanted to fix something, but I couldn't fix anything that was broken."

"Cooper wanted to fix it all, too, but some things are beyond our control." She paused. "I'm glad you finally came home, Andi."

"I'm not sure I would call LA home, but I'm back."

Joanne nodded in understanding. "Your father can be a tough person to like. I knew some of what your mother went through, and since then I've seen a few other crying women going in and out of your father's house."

"Do you ever talk to him?"

"I don't go out of my way not to, but even though he's lived across the street from me for thirty-five years, I can't say I know him at all. I was your mother's friend, and I think he realized quickly that I knew too much about him."

"I know too much about him, too. That's why I really don't want to spend any more time with him. Anyway, if I missed anything about the place where I grew up, it's this house, not the one I lived in. You always made me feel happy and safe here."

"I'm so glad. Now, don't be a stranger. You can always come by to visit, with or without Cooper."

"I appreciate that." She gave Joanne another hug and then walked out to the car.

Cooper and Monica were on the sidewalk talking to Kim, but their conversation ended as soon as she drew near.

"Ready to go?" Cooper asked.

"Yes." She turned to Monica. "I'll definitely stop by your bakery as soon as I can."

"That would be great," Monica said.

Andi couldn't tell exactly how Monica felt about her. She wasn't as hateful as Cooper, but she was not as welcoming as her mother.

"I hope you find that little girl, Andi," Kim said.

"I will," she said confidently. "There's no other option."

She walked around the car to get in on the driver's side.

Cooper opened the passenger-side door, and she heard Kim's shrill laugh once more as she and Monica found humor in something. As she fastened her seatbelt, an old memory niggled at the back of her mind. And then it came to her.

"Oh, my God!" she said. "That laugh. It's the same one."

"What?" Cooper asked as he shut the door, cutting off the sound of Kim's laughter.

"It was her," she added, shocked by the realization.

"What are you talking about?"

She watched as Kim and Monica hugged, then Kim moved down the street while Monica got into her car.

"Andi?" Cooper pressed. "Where are you?"

"In the past." She turned back to him. "I was about twelve, I think. My mom called my dad one night, looking for him, which she did a lot. He always ran errands or took walks or went on runs at night, but that night he'd been gone for hours, and she was getting worried. When he answered his phone, we heard a woman laughing in the background. It was a shrill, high-pierced laugh. My mother asked him where he was, and he said he'd walked to the store and was coming home soon. When she hung up, her eyes were burning with anger, and she said, 'I can't believe it's her. And he thinks I'm that stupid.'"

Cooper gave her a thoughtful look. "Are you suggesting your father and Kim were having an affair?"

"Yes. That laugh is the same one I heard on the phone that night, and my mother was convinced my father was not at the store."

"Kim has an irritating and distinctive laugh, but you're making a leap, Andi. I'm sure there are other women who laugh like that. And even if your dad was with Kim at that moment, they both could have been at the store."

"My father admitted to cheating on my mom, Cooper. I never got names, but I know there were at least three, because my mom told me one would have been forgivable, but three women was just humiliating." Her gut churned at the thought of Kim and her dad hooking up. "And if it was true, how disgusting was that? They were both married. Their kids went to the same school and were all friends. Kim was on the PTA with my mom at one point."

"My mom, too," Cooper said. "Everyone knew each other around here."

"Maybe Kim and my father knew each other a little too well. It makes sense. Kim's husband, Steve, travelled a lot. And TJ and Will were probably oblivious to anything their mom was doing."

"Probably," he agreed. "They got high a lot."

"I should have tried that. I wanted to be oblivious to what was going on in my house. I wanted my mom and dad to be normal and boring, like everyone else's parents. I didn't want the fighting, the accusations, the car leaving in the middle of the night, my mom crying, my dad apologizing, and then more yelling. It was either tensely silent, politely fake, or just weird. I wanted a family dinner that was warm and filled with conversation and laughter, like yours always were. Even today, even with all the animosity and history between us, your parents welcomed me in." She cleared her throat, feeling a little choked up. "I'm still surprised they did that."

"My parents have always been generous people."

"You're lucky, Cooper."

"I know," he said, meeting her gaze. "I should probably try to be more generous, too."

His words and the look in his eyes twisted her stomach again in a different way as she remembered the tension between them in his bedroom before his mother had interrupted them.

And then her personal phone dinged with a text. Her father —again! "We seem to be on our parents' radar," she muttered.

She read his text, which was long and more detailed. Her father had some of her old things that she'd left behind when she was a kid and now that she had her own apartment, she should come and get them. He was going to put the house up for sale, and he wanted her boxes out. If she didn't come and get them, he'd throw them away, but he didn't want her to get angry if he threw away something she might want, like her favorite books, and her old journals. He added that he was going out of town and would be back on Sunday and to call him then.

"What does he want?" Cooper asked.

"He wants to get rid of some stuff I left behind when my mom and I moved. I'm surprised he hasn't done it before now." She looked from the phone to him. "Do you remember the journals I used to write in when I was working on a case?"

"Of course. You were always officially taking notes."

"I stopped all that when I moved. I left them behind and never really thought about them since then."

"Do you want to get them now? We won't be any closer."

His words almost made her look at her old house, but she stopped herself from turning. "No. He said he's going out of town until Sunday. I'll deal with this next week." She picked up her phone and sent a brief text that she wanted her things, but she was working an investigation so she'd set up a time next week when he was back, and her case would hopefully be over. She hit send and then started the car. "It's time to refocus on the case. Break is over."

CHAPTER FIFTEEN

THEY ARRIVED at Solange's house, a one-story home in a modest neighborhood in south LA a little before three. The yard was neatly kept, and there was a large vase of flowers by the front door.

When Solange opened the door, she gave them a wary look. She wore faded jeans and a sweatshirt, and her brown eyes were stressed, her face pale. "Have you found Elisa?" she asked.

"Not yet. May we come in?"

"I don't know what else I can tell you." Solange waved them into the living room. It was a comfortable room with two large, pillowy couches and a big TV taking up most of the room. There were toys in one corner that Andi's eyes immediately strayed to.

"My granddaughter comes over sometimes," Solange said quickly. "She's two. My oldest daughter's child." Her gaze moved to Cooper. "Why are you here, Dr. Bradford?"

"Agent Hart has a few more questions for you, and I wanted to tag along," he said.

"I wish I could help, but I wasn't at the house yesterday morning. I didn't see anything."

"Where's Daniel?" Andi asked. "I know my office spoke to

you earlier, and you said you haven't seen him since last night. Is that true?"

"Yes. He went out with friends. He does that sometimes. He's twenty years old. He's an adult. Why are you looking for Daniel? He was at the gym yesterday. He didn't take Elisa. He wouldn't do that. He loves her."

"Then there's no reason for him not to talk to us," she said. "But he hasn't returned our calls. Why don't you call him now? Ask him to come home. Tell him you need to see him, that you're upset, whatever will get him to come back here."

Solange stared at her, clearly weighing the possibility of her son being in trouble with her need to find Elisa. "Daniel is a good boy. He just drinks a little too much. Ever since his father died, he's been struggling, but he wouldn't hurt a soul."

"You need to call him, Solange," Cooper said, drawing the older woman's gaze to his. "Neil would really appreciate your help. And Claire is desperate to get her daughter back. The sooner Agent Hart talks to Daniel, the sooner we can move on to someone else."

Andi saw Solange waver. It bothered her that Cooper's words were more compelling than hers, but he had a history with the woman, and whatever got her cooperation was all that mattered.

Solange walked over to the table and picked up her phone.

"Don't tell him we're here," Andi said. "And put the phone on speaker."

Solange drew in a breath, then called her son. They heard a phone ring somewhere else in the house.

Andi's stomach turned over. "His phone is here."

Solange headed down the hall, and she and Cooper followed. The ringing phone sat next to an unmade bed. The room was a mess, clothes everywhere along with some dirty dishes and empty beer bottles.

"He must have forgotten to take his phone," Solange said. "I'm sure he'll be back soon."

She wasn't sure at all, and she didn't think Daniel had forgotten his phone. "When's the last time you saw him?"

"It was around six last night. He was going to meet friends. I don't know who. He doesn't tell me. But he's not a kidnapper. He wouldn't hurt a child, especially not Elisa. He knows her. He has played with her."

Solange's words only made her more suspicious of Daniel. Elisa hadn't cried when someone had picked her up out of her crib, at least, not according to Kristine. That could mean Elisa felt comfortable with the person picking her up.

"Does Daniel have another phone?" she asked Solange.

"I've never seen one."

She walked over and picked up Daniel's phone. It was password protected. "Do you know his code?"

Solange shook her head. "I don't invade his privacy." She hesitated. "I can't let you take it, unless you tell me you have the legal right to do so?"

Without Solange's help, getting probable cause and access to the phone would take more time than she had, and she suspected it would lead nowhere. Daniel hadn't left the house without any way to communicate with his friends. He had to have another phone, probably one that couldn't be traced.

She set down the phone, then turned to Solange. "Does he have a car?"

"No."

"How did he leave last night?"

"Someone picked him up. I'm not sure if it was a friend or a ride share."

Everywhere she turned, she ran into a brick wall. She changed directions. "What can you tell me about Kristine Rozic? Do you know anything about her private life? Her friends? Where she goes on her days off?"

"No. Kristine doesn't talk to me much," Solange said. "She keeps to herself."

Solange was giving her nothing, whether that was because

she had nothing or she was hiding something, Andi couldn't tell. "We really need to talk to Daniel," she said again. "If he comes home, call me right away." She pulled out a card and handed it to Solange. "It's better for him to cooperate than to stay out of touch for whatever reason he might have."

"I understand, but sometimes, Daniel is gone for a few days at a time," Solange said. "And he doesn't tell me where he's going or when he's coming back."

"I understand. Do his siblings know more about his activities than you do?"

She sighed. "No. They've gotten annoyed with him because of his...drinking. He hasn't been talking to anyone in the family the last several months."

She suspected that Daniel's drinking was just part of a bigger problem with substance abuse. But Solange didn't want to put her son in an even worse light. She might need to track down the siblings and get their take on their brother.

"How's Daniel doing at the gym?" Cooper asked. "Is he enjoying the boxing? I hope it's giving him an outlet for his grief and anger."

"He has been better since he started there," Solange admitted. "I guess punching something helps. He was really upset by his father's death, and I was so lost in grief I didn't help him the way I should have. If he's in trouble, it's my fault."

"Let's hope he's not in trouble," Cooper said. "I know you're worried about your son, just as Neil is worried about Elisa. The best way for us all to move forward is to be honest and forthcoming. You believe Daniel is innocent, so there's no reason to try to protect him. The truth won't hurt him."

"I understand. I'm not trying to protect him. I don't know where he is." Solange walked them to the front door. "Does Neil think Daniel is involved?" she asked.

"I'm sure he doesn't," Cooper answered. "Agent Hart is focused on everyone who has been in the house. Daniel is the only one we can't find, and that's troubling."

"He didn't know he had to stay home. No one told us that. He talked to someone yesterday. He thought he was done."

"I understand," Cooper said. "I realize this is upsetting, Solange, but as a mother you know what Claire is going through, and I'm sure you want to help."

"I do. I really do."

Seeing Solange respond to Cooper reminded Andi of how good Cooper had always been at charming people. His easy-going manner, the way he looked someone straight in the eye, and his soothing smile had always made people loosen their guard. While her impatient desire to get to the truth had made her less interested in soothing and more focused on ruthlessly dragging answers out of people. That hadn't always worked well.

She'd gotten better at varying her interrogation tactics over the years, but she had to admit it had been a while since she'd talked to anyone in such a slow, soothing, compassionate way. There was rarely time for that. Her cases always moved fast, at least at the beginning, when they knew their best chances for finding a child were in the first twenty-four hours.

Unfortunately, they were past that now, and they were no closer to finding Elisa than they'd been yesterday.

Hopefully, they'd have more luck with Shana Grier.

Andi was frustrated. Cooper could tell that by the way she drove them to Shana Grier's office, jumping between the gas and the brake with a very heavy foot. He was feeling the same way. Every step they took to move forward either just left them stalled or sent them backward. They were getting nowhere fast, and he was beginning to realize just how many more people would need to be interviewed, how many more times they would have to ask the same questions and probably get the same unsatisfying answers. Because they didn't have any good leads.

Maybe this one with Shana would pan out, but he doubted it. He couldn't see Shana kidnapping her ex's kid. It seemed like she'd be more likely to try to destroy him another way, like stealing his business or something.

On the other hand, Shana had been incredibly hurt by Neil choosing to have a baby with another woman while refusing to give her a child. Who knew what that had done to her emotionally? It could have hit her so hard that a part of her had broken, which might have led to an irrational and impulsive decision.

Andi pulled into the underground garage for Shana's building, and they took the elevator to the third floor. He'd been in this office once before when he'd first discussed his book with both Neil and Shana. It hadn't changed much. There was a young woman sitting at a reception desk. She waved them toward a small couch to wait until Ms. Grier was off the phone.

There were film and television posters on one wall, some of which had been done when Shana was still working with Neil, although there were some newer projects as well.

"What can you tell me about Neil and Shana?" Andi asked as they sat on the couch together.

"I know they met in their twenties. Shana was an actress. Neil was writing a screenplay. They were both moonlighting as servers in a restaurant. Together, they pitched one of Neil's scripts to a production company. It almost got into development before being scrapped. But from that venture, they made valuable connections and ended up getting a backer and taking the project to market themselves. The film was a modest success and brought them enough funding to do other projects. They spent the next thirteen years together as husband and wife and business partners."

"Maybe that was too much togetherness," Andi said dryly. "Was Neil cheating on Shana with Claire?"

"I don't know. He told me that he met Claire after he and Shana separated, but they weren't divorced yet."

"I wonder why Neil decided to have kids with Claire when he didn't want them with Shana."

"He was just at a different point in his life. When he was with Shana, they were working a lot, traveling for productions. He told me it just didn't make sense. But when he got together with Claire, his feelings changed. Plus, Claire really wanted a baby, and he really wanted Claire."

"He wanted to make Claire happy but didn't feel the same way about Shana."

"Maybe, but no one knows what goes on inside a relationship besides the two people involved, and we're here based on an anonymous tip, which could be completely wrong."

"You're right. I'm just considering motivations."

He jumped to his feet as Shana entered the lobby. Shana had a much different look than the blonde and waifish Claire. Shana was tall and fit, with dark hair and olive skin. An energy radiated off her.

"Hello, Cooper," she said, then turned to Andi. "I understand you're from the FBI. I assume this has something to do with Neil's daughter?"

"Yes," Andi replied. "I'm Agent Hart. I'd like to ask you a few questions."

"Let's go into the conference room." Shana led them into a nearby room with a long table and a dozen chairs and closed the door. As they sat down at the table, she added, "I don't know what I can tell you, but if you have questions, fire away."

"Do you know anyone who would have a grudge against Neil, who would use his daughter as leverage?" Andi asked.

Shana gave her a direct look. "Are you talking about me? Do you want to know if I have a grudge against Neil and if I'd kidnap his daughter to somehow punish him or hurt him? Is that what you really want to know?"

"I'd be happy to hear your answer to any of those questions," Andi said evenly.

"Look, Neil and I had a bad ending. We started out wanting the same things and ended up with dreams that were far apart."

"Did you want a child with Neil?" Andi asked.

Shana didn't even flinch. "Yes, I did. I wanted a family. Neil kept putting me off. It wasn't the right time. There was a new production about to start. We had business trips somewhere, but, clearly, he just didn't want to have a baby with me. He felt differently after he married Claire. That hurt. But Neil was and is a selfish person. He wanted what he wanted when he wanted it. I'm sorry their baby has been taken. I certainly didn't do it, and I have no idea who else could be involved. Neil can piss people off, but I can't imagine why someone would take his child. I assume it must be about money. Neil's last two films have been very successful. Maybe someone wanted a piece of that." Shana frowned. "And, no, I'm not that someone. I'm doing fine on my own. I actually prefer not having to answer to Neil. We started together, but at some point, he thought he was in charge. Now, I call all the shots."

Cooper couldn't help but admire Shana's direct candor. It was refreshing, and it felt remarkably honest.

"What can you tell me about Larry Friedman and his problems with women?" Andi asked, changing the direction of their discussion.

"How much time do you have?" Shana asked cynically. "Larry is a pig. He's a known harasser and predator, and while no one has come out and called him a rapist, I would not say that is out of the question."

"I understand Jillian Markham is trying to get some accusers together."

"She reached out to me, but the truth is I didn't work a lot with Larry. His partnership with Neil didn't start until after we divorced."

"Neil's defense of Larry seems to have made Ms. Markham very angry," Andi said.

Shana tilted her head. "You think she would kidnap Neil's

child because Neil is defending Larry? That's ridiculous. Although, she might have done something stupid because I think she's crazy in love with Neil."

"Did she tell you that?" Cooper asked in surprise.

"Of course not. But she said they hooked up, and I believe her, but Neil has never been a faithful person." Shana gave him a questioning look. "What's your involvement in all this, Cooper? I thought you hated the FBI."

"Neil asked me to make sure everything that needed to be done was being done."

"So you're looking over Agent Hart's shoulder." She looked at Andi. "You must love that."

"Dr. Bradford has actually been helpful," Andi said, shocking him with her words. "Is there anyone else you can think of, Shana, that would go after Neil in this way, because it feels very personal. Whoever took Elisa knew the layout of the house, how to get in and out without anyone seeing them."

"I can't think of anyone."

"What about Solange's son, Daniel?" he asked. "You must have known Daniel from the time Solange worked for you."

"Of course. Daniel was a good kid until his father died. Then his issues with drugs got bigger. I'm pretty sure he stole some jewelry from me. I couldn't prove it, and I confronted Solange about it. She denied it, said she checked his belongings, and then she quit. I would have pursued it, but it wasn't a big loss, and I felt sorry for Solange. I told her I didn't think she was helping her son by not admitting he had a problem. She said I was wrong, but I don't believe I was." Shana paused as her cell phone rang. "Hold on. Hello? Yes, I need to talk to you. One second." She put her hand over the phone. "I need to take this call. Are we done?"

"For now," Andi said. "Thanks for your help."

"I'm not sure I was of any help, but I hope Neil gets his kid back."

There wasn't a tremendous amount of empathy behind her

words, but then Shana hadn't tried to hide her feelings about anything.

They walked out of the office and back down to the car. They'd no sooner gotten inside when Andi's personal phone dinged with several more texts in a row.

"Your father?" he asked.

"No. My furniture was supposed to be delivered tomorrow morning but now it's coming in less than half an hour. Damn."

"What's the problem? We can be at your place before they get there."

"If you want to get out and get a ride to your car, you can do that. You don't need to go to my apartment."

"I want to keep working with you. This won't take that long, right?"

"Probably not."

He could see that Andi didn't want to take him to her place. She'd always been prickly about where she lived. When they were kids, he'd chalked that up to her just hating to be at home. But it had probably been more than that. She'd never wanted to hang out at her house. Even when her parents weren't home, she'd always wanted to go somewhere else.

"What are you so angry about?" he asked, seeing the stony set of her profile as she drove home.

"It's inconvenient and I hate when people don't do what they say they're going to do. They said they would deliver tomorrow."

"I get it, but what's really bothering you is that I'm going with you, right? You don't want me in your apartment. You hated when I'd come to your house. You never wanted to hang out there."

"Because my parents were always fighting. It was embarrassing."

"Even when they weren't around, you insisted on going somewhere else. I used to tease you about it, remember?"

"I remember punching you when you annoyed me. I wouldn't make the same mistake."

He grinned at her sharp comment. He'd always liked the fire Andi brought. She could be irritating as hell, but she had always made his life more interesting.

His smile faded as he realized he was doing it again, forgetting why he hated her. Spending so much time with her was dimming his anger, his feeling of betrayal. He needed to remember the end of their friendship, not the six years before that. In fact, he felt a little desperate to hang on to the dislike, because hanging with Andi in his old bedroom, wanting to kiss her like he had when he was a kid, was messing with his mind. Kissing her had seemed impossibly complicated when he was fourteen, and it was even more complicated now. Maybe he should have gotten a ride to his car, instead of going to her house. Wasn't that just going to entangle them even more?

That question still echoed in his mind when Andi pulled up in front of a two-story townhouse in Santa Monica. It was at the end of a development of six matching homes, and it really didn't seem to suit her, because Andi had never been like everyone else. She'd always been one of a kind.

"I'll leave the driveway for the moving van," she said, as she got out of the car.

"Makes sense." He followed her into the house, the very empty house. There was no furniture in the living room, just a shiny hardwood floor and very white walls. The kitchen was slightly better with a bowl of fruit on the counter, along with a coffeemaker and a box of oatmeal.

"Looks like this delivery is coming in the nick of time," he said dryly. "How are you even staying here?"

"I have a bed upstairs and a coffeemaker. That has gotten me through the past two days. I got in late Monday night, started work Tuesday, and I've barely been home since then."

He moved toward the stairs.

"Where are you going?" she asked.

"I want to see your room."

"There's nothing to see," she protested, as she moved up the stairs after him.

He walked into the large master bedroom and realized she was right. Besides the bed which was only covered with a sheet and a blanket, there was nothing else in the room. There were a couple of suitcases by the closet and a single rack of clothes, but that was it.

"I told you, Cooper," she said.

He moved toward the window, which looked at another building about thirty feet away. "Why didn't you go for a beach view? You always said you wanted to live by the beach one day."

"I didn't see the point of paying extra for that. I work a lot. I don't have time to sit around and look at a view."

"But you must have told me a million times that one day you were going to live by the sea."

She frowned. "I can't believe you remember that."

"Like I said, you said it a million times. We'd ride our bikes to the top of Ridgeview Avenue, where we could almost see a sliver of the ocean fifteen miles away."

"I loved going up to Ridgeview. Even though we couldn't really see the ocean, we did have a great view of the city, and I liked having a bigger world to look at. It made me feel that there was more to life somewhere out there."

"So, why not pay the extra bucks?"

"The beach is six blocks away. I can walk there."

"It's not the same."

"What about you? Do you have a beach view?"

"As a matter of fact, I do," he said. "It's amazing."

"Well, you probably have a few more extra bucks than I do. You've sold a lot of books."

He wasn't going to tell her that he'd thought about her when he'd bought his condo, when he'd stood on his deck and looked out at the crashing ocean waves.

"It was nice to be able to buy a place that spoke to me. I've always wanted a bigger world view, too."

As their gazes met, something shifted between them. He took a step forward, and he thought she'd move back, but she didn't, and they were suddenly too close. He could hear her breathing. He could smell her scent. His blood began to race through his veins. A million voices in his head were screaming at him not to do what he very much wanted to do. But he shut them out.

He didn't know if he moved or she did, but his mouth was suddenly on hers, and she tasted better than he'd imagined. She also kissed him back like a woman who knew what she wanted, a woman who wanted him, and every single wild fantasy he'd ever had about her was coming true. It felt like a dream, but it was real.

Until she pulled away, until their eyes met in a clash of uncertainty and desire.

"That was…" her voice trailed away uncertainly. "You shouldn't have kissed me, Cooper."

"You kissed me back, Andi. You know you did."

She stared back at him. "I shouldn't have."

"Why not? You're single, right?"

"Yes, but—"

"So am I. We kissed. What's the problem?"

"The problem is that you hate me, Cooper."

The problem was that he didn't. He blew out a breath. "I want to hate you," he said. "But I'm having trouble getting there now."

Her phone suddenly dinged. She pulled it out of her shoulder bag. "Oh, great. The furniture won't be here for another twenty minutes. Maybe you should go. Get a ride, get your car, do something else."

"I want to go with you to the gym."

"I think we should spend less time together, not more."

"Because of a kiss. Was it that big of a deal?"

"No, of course not. It was just a kiss. It's not like I haven't kissed anyone, and I'm sure you've kissed a million people."

"You might be giving me a little too much credit," he said dryly.

"But we're working together, and we should keep it professional. I'm going downstairs to wait for the truck." She practically ran out of the room, belying her statement that their kiss was no big deal.

He waited a minute, needing a moment to regroup. Then he walked out of the room and moved slowly down the stairs. Andi was standing in the kitchen. She'd pulled her phone out of her bag, which was on the counter next to her.

"Any more news?" he asked, as he hit the last step.

"No," she said, putting her phone in her pocket. "I'm going to wait outside." She headed toward the door.

"You don't have to leave your own home just to get away from me," he said.

She paused, looking back at him. "That's not what I'm—"

Her voice was cut off as a massive explosion lit up the air, rocking the house, forcibly throwing them off their feet as the front door blew off the building in a rain of fire and debris.

CHAPTER SIXTEEN

COOPER'S EARS throbbed from the roar of the explosion. It took a minute to realize he was in the hallway and the front of the house was on fire and smoke was choking his lungs. He struggled to sit up, and then his heart stopped as he saw Andi laying in the kitchen, blood on her face. She was so still. Terror ran through him. He jumped up, the heat of the fire burning his skin, as he ran toward her. Dropping to his knees, he put his hand on her chest, almost weeping when he felt the soft fall and rise. Leaning over her breath lightly touched his face. She was breathing. She was alive.

He put his hand on her shoulder, afraid to move her, but also afraid to stay where they were. A bomb had gone off outside the front door, and he didn't know if there was another one coming. The fire was also spreading quickly. He thought he heard sirens, but they were very far away.

"Andi," he said. "Wake up." He put his mouth right next to her ear. "I need you to wake up."

He needed her to be okay, too. He felt almost desperate and overwhelmed with that need. He moved his gaze to her lips and put his mouth against hers. He needed to bring her back to life before the fire consumed them.

She started, and then her eyes slowly fluttered open. She looked at him with a dazed, confused expression. "Did you push me down?" she mumbled. "Did you just kiss me?"

He was incredibly relieved that she was awake and immediately annoyed. "A bomb went off. We need to get out of the house."

At his words, her gaze moved past him, and she sat up.

"Are you okay?" he asked. "I don't know if you should move. But we also can't stay here."

"I'm all right."

He doubted she had any idea if she was all right as blood dripped down her face from cuts that marred her beautiful skin. There was glass and plaster in her hair. Her black slacks and jacket were covered with white and gray soot. And he probably looked just as bad. He could see blood on his arm, but he didn't care about any of that.

Andi scrambled to her feet. "I'm okay," she said. "There's a back door." She grabbed her gun from the floor where it had gone flying and her bag from the counter and then they ran through the kitchen and laundry room to a door leading into the small yard behind the house. They got as far away as they could before collapsing onto the grass.

Andi put a hand to her face, coming away with blood. Her gaze widened as she saw it on her fingers. "Where am I bleeding?"

"Your scalp is cut," he said. "You have some scratches on your face." His gaze dropped. "And your neck. There's blood on your shirt." He suddenly worried that she was far more injured than he thought. "Do you feel pain anywhere?"

"I don't think so," she said slowly. "You're hurt, too."

"I'm fine. I was farther away than you." The sirens were getting louder now. "I think the fire department is almost here."

She pulled a phone out of her pocket and pressed a number. Then she said, "Flynn. Someone just set off a bomb at my house." Pausing, she added. "Cooper and I are okay. We're in the yard.

Police and fire are coming. You should, too." She waited a moment and then said, "Okay," and ended the call. "He's on his way." Her gaze moved to the fire that was leaping through the roof at the front of the house. "I can't believe someone put a bomb outside the front door."

"Thank God we weren't any closer. You were headed straight for the door." He shook his head as chills ran through him at the thought of how close she'd come to dying. "When I saw you laying on the ground so still..." He drew in a shaky breath. "I wasn't sure you were going to wake up."

"But I did," she said.

"Yes, you did," he said tightly.

"There's plaster in your hair, Cooper. And you have a cut on your forehead."

"Superficial, I'm sure. But you don't look any prettier than me, which is a first."

"No, not a first. You grew into your looks way before me. I was an awkward fourteen-year-old. You were already becoming the hot guy in our class."

"But you didn't notice."

"I was trying hard not to." She paused. "Did you kiss me when I was unconscious?"

"Yes. To wake you up—like Sleeping Beauty."

"I thought I was dreaming," she said in bemusement.

"I wasn't trying to take advantage. I was really...scared."

Their gazes clung together, and then she said, "Thanks for waking me up. I shouldn't have brought you home with me. You could have been killed."

"You couldn't have seen this coming. It was a bomb, Andi. Who would do this? Why would they do this?"

"To get rid of me."

"Or both of us."

"I think you were just going to be collateral damage."

"Well, it wouldn't be the first time," he muttered, drawing a frown to her face. He immediately regretted his statement. He hadn't meant to give her a dig, not now, not after almost dying. Before he could say anything, firemen were coming through the side yard, and they got to their feet.

For the next half hour, they were attended to by medics and answered questions from the police and from Flynn and several other agents. After getting first aid and bandages for their thankfully superficial cuts, they both refused further treatment. He wasn't sure that was the best idea, but he was sticking close to Andi, and she was adamant that she wasn't going to waste time in an ER.

As the FBI took control of the scene, Flynn and an agent Andi called Savannah urged them into an SUV and drove them to another house that was apparently considered a safe house.

The two-story home was in a wooded area called Rustic Canyon in the hilly Palisades area just north of Santa Monica. It was a standalone home with shrubbery and tall fences on either side providing privacy from nearby homes. There were cameras all over the property and advanced locks on the doors, as well as a security system that was better than anything he'd ever seen. Unlike Andi's townhouse, it was also fully furnished.

They sat down together in the living room, and for the first time in an hour, he took a full breath. They were alive and safe and while there were a million more questions now, that was really all that mattered.

Savannah handed them each a bottle of cold water. He opened his and took a long, thirsty drink, while Andi did the same. Savannah and Flynn sat down on the chairs facing them.

"My furniture," Andi said suddenly. "It never came, did it?"

"There was a furniture truck that arrived," Savannah said. "I sent them away."

"Well, at least my furniture wasn't blown up," Andi said, making a weak joke that he didn't find at all funny.

"Do you think you were followed home?" Flynn asked.

"I never saw a tail, but maybe I wasn't looking closely enough. Because I don't know how else anyone would know where I live. Although, the furniture company had my address, and it is weird that they weren't supposed to deliver until tomorrow, but suddenly they were coming today, which is why I went home. I have no idea, though, how anyone could have contacted them or known that I had a delivery coming. It's not like I've been talking about it with anyone."

"They could have hacked your phone, your email," Flynn said.

Andi frowned. "That's true."

"It appears that the device was activated remotely once you were in the house," Savannah said. "But the good news is they weren't able to plant it inside your home where it would have done more damage."

"That's the good news?" Cooper cut in. "Andi was almost killed. She was knocked out. I thought she was dead."

At his words, all three of them looked at him with varying emotions in their eyes. Flynn appeared sympathetic, Savannah was curious, and Andi flushed like she was guilty of allowing herself to almost be blown up.

"I realize you're all more used to this than I am, but someone tried to kill her. We're all agreed on that, right?"

"Not just her—you, too," Flynn said. "That's why you're both here."

"I'm not going to stay here and hide," Andi said. "I have work to do. I won't drop this case. Then they would win. They'd get me out of the way, which is exactly what they want."

"You're not dropping the case, but you're going to need to stay here tonight while we regroup," Flynn replied.

"I'll be safe at the office. At least there I'll have more resources."

"There's an office here that's set up with everything we have downtown," Savannah said. "It's just down the hall."

"And here you won't be making the rest of the team a target," Flynn added.

Andi had been about to protest before Flynn's latest argument. Now she gave a resigned sigh. "All right. I'll stay put for tonight. But I'm not making any promises about tomorrow." She paused, looking at her watch. "It's after six. I was going to go to the Fourth Street gym. Tyler, the employee who drove Flores's car last night, is supposed to be working tonight."

"I'll check that out," Flynn said. "I'm bringing everyone in to work on this case, Andi. Whatever you need."

"Thank you."

The doorbell rang, and Flynn got up. "That's Caitlyn," he said. "She's bringing supplies."

A moment later, a dark-haired woman entered the room with two large bags of groceries, while Flynn carried a duffel bag.

"Groceries," the woman said. She gave Cooper a smile. "I'm Caitlyn."

"Cooper."

"I know."

"And there are some basic clothes in here," Flynn added, pointing to the duffel bag that he set on the floor by the coffee table. "That should hold you both until tomorrow. Hopefully, this won't have to last longer than that."

"It won't last longer than that," Andi said emphatically. "Elisa is still missing and someone going after me should not slow the investigation down. I can take care of myself."

"Well, you're not by yourself. You have a team behind you," Flynn said.

"I'll put these bags in the kitchen," Caitlyn said.

"I'll help." He grabbed one of the bags out of her arms and followed her down the hall to the kitchen. As they unpacked the bags, he realized Caitlyn had brought the basics, eggs, milk, bread, butter, coffee as well as fruit, steaks, frozen pizza, salad fixings, dessert, and two bottles of wine, one white and one red. "You did good," he said approvingly.

She smiled. "I've had to put some time in at a safe house. I know what's important."

"How long was your stay?"

"A couple of days."

"Do you think we'll be here that long?"

"I hope not. But all you can do is take it one step at a time. There's a first aid kit in the master bathroom. You look like you might have some scrapes that haven't been looked at.

"I'm okay."

"Make sure you put some antibiotic ointment on those cuts."

"Will do."

When they returned to the living room, Savannah, Andi, and Flynn were standing by the front door. As soon as the agents left the house, Andi turned two deadbolts and pushed a button to set the alarm.

"Looks like we're all tucked in," he said. Andi stared back at him with brown eyes that were still a little too dazed and a face that was far too pale. "Are you really okay?"

"I'm fine," she said, but he couldn't help noticing that she looked a little unsteady as she walked back to the couch.

He sat down next to her. "Caitlyn brought us a lot of food."

"I'm not hungry. I'm frustrated and pissed off. And I'm stumped as to who would have done this and why."

"What's your gut telling you?"

"Nothing," she said with annoyance. "Which is unusual. I always have some idea, but my brain is empty."

"Maybe because your ears are still ringing. I know mine are. That was close, Andi, too close."

She met his gaze. "I know."

"I feel like it's partly my fault that you were so close to the door."

Her eyebrows shot up. "Why would it be your fault?"

"I kissed you, and you couldn't get away from me fast enough. You didn't want to stay in the house. You wanted to go out front and wait for the truck."

"I wasn't running away from you. I was just impatient to get the delivery and mad that they were going to be late after we raced back to meet them. That bomb wasn't your fault, Cooper. If anything, it was mine. I missed something."

"Like what?"

"Whatever I said or did that got someone thinking I know more than I do," she replied.

"You've talked to a lot of people, but it's not like you accused anyone of anything. You just asked questions."

"And got very few answers." She paused. "I don't think someone followed me home last night or today. I always look in my rearview mirror. It's automatic for me. It's like fastening my seatbelt. I never forget to check for a tail."

Her words reminded him what different lives they led.

"So, someone knew where you lived and wanted to send you a message."

"The car last night was a message. This was more. This was attempted murder."

A shiver ran down his spine. He'd spent most of his adult life talking to criminals, reviewing details of some of the most heinous crimes, but he'd never been a victim. He'd always been a spectator, an analyst, a critical observer. But today, he could have died. And Andi could have died, too. He shook his head in bemusement. "Remember when we were kids, and my mom said that sticking our noses into other people's business could get us into trouble. She was right."

"She was. But to save lives, it's a necessary risk."

"Have you been in danger a lot?" he asked curiously.

"Depends on your definition of a lot."

"That sounds like a yes."

"It's part of the job."

"You always had a hell of a lot of courage, Andi. Even as a kid. When you were determined to right a wrong, you were not going to stop, no matter what obstacles you faced."

"I don't know any other way to be. I just wish I knew what I missed, because I obviously present a danger to someone."

"Maybe Daniel and his friends. They seem the most likely

suspects. We know he's connected to the gym, and the car that almost hit us is also connected to the gym. Daniel's drug problems, his inside information on Neil's house..." He shrugged. "He's at the top of my list."

She nodded in agreement. "We need to find him."

"I don't think we're going to do that, at least not tonight. Unless you're planning on bailing on our safe house?"

"I was considering it," she admitted.

"Well, I think you should eat something before you make any decisions. I may not be as good a detective as you are—"

"May not?" she challenged.

"Okay, definitely not," he conceded. "But I'm a decent cook, and Caitlyn picked up some good steaks. Will you let me make you dinner before you take off anywhere?"

"You don't have to cook for me. I can help."

"I've got this. You think about what we need to do next."

CHAPTER SEVENTEEN

ANDI COULDN'T THINK about anything else but what she was missing, and that was a frustrating wheel to be trapped on. She could have spooked any number of people, but a bomb…that seemed completely out of left field for a child kidnapping case. There had to be more at stake than one child's life. Elisa had to be the tip of an iceberg. This was about more than just her, which raised all kind of speculative theories in her head, especially a human or baby trafficking ring. That didn't sound like something the twenty-year-old Daniel Guerrero would be in charge of. But he could definitely be working for a bigger organization. Hell, maybe the whole gym was a front for a criminal enterprise.

But she needed more than an idea; she needed proof of something. And that's what she didn't have. Or at least, she didn't think she had.

As her head spun in a frustrating circle, she became more aware of stinging pain in her face, so she got up and went into the downstairs guest bathroom to look in the mirror.

No wonder everyone was treating her like an invalid. Her right eye was swollen, there was blood seeping through a bandage on her forehead, and she had tiny, bloody knicks all over her face and even her throat. Her blouse was torn in several places, revealing some cuts and dried blood, mixed in with the dirt and smoke of the fire.

She could still feel the heat of the flames, the ringing in her ears, the force of her body hitting the ground. She would probably have some aches and pains twenty-four hours from now. Her head was already throbbing, but she wasn't going to mention that to Cooper. She'd had a concussion before, and this wasn't that bad, although, according to Cooper she'd been completely knocked out for a few seconds. But she was fine. She didn't want to go to a hospital. She just wanted to take a shower and clean up.

Returning to the living room, she looked through the duffel bag finding a mix of new men's and women's clothing. Caitlyn had thought of everything. She grabbed undies, black jeans that were her perfect size, a thick sweater, socks, and tennis shoes and then went up the stairs to the master bathroom where she took a long, hot shower.

It felt great to be clean again, and she was thrilled to find lotions in the bathroom drawers as well as a first-aid kit. She checked out the rest of her cuts but nothing besides the one on her forehead was that bad. She changed that bandage and then dried her hair and got dressed.

She left her dirty clothes in a hamper in the bathroom, but took her gun, badge, and phone down the stairs with her. When she got into the kitchen, she found Cooper looking remarkably comfortable as he sauteed a steak with butter, while mushrooms and onions sizzled in a nearby pan. She probably shouldn't be surprised he could cook. His mom had insisted that her kids know how to provide for themselves, and while Monica had veered toward baking, Cooper clearly knew his way around a stove.

She slid onto a stool at the island and put her gun and phone on the counter.

Cooper set down his spoon to turn to the opposite counter

where he poured her a glass of red wine and then placed it in front of her.

"This restaurant has good service," she said lightly.

He gave her a grin that was so Cooper, her heart clenched. Sometimes, she could still see the boy in him that she'd loved beyond belief. Other times, she could only see the man he'd become, but she was starting to like that man, too. Not that she was going to let herself think about their kisses. In some ways, they'd been more explosive than the bomb that had gone off minutes later.

"You deserve a glass of wine after today," he said. "You look a lot better now."

"You should grab a shower, too."

"After we eat."

"I am hungry. I just hate to take time off when there's so much that needs to be done."

"It's almost eight o'clock at night. There's not much else you can do tonight. You have to pace yourself and remember that you have a team behind you."

"I know. But it's my case, and I want to solve it."

He smiled again, and she couldn't help but grin back at him. "Okay, I know I'm too stubborn and competitive, but I like to win, especially when the stakes are as huge as they are now. Elisa's life is on the line. And here I am drinking wine. It never feels right."

"There's an office down the hall. I'm sure you can get some work done tonight, even after drinking a glass of wine. But in the meantime, you can relax, get your head together, and enjoy a nice meal."

"It smells good. Your mother trained you well."

"None of her children were going to say they didn't know how to cook. Even Kyle could whip up dinner if he had to."

"Kyle always liked breakfast for dinner."

Cooper's hand stilled at her words, then he continued

spooning butter over his steak. "Scrambled eggs with cheese and bacon was his favorite meal." He took the steaks off the heat and pulled them out of the pan to rest. Then he looked at her. "Waffles, too. My mom let us each choose a meal to make once a month for the family, and breakfast for dinner was always Kyle's."

"I remember. I liked it. No one ever made breakfast at my house, so I was thrilled to get it for dinner." She took a breath, feeling like she was walking on the edge of a cliff, but she had to keep going. "If I ask you to tell me more about Kyle's life, would it be too painful?"

He sucked in a breath, resting his hands on the counter. "What would you want to know?"

"Did he go to college? Have a job? Did he live away from home? Did he have a girlfriend?"

"He had a girlfriend for about a year and a half when he was in his twenties. Her name was Georgia Blake. She was a kindergarten teacher, sweet as could be, and she really cared about him. But Kyle had a lot of personal demons that went along with his depression, anxiety, and bipolar disorder. He also had trouble with communication, which made relationships and jobs hard for him."

"So he had a job. What did he do?"

"He worked at several jobs, mostly with computers. He was good at coding, and he liked not having to interact with humans." Cooper took a breath. "He'd do well for a while, but the mood swings always came back. Medications would help for a while and then need to be changed. Sometimes he'd bounce all the way back and feel like he was completely normal. He'd be the brother I always wanted. And then other times, he'd disappear for days at a time and then he'd get fired. It was an agonizing circle he couldn't get out of. I really wanted to help him, Andi."

"I know," she said softly.

"That's really why I went into psychology. It wasn't just about understanding criminals. I thought if I could understand Kyle better, I could help him. I could…"

"Fix him?" she asked, as he appeared to be searching for the right words.

He met her gaze. "Yes. I wanted to make him better, make him happy, make him whole. But I wasn't smart enough. I couldn't make it happen." He paused again. "But I don't want to downplay the impact the false accusations had on his life. He suffered from a lot of hatred for no reason for a very long time. Even years later, someone would suddenly say something about the kidnapping, make others suspicious of him. He moved away when he was twenty-three for about three years. He was in a small town in Arizona. That's when he was with Georgia, but then a friend of hers from LA said she'd heard his name in conjunction with the kidnapping. I don't think Georgia believed he did it, but it changed things between them. That's when he realized he would never escape the past. He came home and for the next year, I watched him struggle even more. That's when I realized he wasn't the only person who'd ever had to deal with being falsely accused."

She was sorry they'd come back to that part of his life, but she was realizing she could never fully escape from that circle, either.

"What about you?" she asked changing the subject. "I know about your professional life, what about personal? Have you ever been in love? Ever lived with anyone? Thought about getting married?"

"I think we should eat," he said.

"The questions are not that difficult."

"But I'm hungry, and I could use some wine, too. Let's sit at the table."

She slid off her stool and joined him at the kitchen table where he set out a meal that was restaurant worthy, and suddenly she was more interested in eating than hearing about other women. In fact, she wasn't sure why she'd even asked about his love life. She didn't need to close the distance between Cooper and herself; she needed to widen it. While he had a lot of reasons to still hate her, she was finding it more and more difficult not to like him again, and that couldn't end well. So, she focused on her food, which was easy to do. The steak, mushrooms, and onions were delicious, perfectly seasoned, and just the right temperature. The salad was beautiful and fresh, and she enjoyed every bite.

"I can't remember the last time I had a home-cooked meal," she murmured as she cleaned her plate.

"Really? You don't cook at all?"

"Hardly ever. And when I do, it's quick and basic. Unlike you, my mother did not teach me how to cook, and dinner wasn't a meal I enjoyed growing up. That was usually when the fights started and, by dessert, I had an upset stomach."

Cooper gave her a compassionate look. "I knew it was bad, but I don't think I realized how bad."

"I didn't want you to know. I didn't want anyone to know. It made me feel like we weren't normal, which I guess was true."

"No family is normal. That's something I have learned in my study of psychology."

She smiled and sipped her second glass of wine, which had definitely mellowed her. "I have also realized since I grew up that even families that look good from the outside aren't always good on the inside. There's almost always a secret. Sometimes, that secret is nothing big. Other times, it's huge."

"Do you think Neil and Claire have a secret?" he asked curiously.

"He had an affair with Jillian. That was a secret."

"Good point. I don't think my parents ever had secrets, though."

"Or they're still secrets," she said. "But they do seem to really love each other, and they have respect and trust. That's so rare."

"What about you? Have you been in love, lived with anyone, thought about getting married?"

She shook her head. "No way. You didn't answer those questions. Why should I?"

He rested his arms on the table and smiled at her. "All right. I'll answer first. I've never lived with anyone, never considered getting engaged. As for love, I've been close a couple of times, but I haven't crossed the finish line."

"Why not? Afraid of commitment?"

"I don't think so. I grew up with a good example in front of me. Maybe my parents set my expectations too high."

"Maybe," she agreed. "And my parents set my expectations very low. I don't trust easily. I can easily assume someone is lying even when they aren't, which doesn't work well in a relationship. I also love to work, which takes up a great percentage of my time and my energy. I haven't found any men who enjoyed being second."

"So, your work is your relationship, isn't it?"

"Uh-oh, I sense we're venturing into psychologist couch category."

He grinned. "More like I've known you since you were eight category."

"I didn't work when I knew you."

"Not for money. But you threw yourself into neighborhood mysteries with a passion equal to a job."

"I suppose that's somewhat true. When I'm on a mission, I don't like to be stopped. Like tonight, having dinner, drinking wine. It's great, but it's also eating at me. I should be doing something more important than this."

He gave her a thoughtful look that made her even more uneasy. "What?" she asked, when the silence lengthened between them.

"You used mysteries and projects as distractions when you were a kid. You didn't want to slow down, because then you'd have time to think and thinking made you sad. Maybe that's what you do now, too. If you never stop running towards the next goal, you never have to assess your life, deal with your emotions, or have a relationship, develop a trust that can only happen with time."

She frowned, wishing he wasn't so good at reading her. "I love what I do. And I'm good at it. Why should I stop to reassess anything when I'm doing what I want?"

"Because I don't think it's physically or mentally or emotionally possible to never give yourself a pause. Eventually, you're going to run out of gas and then where will you be?"

"I guess I'll find out then," she said, her words putting a small smile on his face.

He tipped his head. "I guess you will."

"It's my life. I get to live it how I want. And I thrive in my job."

"It's great that you love what you do, because that's rare. You might thrive in a relationship, too, if you're willing to take a risk. But love scares you more than anything, more than a bullet or a bomb, I'm guessing. You can risk your life for your work, but your heart is a different story. You guard that like it's Fort Knox. No one gets close enough to break it."

He was shockingly right. She took in a breath as his words rang around in her head. "I don't know if I should be impressed by your analytical skills or if I'm really easy to read," she said lightly, trying to downplay the drama of his words."

"Like I said, I know you."

"But you don't know me," she argued. "And I don't know you. We're grown up. We're not kids anymore."

"We're older and taller, but our personalities aren't that different. I saw how much you were hurt by your parents' divorce. It has to have affected your relationships, your ability to trust, your view of love."

"I said I don't trust easily, and I know that has something to do with living with my father, a man who lies and cheats with a straight face and a very believable demeanor. He didn't just lie to my mom or to me but everyone I ever saw him with. It still stuns me that so many women have fallen for his lies. I don't want to get taken in by a man who's as good at lying as my dad."

"You never would. You're too suspicious and discerning. Any man is going to have to jump through hoops to get your trust."

Or maybe fire, she thought, thinking that Cooper, sadly, might be the one person she could trust. But he could never trust her.

Since that stung, she made a joke instead. "Wow, what a great compliment," she said dryly. "I'll have to put that on my dating profile—suspicious and discerning."

He grinned. "Do you have a profile?"

"No. With my job, I can't be that public. I have to be very careful about who I let into my life. I can't risk that someone might use me in some way." She paused. "And considering you're as single as I am, I'm not the only one who has had trouble finding the perfect partner. What are you looking for that you haven't found?"

"Someone I can trust."

Her heart flipped over as his words echoed the thought that had just run through her mind. "Did my betrayal make you afraid to trust other girls, other women?"

"Yes," he said flatly.

She felt like he'd just stabbed her. She sat back in her seat. "That was direct."

"It had a tremendous impact on me."

"I'm sorry. I know those words will never be enough, but I'm speaking from my heart. I wish you could believe me."

"I believe you," he said, surprising her with his words.

"But you just said—"

"I said that what you did made me afraid to trust other people, and that's true. But I also know now that I didn't see the situation with as much clarity as I do now. Being with you the past two days has been an eye-opener. I know you're sorry. I just don't know how to fully let go of the anger, Andi."

Her gut clenched in sorrow with the truth of his words. He

might have clarity, but forgiveness was still out of reach. "Do you really want to let the anger go, Cooper?"

He nodded. "Yes. I want to forgive you, Andi. I just don't know how."

She stared back at him, watching a mix of emotions play through his eyes. "I guess kissing me didn't help."

He sucked in a quick breath. "That was better than I imagined."

"Which only complicates your feelings, right? How can you physically want someone you hate?"

"Or how can I hate someone I want so much?" he countered.

She swallowed hard. "I don't think we should kiss again until we have an answer to at least one of those questions."

"Do you feel the same way, Andi?"

"Conflicted?" she asked. "Yes. And confused. Because I never thought about you in this way when we were kids."

"You don't have to keep rubbing that in," he said dryly.

At his rueful smile, she grinned, grateful their deep conversation had suddenly gotten easy again. It would probably always be this way with Cooper. One step forward, one step back, the good and the bad and then the good again. Since they had to spend time together, she'd rather stay on this lighter note. "I was not as advanced as you were back in high school."

"I was not advanced. I was awkward and uncomfortable and the more time we spent together, the worse that got. That's why I wasn't as available to hang out with you. I was trying to figure things out when you weren't in my presence, fogging up my adolescent brain."

"And I just thought you were getting bored or annoyed with me."

"Well, you were annoying. We already established that."

She threw her wadded up napkin in his direction. "You were annoying, too, and you still are."

"But we make a good team."

"I'm not sure I'd say that."

"I saved your life. I pulled you out of the fire. That's twice in two days I've had your back."

"You woke me up, but I got myself out of the fire," she argued.

"It's always picky semantics with you. You hate to be weak."

"And you like to be the hero."

"We both like that," he corrected. He took a breath, his expression changing once more, his gaze getting contemplative. "Did you forget about me over the years?"

"I tried really hard to forget you, because remembering our friendship hurt way too much. You were my best friend. I don't think I've ever had a friend like you since then. We talked about everything."

"We did," he agreed.

"But those days are gone. We can't get them back."

"We can't recreate the past, but we might be able to redefine our future."

"You just said you don't know if you can ever forgive me. I don't see us redefining anything."

"I said I want to forgive you. I just don't know how, but I'm thinking more kissing might help."

Her pulse leapt, but she shook her head. "It's only going to make everything more complicated and the last time we kissed, there was an explosion at the end of it. I take that as a bad sign."

He grinned. "I thought our kiss was more explosive than the bomb."

"Why did you have to grow up and be so attractive?" she asked in frustration. "So sexy and charming."

"I was thinking the same thing. Well, not the charming part, because you're very prickly, but the sexy part—definitely," he said, as he inched closer to her.

And then her phone rang, making them both jump.

"Did you time that?" Cooper asked.

"I wish I had thought of it. But saved by the bell. And it's Flynn." She answered the call. "What did you find out?"

"Tyler, the kid at the gym is in the hospital," Flynn said. "He was jumped in an alley behind his apartment and beat up. He was barely able to speak, said two guys jumped him, but they were wearing masks and he didn't know who they were. He also said he was driving alone last night. There wasn't anyone in the car with him. He didn't think he hit anyone, but he was texting while he was driving, so maybe he wasn't looking."

"Maybe it was an accident."

"Or the beat-down came after instructions not to say who was in the car with him. He looked nervous and terrified," Flynn added. "We're still looking for traffic cam footage. Hopefully, we can pick up the car at another location."

"What about the Benedicts? Have you spoken to them again? They're going to wonder where Cooper and I are."

"I said you were working on the case. There's nothing new with them. And nothing more you can do tonight, so stay put, and we'll talk in the morning."

"I'll stay here tonight, but I make no promises for after that. I can't just hide. I need to work."

"I get it. We'll touch base tomorrow."

She hung up the phone and met Cooper's gaze. "What do you think?"

"That Daniel was probably in the car," he said heavily.

"Daniel or someone else. I don't believe Tyler was alone, but I need evidence not thoughts. I'm going to get on the computer and see what else I can find." She stood up, then paused. "What we were just talking about…"

"Can wait," he said quickly. "For a better time."

"What if there isn't one?"

"Then that will be our answer," he said cryptically. "You get to work. I'll clean up here."

While Andi got on the computer in the office, Cooper cleaned up the kitchen. He'd just started the dishwasher when his phone buzzed. It was Neil.

"Where are you Cooper?" Neil asked, an angry note in his voice. "Why haven't you checked in with me?"

"I was about to," he lied. "The FBI assured me they were keeping you up to speed."

"They've told me next to nothing. Solange called me and said she thinks she needs a lawyer. They're asking her a lot of questions about Daniel."

"Has she seen Daniel?"

"No. But she can't believe he would hurt Elisa, and I can't, either. I've known that kid since he was ten years old," Neil said. "He's a little wild, but he's not a bad person. He wouldn't kidnap a child."

"He has a drug problem, Neil. Sometimes that changes people."

"You think he's the one who did this?"

"I don't know, but Solange doesn't know where he is, and that's concerning. What about Kristine? Has she come back to the house?"

"No, and that's worrying me, too," Neil replied. "I've called her a couple of times and left messages. The last time I tried, her phone didn't even ring."

His gut tightened. That meant Kristine's phone was off. "Did you tell the FBI that?"

"Yes. They said they're looking for her. They're very focused on Kristine and Daniel. I have trusted Kristine with my child for months now. Why would she suddenly do something? And Daniel—I used to throw baseballs to him when his dad was sick, and he needed to practice. These are people I've let into my life, Cooper."

He could hear the growing sense of betrayal in Neil's voice, and he knew exactly what that felt like. "How's Claire doing?"

"She talked to her doctor, and he convinced her to take a sedative. She's sleeping for the first time since this all happened."

"You should try to get some sleep, too."

"Every time I close my eyes, I see Elisa's face, and my brain takes me to a dark place. Like maybe I'm never going to see her again."

He wanted to tell Neil to stay positive, but it felt pointless. He knew firsthand not every missing kid came home. "There are a lot of people working hard to get Elisa back," he said instead. "I can promise you that."

"So, where are you?"

"I'm with Agent Hart. Has anyone else contacted you, Neil? I'm not talking about ransom specifically, but maybe someone you haven't heard from in a while, someone who suddenly seems unusually interested in what's going on?" There was a silence at the other end of the line. "Neil?"

"Michelle, Larry's ex-wife, stopped by. I haven't seen her since they divorced. She said she'd come to check on Claire. I told her Claire was asleep, and she started asking me a bunch of questions about what happened, what we know. I couldn't tell her anything because I don't know anything. Then she said something odd. She asked me if I thought Larry was having an affair. That she'd seen him with a young blonde woman who looked like my nanny."

He sucked in a quick breath. "Larry and Kristine? Is that possible?"

"I can't imagine that it is. He couldn't have spoken to her more than a couple of times, although…"

"What?"

"Larry is in a run club, too. I don't think it's the same one as Kristine. But I don't know for sure. Neither Larry nor Kristine has ever mentioned that they've seen each other somewhere else. Larry is twenty-five years older than Kristine. And even if he was seeing her, he wouldn't steal my kid. I've been standing up for him."

"It doesn't make sense," he agreed. "And we don't even know if it was Kristine or why Michelle felt the need to talk to you about it when clearly you have other issues on your mind."

"Exactly." Neil let out a sigh. "Elisa isn't coming home tonight, is she?"

"I don't think so, but I hope it's soon."

"I'm trying to cling to the idea that because they took her clothes and toys, they're taking care of her."

"That's a good thought to cling to. Get some rest. I'll check in with you in the morning."

He slipped his phone into his pocket and moved down the hall to the office. Andi was pressing her hands to her temples as she stared at the computer screen.

"Any luck?" he asked.

She started at the sound of his voice. "Nothing. I've been looking at traffic camera footage around the gym, the bar, and Neil's house. Aside from that one clip by the bar where Enrique's license plate was captured, there's nothing."

"Does your head hurt?" he asked.

She dropped her hands with a self-conscious frown. "No, I'm fine."

He didn't think she was close to fine, but she'd never admit that. Andi didn't like to be perceived as weak. Her mental strength had always been her armor. "I spoke to Neil. Solange asked him if she should get a lawyer. I guess your team has been talking to her."

"I spoke to Flynn a few minutes ago. He said they brought her in, but they don't believe she knows where her son is. Did Neil say anything else?"

"He said Larry's ex-wife dropped by to check on Claire but then made a point of asking if Larry was having an affair with a young blonde, maybe his nanny."

Andi's brows shot up in surprise. "Seriously? Larry and Kristine."

"Neil doesn't believe it's true, although he said Larry is a runner, too."

"I guess that's another angle to check, but it seems odd. Why would Larry's ex-wife even bring that up to Neil with everything else Neil is dealing with?"

"That didn't make sense to me, either." Pausing, he added, "This is quite the setup." He waved his hand toward the bank of monitors showing every angle of the house. "I wonder how often this place is used."

"Probably quite a bit."

He couldn't help noticing the gun on the desk beside her. "Do you think you're going to need that tonight?"

"I think I'd be a fool not to have it with me at all times," she returned.

"Maybe I should have one, too. Since we're together, and you're a target."

"Do you know how to shoot?"

"I do. I've gotten to be friends with a private investigator who has helped me with research, and he's taken me out to the range a few times. I can hold my own."

"Shooting at the range is very different than a real-life situation."

"I'm sure, but I still think I need a weapon."

"And I think we should talk about your involvement going forward."

"No," he said, cutting her off with a decisive shake of his head. "I'm in on this. I'm not walking away."

"Cooper—"

"Don't even bother. I'm not hiding out somewhere until this is over. I was in your house, too. I could have been killed. I want to catch the people who took Elisa and tried to kill us. I'll follow your lead. That's the only concession I'm making." He was suddenly distracted by a movement on one monitor. "Hey, what's that?"

Andi's gaze followed his to a shadowy figure approaching the back of the house. She jumped to her feet. "That is not good."

"Shit! There's one in the front, too," he said, tipping his head to the other monitor. A flash of light showed an armed figure with a hat pulled low over his head. "They can't get in, right? This is a fortress. We should call 911."

Before they could do that, they saw one of the figures punch in some numbers on the keypad by the front door.

"Dammit," Andi swore. "They have the code."

"How the hell would they have the code?"

She didn't answer, just grabbed her weapon and ran toward a door that he thought led to a closet. She put in another code and opened it, then waved him inside. As she slammed the door, he heard a hail of gunfire. Andi dropped to her knees, put in another code and pulled up a trapdoor. "Go," she said, steel in her eyes. "We have to get out of here now. We're out of time."

CHAPTER EIGHTEEN

"You first," Cooper said, afraid she would stay behind to fight once he left. "You know the way."

As the gunfire got louder, Andi climbed onto the ladder and turned on the flashlight on her phone. She hurried down the rungs, and he followed, pulling the trapdoor closed behind him. They must have gone down twenty feet. He could hear bullets bouncing off the metal of the door leading into the closet. If there hadn't been an escape hatch, they'd already be dead, a fact that he couldn't even grasp at the moment. There was too much adrenaline running through his veins.

They hit the ground a moment later and made their way through a long, dark tunnel that seemed to go on forever. He kept waiting to hear someone coming after them. They reached another ladder, and this time, he wanted to go first.

"I've got this," he said, jumping in front of her. He climbed up to the top of the ladder, where he faced another lock. "Give me the code."

She rattled off six numbers, which he punched into the lock. It clicked open. "Before I push the door up, do you have any idea what we're walking into?"

"I think it's a bathroom at a baseball field. There shouldn't be anyone there at this time of night."

"Unless whoever got into the safe house knows about the tunnel and the exit."

"Unless that," she agreed. "I have the gun. Let me go first."

"I'm already here. And I don't think one gun is going to be enough. There were at least two people, maybe more at the house."

He pushed up the door, which reached a certain level of opening and then sprang open. He climbed up and onto a floor. Using his own phone for light, he looked around. They were in a bathroom, in what had once been a stall but was now empty.

Andi climbed up behind him. He pushed the stall door open. The bathroom was dark.

"Let's keep the lights off," she murmured.

He clicked off his phone and they let their eyes adjust to the dim light coming through a tall window. Then they walked past a urinal trough and a couple of sinks to another door.

Andi got there before him. She motioned for him to open the door, while she readied her weapon.

He pulled the door open, and she slid out. He moved behind her. To their right was a backstop for a baseball field. To their left was a thick line of trees.

They moved through the dark shadows and into the trees, which were in the opposite direction of the safe house. A few yards later, the backyard of another house butted up against the trees. Andi hopped over a low fence, and he quickly followed. They headed through the yard without saying a word, and he couldn't help feeling like they were playing out one of their summer night adventures, only it wasn't summer, and this wasn't a game. This was very real.

Andi peeked through the side gate. "I don't see anyone."

"Do you know where we are?"

"Flynn said the ball field is a quarter mile south of the safe house."

"Did he happen to leave a car parked nearby?"

"He did. But I don't think we should take it."

"Why not? We need to get farther away."

"Someone knew the code to the safe house. They might know about the car."

"They haven't found us yet. Maybe they didn't know about the tunnel or the car." She didn't appear convinced. "What are our other options?"

She thought for a moment. "Let's walk."

"We're just going to walk down the street? That doesn't sound like the best plan."

"Well, we can stand here and argue until they find us," she snapped.

"Lead the way," he said.

She moved through the gate. Staying close to the houses, they made their way down the street. Like all the streets in this area, it was heavily wooded and not very well lit, which worked in their favor. In the distance he could see traffic lights and cars, and that was clearly where Andi was headed.

His heart jumped as a car came around the corner and pulled into a driveway. Andi froze behind a bush, which he didn't think would provide much cover from an array of bullets, but a man got out of the vehicle and went into his house.

They kept going, one block after the next, until they ended up on a busy street, and it was easier to blend in between people and cars.

A few minutes later, she moved into a bar, which crowded and dimly lit. She turned to him. "What kind of cash do you have?"

He pulled out his wallet and checked the bills. "About a hundred and sixty bucks. But I've got plenty of cards."

"Give me twenty."

"What are you going to do?"

"Get someone to call us a taxi."

"We both have phones," he said, but realized quickly that she didn't want to use their phones.

"We need to turn them off." She took out her phone and powered down.

He did the same.

Andi then walked up to a female bartender at the end of the bar. They spoke for a few moments. Andi put the twenty on the bar, and then the woman grabbed a phone from under the counter and made a call. She said something to Andi and handed her back the twenty. Andi smiled and walked back to him, then motioned for him to follow her out the door.

"Taxi is on its way," she said.

"She didn't take your money."

"I told her I lost my phone and my bag, and she felt sorry for me."

A taxi pulled up a moment later, and they got inside. Andi directed the man to a Hyatt hotel by the Santa Monica Pier.

He started to ask her why they were going there, but she gave him a look that suggested they not talk. He sat back and hoped she had a plan, and that it would be better than the ones she'd come up with when she was fourteen.

When they got out of the taxi in front of the Hyatt, it was almost midnight. Andi waited until the cab pulled away and then headed away from the front door of the hotel.

"We're not going inside?" he asked.

"Nope. We're going to the motel down the street, the one we can afford to pay cash for. We can't use a credit card, and there's nothing open right now so I can't get a burner phone."

"What if I call my sister and ask her to book us a room?"

"We can't take the chance that her card and phone wouldn't be traced. Right now, we can't trust anyone, Cooper."

"Do you think someone in the FBI sold you out?" he asked.

Her mouth drew into a tight line. "Yes. And I might have an idea who, but right now I just want to get us somewhere safe."

Several minutes later they walked into the lobby of the Lucky Motel, which was a dumpy, run-down building that advertised rooms for $39 a night. They got one room, for which he paid cash, and Andi signed the register with the name Whitney Hayes. He almost laughed at the sight of her childhood alias. For some reason, she'd thought the name Whitney was the perfect alias. Apparently, some things never changed.

The bored clerk barely looked at them as he gave them a key and they walked up the stairs to a second-floor room with a view of the parking lot. The door had a deadbolt, which was probably the best thing about it. There was a king-sized bed, a dresser, a very old television, and a small bathroom. It was nowhere he would have ever wanted to stay, but it felt like the safest place they could be.

Andi closed the blinds and sat down on the end of the bed.

"Are we done running for the night?" he asked.

"I think we'll be okay here. No one could have followed us."

"I agree, Whitney."

A smile lifted the corners of her mouth. "It's still my go-to name."

"Maybe you should have used another one if you think someone from the FBI is after you."

"No one on my current team would know that's the name I use. I just started two days ago. I can't believe it's only been two days."

"Two very long days," he murmured. "You did good getting us here. How did you know about the closet, the trap door, and the tunnel?"

"Flynn told me when you were in the kitchen with Caitlyn. Thank God, he did," she said.

"Do you think they know what happened by now?"

"Yes. The alarms at the house would have gone off, and they would have responded to the scene."

"Why didn't they have someone watching the house?"

"They thought they'd built a fortress. Flynn said they'd never had a breach."

"Well, they had a big one tonight." He paused. "Who do you think sold us out?"

"I don't believe it was anyone on my team. Even though I haven't worked with them very long, I went through Quantico with most of them. We were friends. We trusted each other."

"That doesn't mean anything. Anyone can betray you, even your best friend." As he said the words, he realized how often he went back to her betrayal. But it really wasn't even close to the same thing as what had happened tonight.

"Well, I still don't think it was one of them," she said, not bothering to defend her actions.

He couldn't blame her. She wanted to get off that endless circle, and so did he. "Then who?" he repeated.

"Agent Burnett."

He was more than a little surprised. "Why would he sell you out?"

"I'm not entirely sure, but we had a strange conversation this morning. God, I can hardly believe it was only this morning. So much has happened since then. He was angry that he wasn't handling the investigation into Elisa's disappearance. He blamed you for that, and he couldn't understand why I would have been a better choice when you hated me. He's the one who outed our relationship to Damon and Flynn."

"And you think he'd send shooters to a safehouse to take you out because he didn't get a case?"

"Yes. The only person who could have known where we were was someone connected to the bureau, and he made it clear that he'd wanted the investigation into Elisa's disappearance." A sudden gleam entered her eyes. "That's it. He didn't just want the investigation; he had to have it. But I was standing in his way."

"Why would he have to have it?" he asked, realizing the

answer as soon as he'd asked the question. "You don't think he's involved, do you? Why would he be?"

"I don't know. But there was another case he ran that he didn't solve."

"This can't be about Hannah. After all this time?"

"The mode of kidnapping is very similar."

"But there's an eighteen-year gap."

"Maybe there isn't. Maybe those are just the two we know about."

He thought about her suggestion. "Okay, let's say you're right, and the two cases are connected. Why does Burnett suddenly start going after you and me? We really weren't even thinking about him."

"Because if I was out of the picture, he'd probably get the case. He could protect whoever kidnapped Elisa, the way he did for Hannah. Think about it, Cooper. No one else we talked to would have the connections to get a bomb planted, to attack a safehouse. It had to be someone on the inside."

"You might be right," he admitted. "What do we do about it? I don't know how the FBI works, but I don't think you can accuse a seasoned veteran of Burnett's stature without evidence."

"Which is why we have to get some. I need to think about it." She let out a sigh and scooted up the bed, so she was leaning against the pillows and the headboard. "But I have to admit my head hurts."

"We passed an all-night drugstore on our way over here. I could pick you up something."

"No, I don't want you to leave. It's better that we stay together. I just need to rest a little."

"Or a lot." He got up and turned off the light, then stretched out on the other side of the bed.

She did the same, as they faced each other in the shadowy light of a shitty motel room. There was a brightly lit sign across the street from the motel that cast a glow through the broken blinds, making it easier to see her face.

"Never thought we'd end up together in a place like this," he muttered.

"Life is strange," she agreed. "I never thought I'd see you again. But here we are."

"On a case, just like when we were kids, only there are real people's lives at stake, real bullets flying. Not that that bothered you. You were calm and cool. You never looked scared or uncertain. You just acted. It was impressive."

"I've had good training."

"Training doesn't account for everything. Take the compliment, Andi."

"I will, because you don't hand them out very often. You've been a really good partner, Cooper. You were the first one to spot the intruder on the monitor. That gave us valuable seconds."

"That was luck."

"Better to have good luck than bad."

"I can't argue with that."

"Finally."

He smiled as he dragged the pillow under his head so he could support his neck and see her better. "Look who's talking. You're the champion of arguing."

"I can be too competitive," she admitted. "I hate to lose."

"You always have. You take losses too personally. Not everything is a personal failure. Some problems just can't be solved."

"Logically, I know that. Emotionally, I still get a sick feeling in my stomach when I can't make something right."

"You do more than most to right a wrong. I've always admired that in you, Andi." He paused. "Now tell me something you like about me."

Wariness entered her gaze. "Why would I do that?"

"Because after everything we've been through today, we should let go of the bad feelings."

"Can you do that, Cooper? You have far more bad feelings about me than I do about you."

He thought about that for a moment. "I have to admit that

hating you has become a habit, maybe even a reason to not look at the real truth, at my own failures."

"You're going to have to explain that."

He rolled onto his back and stared at the odd shadows dancing across the ceiling from the light outside the room. Then he said, "I couldn't make things good for Kyle. I wanted to make him okay, but I couldn't do it."

"I know you tried," she said softly.

"It's taken me a long time to make peace with his death, to acknowledge that it wasn't just about the horrible time when he was accused of kidnapping and other heinous crimes. That experience was traumatic, and it haunted him. I won't say it didn't, but there were other issues, too. Instead of spending so much time fighting and hating people who didn't treat him well, I should have tried to get him more help." He still felt a frustration that he didn't think would ever go away. "I used to feel guilty that he was messed up and I wasn't. It seemed unfair. We both came from the same parents. Why didn't I have to carry his burden?"

"Because you couldn't. You were you. Kyle was Kyle. Your parents loved you both and Monica, too, of course."

"They were good parents. They tried hard to give Kyle the best life. But they didn't see everything that was happening. I was at school with him. I was his age. I saw more than they did. Sometimes, I just didn't want to see it."

"Like his car the night of the kidnapping," she said quietly. "You knew it was Kyle, just like I did."

"Kyle didn't take Hannah."

"That wasn't what I said."

He rolled back to face her. "I honestly thought you were wrong, Andi."

"Then or now?" she returned, her gaze boring into his.

"You always ask the hard questions."

"You don't have to answer. You started this conversation."

She was right, but he did have to answer. "Then," he said. "I honestly didn't believe Kyle was anywhere near our street that night. And no one ever proved that he was."

"Okay. Then why does it feel like there's a but coming…"

"But," he said. "Kyle's story did change a lot. He couldn't say exactly when he left the concert. Will said Kyle left early, but Kyle claimed that Will took off first. Later, he told me that he'd gotten mad at Will that night and left because Will was high and acting like an asshole. Which made me wonder if you did see Kyle's car that night. It wasn't at the house when I got back, but Kyle could have just been driving around."

"Did you ever ask him flat out if he saw Hannah that night? I'm not talking about when it happened, but later, when everyone was older, when time had passed?"

"No. I never asked him flat out. I didn't want him to think I ever had any doubts about his innocence."

"So you stuck to the story that I was the bad guy, even though you knew Kyle wasn't very clear on his actions that night."

"That was my story," he admitted, seeing the pain in her gaze. "I had to tell myself that. I had to hate you."

"Why?" she asked in bewilderment. "Why did you have to hate me?"

They were venturing into dangerous territory and into thoughts he'd never spoken aloud to anyone. But this was Andi. This was the girl he used to tell everything to. "Because," he said, his voice so thick he had to clear it before continuing. "You hurt me. I didn't understand why you couldn't stand up for me or my family, why you couldn't protect us. You were my best friend. I felt betrayed."

She bit down on her lip, his words obviously hitting her hard. "I didn't know in the beginning that I would get Kyle in horrible trouble. I thought maybe he had just seen something. It snowballed after that. I made mistakes. I know I did. I talked too much to the wrong people. I thought I was standing up for Hannah, for justice, for truth. But I wasn't thinking enough about what my actions were doing to you, and I did regret that. I just didn't think I could fix our broken relationship. I still don't. Even when we have a laugh together, there's a moment where you suddenly realize how you really feel about me. You'll never forget what's between us."

"I've never wanted to forget it…until now."

"Why now?" she challenged.

"Because I don't want the past between us anymore." His heart started pounding hard against his chest. "I want to see what else could happen with us."

Her eyes glittered in the dim light. "Could you really take that risk with me? Because I don't know if I could take it with you. It was hard to get over you, Cooper. I missed you for so many years. I don't want to start something now that's going to end up in the same horrible place of pain and unhappiness."

"It would never be the same place."

"It could be worse. It's not worth it."

"It could definitely be worth it."

At his words, a spark lit up her eyes. She was hesitant, but she was also tempted, and it was nice to know he wasn't the only one feeling that way.

"I think we should just go to sleep." Her words sounded a little desperate now. "There's too much at stake. And it could go bad. Because it's you and me, and we'll be good and then we'll be bad."

He waited until she ran out of steam and then put his hand on her arm. "Or it could be amazing. And consider this. We've already risked our lives twice today. Maybe tonight is all we have. If that were true, would you want to spend it sleeping?"

She shook her head and let out a sigh. "You're pulling out all the stops."

He smiled. "You told me earlier today that I move too slow. Let's speed things up. You like speed. You like danger. You like to feel like you're living on the edge."

"You know exactly how to play me, Cooper."

"Which bodes well for what could happen next."

A smile lifted her lips. "I know a few things about you, too."

"Why don't we just start with a kiss and see if either of us wants to take it further? You can say no at any point. You know that, right?"

"Of course, I know that. But let's say the kiss goes as well as the last one. Let's say we want to take it a lot further. We're going to see each other naked. Are you ready for that?"

He laughed. "While that thought would have grossed me out at eight, I was intrigued by the idea at fourteen and even more so now. Are you interested?"

"Very interested. But ready? Not sure. I feel nervous. Like I've never done this before."

His pulse was already racing fast. "Me, too, but I think we could be good together."

"Or horrible. It could go either way."

"There's the pessimist I know so well."

"Realist," she corrected. She put her hand on his waist as she leaned in for a kiss. "Let's see what you've got, Cooper."

"Let's see what you've got," he returned.

She gave him a cocky smile. "You know I like to be good at everything I do."

"And I hope you know that you're not going to call all the shots."

"We'll see."

"You'll see," he promised as their mouths met.

They started out slow, slightly tentative, curious, exploring, but the heat built fast. One kiss led to two, then three. His hands roamed her body, exploring her curves, sliding under her sweater to feel the warmth of her skin.

Andi got impatient quickly, tugging at the hem of his shirt, until he pulled it up and over his head. Then her hands were on him with an eagerness that sent a jolt of desire through every nerve ending in his body. He loved the way she touched him, kissed him, moved against him. They were running hard and fast toward the edge of a cliff.

He didn't want to stop. He didn't want her to want to stop. Because every dream he'd ever had about her was coming true, only it was so much better than he'd imagined.

Every kiss, every taste, every touch stoked the fire that had been simmering for years. But as he'd told her, this time he was calling the shots, so he flipped her on her back and smiled into her surprised eyes. Then he pulled her sweater up over her head and unfastened the clasp of her bra, feasting on the sight of her luscious curves. His hands led the way, his mouth following as he kissed his way down her body, taking his time, savoring every moment, as he stripped off the rest of her clothes.

One high led to another, until she wanted her turn with him, until they were both naked and impatient to have no more barriers between them, until they were both gasping for air, their bodies singing with a song that only they could make.

CHAPTER NINETEEN

LAYING in Cooper's arms after a firestorm of feelings and emotions, Andi couldn't quite believe what had just happened. Her pulse was finally starting to slow down, but her body tingled all over, her mind still remembering every touch of Cooper's mouth and hands, the way he'd moved against her, inside her. How perfectly they'd fit. How in sync they'd been, reading each other's minds the way they'd always done, but in a way they'd never done before.

It should have felt strange, awkward, but it hadn't been either of those things. It had felt exactly right, like it should have happened a million times before. Maybe it would have if they hadn't fallen out, if their world hadn't changed. Or maybe it had been sweeter because of everything that had happened between them.

Whatever the reason, Cooper had kissed like a dream, and she was only realizing now that she'd had this particular dream before. She'd just never been able to see the face of her phantom lover. He'd always been in the shadows. *Had it really been Cooper all these years? Was that why no one else had ever made her want to get serious, to move in, to be committed?*

But that was crazy. She could not have been pining for him for eighteen years.

And she was getting way ahead of herself. They'd just had sex, really good sex. She had no idea where anything went from here. Maybe nowhere. Maybe that was okay.

Frowning, she actually didn't think it would be okay. Because now she knew how they could be together, and it wouldn't be easy to forget him. But she didn't have to forget him yet. Not now with her head resting on his broad chest, her legs entangled with his, one arm around his waist.

"So, naked is good," Cooper murmured.

She lifted her head to look at him. "Yes, and no one started laughing."

He gazed back at her with a tender smile. "I definitely didn't feel like laughing. How are you doing?"

"I'm great. And thanking God you had a condom in your wallet. But then I shouldn't have been surprised. You were always a better planner than I was."

"I sure didn't plan this. If I had, I would have chosen a much better location."

"It's perfect. You got lucky at the Lucky Motel," she teased.

"Or maybe you got lucky."

"I can't argue with that," she said, as his magic fingers stroked her bare back, stirring up the desire she'd thought she'd vanquished. "You better stop that, or you're going to have to check out that 24-hour drugstore down the street."

"I would go there in a second, except that I wouldn't want to leave you alone here."

"We need to stay together," she agreed.

"Just like this," he said with a laugh. "Or maybe even a little closer."

She grinned. "Behave."

"Why? It's so much more fun to be bad. And there are other things we can do without a condom."

"I know. We already did some of them."

"I bet you have other ideas. You always have ideas, Andi."

"Maybe a few," she admitted. "But—"

"No," he groaned, cutting her off. "It's too soon to think of all the reasons why this was a mistake. We're living in the moment. Let's stay there."

"Okay." She wasn't that interested in talking, either. She just wanted to enjoy being with Cooper for however long they had.

"That was almost too easy," he said suspiciously. "You're not going to wait for me to fall asleep and then bounce out of here, are you? Because putting what just happened aside, we need to be together."

"I'm not bailing on you," she promised.

"Good."

She put her head back on his chest and drew in a happy breath, then let it out, feeling remarkably relaxed and more content than she'd felt in a long time. The problems would come flooding back with daylight, but here in this moment, she was exactly where she wanted to be.

"Do you want to go to sleep?" Cooper asked.

"I think so. There's a beautiful dream still going on in my head."

"Mine, too," he whispered, as his arms tightened around her. "Let's meet there."

"In our dreams," she murmured. "Just like before."

"Before?" he asked.

She heard the question, but she couldn't answer it, because she was already drifting away…

Andi woke up Thursday morning to bright sun and a cold, empty bed. The man whose arms she'd slept in was gone, and her heart skipped a beat. She jumped to her feet and moved toward the bathroom. It was empty. *Where the hell was Cooper?*

She told herself he was fine. He'd probably just left to get coffee, which was stupid, since he shouldn't have gone anywhere without her. A quick glance at the bedside table revealed that her gun was still there. She didn't know whether to be happy about that or not. But clearly, he hadn't wanted to leave her unprotected. However, he had left her in a funky motel room without the dead-bolt engaged, which wasn't smart. She thought about using it now, but she wanted a quick shower and didn't want to lock him out.

She took her clothes into the bathroom and took a very quick shower. When she returned to the bedroom, she found Cooper walking in with a tray of coffee and a bag of food.

"Where did you go? Why did you leave without waking me up so I could lock the door?" she demanded.

"Oh. Sorry. Damn! I forgot."

"You forgot a lot of things," she snapped. "Like how we were going to stay together."

"I also forgot how angry you get in the morning when you haven't had any food." He set the tray down and handed her a coffee. "I was only gone for fifteen minutes, and I did try to wake you up, but you were out, and I figured you could use a little more sleep." He frowned. "But you're right about the deadbolt. I should have thought about that."

She grabbed the coffee and took a long sip. The hit of caffeine gave her a much-needed punch of clarity. She was hungry and she never did her best work on an empty stomach, so she grabbed the bag and pulled out a breakfast egg sandwich.

"Am I forgiven?" Cooper asked dryly, as she took a bite.

"I suppose. But you should have woken me up. We don't know who we're dealing with, but it's a sophisticated operation. No one breaks into an FBI safehouse unless they are well-connected. We can't afford to be careless."

"It won't happen again. Where you go, I go."

"I'm not sure about that. I still want to get you somewhere safe."

"Where would that be? I won't endanger my family, and

there's no one in law enforcement I'm going to trust except you. So we watch each other's back."

"We'll see how things go," she said, not wanting to commit to a long-term plan. "What we need to do first is get a phone. I'm going to need some of your cash for that."

"Already done," he said, putting the smaller bag in his hand on the counter. "I bought it while I was out. The strip mall across the street had everything."

"Great," she said, ripping the plastic off the phone. "We're going to need this."

"I figured." He grabbed the other breakfast sandwich and took a bite. "What's next?"

"I need to talk to Agent Burnett. I have his number on my phone, but I don't want to start my phone until we're away from here. Then I can grab the number and call him."

"We're going to talk to the guy you think hired people to kill you?" he asked in surprise.

"I'm not going to tell him I think he's trying to kill me. I'll just see if I can set up a meet and go from there."

"Maybe Flynn should talk to him for you."

She shook her head. "This is my job, Cooper. This is what I do."

He frowned, then nodded. "All right. Your call."

She finished her sandwich, took several more sips of her coffee, then said, "Are you ready to go?"

"One second." He crinkled his empty food wrapper and tossed into the bag. Then he stepped forward, put his hands on her shoulders and pulled her in for a kiss.

His lips were salty and tasted like bacon. Hers probably did, too. But the hunger that instantly burned between them had nothing to do with food. She'd thought—hoped—their desire might have burned out, but she'd been fooling herself. It was even stronger now, because she wasn't trying to fight the attraction, and neither was he.

"That was the way we should have started this morning," he said as they came up for air.

"Yes," she agreed, her voice a little breathless. "But that can't keep happening today. We can't be distracted. We have to focus."

He smiled. "You used to say that to me all the time when we were kids. Like when I was focused on throwing strikes against my garage door, and you wanted to figure out whether the school cafeteria was actually using whole milk or nonfat."

"Exactly," she said, as he referred to her first feature story as a freshman on the school newspaper. "You couldn't focus then but you must focus now, because we're not dealing with milk."

"I'm very aware of the gravity of our situation," he said. "And what's at stake—not only our lives, but Elisa's. Don't think for a second that I'm taking anything lightly. That said, I'm glad we spent the night together, and for the record, I picked up a few more condoms in case we want to do any more exploring when this is all over."

Tingles ran down her spine. "When this is over," she echoed. "Maybe."

He gave her a cocky look. "I don't think there's a *maybe* about it, but it's time to get serious, and that's what I'm going to do."

"Then we should go."

With her gun tucked under her sweater and her phone in the pocket of her jeans, they headed out the door. They made their way to the Santa Monica Pier where amidst a crowd of strangers, she opened her work phone and saw several text messages. One was from Agent Burnett.

"Burnett sent me a text," she told Cooper.

"What did he say?"

"We need to meet tomorrow. Matter of life and death. Text me back. I have important information for you and only you. Don't trust Flynn or anyone else on his team."

"That sounds disturbing."

She sent Burnett a reply. "Where and when?" Then she waited. When no message came back, she grabbed Burnett's number and Flynn's and copied them into her burner phone. She waited another minute or two, but there was no reply. "He's not getting back to me."

"What time did he text you?"

"This morning at six-twenty-three. It's after nine now." When another minute passed, she shut down her phone and then motioned for Cooper to follow her down the pier. She wanted to change their location in case anyone was tracking her phone. Then she took out her burner phone and called Burnett. "I'm going to try him again." Her call went to voicemail. "He's not answering," she said with frustration.

"Now what?" Cooper asked, as his gaze swept the area around them. "Are you going to call Flynn? Or follow Burnett's suggestion that you don't trust Flynn or anyone on your team?"

"I'm conflicted," she admitted. "I trust Flynn and the people I went to Quantico with, but I don't know everyone in the office. There could be an analyst or a lower-level admin that's leaking information. I'd rather not risk anything right now. But I need to find Burnett. I'm going to try the office." She looked up the general number for the LA office and then made the call. She was re-routed through two people before getting to someone who told her that Agent Burnett was not in the office. She chose not to leave a message and ended the call. "He's not answering his phone, and he's not at his office."

"Maybe we should check his house," Cooper suggested.

"I have no idea where he lives."

"And that's why you need me. I know his address."

"How is that possible?" she asked in surprise.

"I've done a lot of research on the man who falsely accused my brother. Several months ago, when Neil and I were trying to talk to him, and he kept putting us off, I followed him home from work one day and we had a chat in front of his house."

"That can't have gone over well."

"He was furious and defensive. I told him I just wanted to hear his side of the story, but he wasn't interested in telling it."

"Where does he live?"

"Brentwood. We're going to need transportation to get there. I could borrow my sister's car."

"No, nothing that ties to your family. We have enough cash for a cab."

"That's true, but…" He thought for a moment. "How about a car that belongs to a man who has an office in the building where I record my podcasts?"

"Are we going to have to steal it?"

"Borrow it. I have his keys. We share a tandem garage parking spot, and he's out of town."

"Okay, that will work," she said, relieved to have one problem solved. "We'll take a cab to where the car is parked, but we'll need to get in and out quickly. Someone could be watching your building."

"It's not where my office is. It's a studio space for podcasters. I don't know if anyone would know I use it."

She felt even better hearing that. They walked out to the street and found a cab. Fifteen minutes later, they arrived at a two-story building in El Segundo, that was surrounded by industrial shops and wholesale stores. Cooper let them into the building, giving her only a quick glance at the studio space before heading into the garage. Since his car was still parked down at the LA FBI Office, there was only his coworker's car in the space, a dark-gray Kia Sport.

"I'm driving now," Cooper told her.

She didn't bother to argue, just got into the passenger seat, and locked the doors. As they drove out of the garage and got on the freeway, she kept an eye on the sideview mirror, watching for any cars that might be tailing them, but nothing appeared to be suspicious.

As she cast a quick glance at Cooper, she had to admit that he looked happy to be in the driver's seat. She had to appreciate the fact that he had been following her lead the past several days. Even with everything between them, he respected her abilities.

In fact, he'd always respected her. She probably hadn't recognized that enough when they were kids, but Cooper had had her back for just about everything she'd ever done, except when it had come to Hannah.

She was glad they'd talked things through last night. She hoped things would be different now, but she was very aware that having sex with her was one thing, trusting her completely was another.

As her thoughts went back into the past, they returned to Agent Burnett, who was a big part of their history. Eighteen years ago, Jim Burnett had been a much younger and less seasoned agent. It was difficult to believe he could have been involved in Hannah's disappearance or in Elisa's, but he was a common denominator in both cases.

He'd also barely been able to hide his anger toward her when they'd met yesterday morning. It didn't make sense that he would have been that angry to lose the investigation when he'd had a run-in with both Neil and Cooper. Of course, Damon wouldn't want him on the case. With all his years of experience, he would have known that was the only move Damon could make.

But Burnett hadn't accepted the decision. He'd given her a tip that had proved to be true but had also sent her down a different path toward Claire. That could have been the point of his lead, to slow her down, distract her, and send her in another direction. But that hadn't worked. She'd kept digging into Daniel and the gym, into Kristine, and also to Jillian. He could be involved with any one of them. But none of those people had been around eighteen years ago. Which was where her theory of Burnett's involvement fell apart.

On the other hand, the only way her safe house could have been exposed was through a leak. She had no idea if Burnett would have known about the house, since Flynn ran that property. Maybe it was someone on Flynn's team who she didn't know, didn't trust. But she couldn't come up with a motive for someone on Flynn's team to want to get rid of her. She hadn't taken anyone's job. Bree, their kidnapping expert, was on maternity leave, so she didn't care.

"What are you thinking about?" Cooper asked, breaking into her reverie.

"Too many things. My mind is going around in circles."

"Can I help?"

She thought about that. "What else can you tell me about Agent Burnett? You've obviously studied him more than I have."

"I know everything about him. He was born into a wealthy family. Father was a plastic surgeon in Hollywood, so you know that brought in the bucks. His mother came from money, too. Her father was the CEO of an energy company, and she was heavily involved in fundraisers and charity events. Agent Burnett went to USC where he studied finance. After graduation, he got a job with a venture capital firm where he worked for about six years. When he first joined the FBI, he handled mostly financial crimes. Because of his connections in that world, he did very well. He was six years into his career as an agent when Hannah went missing. Her case was the first kidnapping case he worked. The other agent on the case, Agent Ralston, told me that Burnett asked to join the investigation because he wanted to get out of financial crime."

"You do know a lot about him," she said in surprise. "I looked at the investigation he conducted but not at his background. I didn't know it was his first kidnapping case. What about his personal life?"

"He's been married and divorced twice. He has no children. He likes to gamble and spends a lot of weekends in Las Vegas. He also has a financial stake in a couple of racehorses. One of them was supposed to make it to the Derby this year but came up lame and is now out to pasture somewhere. That happened recently." Cooper paused. "What else do you want to know?"

"I'm not sure. Gambling habits can make an agent vulnerable to bribes and blackmail. But he has worked for the Bureau for more than twenty years, so it's hard to believe he could keep that kind of bad behavior a secret for so long." She paused. "I'm also still thinking about the fact that Hannah was the first kidnapping victim he'd ever dealt with and that he asked to be on the case. From what I read, Agent Ralston took a backseat almost immediately. I wonder why. She would have had more experience than Burnett."

"I asked Agent Ralston that. She said she was pregnant at the time and had to take a step back. They were shorthanded, so Burnett ran with it. Apparently, his superiors had a lot of respect for him, and she told me she has never had any reason to believe he didn't do everything by the book. She said she supported him a hundred percent. That's where our conversation ended." He took a breath. "That's where every conversation that I had with anyone connected to the FBI ended. The ranks closed around Burnett."

"But this time when a child disappeared, Damon took the case away from Burnett, and that made him very angry."

"His text implied that he wants to help you."

"Or he wants to set me up in some way."

"Aren't we playing into a setup by going to his house?"

"I don't think he'd expect me to show up at his home. There's probably a small window of time where I can take him by surprise. If he was behind the attack on the safe house, he'll think I'm laying low. And I don't believe he would go after us himself. He has the resources to hire people to do his dirty work. He wouldn't want to take us down at his own house. In fact, I'm sure he'll feign outrage and threaten to report me and tell me I'm out of my mind. That's more likely to be in his playbook."

"If he thinks you're lying low, then he doesn't know you at all. I would never assume that."

"Well, he doesn't know me. But we're about to get better acquainted."

When they got to Burnett's Brentwood neighborhood, she had Cooper do a pass down the street and then back before they parked a few houses down from Burnett's home. They didn't leave the vehicle immediately, instead watching the property for several minutes. There was no movement visible in the house. The blinds were open on the second floor but closed on the first floor.

It was after ten now on a Thursday, so there wasn't much activity on the street, save for a gardener blowing leaves off a driveway three doors down.

It was an upscale neighborhood with mostly two-story homes set back from the street with lots of fences and high shrubs providing privacy. It was probably a good thing Burnett came from money, because she doubted that he could afford a house like this on his salary alone.

"I'm going to check the house," she said.

"We're going to do that," Cooper corrected.

"I think it's better if I go alone. If I run into trouble, call Flynn."

She tried to hand him her phone, but he refused to take it. "I'm going with you. We're not splitting up, Andi."

"I don't know that I can protect you," she said honestly. "And I don't want anything to happen to you."

"I can take care of myself. And I trust you to do your best for both of us. But I'm not sitting in the car while you do this alone."

Seeing the stubborn light in his eyes, she knew she was fighting a losing battle. "Okay. But try to stay behind me."

They got out of the car and walked down the street. When they reached the porch, Andi pulled out her weapon. She was about to ring the bell when she saw that the door was slightly ajar. That was disturbing. She knocked on the door. She didn't hear anyone inside. Knocking again, she pushed the door open. Moving into the house, she called out. "Agent Burnett? Are you here?"

There was no sound except the loud tick of a grandfather

clock in the entryway. Cooper stayed close to her back as they moved into the house, making their way into the living room, dining room, and finally the kitchen where the smells of bacon and coffee were thick in the air.

Her gaze was drawn to a seeping pool of red coming from around the island, and her heart stopped. She moved around the counter, staring in horror at the man lying face-down on the floor, a pool of blood pouring from a bullet hole in the back of his head.

CHAPTER TWENTY

"OH, MY GOD," she muttered as she dropped to her knees to check for a pulse.

"Is he dead?" Cooper asked, a grim expression on his face.

She gave a quick nod. "Yes. It couldn't have been that long ago."

"Do you want me to call 911?"

"No. I need to call Flynn. He and Damon should handle this." Despite her words, she didn't reach for the phone. "Let's take a look around first. Don't touch anything, Cooper."

"Are you sure we shouldn't just get out of here?"

"We will soon. I just need a minute." She made a quick perusal of the first floor, which didn't seem all that lived in. It felt more like a decorator showcase than someone's actual home. When she reached the second floor, everything changed. The office had been ripped apart in what appeared to be a violent and hasty search, with files and papers strewn on the floor. The guest bedroom next door was untouched but the master bedroom at the end of the hall had also been trashed.

"What were they looking for?" Cooper muttered.

She met his gaze. "Whatever they killed him to get."

His lips tightened. "Does this mean he wasn't in charge, wasn't the one calling the shots, trying to get us killed?"

"There's definitely someone else in charge, but he still could have given out our location. At some point, he became less valuable." She wandered over to the chair by the desk where a jacket hung around the arms of a chair, the same jacket she'd seen Burnett wearing the day before. She instinctively searched the pockets, not sure what she was looking for, but when she found a receipt, she pulled it out. It was time-stamped yesterday, Wednesday at one thirty. Burnett had bought several pacifiers and a baby blanket.

"What's that?" Cooper asked.

She handed him the receipt. "Burnett bought baby items. But he never had kids, so what's that about?"

"Could he be buying supplies for Elisa? But even if he was tied into her case, wouldn't someone else do that? Someone less obvious than an FBI agent?"

"Good point. But we need to check out that store."

She led the way down the stairs and out of the house. They walked quickly to the car. Once inside, Cooper started the engine and pulled away.

When they were three blocks away, she took out her phone and called Flynn. "It's me, Andi."

"Are you all right?" Flynn's voice was tense. "I've been worrying about you since the alarms went off last night. I take it you got out through the tunnel."

"Yes. I'm very glad you told me about it. There were at least two gunmen."

"We were able to replay the video from here. Couldn't identify the shooters, but they knew what they were doing. Why didn't you take the car?"

"I was afraid to. Someone sold us out. I don't know who. But they had the code to get into the house. How many people have that?"

"Not many."

"What about agents in the LA office? What about Damon?"

"There are a couple of agents in that office who know about it. We held someone there on another joint investigation last year."

"So it's not as secret as it could be."

"No," Flynn agreed, a terse note in his voice. "Where are you now?"

"It doesn't matter. You need to go to Agent Burnett's house. When you get there, you'll need to call the coroner."

"What happened, Andi?"

"I don't know, but Agent Burnett was shot in the head, and his house looked trashed. I think Burnett might be involved in Elisa's kidnapping, maybe other cases as well, like the one from my past. He was very angry when Damon took him off the case and gave it to me. There's something big going on here. Something with huge stakes."

"I figured that out after the attacks on you yesterday. Let me get you to a safer location."

"I'm safer on my own."

"Are you on your own, or are you with Bradford?"

"I'll check in with you later. Be careful what you say to Damon. If Burnett is dirty, he might be, too."

"I'd bet my life that Damon is not dirty."

"Just don't bet mine. Don't try to find me. I'll get back to you." She ended the call and blew out a breath.

"You didn't tell him about the store," Cooper commented.

"No. And I didn't forget." Their gazes met for a quick moment. "It's going to have to be just us for a while longer. I don't know who else I can trust."

"That works for me."

The Baby Time Boutique was located on a side street off the Sunset Strip. There were three businesses, a printer, a laundromat, and the clothing store, which had a parking lot adjacent to the building. Cooper parked in the lot. There were three other vehicles nearby, a back door to the store, and a large dumpster. She didn't see any security cameras by that back door, but hopefully there was one in the front, so they could verify Burnett's presence at the store. But even though he'd had the receipt, he could have simply sent someone to pick something up, and they'd given him the receipt when they'd dropped the items off. That didn't make a lot of sense, though, since it seemed doubtful anyone was keeping receipts for any reason.

She might be on the wrong track. But at this point, she didn't have many other leads to work, so she might as well follow it through.

When they reached the front of the store, she didn't see any cameras there, so video footage would not be available. But maybe someone in the store would remember an older man buying baby supplies.

The store was busy with shoppers, so they wandered around, waiting for the line at the front desk to disappear so they could talk to the clerk. Toward the back of the store, she saw a cozy sitting area with comfortable chairs, a tea and water station, with a tray of desserts and a sign encouraging mothers-to-be to rest, have some tea, and enjoy some complimentary reading. There was also a large bulletin board with various community notices, a prenatal exercise class, mommy and me yoga, a tour of the new hospital maternity wing at St. Mary's, and a flyer urging parents to learn about surrogacy and adoption.

Cooper moved in closer to her. "What are you looking at so intently?" he asked.

"That flyer about adoption. I wonder if the store has a connection to an adoption agency." She paused, hearing loud voices coming from the hallway near the restrooms and what appeared to be a half-open door leading into the back room of the shop. Two women were speaking loudly in another language. It was Russian, she thought, her heart speeding up as she strained to pick up a couple of words. She knew a little Russian, but she couldn't make out what they were saying. They were talking too fast. Then the voices dimmed. A door slammed, and it sounded like one or both of the women had left the building.

"Did you understand any of that?" Cooper asked.

"It was Russian. Kristine was originally from Belarus."

"That's right," he said, a gleam in his eyes.

"It might not mean anything, but it's interesting." She paused as a middle-aged woman approached them. She was blonde with blue eyes, and her name tag said her name was Veronica.

"Hello," Veronica said with a warm smile. "Can I help you find something?"

"Maybe," she replied, deciding on the spot to try something different. She'd have to reveal she was an FBI agent if she asked about Burnett, and that didn't seem like the best plan. She looked over at Cooper, then took his hand. "My husband and I have been trying for a long time to have a baby, and it's not happening." She drew in a shaky breath, blinking her eyes until they watered. "We're kind of losing hope. We registered at an adoption agency, but we're really far down on the list. I noticed that you have flyers about adoption on the board, and I wondered if you know of someone we could try. We're pretty desperate."

Veronica hesitated. "We try to share whatever information we have on the board. You should go to one of the seminars. They're very good."

"I'm sure they are. But that one isn't for another few weeks, and I just don't know how long I can wait."

"It's going to be fine, honey," Cooper said. "We'll do whatever it takes to become a family, whatever it costs."

"I know," she said, looking at him with an adoring gaze. Then she turned back to Veronica. "I'm sorry. I didn't mean to get so emotional."

"I understand. We see a lot of emotional women here." Veronica hesitated. "I do have a business card for an attorney who works in adoption."

"Could you give me his name? That would be amazing."

"Of course." Veronica walked them back to the front of the store and pulled a card out of a drawer behind the counter. "His name is Sergio Molina. Here's his information. I hope he can help you."

"Thank you so much. I really appreciate it."

"Good luck," Veronica said.

Another customer stepped up to the register, so Andi moved away from the counter and headed out of the store.

"That was a quick improv," Cooper said as they left the building. "Why didn't you ask her about Burnett?"

"I would have had to identify myself as FBI to get information, and I didn't want anyone to realize we have a connection between Burnett and this store."

"Which we still don't know that we have."

"True. But we have the name of an adoption attorney, and that might be even better."

As they walked around the building and into the parking lot, she saw a young woman come through the back door of the shop. She was short and thin, wearing tight jeans and a sleeveless crop top, her blonde hair flowing halfway down her back. She threw an empty box into the recycle bin and gave them a tentative smile as she moved toward a small coupe parked next to their car.

"Hello," she said.

"Hi," Andi said back, her heart skipping a beat as she looked into the girl's bright blue eyes and a completely irrational thought came into her head. That thought got even wilder when she saw the thin-lined scar running down the girl's arm. She sucked in a breath. "Hannah?" she asked in shock. "Is that you?"

The girl gave her a startled look. "Uh, no. Sorry. I'm Natasha."

"Natasha?" she muttered in confusion. Her blood was roaring so fast through her veins, she couldn't even think. "I thought you were someone else."

"I'm not. I have to go," the girl said, as she opened her car door and got in. She quickly backed out of her space and drove away.

"What the hell was that?" Cooper asked. "Why did you call her Hannah?"

"Because I think that's who she is, Cooper. I think that girl is Hannah."

———

Cooper stared at Andi in shock and confusion. "Hannah?"

"We have to follow her," Andi said, running to the car. "Hurry."

He jumped behind the wheel and started the engine, speeding out of the lot as fast as he could. Thankfully, he could see her car stopped at a light a quarter mile ahead. "She's right there," he said, shooting Andi a sharp look. "Why on earth would you think that girl is Hannah?"

"Her blue eyes and the way she smiled. It suddenly felt so familiar. And then I saw the scar on her arm. It reminded me of when Hannah fell off the bars at the park two months before she was kidnapped. I was babysitting her, and she cut her arm. There was so much blood. I almost threw up. Don't you remember? You were there. You were playing basketball and you came running over to help."

"I remember. Dr. Grayson was there with his son. He wrapped Hannah's arm to stop the bleeding and then Hannah's dad came and took her to the hospital."

"I felt so guilty," Andi murmured. "I thought I was watching Hannah so closely, but she still fell. And she ended up with a scar on her arm. That scar was listed on all the missing person posters. Everyone was looking for a two-year-old blonde girl with a scar on her arm." She gave him a pointed look. "Natasha had a scar in the same place."

"Are you sure?" he asked, seeing the doubt in her eyes.

"I think so. I only had a quick look before she took off."

"Well, she said her name is Natasha."

"Maybe she doesn't remember who she is. She was only two years old when she was kidnapped."

He could hear the mix of emotions in Andi's voice, the desperation, hope, fear, uncertainty. It was all there, and the same feelings were running through him as well. It would be a miracle if that girl was Hannah, but he wanted to believe it, too.

"Hannah—Natasha—whoever she is," Andi continued. "She was in the backroom at the store. There were two female voices."

"And they were both speaking Russian. Hannah wasn't Russian."

"It's been eighteen years. She could have learned to speak it. She could have been raised by a Russian family."

"It's so unlikely, Andi." He had always believed in Andi's gut instinct. But he also knew how much she'd wanted to find Hannah, to save her. Was she operating on emotion more than instinct? "What are we going to do? Catch her and tell her she was kidnapped?" He changed lanes, edging closer to Natasha's car as they moved through the next intersection. There were still a couple of vehicles between them, but he thought that was a good thing.

"I'm not sure she'd believe us. She was quick to say she wasn't who I thought she was. But we need to stay with her, see where she's going, who she's meeting. Even if she's not Hannah, she works at that store. Maybe we can pick up another clue before anyone realizes we're on to her."

"She looked a little spooked when you asked her name. She might have already called someone and said some crazy woman called her Hannah."

"Hopefully, she just thought I mistook her for someone else. She was on her way to her car. She was going to leave whether I asked her name or not."

Andi was rationalizing and looking for validation. He normally would have reassured her that she was on the right track, but he didn't know if that was true. He was still grappling with the possibility that they might have stumbled upon Hannah after all these years.

On the other hand, if the baby store was a front for some illegal operation that involved Burnett, maybe it wasn't that unlikely that Hannah would have been there. But he was making as many leaps in logic as Andi was.

"Maybe we just want that girl to be Hannah," he said aloud. "We were both changed by her disappearance. Her kidnapping drove us into the jobs we have now. You've spent your life bringing other kids home because you couldn't bring her home. And I've wanted to find her to prove that my brother didn't hurt her. We both have a lot of reasons to want Natasha to be Hannah."

"I'm aware that I'm acting on emotion right now. It's not the way I like to operate. And I will pull myself together. I just need a minute."

He respected her self-awareness and realized she didn't need him to rein her in anymore. She wasn't a wild, reckless fourteen-year-old with a big imagination, she was a federal agent who knew how to handle herself.

He also needed to get a grip, because he wanted that girl to be Hannah, too. Then he could finally find out what had happened to her. He would know for sure that his brother was innocent.

That thought stole the breath out of his chest. He already knew that. Didn't he?

He hit the brake a little too late and came within a few screeching inches of the car in front of them.

Andi braced her hand on the dashboard. "Do you want me to drive?"

"No. I've got it," he said tersely.

As the traffic surged forward again, he chased the other troubling thoughts out of his head. He had one focus now and that was not losing Natasha. If she had any answers, he desperately needed to know what they were.

CHAPTER TWENTY-ONE

THEY FOLLOWED Natasha to a park in Venice Beach. It was a small city park across from a cannabis dispensary, tattoo parlor, and a bookstore about a block from the beach. Natasha parked in a delivery spot in front of the bookstore and then got out. Cooper slid into another loading spot down the street as parking was extremely limited. But a parking ticket was the last thing on his mind.

"She's getting something out of the trunk," Andi said, checking the rear view through the makeup mirror on the visor in front of her. "Let's get a little closer."

"She's going to run if we get too close."

"Then we won't get too close," she said.

He knew there was no stopping Andi in the mood she was in, so he was going to follow her lead and be ready for any problems that might arise.

They walked across the street, keeping plenty of people between them and Natasha as she moved away from her car. She didn't seem to be concerned that anyone was following her as she walked quickly down the street, the duffel bag in one hand, her phone in the other. At one point, she stopped to type something into her phone, probably texting someone, and then she moved into the park. A few moments later, she stopped by a bench in front of a small children's playground and set the duffel bag on the ground. She seemed to be waiting for someone as she checked her phone again.

They moved behind a tree about twenty yards away.

His heart began to race. He felt like something was about to happen, but he didn't know what. He wanted to be ready. After the explosion at Andi's condo and the attack at the safe house, he needed to expect the worst, but he didn't know how to prepare for that. He also didn't know how he could protect Andi when she was the only one with a weapon.

Andi put a hand on his arm. "It's going to be fine," she said.

"That's usually my line," he replied, looking into her confident brown eyes. "I'm the calm one, remember." It had been easier to be the calm one when they were kids, when the biggest consequence was getting grounded or losing phone privileges. This was so much bigger than that.

She gave him a small smile. "That's true. You were always my North Star. When you were around, I felt safe. I knew everything would be all right."

"Well, you shouldn't feel safe now, because you have the gun, and I can't protect you."

"Then I'll protect you. You have to trust me, Cooper. I know I broke your trust, once, and I'm probably asking the impossible, but I'm still asking. Because we need to be confident in one another. That's the best way for us to survive."

"I trust you," he said.

"Thank you."

"Someone is coming," he added, as he saw a figure moving toward Natasha. The person wore dark joggers, sneakers, and a sweatshirt with a hoodie pulled up over their head. Sunglasses covered their eyes, but there was something familiar. When the person sat down on the bench by Natasha, he saw a glint of gold hair under the hoodie.

"Oh, my God," he murmured. "I think that's Kristine."

"It's all coming together," Andi breathed.

Was it? The two women didn't speak. Natasha continued to stare at her phone, while the other person's gaze was on the playground. Then Natasha suddenly turned and walked away. Kristine grabbed the backpack and took off running.

"Who do we follow?" he asked. But it was a moot question, because Andi was already chasing after Kristine. He quickly followed, passing Andi at the next corner. Everyone had said Kristine was a runner, and they weren't kidding. She moved in and out of crowds of people, staying in front of him, but he was gaining on her. And Andi was holding her own, only a few feet behind him.

And then a woman came around the corner of a building with a dog on a leash. He was able to dodge to the left to avoid them, but Andi collided with the dog and tumbled to the ground. He looked back at her.

"Go," she said, as she untangled herself. "Don't let her get away."

He ran harder, relieved as he began to close in on Kristine. She suddenly looked back, the hoodie falling off her head, her blond hair flying out behind her.

"Stop, Kristine," he yelled. "There's nowhere to go."

"I can't," she said, her voice choking on what sounded like a sob. As she turned back around, she ran straight into an oncoming car. He watched in horror as the car hit her, throwing her body into the air. The duffel bag went flying. People on the street screamed. And then Kristine landed hard on the pavement.

The car came to a halt. A man jumped out of the vehicle, "She ran right in front of me. It wasn't my fault. You saw," he said to Cooper. "You were right behind her."

"Call 911," Cooper told him as he squatted down next to Kristine. Her eyelids were fluttering as she struggled to stay conscious. One leg and arm were bent in a horrific way, and there was blood coming from the back of her head. "Hang in there," he told her.

"I'm sorry," she said. "I never meant for any of this to happen."

"Where is Elisa?"

She tried to answer, but she couldn't get the words out. She was gasping for breath.

"Tell me where she is," he said desperately. "Please, Kristine. Elisa needs her parents."

His words fell on deaf ears as Kristine's eyes closed.

"Is she alive?" Andi asked breathlessly.

"Barely," he said, as sirens rang through the air. He got to his feet as the police, fire, and paramedics arrived. While Andi spoke to the officers, he fell back into the crowd, his gaze moving to the duffel bag laying against the curb, the one that had been in Kristine's hand.

He crossed the street, grabbed the bag, and unzipped it. Inside were baby clothes, diapers, bottles, and cans of baby food.

His gut twisted. He had a feeling all this was going to Elisa, but he still had no idea where she was. And they'd lost their best chance to find her. He'd messed up. He should have caught Kristine, before she ran into the street.

"Cooper?" Andi said. "Is that the bag she was carrying?"

"Yes." He got up and showed her the bag. "Everything to keep a baby going for a while."

"Did Kristine say anything?"

"She said she was sorry. She never wanted to hurt anyone. I asked her where Elisa was, but she slipped away."

"She's still alive. Hopefully, she'll stay that way until we can get more information."

"I'm sorry, Andi."

"What for?" she asked in surprise.

"I should have caught her."

"You tried."

"My effort wasn't good enough," he said tersely. Then his

gaze moved to the man and woman approaching them. "You called your team? What about staying in the shadows? Not knowing who we can trust?"

"The man who was driving the car said you chased Kristine into the street. I need Flynn to take over this scene, so that you don't get taken down to the precinct and interrogated."

He hadn't thought about that. The last thing he wanted was to get put on ice with everything else going on. He wouldn't be able to help if he was in jail.

Savannah went to talk to the police while Flynn joined them, a grim expression on his face.

"Are you both all right?" he asked.

"Yes," Andi said. "We're fine. But we need to keep moving. This is the duffel bag that Kristine got from a young woman who works at the Baby Time Boutique. It wasn't a normal delivery of goods to a customer. It was a drop in a public park. The boutique is involved in this."

"It sounds like it. Did Kristine say anything?" Flynn asked.

"Just that she was sorry," Cooper replied. "She wouldn't tell me where Elisa was. But she had to be going to her with all this stuff. When Kristine doesn't arrive, whoever is holding Elisa will know they're in trouble. They'll probably move Elisa."

Flynn nodded. "Then we better move fast."

"There was a girl at the boutique, Flynn, who looked familiar to me," Andi said. "She was the one who did the drop to Kristine in the park. I believe if we did an age progression photo on Hannah Montgomery, the toddler who went missing in my neighborhood eighteen years ago, we'd find it was a perfect match to this young woman. She said her name was Natasha. But she had a scar on her arm, just like Hannah's."

Flynn looked at Andi in astonishment, and Cooper couldn't help but notice the doubt in Flynn's gaze.

"Are you sure, Andi?" Flynn asked.

"I'm not sure. But it's possible that Natasha has no idea she was kidnapped. She was only two. She wouldn't necessarily remember what happened to her."

"All right. You two head to the boutique. Savannah and I will take care of this scene." He took out his phone. "I'm going to send Caitlyn and Nick to meet you."

"What happened with Agent Burnett?" she asked.

"Damon is handling that scene," Flynn replied.

"Should he really be investigating his own employee?" he challenged.

"Damon will get to the truth, whatever it is," Flynn said flatly. "No doubt in my mind."

He had a lot of doubts in his mind, but none of that was important now. Andi gave Flynn the duffel bag, and then they headed down the street. It took them another ten minutes to get back to their car and fifteen to arrive at the store. The parking lot was empty and there was no sign of Natasha's car. The lights were also off in the store, and when they got to the front door, the doors were locked, and there was a closed sign up.

"We're too late," Andi said with disappointment and frustration in her voice. "They've shut it down. Everyone is gone."

He couldn't believe how fast they'd shut things down. "Let's check out the back. They walked around the dumpster to the back door. It was locked as well. "So, do you have to get a warrant or something?"

"Yes. Which will take time," she said wearily. "The duffel bag Natasha gave to Kristine was filled with baby products, but we can't prove that Kristine was involved in the kidnapping or that the items were for Elisa."

"Kristine said she was sorry," he reminded her.

"Any defense attorney could spin that to mean she was sorry she wasn't with the baby when she was kidnapped. It's too vague. This is a disaster."

He smiled, which made her frown deepen.

"Is something funny?" she challenged.

"No. I just remembered that hitting a wall usually brings out the best in you."

She stared back at him. "You're right, because I never give up."

He liked seeing the fighting light back in her eyes and was happy he was the one to put it there. "What's next?"

She thought for a moment. "Even though we don't have evidence of the store's involvement, there's no way they closed so fast for any other reason than that they figured out who we were, someone spotted us following Natasha or chasing Kristine, and/or they found out Kristine was in an accident."

"Maybe we should try to break in. Your team can cut through the red tape later."

"There's probably an alarm on the building. I don't want to get bogged down here. I have another idea." She pulled out the card Veronica had given her. "Sergio Molina works in private adoptions, which can walk the edge of legality. He sounds like someone who might be involved in this operation. Let's talk to him. Caitlyn and Nick can work on getting a search warrant for the boutique." She took out her phone and texted her team a quick message about the store being closed.

"Did you tell Flynn where we're headed?" he asked curiously. "Are we trusting him again?"

"I'll tell him after."

Andi was still debating her decision to keep Flynn in the dark when they arrived at the attorney's office, which was only a mile away. She did trust Flynn, but she still didn't know who had given up her location in the safehouse. Until she did, she needed to play it as safe as she could.

As Cooper parked the car, he gave her a questioning look. "What's our play? Are you an FBI agent looking for answers, or a desperate woman who wants a baby?"

She thought about that, then shrugged. "I'll decide when we get in there."

"Oh, great. I love it when we improv," he said dryly.

"It's when I do my best work."

The law firm was located on the third floor. When they entered the reception area, it was empty, but she could hear a voice in the inner office. She motioned for Cooper to stay silent as she moved closer to the door that was slightly ajar. A woman inside the office was talking on the phone.

"I don't know where Mr. Molina is," the woman said. "He got a call and told me to cancel all his appointments. I know you've been waiting to talk to him all day; I'm sure he'll get back to you as soon as he can." The woman paused. "Of course, we're going to honor your contract. I understand that you paid a lot of money, but sometimes birth mothers change their minds, and we have to wait for another child."

Andi could hear the anger in the garbled female voice that was screaming into the phone.

"Please, you have to calm down," the woman said. "There's nothing to worry about. Mr. Molina will fulfill the promise he made to you. He never lets anyone down. You really don't have to worry."

Andi moved away from the door as the woman seemed to be wrapping up the call. There was a silence and then she heard the woman start talking again. She slid closer to the door once more.

"Daniel? Where are you?" the woman asked, fear in her voice. "Something has happened. I don't know what to do. Call me back as soon as you can. I'm getting worried."

Andi's heart jumped. *Was she talking about Daniel Guerrero?*

She moved away from the door as the woman came out of the office. She was young, probably in her early twenties and was attractive with dark hair and eyes. She stopped abruptly when she saw them, wariness entering her eyes.

"Can I help you?" she asked.

"I'm Agent Hart with the FBI," she replied. "And you should be worried. Who's Daniel?"

"Uh, he's my boyfriend. Why?"

"What's your name?"

"Ivy Sloan. Why are you here? You don't look like an FBI agent."

"Well, I am. Is Daniel's last name Guerrero?"

The girl's eyes widened. "Is he in trouble?"

"Yes, and so are you. What's going on here? Where's Mr. Molina?"

"He left a little while ago. He said he wasn't feeling well and that I should go home, but the phone keeps ringing. People seem to be upset about something."

"Did he tell you to do anything else before you left?"

"He just said to lock up and not to talk to anyone," she finished. "Can I go?"

"What do you know about Mr. Molina's business? About the adoptions? Where do the kids come from? Who does he work with?"

"I—I'm not sure. I think they come from all over. All I do is answer the phone and make coffee. I don't know anything."

"Does Mr. Molina work alone?"

Ivy hesitated. "I think he has associates, but they call on his private phone. He told me to never answer it. I just answer the office phone."

"Have you ever spoken to anyone from the Baby Time Boutique?"

"A woman named Veronica," Ivy answered. "She calls about once a week. And Mr. Molina says I should always put her through."

"Did you ever hear Mr. Molina mention a baby named Elisa Benedict?"

"No. He never said a word about her."

"But you've heard her name," she said, seeing the truth in Ivy's eyes.

"Daniel's mother works for the family. He was really upset about it."

"Because he was involved? Because he betrayed his mother's employer?"

"No. No," Ivy said quickly, shaking her head. "Daniel wouldn't hurt a child. He's a kind person."

"And yet you just left him a message saying you were worried about him."

"Because he hasn't texted me all day." Ivy paused. "I don't think I should say anything else. Are you arresting me?"

"Andi," Cooper interrupted. "I need to talk to you now."

"Stay here," she told Ivy, as she followed Cooper into the hall. "What's going on?"

"We need to get out of here. I was looking out the window, and I saw a dark van pull up to the building."

The elevator dinged at his words, she immediately pushed open the door to the stairway. They raced down the steps and thru the front door. They were almost at the car when a shot rang out, a bullet sizzling past her ear as it exploded the car window.

She dived inside and ducked down as Cooper pulled away from the curb just as another gunshot shattered the front window.

"Are you hit?" she asked, seeing blood on his face.

"I'm okay," he said, as he sped down the street.

"You're bleeding."

"The glass cut me." He took a corner so fast, she had to brace herself against the door.

She looked out the sideview mirror. The van was coming after them. She really wished she was driving. But there was no time to make a switch.

"Make as many turns as you can," she told him. "Run every yellow light and anything close to a red."

"I got this," he said confidently.

She had no idea where that confidence came from, since she

didn't think he spent a lot of time in car chases, but Cooper had never been one to back away from a challenge.

He slammed on the brakes suddenly and spun around in the middle of an intersection. Her life, as well as every other car and person on the street, flashed in front of her eyes, as the car tilted onto two wheels. It felt like they were airborne, and she was afraid they were going to come down to earth upside down.

CHAPTER TWENTY-TWO

ANDI'S whole body shook as the car finally came down on all four tires, and they were racing down a side street, leaving a blaring of car horns behind them.

Cooper floored the gas, narrowly missing a car pulling out of a parking lot. Her body bounced off the door once more. She gave Cooper a quick look. He was completely focused and determined to win. He made several more breathtaking turns and then got on the freeway. They didn't speak for almost three miles, constantly checking the mirrors, but she never saw the van get on the freeway.

Another five minutes passed before she finally let out the breath she'd been holding.

"I think we're okay," she said.

Cooper flung her a triumphant look. "Of course, we're okay. I wasn't going to let anything happen to us."

"You're the reason we're alive," she agreed. "If you hadn't been looking out the window when they arrived, we would have been sitting ducks. Did you see their faces?"

"I saw two guys in ski masks."

"I hope Ivy wasn't hurt."

"I doubt it. She's probably in on whatever is going on."

"She didn't sound completely in the know, but she knew something."

"You were right about Daniel," Cooper said. "He's involved in this, too. Neil had no idea how many people in his intimate circle of employees were going to betray him." He blew out a breath. "I need to talk to Neil. He probably thinks I deserted him."

"My team will be keeping him in the loop," she assured him.

"I'm supposed to be his eyes and ears. Anyway, where am I going? I feel like we need to regroup. Should we go to another motel? I'm not sure we have enough cash, especially since we'll probably need to get gas at some point. We may need to risk using an ATM."

"I need to think for a minute." She tucked her hair behind her ears as she considered their options. Cooper was right. They needed a safe place to regroup and one that didn't require a lot of cash. She also wanted some resources. "I need computer access and wi-fi. I need to know more about the lawyer, about the store, about Natasha, Ivy, everyone. But I don't think I should go into the office."

"I don't, either. People are finding us too easily. How did they know we were at the attorney's office?"

"Maybe they followed us from the store."

"Or they had someone watching the lawyer's office and called it in when we showed up."

"That's probably what happened," she said, feeling like Cooper's head was surprisingly a little clearer than hers.

"I have an idea," he said suddenly. "You won't like it."

"Then maybe you should keep it to yourself."

"We should go to your old house."

"No way. We don't go anywhere that's tied to either of us."

"I'm not talking about a long stay, but we can't keep driving around. Your father isn't home. You said he left on a trip. I'm guessing that he probably hides the spare key in the same place he always did. And I remember him keeping cash in his drawer to pay the housekeeper and the gardener."

She frowned, absolutely hating his idea as he'd known she would.

"He also has your box of stuff in his house, the old journals you wrote when you were first working on Hannah's case," Cooper added. "Maybe there's a clue there. Maybe you wrote down something about Burnett."

"My dad would hate me breaking into his house, Cooper."

"Does that really bother you?" he challenged. "Doesn't he owe you, Andi?"

She shook her head in bemusement. "I bet you got an A in whatever psychology class taught you how to manipulate someone."

"I did, but I've also known what your hot buttons are for a very long time."

"I hate that, too."

"I know," he said with a laugh.

"You should not be laughing, Cooper. We were almost killed."

"But we didn't die, and that makes me feel good."

"That's the adrenaline."

"It's quite a high," he admitted.

"You will come down."

"I'm fine with that. Right now, I just want to get us off the street. Our car is shot up. If we pass a police car, that won't look good. And while you can probably talk your way out of that kind of trouble, it will take time."

"Time we don't have," she agreed, her gut tightening as he got off the exit near their old neighborhood. "Fine. But we're only going to stay long enough to figure out our next move."

Ten minutes later, they pulled up in front of her old house. The day before, when she'd had lunch at his house, she'd tried very hard not to look at her former home, but now she had no choice. She got out of the car and went up to the porch. On the farthest side from the front door was a loose board under the rail. She squatted down, pulled it up, and was not surprised to find the spare key that her father had kept there forever. She took it out and opened the front door. Cooper followed her into the house.

"We need to get the car into the garage," he said.

They headed into the kitchen and down the steps to the garage. There was one vehicle in the garage, but the second spot was open. She hit the remote while Cooper got the car and drove it inside. Once the garage door was closed, they both returned to the kitchen.

She drew in a breath as she looked around the room. It had definitely changed over time. Her father's latest girlfriend clearly liked a modern look. Where there had once been cherry cabinets and warm stone-colored counters were white cabinets and white marble countertops. There was a fake bowl of fruit on the kitchen table, that felt absolutely perfect for a house with no soul.

"What are you thinking?" Cooper asked, studying her face.

"That I miss the old kitchen, where my mom and I used to do my homework. But then, there were also a lot of fights at that kitchen table. I think my parents were happy when I was really little, like four or five, but by the time I was eleven, my life was a war zone. I hated dinnertime. I was relieved when my father worked late. I preferred when only one of them was in the house. Now, neither of them is here, but I am, which feels weird. I don't think my father would be happy about it."

"He wanted you to come and get your boxes."

"That's true. I wonder where they are."

"Maybe your old room. Shall we see?"

"Not yet." She wasn't ready to go down that road. "I need to check in with Flynn, find out what's going on and let him know what we've learned."

As she spoke, Cooper opened the refrigerator, which was pretty bare, save for some condiments and drinks. However, the freezer was full.

"Food," Cooper said, a happy note in his voice, reminding her of how hungry he'd always been when he was a teenager.

Apparently, that hadn't changed. "Do you mind if I heat up some pizzas? We never ate lunch, and it's almost four now."

"We said we were going to make this quick."

"We will, but we have to eat, and we have free food."

"Fine. Go for it." She sat down at the kitchen table and called Flynn while Cooper pulled things out of the freezer and preheated the oven.

It felt more than a little strange to be in her old house, her father's house, not hers, she reminded herself. But that was just semantics, because this was the home of her childhood and there were a lot of memories here, both good and bad.

Flynn answered, and she straightened in her chair, putting the phone on speaker so she wouldn't have to recap for Cooper. "Did Kristine survive?" she asked first.

"She's alive, but she's in a coma. We haven't been able to talk to her. We have security on her room."

"Damn. I was hoping she told you something."

"I'm hoping you have something to tell me. There were reports of a shooting at an attorney's office with a man and a woman getting shot at as they ran to their car."

"That was us. When we were at the Baby Time Boutique earlier in the day, a woman told me about an adoption attorney they worked with, Sergio Molina. We went to his office. His admin, Ivy Sloan, said he'd left abruptly, and people were calling in upset about something. It turns out Ivy is dating Daniel Guerrero."

Flynn let out a whistle. "I didn't see that coming."

"Before I could get more information out of her, Cooper spotted a van pulling up to the building. Two shooters came after us, probably the same ones who were at the safe house. We obviously managed to get away, but I don't know how they keep finding us so quickly."

"Your life is getting exciting," Flynn said dryly.

"Yes, but the clues are starting to come together, Flynn. The boutique, the attorney, Daniel, and Kristine. Those are at least some of the players. I think Agent Burnett had a role, too."

"But he's out of the operation. Someone else is calling the shots. The boutique is owned by Baby Time Enterprises, LLC. We're digging through the levels of paperwork to find the actual owner. Caitlyn and Nick canvassed the neighborhood and were told that two women ran the store: Veronica and Renee. They didn't know the last names. They said there were at least three or four other employees."

"Did anyone mention a girl named Natasha?"

"No. Her name didn't come up. Do you think she's involved?"

"I would hate to think that, especially if she's really Hannah, but she was at the store and she made the drop to Kristine. We have to consider that she's part of the operation. But when this is all over, we need to figure out who she really is, and whether she was forced into this." She paused. "Have you spoken to Neil and Claire?"

"Yes. They were shocked, horrified, and felt betrayed by Kristine and Daniel. Neil would like to talk to Cooper. At some point, he should give him a call."

"He will. What about Burnett?"

"It looks like Burnett had another identity with a bank account, social security number, the works. He moved significant amounts of money through that account. It's going to take some time to put it all together, but it looks like he was dirty."

"Was Burnett working with anyone else at the bureau?"

"Damon is investigating that. What's your next move? Or do you feel that you can't trust me enough to tell me?" he asked.

"I don't honestly know, Flynn. I'm thinking about everything I've learned. I heard two women speaking Russian at the boutique, and I know Kristine was from Belarus. I'm thinking this could be some kind of international baby trafficking ring."

"But why kidnap a high-profile baby like Elisa?"

"Maybe Kristine was planted with the Benedicts in order to

get access to Elisa, or maybe she was just bribed to look the other way?"

"But why Elisa?" Flynn persisted. "Her parents and grandparents are well-connected. They have money, a level of celebrity, and public interest. Why not go after a child who would draw less attention?"

"That's what we have to figure out."

"We're going to keep working on our end. Are you safe for now?"

"I think so," she said.

"You can trust me, Andi. You can trust your team. I realize that some facts are pointing to the contrary, but we have your back."

"I believe you, Flynn, but my gut tells me that for now, it's better if I just trust myself."

"What about Bradford?" Flynn challenged. "Are you sure you can trust him? Maybe he's the one feeding your location to people. He hates law enforcement. He had a run-in with Burnett a few weeks ago. Don't forget that."

At Flynn's words, she locked eyes with Cooper. He gazed back at her as he leaned against the counter, folding his arms across his broad chest.

"I haven't forgotten anything. I'll check in with you later, Flynn." She ended the call, her gaze still on Cooper.

"Did Flynn plant a seed of doubt in your mind?" he asked, giving her a sharp look.

CHAPTER TWENTY-THREE

"No," Andi said firmly. "If I didn't trust you, Cooper, I wouldn't be here with you. And we've been through the same barrage of fire. But I do wonder why you're sticking with me, because you could be on a plane to Bora Bora right now and far, far away from this mess."

A smile lifted his lips. "Bora Bora sounds sweet. You and me on a beach with some fancy drinks. I could get behind that."

She had to admit she liked that picture, too. "We're a long way from any beach."

"Maybe we go after all this."

That was a future she couldn't contemplate right now. "Maybe," she said with a noncommittal shrug. "I can't think that far ahead. I'm going upstairs. Since we're here, I might as well check my boxes."

"The pizzas will be ready in twenty minutes."

"Good. After that, we should leave and find another location. In the meantime, let's try not to announce our presence here."

"I wasn't planning on throwing a party and we have another hour or two of daylight, so we don't need to turn anything on. Most of the blinds were closed already, so unless someone saw us drive in here, I think we're good."

His logic was sound, but without knowing how they were being tracked so easily, she didn't want to relax too much. But it was nice to take a little breather and regroup and the smell of the pizza cooking was making her hungry. Getting to her feet, she left the kitchen and moved down the hall.

There were a lot of things that were different in the house. The floral wallpaper and family photographs that had once been up in the hall were gone, replaced by more white paint and mini-malistic art. A peek into the living room and dining room revealed the same sensibility. The rooms felt very different now. Her father certainly hadn't put up any reminders of the family he'd once had, the daughter he supposedly loved. She was nowhere in this house, except maybe in some boxes he wanted to get rid of. That seemed sadly ironic.

As she went up the stairs, more old memories stirred within her. The carpeting was gone, replaced by shiny dark-wood floors, but she could still picture herself running up the stairs after school to drop her backpack in her bedroom, change her clothes, and get ready for the next adventure, which, of course, would be outside this house.

The master bedroom was the first room at the top of the stairs. It was also white with a touch of gray in the pillows on the white plush bedspread. The guestroom was next, featuring the same white bedspread but rose-colored pillows. She couldn't imagine that her father liked this look, but maybe he did, because it was very impersonal. It almost felt like the house was a luxury hotel.

Her bedroom had also received the same decorating treat-ment, which made it easier to walk into. Because with all the white, he'd erased the color, drama, and turmoil of her child-hood. She wished she could have done the same erasure inside her head. But she still had her memories and that's what made her feel a little emotional as she walked over to the window and looked out at the thick branches of the oak tree that had been her escape route.

"Doesn't look the same," Cooper said, coming into the room.

"No," she said, as he joined her at the window.

"Our tree is still there."

She turned her head to smile at him. "We spent a lot of time climbing up and down that tree. I don't think my parents had any idea what was going on. The flip side of them not being involved in my life."

"I liked your mom," Cooper said. "But she always seemed sad. And that made you sad, which I didn't like."

"Sad and angry," she agreed, her gaze moving back to the tree. "But when I climbed out this window and down the tree, it felt like I was entering a portal into a different world, a new adventure. And you were part of that excitement. A really good part."

"We had a lot of adventures. And we still are."

She glanced back at him. "The stakes are much higher."

"Well, we're a lot older. We'll get through this, Andi. We will find Elisa and figure it all out."

"I think so, too." Her confidence swelled with his undoubted belief in their abilities.

He moved closer, resting his hands on her hips. "I wish—"

Before he could finish, the oven buzzer blared through the house.

"Damn. My timing sucks," he said with annoyance.

She grinned. "You wanted pizza. But you can finish what you were going to say."

He hesitated. "It will keep. Let's eat. You have to be as hungry as I am."

She was hungry, but as he let go of her, she couldn't help wishing that the pizza had taken a while longer.

Cooper pulled the pizzas out of the oven as Andi grabbed plates and napkins. He was relieved that he hadn't said what he wanted to say, because there was too much going on. This wasn't the time for a deep personal conversation, and that's what they needed to have. They couldn't do that now, not with people shooting at them and his friend's daughter's life on the line.

"I need to call Neil," he said, as they sat down to eat. "He's going to wonder why I've been so out of touch. I'm sure he's called me a dozen times. I'll use the burner phone, but I need to check in. He's my friend, and he must be going out of his mind."

"That's fine. I'd like to know what he thinks about Kristine being involved. Maybe knowing she had something to do with it will have opened his eyes in some way."

"I wonder how Daniel and Kristine were connected. Did they know each other before she took the job at Neil's house? Did they come up with the plan to sell Elisa in some way?"

"I don't believe either one is the brains behind this operation. Kristine was either planted there or paid off in some way. I'm leaning towards planted. She's from Belarus, her employment history is sketchy. I'm not sure why the Weiselbergs even hired her without childcare experience." Andi paused. "I know my team has talked to them, but I haven't heard what they found out. It would be interesting to know what kind of background check they did."

"I thought they met her at a park through another nanny. Maybe they didn't do a check. They just took someone's word for Kristine being a good person. They probably moved just in time. If they hadn't, it might be their child who's missing." He took a breath. "But if she was planted, then that means this was premeditated. It was in the works for a while, at least four months. That seems like a long time."

"Or the operation plants young women in the community in areas where they have access to other nannies, kids, pregnant women. I think whatever we're dealing with is big. The baby boutique would have been a point of access, as well as the nanny, the adoption attorney..." Her voice trailed away. "I'm not sure how Daniel fits in. Maybe Kristine pulled Daniel into this.

She could have known he needed money and used him to get the baby out of the house."

"But Daniel's girlfriend, Ivy, is tied to the attorney, which ties Daniel to Sergio Molina. Maybe Daniel was the one who enlisted Kristine's help," he suggested.

"Good point."

"I really hope Solange is not part of this," he said heavily, thinking about Daniel's mother. "That will kill Neil. She's like a second mother to him."

Andi nodded, compassion in her gaze. "I get the feeling Solange has no idea how far down the dark side her son has gone."

"Okay," he said. "What about the near miss by the bar? Was Daniel in the car with Tyler? Was it Kristine?"

"Good question." Andi thought for a moment as she munched on her pizza. "I wonder if someone from the bar that night contacted Kristine. I asked questions about her before I sat down with you, TJ, and Naomi. We didn't leave for at least forty-five minutes. Plenty of time for someone to sound an alarm about my questions. Whether it was Kristine or Daniel in the car with Tyler, I don't know. I'm leaning toward Daniel, because I think Kristine was in the house that night, solidifying her alibi of being heartbroken about Elisa's disappearance. But she could have called Daniel in a panic, or she contacted someone else who sent Daniel and Tyler down to the bar to scare me or take me out. I'm not sure what the intent was. But it was sloppy and amateurish, completely unlike the rest of the attacks on us. Which suggests a less experienced, low-level criminal."

"So, not Agent Burnett."

"I don't think so."

"Getting back to him—why would someone kill Burnett? What did he do wrong?"

"That's a question that keeps going around in my head. He met with me the day before he was killed. He also sent me a text several hours before someone showed up at his house and shot him in the head. Maybe someone thought Burnett was playing both sides or was going to try to save himself. I do wonder what he wanted to tell me. He was very angry and antagonistic the day before."

"I think he wanted to meet with you to lure you into a trap."

"Except that he was the one who was killed. From what Flynn said, it looks like Burnett had a double life going for twenty years or more."

"Which makes me wonder again why take him out now? We weren't that close to nailing him."

"They might not have known that. The other reason could be the fact that he was taken off Elisa's case. If Burnett couldn't help, then he might not have had any value," Andi said slowly, as she puzzled it out. "He was desperate to get back into the investigation. That's why he fed me information. He wanted me to include him in the case. But I wasn't going to do that, because I didn't trust him."

"And you didn't trust him because you knew he screwed up Hannah's investigation."

"I was definitely a concern to him. It was bad timing that I showed up when I did."

"But even if you hadn't moved back to LA, Damon was going to take him off the case because of Burnett's altercation with me and Neil. He still wouldn't have had the investigation."

"Maybe not, but it only came to my unit because I was there. Our kidnapping specialist is on maternity leave. Without me, Damon would have probably assigned it to someone else in his office, in which case Burnett would have still had some access to the investigation. He could have manipulated facts more easily."

"That makes sense. Do you think this operation is being run by a foreign group?"

"Could be foreign and domestic. I suspect we've only seen the tip of the iceberg."

Her words were chilling. "But that tip can still kill a lot of people," he muttered. "And I'm worrying most about Elisa. Is she somewhere safe? Has she been sold to some loving family and is happily ensconced somewhere? Or is she being held in limbo? That duffel bag of baby items had to be for her, which implies she's still in transit." He frowned at his own words. "God, I hate to think of that sweet little baby being trafficked. It's so cruel. I don't think Neil and Claire will ever be able to forgive themselves if they don't get her back. They'll blame themselves for bringing Kristine into the family, giving her access to their baby. How can they survive that kind of guilt?"

"Let's hope that doesn't happen. As you said earlier, we'll get her back. That's what we need to focus on."

He'd said that with confidence before, but he wasn't feeling that confident now. They'd made some progress, but there was still a lot they had to learn. "And then there's Natasha," he said.

Andi met his gaze. "Yes. I could be wrong about her being Hannah. But I don't think I am. Either way, she works at the boutique. She took the duffel bag. She's involved. One way or another, we have to get her story."

"It would be a huge coincidence for her to have a scar like Hannah's."

"I agree. But what I don't understand is why she would even be in Los Angeles. If this is a human trafficking operation, then she was kidnapped to be sold to a family desperate for a child. But it doesn't feel like that happened. And with all the media reports at the time, why would anyone have kept her in this area? It would have been too risky."

"She could have been gone for a long time and just recently returned."

"True. However it happened, she seems to be part of the organization. She might be complicit in the kidnappings of other kids."

"Without even knowing that she, herself, was taken," he said, thinking that was a bizarre twist. "They would have had to tell her some story about herself. She's twenty years old. She'd have a birth certificate, a social security number."

"I'm sure her entire identity has been created for her. But what she knows about herself is really the question." Andi paused. "Part of me wishes we had split up in the park and one of us had gone after her. But when Kristine ran, all I could think was that she was going to Elisa."

"She was more important than Natasha at that moment," he agreed. "You didn't make the wrong call, and Kristine is alive. With a little good luck, she comes out of this coma and tells us where Elisa is."

"Good luck?" she asked dryly. "We haven't had much of that."

"Are you kidding? We've been almost run over, blown up, and gunned down, and we're sitting here eating pizza with only a few scratches and bruises. I'd call that good luck."

"I can't argue with that." She wiped her mouth and took her empty plate to the sink. "I want to take a quick look through the boxes and see if I want anything. I know I wrote about Hannah's case in my journal. Maybe there's some clue I've forgotten about."

"Good idea. I'll clean up, so your dad will never suspect anyone was here."

As soon as Andi opened the first box, she had second thoughts about going through the reminders of her life. But it was Hannah's case that made her dig through the odds and ends of her childhood that she'd left behind. And sure enough, there was a stack of journals that she'd labeled as Andi's case files.

She smiled at her own silliness. She really had thought she was some kind of girl detective, but she'd accomplished next to nothing as a child. Still, it had prepared her for her current job, which she was pretty good at.

She found Hannah's case in the third book. She took it over to her bed and sat down.

Cooper came into the room. "Did you find it?"

"Yes."

He sat down next to her. "Let me help—like the old days."

Cooper sitting on her bed next to her felt nothing like the old days. Not after the night they'd shared. And having him so close felt like a big distraction.

"Maybe I should read it first, and then you can read it," she suggested.

He gave her a knowing smile. "You're suddenly not thinking about the case anymore, are you? You're thinking about this bed, about me and you, last night…"

She felt her cheeks warm at his words. "Wrong. I wasn't thinking about any of that. And don't distract me."

"Sorry. Read me what you wrote."

Clearing her throat, she looked at the journal and started reading aloud the notes that she'd made.

"Hannah disappeared between eight and ten o'clock at night. Gemma, the nanny, discovered Hannah missing at nine-forty-five but hadn't checked on her since she'd put her to bed at eight." She paused, looking at Cooper. "I forgot the nanny discovered Hannah missing. Just like Kristine."

"That's right. And Gemma was from Sweden. She'd come to the US with two girlfriends after college and they worked for a local agency. She'd been with the Montgomery's for a year when Hannah disappeared. But even though she was the last person to see Hannah, Gemma was never considered a person of interest in the case."

"You read the case files, too."

"I was able to do that, yes," he admitted.

"I won't ask how that happened." She flipped to the next page. Gemma had a boyfriend—Nate Forrester. He worked at a bar called Benji's."

"Burnett wrote only one thing next to Nate's name—alibi checked."

"I'm not sure I need to go through this journal. You know more than I did then, Cooper."

"Keep going."

She looked further down the page and Kyle's name jumped out at her. She closed the book. "I don't want to do this."

"Afraid to show me what you wrote about Kyle?" he challenged.

"What purpose will it serve? It will just make you unhappy."

"Give me the book, Andi."

She hesitated, then handed him the journal. "I'm going downstairs to look for some cash and see if I can get into my father's computer. That will be a lot more helpful. And then we need to go." She paused at the door. "If I can find the spare key, we can take my father's car. That way we won't have to drive with the bullet-shattered glass."

Her words fell on deaf ears as Cooper read through her journal. She couldn't remember exactly what she'd written, but she had a feeling the wall between Cooper and her would be coming back up very soon.

She went downstairs and into the office. Her father's laptop was on his desk. She opened it up and saw it required a password. He'd never been too clever about passwords. She tried a couple of his old favorites and found gold on the last one. As the computer opened, the display showed a background photo of her father and his latest girlfriend, who was wearing a skimpy bikini and looked to be in her twenties. Her father was never ever going to change.

She didn't know why this beautiful young woman would want her dad. Maybe he was attractive, in an older man in his late fifties, kind of way, but he was a player. Married twice with a bunch of girlfriends concurrently and in-between.

She clicked on the internet to get away from that disturbing picture and looked up the baby boutique. She flipped through the site, but there was no information about the owner. As Flynn had said, the business was masked in an LLC.

Frustrated and tired, she looked away from the computer to dig through her father's drawers. In the first drawer, she found a brochure from Lassiter Realty. She pulled it out and set it on the desk. There was a note attached and addressed to her father, Tom. It said: Will would love to sell your house. He'll do a great job for you! Call him. Kim.

It wasn't a love note but it still made her wonder again if her father and Kim had had an affair. But if they had, it had been years ago. Kim was no doubt too old for her father's taste these days.

She looked back in the drawer and found a hundred and thirty dollars in cash, which would come in handy and a couple of keys, one of which hopefully went to the vehicle in the garage.

Grabbing the keys, stuffing the cash into her pocket, she went down the hall, through the kitchen, and into the garage. A blast of cold air caught her by surprise. Her gaze swung to the door leading into the garage from the side yard. It was open.

Her heart jumped. She felt a movement behind her, started to turn around, and then something hard and heavy came down on her head.

CHAPTER TWENTY-FOUR

ANDI'S JOURNAL was making him angry, but Cooper couldn't stop looking at it. He was torn between wanting to let go of the past and the feeling that there was something important in her teenage writings that he needed to understand.

The page devoted to Kyle's actions that night was upsetting and confusing. Andi reiterated how Kyle first said he'd left the concert early and had gone straight home. The next time he said he'd stopped to smoke a cigarette, which he couldn't do at home. And in one other conversation, he'd said that Will had left the concert early, and Kyle had stayed to the end and then gone home alone.

He was aware of the times his brother had changed his story, but that's because Kyle got confused when he was under pressure, and when the FBI had searched Kyle's car and asked him where his cigarettes were, Kyle had stumbled, and then said he hadn't been smoking at all.

The day of the search had been horrible and still lived in his brain in vivid detail. He could still feel the shame he'd experienced when the FBI had entered their house, and the neighbors had watched with suspicion in their gazes. He could still see Andi standing across the street. She'd sent him a pleading smile, but he'd looked away. What was happening to his family was her doing.

He swore under his breath, not wanting to get caught up in the circle of hate again, and he was relieved when he turned the page and saw a new section focused on the scene of the crime and the neighbors. Andi had written detailed notes about everyone on the block and their actions that night. Some of them he remembered. Some he didn't.

TJ Lassiter had come out of the house. He'd been playing videogames when Mr. Montgomery pounded on the door, yelling that Hannah was missing. TJ was the only one home at the time. He'd let Mr. Montgomery through the side gate so he could check their yard. Then TJ had gone back into the house until he saw the police lights and the crowd gathering outside.

TJ's older brother, Will, arrived a few minutes after he and Andi had gotten to the scene. Will told them that Kyle bailed on the concert, left him alone there. He said Kyle was in a strange mood. Andi had put a star by that notation.

Mrs. Lassiter had arrived home next. She'd joined them on the sidewalk, asking what had happened. She'd been working late at her travel agency. Her husband, Steve, was out of town.

The house across the street from Hannah Montgomery was rented by Rose and Walter Voltman, an older couple in their seventies. They'd come out of the house in their pajamas and robes, saying they'd been woken up by the sirens.

The house next to the Voltman's belonged to the Connors. They were on vacation. The house next to them was owned by the Madison family. They had two older teenagers who were in college. The Madisons were not living in the house, because they'd recently staged it and put it up for sale. While that was happening, the Madisons were staying with relatives out of town.

On the corner lived a middle-aged man, John DiVincenzo. He said he was asleep and didn't know anything until the next morning. Andi had made a note that John had recently been laid off from his job at a local printing warehouse and his wife had left him a year earlier.

He hadn't heard anyone talk about DiVincenzo when Kyle had been under the microscope. Mr. DiVincenzo seemed like someone the FBI should have questioned. But clearly, Burnett had just wanted a scapegoat to protect the real kidnapper. He'd had no reason to look any further than Kyle, who was a great target for him.

As Cooper re-read Andi's notes about the neighbors, something niggled at his brain. The Madison's house had been up for sale. *Why did that bother him?*

And then he knew why. Andi had told him the house behind Neil Benedict's property was for sale and because of that, their security cameras were not in operation. She'd thought that the kidnappers might have left Neil's property through the back of his yard, ending up on the street behind the house.

Was that just an odd coincidence or did it mean something?

The police had searched the neighborhood for Hannah, just as they had done for Elisa. They'd gone door to door, looking in backyards.

Would they have gone into a house that was up for sale? Maybe that would have been difficult if the owner wasn't present to let them in.

A crazy idea took root in his brain. *Was it possible that each child had been kidnapped, taken to a nearby house for sale, where they were hidden away until the smoke cleared, and then moved to another location?*

The FBI might not have been able to access those houses within the first twenty-four hours, especially if they had no probable cause to go inside. It would have taken longer than that to get in, and by then, the child could have been moved again, but during a time frame when no one was looking.

His pulse raced. He felt like he was on to something. Jumping off the bed, he jogged down the stairs to find Andi.

The computer was open on the desk in the study, but there was no sign of her.

His heart sped up for a different reason. It seemed suddenly far too quiet.

"Andi?" he said, his own voice echoing back to him. He entered the kitchen, saw the open door leading into the garage. When he went down the stairs, he saw keys on the cement floor behind her father's car. Across from him, the door leading into the side yard was wide open.

Fear stabbed him in the heart.

Someone had broken in.

Someone had taken Andi.

Andi woke up with a start, the back of her head throbbing with pain, her arms aching from being stretched out in front of her. She tried to move them, but they wouldn't budge. She blinked her eyes open in confusion.

The room was dark, but there was some moonlight coming through a high window over her head, enough dim light to see that she was lying on her side on a bed, fully dressed, her arms stretched out in front of her, a zip tie around her wrists and handcuffs attaching her to the headpost of the bedframe. One of her legs was bound to the post at the end of the bed. She tugged hard, but she couldn't move more than an inch.

Anxiety ran through her. She tamped it down. She couldn't panic. That wouldn't help. She needed to think. To remember what had happened.

She'd gone into the garage. The side door had been open, cold air hitting her face. She'd started to turn, to run back inside, but someone had hit her on the back of her head and knocked her out.

Her breath came a little faster as she thought about what might have happened next. Clearly, they'd brought her somewhere. They could have killed her on the spot. But they hadn't. *Why?*

She couldn't think of a good reason.

She also couldn't think because Cooper's image was suddenly racing around in her head. *Had the person or people who had kidnapped her gone into the house? Had they grabbed Cooper?* She tried to twist her head to look behind her, but she couldn't see much.

"Cooper," she said softly, hoping he was in the room with her, but there was nothing but cold silence.

He wasn't here. Maybe they hadn't gone into the house. He could be fine.

She tried to hang on to that thought, but she couldn't. *What if he wasn't fine? What if they'd shot him? What if he was lying in a puddle of blood dying? What if she'd let him down again?*

She'd left the bedroom. She'd gone downstairs to get away from him. She'd gone into the garage without telling him she'd found the car key. All those decisions could have led to something horrible happening to him, and she couldn't bear that thought.

The rational part of her brain told her to get a grip. She couldn't help Cooper until she figured out how to help herself.

That seemed like an impossible challenge.

Then she heard voices nearing the door. They were talking in Russian. Two women—again, just like in the store. Was one of them Natasha?

In the distance, she heard louder sounds, heavy thuds, shuffling feet, loud bangs. There was a lot of action going on, and it felt like the noise was coming from a big cavern. She appeared to be in a bedroom, but was she?

There was bedroom furniture, but now she realized there were two dressers in front of her, one white, one brown. There were several different vases on top of those dressers. In the corner were two chairs, one armchair, one hardback. She was in a furniture warehouse, she realized.

She heard more voices, mostly female in nature, one sounded hysterical. And then she heard the sharp, piercing cry of a baby.

Was that Elisa?

More Russian words followed. She picked out a few of them. Mothers, babies, truck.

It felt like she was in a holding area, maybe a point through which they moved babies and kids. *But why bring her here?*

The answer to that question wasn't a good one.

They'd shut down the store. They were dismantling the operation, probably to restart somewhere else. They were going to destroy any evidence left behind and any other loose ends, like an FBI agent who would never stop looking for them.

"What's going on?" a new female voice asked in English, her tone hesitant, unsure.

"It doesn't concern you, Natasha."

At the mention of Natasha, Andi's pulse leapt into overdrive. "Your name isn't Natasha," she yelled. "It's Hannah Montgomery. You were kidnapped when you were two years old."

"What is she talking about?" Natasha asked.

"She's just trying to upset you. Come along now."

She heard them move away, and she felt a wave of despair. Five minutes later, the door opened and quickly closed. Natasha moved into the room.

"Why are you telling me lies?" Natasha asked suspiciously.

"I'm telling you the truth. I used to babysit you. Your name is Hannah. We built forts in your bedroom and took flashlights under the blanket and sang songs." She knew she didn't have much time, but she was desperate to convince Natasha. Maybe she couldn't save herself, but hopefully she could save this girl who had been missing for so long.

"We made up a silly song," she continued, trying to remember the words. "It went like this: We're sitting in our tent, drinking our tea, Hannah and her elephant, her turtle, and me," she said. "We would have tea parties with your stuffed animals. Your mother's name is Shari. Your father's name is Ray. Your last name is Montgomery. I lived up the street from you. I'm Andi. I took you to the park when your nanny, Gemma, was busy. The park had a big slide, and you loved it. You would climb up and down the ladder without ever getting tired. But one day at the park, you fell, and you cut your arm. That's where your scar came from."

Natasha shook her head. "That's not true."

"It is true. I think deep down you know it is. That's why you came in here. When you were two years old, someone took you out of your crib, and I never saw you again until earlier today. I didn't know what happened to you, but now I do. The people you think are your family either kidnapped you or accepted a stolen child."

Natasha shook her head. "It's not possible. My mother is my mother. We both have blonde hair."

"That's not enough, Natasha, and you know it."

"I have to go. I have to help. The babies are scared."

"They're scared, because they've been stolen. You gave a duffel bag to a girl named Kristine in the park. That was for a baby named Elisa. She was taken from her crib Tuesday morning."

"No. We don't kidnap children. We just help move the babies from poor mothers to those who can take care of them. We're doing good. We're helping people who can't get help other places. And we're helping the mothers, too. They don't have anything when they come here."

"Where do they come from?"

"I can't talk to you anymore."

As Hannah headed to the door, she said, "Wait. If you don't believe me, look up your name on your phone—Hannah Montgomery. I'm sure your baby pictures are there from when you were kidnapped. You'll see your parents. Maybe you'll recognize them, but even if you don't, you might recognize yourself, and you'll know I'm not lying."

"I—I can't," she said nervously. "You're telling me stories, because you're crazy."

"I'm not crazy, Hannah. I'm a federal agent. I work for the FBI. What's happening here is against the law."

"No, you're trying to kidnap a baby. They told me you'll do anything to get your hands on a child. You were at the store with your husband. You were desperate."

"I just told that story so that someone would tell me what's going on. You have to believe me. I need you to call the FBI or the police. Tell them to come down here. Tell them Agent Andi Hart is in trouble. Please."

Hannah didn't answer. She just backed out of the room and shut the door behind her.

Andi groaned in frustration. She hadn't made her case. She hadn't convinced Hannah what was really going on.

How could the girl be so naïve? How could she believe the story they'd told her?

She must have been brainwashed, raised to believe that lies were the truth.

Although, she wondered again why Hannah hadn't been sold. *Why had they taken her and kept her all these years?*

Her questions weren't going to matter unless she could get herself out of here. She yanked her arms again, which only resulted in sending a shaft of pain through one elbow. The noises outside were getting fainter. They were abandoning this location and she didn't think they were going to leave it standing behind them.

She stiffened as she heard someone coming down the hall.

The door opened once more, but this time it wasn't Natasha who entered the room.

Andi's jaw dropped in shock. "You?" she breathed.

CHAPTER TWENTY-FIVE

COOPER STALKED AROUND THE HOUSE, fear racing through him. He needed to find Andi, to put it all together and figure out where she was. But a wave of hopeless despair ran through him. Andi could be anywhere. And he was one person. He needed to get help. He ended up back in the office, looking for her phone.

As he moved around the desk, his gaze fell on a brochure for a realty company—Lassiter Realty. The note attached suggested that Andi's dad should hire Will Lassiter to sell his house, and the note was from Will's mother, Kim.

He opened the brochure and found an older version of Will smiling as he stood in front of a for sale sign and touted his company's work. The realty company provided all services, appraisals and inspections as well as staging services from Pacific Coast Staging.

He suddenly wondered if the house down the street from the Montgomery's had been listed for sale by the Lassiter's.

Back then, Will's dad, Steven, had run the company. It was more than likely he'd had that listing and that Will, who'd been working in the office with his dad on weekends and summer vacations, would have had access to any houses listed for sale.

What if it had been Will all along?

His heart raced with that thought. Andi had noted in her journal that Will had walked down the street shortly after they arrived at the scene. He remembered that now. Will had come from the opposite direction on foot. He hadn't been in his car. Although, it was possible that he just hadn't been able to drive down the street with the police cars blocking the road.

Still, Will was just as good a suspect as Kyle was. He lived next door to Hannah. He was a stoner. He couldn't account for his whereabouts that night, either, but he hadn't been interrogated the way Kyle had, because Will had been perceived as normal and Kyle was the weird kid on the street.

Maybe Burnett was tied to the Lassiters. And that's why Will had gotten a pass.

He shook his head, his thoughts racing fast. Even if he was onto something about Will being involved eighteen years ago, what about now?

Will could have seen him and Andi arrive. Or someone else in the neighborhood had. He'd thought they'd be safe here for a few hours, but this had been the worst place they could have come.

He pushed away the guilty, punishing thoughts, because they wouldn't bring Andi back. He had to do that. They'd taken her alive. They could have shot her in the garage, like they'd shot Burnett. But they hadn't done that, so he had time, maybe a very small window of time.

He grabbed the phone she'd left on the desk and called Flynn. It was after seven now, and Flynn didn't answer. Dammit. He left a short message for Flynn. "This is Cooper. Andi was grabbed from her father's house. I don't know where she is, but she's in trouble. There might be a link between the house for sale behind Neil's house and the kidnapping. You need to check into Lassiter Realty. I'll explain. Call me back." As he ended the call, he thought about calling 911, but he had no idea where to tell anyone to go, and he didn't know who else to call, who else to trust.

He pulled out his own phone and turned it on, no longer concerned about someone tracking him. If they'd wanted him, they would have come in the house and grabbed him, too. As his phone lit up, he saw the dozens of messages that he'd missed, including one from TJ that had come in an hour ago, asking him to meet him for a drink.

Was that a coincidence? Or was TJ luring him into a trap? God! It seemed crazy to believe that a family who had lived around the corner from him could be involved in all this. Maybe he was wrong, jumping to wild conclusions. That was more Andi's style than his. He really wished she was here to help him sort things out.

He punched in TJ's number. It went to voicemail. He sent him a quick text: *Where are you? Would love to meet up.*

No answer.

He tried to remember what TJ had said about his life when they were having drinks. He had an apartment in Santa Monica. And he had a small music studio in a warehouse in Culver City.

Cooper looked up studios online and came back with two in Culver city, and one was called Wave Studios. That was it. TJ had talked about his three favorite things: surfing, smoking, and making music. TJ didn't seem like a criminal mastermind. Maybe he was just caught up in the family crime business.

Or maybe he was completely wrong about the Lassiters. One way or another, he needed to find out, and TJ was his best lead.

"You should have stayed away. But you always have to stick your nose into it, don't you? Didn't your mother ever tell you curiosity killed the cat?"

Andi stared in confusion at the blonde woman, who had once been one of her friend's mothers, the helper in her third-grade classroom, the maker of the best brownies at the school bake sale. She had even bandaged up her skinned knee when she'd crashed her bike in her front yard.

"I don't understand," she murmured. "You're involved in this?"

Kim Lassiter stared at her with a coldness she'd never seen before. "We've helped a lot of people."

"You've hurt a lot of people," she countered. "You stole Hannah right out from under her parents, your neighbors, your friends, the people you had barbecues with and shared holidays. How could you do that to the Montgomerys?"

"It was a desperate situation. Hannah was well-cared for, as you've seen."

"She's going to figure it out one day."

"No, she won't. She doesn't remember anything."

"How was it a desperate situation?" she asked. "I'm pretty sure you're trafficking babies and toddlers for illegal adoption, so what was the deal with Hannah? Why is she part of this?"

Kim gave her a knowing smile. "You want to get me talking, give your team a chance to find you. It won't work. No one knows where you are."

"Cooper will figure it out."

"He won't," Kim said. "He can't."

Her heart twisted at Kim's words. "Why would you hurt him?"

"If he's hurt, it's because of you. You were always trouble for him and for his family. I knew you would end up at your father's house, that you'd want to get your little journals. I encouraged him to contact you, to make sure you knew that he had them, that he wanted to give them to you. But after speaking to you the other day, I wasn't sure you'd do it. You were so angry with him. But in the end, you couldn't resist. You played right into my hands. Then I sent someone to get you."

"Why? Why bring me here?"

"Because I can't take the chance that you won't keep looking for us. Once you're dead, and the evidence is destroyed, there won't be anyone else to find our trail."

She felt sick to her stomach because the way Kim was talking, it sounded like Cooper was dead. But she couldn't let her see that her words were destroying her. She couldn't give her that satisfaction. "Why didn't you just have someone kill me in the garage?"

"Because I wanted to see you. I thought after all your stubborn investigating, you deserved an answer before you died. Call me sentimental. I also couldn't trust that you wouldn't get away again. I needed to see you trapped with my own eyes."

Kim wasn't sentimental; she was evil, and maybe overconfident. Because as long as Andi was alive, there was a chance she could still get out of this. She did need to keep Kim talking. Maybe no one was looking for her, but at least she'd get more answers. "I assume you're the one who sent someone to blow up my apartment and then try to shoot me."

"I tried to warn you off, but that didn't work. You're too stubborn, so I had to take stronger action. Unfortunately, you proved to be elusive, and my people proved to be incompetent."

"Was one of your people Agent Burnett?"

Kim smiled again. "You figured that out, did you?"

"How did you make that happen? Did you involve him after the kidnapping or before?"

"Before. I made him an offer he couldn't refuse, actually more than one offer," she said cockily. "We got very close over the years."

That thought turned her stomach. "Why did you kill him if he was working with you?"

"Because he couldn't help me anymore," she said pragmatically. "Jim knew too much, and he was getting soft, worrying about himself. He wanted to magically "find" Elisa so he could win back his boss's respect and save the day. Then he tried to persuade me that that action would get rid of you. But the baby was worth far more to me than his offer, so I started following his communication channels. I kept up with who he was calling and texting."

"And you saw that he had called and texted me. You're insane, Kim."

"I'm smart. That's how I've built one of the biggest operations in the country in the past twenty years."

"What about your husband?" she asked. "Was he part of this?"

"Of course, Steve was part of it," she said with a shrug. "This started years ago."

"Did he actually die two years ago, or did you kill him, too?"

"You have a mouth on you, don't you?"

She ignored that. "What about my father? Did the two of you have an affair while he was married to my mother?"

"Yes. He was a very lonely, unhappy man, and your mother was a cold, unfeeling bitch."

"My mother is a wonderful person. And you were her friend. You betrayed her. You're the cold, unfeeling bitch. And someday everyone will know it."

"Shut up," Kim said, obviously not liking that she was losing control of the conversation.

"I'm not going to shut up. You brought me here to talk. So let's go back eighteen years. Who kidnapped Hannah? Was it you? Was it your husband? One of your boys? How did you get Hannah out of the neighborhood? Was she at your house? But she couldn't have been, because the police looked through your home, all the neighbor's houses…" Her voice trailed away, as she remembered the search, and the fact that one house wasn't looked at for two days, because it was for sale, and the owners were out of the country. "Your husband's firm had the listing on the house for sale across the street. He told the police you couldn't reach the owner for consent to search. When you finally got that consent, there was no one there. You'd moved Hannah somewhere else."

"So, you've figured it out. Bravo." Kim gave her a mocking clap. "It's too bad no one will ever know how brilliant you are."

"I still don't understand why you took Hannah and then raised her within your smuggling ring. It doesn't make sense."

"Hannah was sick when we took her. She developed a high fever and a rash and the family she was supposed to go to wouldn't take her when they realized she had medical issues, so we took care of her until she was better. And then..." Kim's lips tightened. "The woman taking care of her didn't want to let her go, so she kept her. She was well-treated. I have nothing to feel guilty about."

She doubted the narcissistic Kim ever felt guilty about anything. "You're an evil person, Kim."

"I'm not evil. I'm a businesswoman. I had no other choice. I had two small kids and a lousy husband who ran up gambling debts so high I was going to lose everything. All I had to do was get a few girls into the country, a few poor, desperate girls, who could have a better life by providing a baby to a couple who were also desperate to be parents. It was a win-win."

"It wasn't a win for the Montgomerys. Why did you take Hannah if you were bringing pregnant girls into the country?"

"There were a couple of instances where a deal fell through, and there was a lot of money on the line, so we had to improvise. Find a child who was the same age, with the same features. Blonde, blue-eyed children are very popular."

"Hannah was an improvisation? Was Elisa Benedict as well?"

"Yes."

"Is TJ part of this?"

"No, my youngest son is adorable but a complete idiot and often too stoned to know what he's saying."

"I can't believe he doesn't know."

"I don't care what you believe. And we're done talking, Andi. Soon, you'll smell smoke. The room will get hotter. You'll wonder if anyone will notice that there's a fire burning. Maybe you'll even think someone will rescue you, but that won't happen. You're not going to survive, Andi. Not this time. This is your last case."

Kim pulled out a small device of some kind and hit a button.

As she did so, Andi heard the sudden sound of a ticking clock.

"You have about eighteen minutes to figure the rest out," Kim said, with a dark smile.

Cooper parked in front of Wave Studios, disappointed to see no lights on in the building. He tried the front door, but it was locked. The blinds were closed.

Andi could still be in there. But it felt wrong. He'd made a mistake. She wasn't here. His heart sank. She'd already been gone an hour, and he didn't like her chances of surviving anything that went on too long.

His gaze swept the industrial area, which was comprised of big stone buildings, one a tile company, another with bathroom fixtures, and a third belonging to a printer. There was a large warehouse a block away with a sign that read Pacific Coast Staging, and he remembered the flyer he'd seen on Andi's father's desk, that Lassiter Realty was a full-service company, with staging services provided by Pacific Coast Staging. It couldn't be a coincidence that it was on the same block as TJ's sound studio. TJ had mentioned that his mother had helped him find the perfect studio space.

He started down the street, thinking a warehouse would be the perfect place to hide someone. He'd no sooner taken a few steps when a figure came running around the corner, barreling into him. As he grabbed her arms, he looked into her face and got another shock. The blonde woman in front of him was Natasha, but she didn't look like the young woman he'd seen earlier. Her clothes were ripped and dirty, and there was blood on her face and on her arms.

"Natasha? Are you all right?"

"You're her boyfriend or something, aren't you?" Natasha asked.

"I'm Cooper. Do you know where Andi is?"

"Yes, but there's no time. Hurry." She ran toward the staging warehouse and as they moved around the side of it, he saw flames dancing in a window. "They set a fire on the first floor, and there's a bomb on the second floor. It's going to go off soon." The words flew out of her mouth in a panicked rush.

"Where is Andi?"

"On the second floor. She's tied up. She told me who I was. I didn't want to believe her. But I know she's right. I'm Hannah."

"We're going to talk about that, but I need to get Andi out first."

He yanked open the door, and they ran into the smoky building. A fire had been started a few feet away, and it was getting bigger by the second. They were in a huge furniture warehouse with plenty of fuel, but he couldn't worry about that now. "Where is she?"

Natasha turned on the flashlight on her phone and led him to the stairs. He turned on his light, as it was dark and smoky and difficult to see. But when they reached the second floor, he was relieved to see there was no fire here—not yet.

The door in front of him was locked, but that wasn't going to stop him. "Stand back," he said. He gave himself a little space and then kicked the door. It didn't budge, so he threw his whole body against it until it flew open. He ran into the room, his light dancing off more furniture until it found the woman on the bed.

Andi stared at him in shock and fear. Her hands were tied together and cuffed to the metal bed frame.

"Cooper, no," she said, shaking her head. "You have to get out of here right now. There's a bomb. Its behind me on the floor. I don't know how much time is left. Kim said eighteen minutes, but that was a while go."

"Kim?" he echoed.

"Yes. Kim is probably running this whole thing, or maybe she has partners." She paused as her gaze moved to Hannah. "Hannah?" she said in shock. "You came back?"

"I had to save you," Hannah said. "I didn't believe you, but then I remembered the song we sang, and I knew you were telling me the truth. I also knew they were going to kill you. I jumped out of the van and ran back here to try to save you."

While Hannah was talking, he flashed his light around the room until he saw the timer and device on the floor behind the bed. It looked like a very large explosive. And he had no idea what to do about it.

"Both of you need to leave," Andi repeated.

"I'm not leaving without you," he told her. "Maybe I can break the bed frame."

"You can't."

Ignoring Andi, he turned to Hannah. "Go outside. Call 911. Tell them FBI Agent Andi Hart is trapped in a warehouse. Give them the address. And stay away from the building."

"Wait," Andi said, as Hannah moved toward the door. "Where are they going, Hannah? Where are Kim and all the others going?"

"To a private airfield in Van Nuys. They're leaving the country tonight."

"Tell the 911 operator to call Damon Wolfe at the LA Field Office with that information," Andi said.

"Okay. But I don't want you to die."

"And I don't want you to die," Andi told her. "Go now."

As Hannah ran out of the room, Cooper pulled the burner phone out of his pocket and called Flynn again. This time the agent picked up.

"I just got your message," Flynn said. "I was about to call you."

"I found Andi." He explained quickly and tersely where they were, what they'd found out, the need to stop the group at the Van Nuys airport, and finished with the fact that a bomb was set to go off in less than nine minutes.

"Tell me what the device looks like," Flynn said, not wasting any time.

He described it as best he could, but the ticking clock and the thick smoke made it difficult for him to see and to breathe.

"Okay, I think I know what you're dealing with," Flynn said. "I've texted my team and Damon to get to the warehouse, but you're going to need to disarm it."

"All right. What do I do?"

"You'll need to pull out three wires in the right order. Can you do that?"

"I think so."

"No," Andi said, terror in her eyes. "Cooper get out of here. I don't want you to die with me."

"We're both going to live. Tell me what to do, Flynn." He squatted down in front of the device, turning his light on it.

"There should be a longer wire in the back connecting to the clock. It's probably black."

"I see it."

"Disconnect the end going into the clock."

He held his breath, forcing his hand to be steady as he pulled the wire. Nothing happened, and he felt a rush of relief. "It's done."

"How much time is left?"

"Six minutes, eight seconds."

"Do you see a yellow wire on the left side?"

"I do."

"And a silver one behind that?"

"It looks like two silver ones, or maybe one is gold. I don't know."

"Let's concentrate on the yellow. It should be connected to what looks like a bracket."

"Got it." He gave it a pull and was met with the same relieving silence. "That's done."

"Last one," Flynn said. "But it has to be the silver, not the gold."

"The light is bad in here," he said.

"Take your time."

"I don't have time." The clock had ticked down to four minutes.

"You have to go, Cooper, please," Andi begged, trying to look over her shoulder at him. "I cannot be the reason your mother loses another son."

Her words made him sad, but he knew one truth, and he spoke it. "I'm not leaving you, Andi."

"Bradford," Flynn said. "Silver wire. You have to do it now. No one will get there in time to help you."

"I know. I'm going to do it." Before he moved, he looked back at Andi and met her gaze.

A tear fell from her eyes. "If it doesn't work, Cooper," she said. "I'm sorry for what happened to Kyle, for my part in it. I never wanted to hurt you or your family. I love you. I always have."

"It's going to work. Our story doesn't end here, not now, not like this." He turned back to the bomb and put his fingers on what he desperately hoped was the silver wire...

CHAPTER TWENTY-SIX

ANDI'S BLOOD raced through her veins as she waited for the end of the world. A million thoughts ran through her mind, all starting and ending with Cooper, with this man who she had loved and hated and everything in between. She didn't want him to die with her. But he wasn't leaving, and that fierce determination to save her life made her want to cry.

She couldn't see what he was about to do, but she could feel the tension emanating off him. He was trying to be confident, and she needed him to know that she believed in him, too.

"You can do it, Cooper," she said. "I trust you."

"I hope I don't let you down, Andi. Here goes."

She tensed for whatever was about to come, but there was one, two, three more clicks of the clock, and then there was silence.

"Oh, my God! It worked," Cooper said with massive relief. "It worked," he said again more loudly, more confidently. "The clock stopped."

She heard Flynn say something else, but it didn't even register. Her gaze was on Cooper as he came around the bed and wrapped his arms around her.

"I did it," he said.

"I knew you would."

He kissed her with all the pent-up emotion of the last few minutes: the fear, the relief, and the gratitude. It was all there and so much more. She felt overwhelmed by her feelings for him, and she savored each kiss, made so much hotter by the knowledge that they'd almost lost each other forever.

It was only the pounding of feet and shouts from people entering the building that broke them apart. Cooper ran through the thickening smoke to the doorway, flashing his light as he yelled, "We're here. We're here."

Several minutes later, firefighters entered the room. It took a few minutes to free her, and when she was finally released, pain shot down her arms and into her fingers, but it was a great feeling, because she was alive, and this could have been so much worse. They were rushed out of the building as more firefighters attacked the flames.

It was a relief to feel the cool night air on her face, to take a deeper breath without coughing. The medics ran to her and Cooper, offering them both oxygen, but she waved them off, saying they were fine. Then she turned to Cooper with questions she needed answered.

"I know you ran into Hannah and that's how you knew where I was," she said. "But why were you even in this area? How did you know to come here?"

"When I was reading your case notes, I had an epiphany. You mentioned the house for sale across the street from Hannah's house, and it reminded me of the house for sale behind Neil's house. Then I re-read what you wrote about Will coming from the opposite direction. And I thought what if Will, who was working for his dad's realty company that summer, had access to that house for sale?"

"Which is exactly what happened. Kim told me that Will took Hannah and stashed her in the house. Her husband stalled on finding the owner and getting consent for them to search the house until Will could move Hannah the next day. It was a family operation. Mr. Lassiter was in on it, too. Apparently, he had a lot of gambling debt, and Kim did it for the money. She said TJ was too stupid and stoned to be included."

"Well, I'm kind of glad about that, but hard to believe he didn't know something. Anyway, when I realized someone had grabbed you and I saw the flyer on your dad's desk about using Will to list his house, I decided to find TJ. He'd told us he had a music studio in Culver City, and I found one named Wave, and that's where I went. It's just down the street. TJ wasn't there, but I saw the sign for the staging company and was thinking about that when Hannah ran into me. We finally found some good luck."

"I'll say." She looked back at the building. "I didn't realize it was a warehouse for furniture staging but that makes sense. I hope some evidence survives the fire."

"I hope your team stops that plane before it takes off." He paused. "Speaking of which…"

She turned her head as Flynn and Savannah joined them. Savannah gave her a hug while Flynn shook Cooper's hand.

"That was too close," Flynn said, moving away from Cooper to give her a brief embrace. "Are you all right, Andi?"

"I'm fine now. Thanks for helping Cooper."

"He did the heavy lifting. There was a second there when…" Flynn couldn't finish his statement.

She nodded in understanding. "I know. It's almost worse to be the person on the phone, to give the control to someone else."

"It's definitely not worse," Cooper interjected.

Flynn grinned. "You're right. Not worse, but still not fun."

"Where's Hannah?" she asked, suddenly realizing she hadn't seen her yet.

"She's talking to Nick." Flynn tipped his head to the pair standing across the street.

"What happened at the airfield?" Cooper asked. "Did you get them?"

"Yes," Flynn replied. "Caitlyn just texted that they took over the plane before it could leave and have twenty plus people in custody including several pregnant women and two babies, one of whom they believe to be Elisa Benedict."

"Thank God," Andi said, as relief ran through her. "I was hoping Elisa would be with them, but I wasn't sure if they'd already sent her to a buyer. It's a baby smuggling, illegal adoption operation that spans several countries, I believe. I don't know if Kim Lassiter is the boss, but she's high up in the organization. Kristine was involved, Daniel, the employees at the Baby Time Boutique, the lawyer, Sergio Molina, and I don't know who else."

"We'll get to the bottom of it. The group will be taken down to the LA office where there is more space for holding and interrogation."

"I need to talk to Hannah," she said.

"So do I," Cooper said.

"Go ahead," Flynn told her. "But be aware that we have to take Hannah into custody as well, until we know her involvement in all of this."

"She saved my life, Flynn. She jumped out of a moving car to do that, and she gave everyone up. Plus, she was kidnapped when she was two. She's a victim."

"She's also a participant," he said. "But all that will work in her favor."

She understood what he was saying, but she was going to do everything in her power to make sure Hannah didn't pay for a crime she was forced into. They walked down the street to join Nick and Hannah.

"Glad to see you're in one piece," Nick said.

"Thanks to Hannah," she said again. "I need a few minutes with her."

"Go ahead," he said, stepping away.

"I'm so glad you're alive," Hannah told her.

"I'm alive. Cooper was able to disarm the device."

"How did you do that?" Hannah asked Cooper.

"Very carefully," he said. "I'm really grateful to you, Hannah. I never would have found Andi if you hadn't come back to save her."

Hannah bit down on her lip, clearly holding back tears. Andi was once again caught by the familiarity of the moment. Hannah, as a two-year-old, had never liked to cry. Even when she got hurt, she tried to hold it in, like she was holding it in now.

"I'm sorry I didn't believe you right away," Hannah said. "I'm even more sorry I told my mother that you called me Hannah. I think that's when they realized you were a threat."

"They knew that long before you said anything, Hannah. It's not your fault. Who did you think was your mother?" she asked.

"Her name is Veronica Kuchova. I really had no idea she wasn't my mother, that I was kidnapped as a child. But now I think back to little things, like my mom never wanted to talk about my dad, who died before I was born. She also didn't care to talk about my birth or how I was when I was a baby. I thought she just didn't remember, or it was too painful, because she remembered being alone, without my father. But now I realize she didn't know anything about my birth, because someone handed me to her. I don't know why they gave me to her." Hannah shook her head in confusion. "There are so many things I don't understand. Like my mom, Veronica, she said she'd lost a baby once, and it was the most horrific thing she'd ever been through. Having me was the only thing that kept her from going crazy. But I wasn't hers. And as a mother, I don't know how she could live with the fact that she'd taken someone else's child. I don't know her at all."

"It will take time to figure it all out," she said, putting a hand on Hannah's shoulder. "Are you hurt? Do you need to go to the hospital?"

"I don't want to go to the hospital. They might look for me there."

"They've all been arrested, Hannah. Everyone on the plane."

"Everyone?"

"Yes. You're safe now, Hannah. I won't let anything happen to you."

Hannah didn't look completely convinced, probably because she'd seen her tied up to a bed only a few minutes earlier.

"Do my real parents think I'm dead?" Hannah asked.

"I don't know," she answered honestly.

"You didn't tell them you found me?"

"Not yet. I didn't have any proof it was you, just my instincts. I didn't want to raise their hopes."

"So, there's a chance I'm not Hannah?" she asked in confusion.

"I think you are. The scar on your arm is very significant. But a DNA test will take all the doubts away."

Hannah nodded. "I can't have any doubts. I don't want to see them until I'm sure I'm their kid."

"I understand." She paused. "My FBI team is going to need to talk to you at length, Hannah. You'll go down to the offices and you'll go over everything you know. You need to be completely honest and open. Don't try to protect anyone, not even your mother."

Hannah gave her a troubled look. "I heard her scream for me when I jumped out of the van. I think she did love me."

"She can love you and still have made bad decisions."

"She loves babies. She runs the boutique. She has always wanted to help women become mothers."

She could see that Hannah was trying very hard to weigh what she thought she knew against what she'd seen in the warehouse, namely her being tied to a bed with a bomb next to her head.

"Am I going to be in trouble for what they did?" Hannah asked. "Because I did some things, too."

"What exactly did you do?" she asked. "Can you tell me what was going on?"

"Aunt Kim would fly in pregnant girls from poor countries,

and then some midwives would take care of them in the ware-house until they gave birth. Then they would pay them and send them back home. Their babies would be adopted by parents who were having trouble getting kids through the normal channels. I thought everyone was getting what they wanted. The girls weren't mistreated, and the babies went to loving homes. I some-times took supplies to the warehouse."

"You said Aunt Kim, but she's not really your aunt."

"Everyone called her Aunt Kim. I don't know why. I just grew up knowing her that way. I didn't think she was that nice to my mom and she was never friendly to me."

"Maybe she was afraid of getting too close to you, because she lives next door to your real parents. Every day she saw your mom and dad she knew you were alive and living a lie with someone else." She shook her head in bemusement. "It's hard to believe."

"Aunt Kim wanted you to die. She said it was time to get you out of her way. She mentioned an explosion was coming soon. That's when I knew I had to get out of the van. When it slowed down, I threw open the door and jumped."

"You could have been killed."

"I didn't think about that. I just knew I had to get away. I thought they might follow me, but they needed to get on the plane and leave the country. So, I guess they let me go."

"I'm really glad you took such a courageous leap to save my life, Hannah."

"I think you saved mine, too."

Andi moved forward and wrapped her arms around Hannah. "It's going to be okay now. Everything will be fine. I'll make sure of it." As she stepped back, Flynn and Nick came over.

"Nick will drive Hannah to the office," Flynn said. "Why don't you and Bradford head over to the Benedict's house? An agent will meet you there in about twenty minutes with Elisa.

And Andi, I don't want to see you in the office until tomorrow at the earliest," he told her. "Get some rest. You look like hell."

"There's so much to do," she protested.

"And you'll be doing a lot of the wrap-up, but not tonight. I think you're out of danger. Whoever wasn't on that plane is probably more concerned with saving themselves, than hurting you."

"I think so, too." She gave Hannah an encouraging smile. "I'll see you tomorrow. Just tell the truth. That's the best thing you can do now."

"I will," Hannah said.

She turned to Cooper. "Let's go deliver some good news."

It was past ten o'clock at night when they pulled up in front of the Benedict's house. Andi had forgotten to ask Flynn if anyone had notified the family but judging by the lights blazing in every room in the house, everyone was up, so they must have gotten word.

As they got out of the car, a black SUV pulled up behind them, with Beck behind the wheel. Caitlyn got out and opened the back door. Andi ran down the sidewalk to catch her first glimpse of the smiling face of Elisa Benedict, who was grabbing her toes and looking absolutely perfect, not a scratch on her. A wave of gratitude ran through her. This story was going to have a happy ending.

"Why don't you do the honors?" Caitlyn said, as she pulled the baby out of the car seat and handed her to Andi. "Beck and I are heading to the LA office to help with the interviews."

"Happy to do so," she said, cuddling the wide-awake baby, who was giving her a sweet smile. "You're home," she told Elisa. "Back where you belong."

They walked up to the house and had no sooner stepped

onto the porch when the door opened, and Neil and Claire ran out.

She handed Elisa to Claire, who was sobbing again, but this time they were happy tears.

"Oh, my God! Oh, my God!" Neil said as he put his arm around his wife and child.

His parents came onto the porch next and told them all to come inside.

She and Cooper followed the family into the house. As Claire and Neil's parents went into the living room, Neil turned to them with a grateful and weary expression.

. "Thank you," he said, his eyes filled with moisture. "When Agent MacKenzie called, I still wasn't sure it was true. But you brought our girl home. And I can't tell you how thankful I am. I know I didn't treat you very well, Agent Hart. I was suspicious, angry, and hostile—"

"You were afraid for your daughter," she interrupted. "That was completely understood and never a factor in our investigation."

"Agent MacKenzie said you'd give me the details, but all I really need to know right now is if she was hurt in any way." He licked his lips. "I don't even want to say it, but—"

"It doesn't appear that she was abused at all," she reassured him. "She was very well cared for, because she was going to be given to a family who wanted to adopt a baby. Those parents probably would have had no idea that she had been kidnapped. She would have gone with a new identity."

"How is that even possible?" Neil asked in amazement. "Who takes a baby without knowing everything about them, who their parents are, where they came from?"

"Someone desperate," Cooper said. "But all that matters is that Elisa is home."

"I don't know that I'll ever take my eyes off her again. The FBI told me Kristine was involved and Daniel Guerrero, too. They were people I trusted. I guess Solange didn't know anything about it, but I don't know that I can ever trust her again. I don't know that I can trust anyone except my family to be in my house, to take care of my daughter."

"She's safe now," Cooper said. "That's what matters. Go. Be with your daughter. We'll talk to you tomorrow."

"I will." He paused. "Agent MacKenzie told me that you ran into some trouble, and by the looks of both of you and the smell of your clothes, I can imagine that it was bad. I brought you into this. I put your lives in danger."

"We're fine," Cooper said. "We feel better than we look."

"Well, thank you again."

As Neil went to join his family, they left the house. They'd just gotten into the car when a news van pulled up in front of the house.

"Looks like the story is out," Cooper said.

"A good story this time." She settled back in her seat, the adrenaline starting to drain from her body, leaving her feeling overwhelmingly tired.

"Where to?" Cooper asked. "Do you want to go back to your dad's house? Or we could go to a much nicer hotel if I can use my credit card now?"

"You can. The danger is over, and I don't want to go to a hotel or my dad's house. What about your place? Will you take me home, Cooper?"

He smiled back at her. "I can do that."

CHAPTER TWENTY-SEVEN

THEY ARRIVED at his condo about twenty minutes later. He'd bought the luxury two-bedroom home, which was located on the top floor of a three-story building overlooking the Pacific Ocean, three years earlier. Like Andi, he'd always wanted to live at the beach, and he'd finally gotten there. He parked in the garage, and they took the elevator up to his unit.

When he let Andi into his home, he felt like he could finally relax. It had only been a few days since he'd been home, but it felt like a lifetime had passed in between.

Andi wandered around, noting the floor-to-ceiling windows, and the bright, airy, beachy space with an approving gaze. "This is really nice, Cooper. Beautifully decorated, too. Did you do it yourself?"

"I had some help from a friend."

"Your friend did a great job. It's comfortable and inviting. I bet you have a great view."

"Phenomenal," he said. "Are you hungry? Do you want anything to eat or drink?"

"No. I think I just want to go to bed."

He nodded. "You should sleep. You can have my bed. I'll stay in the guestroom."

She shook her head. "That's not going to work for me."

"Well, I'm not letting you sleep in the guestroom after everything you've been through tonight. You haven't said anything about your head, but since you were knocked out, I'm fairly sure you have a headache."

"It's gone down to a dull ache," she admitted. "But I don't want to sleep in the guestroom, either. I want to sleep with you, Cooper. I want to hold you, and I want you to hold me, and…" She gave a weary shrug. "That's really all I want."

"That's all I want, too." He took her hand and led her upstairs to his room.

"This is also amazing," she said, as her gaze swept the large room, which had incredible views in the daylight. She kicked off her shoes and sat down on the edge of the bed. "The mattress is so soft and comfortable."

"Stretch out. Make yourself comfortable."

"I'm dirty. I smell like a fire. I should take a shower, but I don't know if I have the energy."

They both smelled like smoke, and he'd sweated bullets when he'd dismantled the bomb, so a shower was a good idea. But he had a better one. "How about a soak in my jacuzzi tub?" he suggested. "Whirlpool jets, hot water, some nice smelling bath salts that my sister gave me for my birthday that I'll never use."

Andi smiled. "Monica gave you bath salts? Do you even take baths?"

"More since I got the big tub. You'll love it." He walked into the adjacent bathroom and turned on the water and the jets, then threw in the bath salts.

Andi came into the bathroom a moment later. "The bathroom is just as spectacular as everything else. I feel like I'm in a five-star hotel."

"Well, I plan on giving you five-star service." He put his hands on her waist as he took a kiss.

"I like the way it's going so far," she said with a smile. "But I'll need a little help in the tub. Will you join me?"

He pulled off his shirt in response, and she laughed.

"I guess that's a yes," she said.

He stripped off the rest of his clothes, while she got undressed, and then they got into the tub together.

"Oh, my God, this is heaven," she said, then dunked under the water completely, coming back up with another smile. "I already feel better."

"Me, too," he said, as he sank under the bubbles, rinsing off the last of the smoke.

When he came up for air, Andi's smile was even bigger now. "What are you grinning at?" he asked.

"I can't believe we're taking a bath together. Me and Cooper in a tub. Who would have thought this would ever happen?"

"I had some thoughts about it when we became teenagers. A tub wasn't on my mind but seeing you naked was definitely on the menu. Of course, you weren't thinking about that at all."

"I was immature. I was a tomboy. And the idea of falling in love while my parents were fighting a war in my house wasn't at the top of my list."

"I know. You had a lot going on. You weren't ready. That's why I never said or did anything."

"We've come a long way, Cooper."

"Yes, we have."

Her smile suddenly dimmed. "Do you think that Kyle will always be between us? Can you ever look at me and not think about him and what happened?"

"A few days ago, I would have said no," he admitted, hating the disappointment that ran through her pretty brown eyes. "But that's because I'd built you up in my head to be this terrible person who betrayed me. When you came back to town, I couldn't see that image anymore, because the real girl was standing right in front of me. And I liked her." He paused, wanting her to understand the complexity of his feelings. "I'll never not miss Kyle, not wish he was here, but I know so much more now about everything that happened. I don't blame you,

Andi. You're not responsible for Kyle's death. It was unfair of me to put that on you. I know he had other problems, deep-rooted issues that would have surfaced if that night had never happened. I was just so locked in on the injustice of it all, so filled with guilt that I couldn't let it go. Blaming you took some of the pressure off of blaming myself."

"You weren't to blame, Cooper. You wanted to help Kyle, to fix his problems. I understand that because you and I are both fixers. Your mom told me that the other day, and she was right. We can't stand it when something breaks. It drives us even more crazy when we can't put it back together. But some things that are broken just can't be repaired." She paused. "But you know all that, because you're very smart and you've made a living studying people, their motivations, and their actions."

"I had a blind spot when it came to Kyle. But some good has come out of my tunnel vision. I still believe there are biases in the law enforcement system and repairs that should be made."

"I can't disagree. Look at Agent Burnett. He was supposed to be someone we trusted. But he was dirty. He was selling out innocent kids for money."

"I wonder why they killed him?" he mused.

"I know the answer to that. Kim said that Burnett thought the heat was on him because he was taken off the case. Then he wanted to ruin everything by saving Elisa and taking the credit, so he could come off the hero and allay any suspicions. Kim wasn't going to give up the payday that Elisa's illegal adoption would bring in. She was worried that Burnett was going to sell her out, so she started tracking his communications. When she saw him reaching out to me, she decided he was no longer of use to her. So, she took him out. She said it coldly, not a trace of emotion in her voice, even though she implied that they'd had a personal relationship going back twenty years. I couldn't believe I was looking at the woman who made the best brownies at the elementary school bake sale. It's like she was a completely different person. She was completely without remorse. It was all about business and money."

"I wondered why she didn't have someone shoot you in the garage. Why kidnap you? Not that I'm not happy that's the path she chose," he said.

"Kim said she was tired of me getting away and not being able to trust that I was going to be gone for good, so she wanted to see me face-to-face. I think she wanted me to know how brilliant she'd been in helping to create this international operation."

"Well, I never would have guessed the Lassiters were involved in something like this," he admitted. "Especially not Kim. She really did lead a double life. She lived next to the Montgomerys and witnessed their pain every day, and she never said a word. That's shocking."

"I said that to her. But she just said Hannah had a good life and was well taken care of. She didn't take her neighbors' pain into consideration at all."

"I have to say, though, that Will should have been as big of a suspect as my brother. They basically had the same messed up alibi, but everyone thought Will was normal and Kyle was the weird one."

"Will is going to pay for what he did. They all are. And we'll figure everything out in the days to come. Nothing else has to happen tonight. We don't need to talk about it anymore." She paused. "Unless you want to talk about it. I shouldn't be telling you what to do."

He grinned. "You love telling me what to do. You always have."

"You're right. I love telling everyone what to do," she said with a laugh. "I'm still bossy."

"But you're a lot of other things, too. You're a fierce fighter for right, a protector of the weak and the innocent, a true warrior, and a great detective."

Her eyes watered. "That's the nicest thing you've ever said to me."

"Well, get used to it, because there's more where that came from."

"You're amazing, too, Cooper," she said. "You're insightful, calm, smart, and talk about brave—you risked your life for me tonight. I don't know why you did that. I don't know why you didn't leave me there. At the beginning of this week, I was your mortal enemy."

"And now you're the woman I've fallen in love with." He looked deep into her eyes. "I love you, Andi. I should have said that before I pulled the wire. Because it would have sucked if you'd never heard me say the words. I just didn't want you to think I was telling you I loved you because you'd said it first. Stupid."

She slid across the tub and framed his face with her hands. "Don't call the man I love stupid. I won't stand for it."

He smiled. "Then don't call the woman I love bossy."

"I love how you know me, Cooper. No one has ever known me the way you do."

"No one has ever known me the way you do, Andi. I think I fell for you when I was eight years old—the first day we met. You were digging for worms, and I had never met a girl who wasn't afraid of a worm."

"And I had never met anyone who wanted to make all my crazy ideas come to life. When things were hard, I escaped to you. You made me feel safe and heard and cared for. You were there for me when I needed you."

"Until I wasn't."

"Until I wasn't," she countered. "Which brings me back to the same question I asked you a few minutes ago. Can we move forward without feeling the pain we caused each other? I'm afraid we're living in euphoria right now. We're grateful to be alive. Will the hurt come back when the euphoria is gone?"

"Not for me," he said with certainty. "I don't want to look back anymore, not unless it's to remember something good. I don't need the past, I need the future, and I need it to be with you. You're the reason no one else has ever been good enough. It was always you, Andi."

She leaned in and gave him a long, loving kiss. "That was the perfect answer. I need you, too, Cooper." She took a breath, giving him a wicked smile. "So, can I be bossy again?"

"Am I going to like it?"

"Oh, you're definitely going to like it." She slid onto his lap and gazed into his eyes. "I want us to be as close as we can possibly get."

"I can make that happen." He wrapped his arms around her, knowing that he was never going to let her go.

Andi woke up Friday morning in Cooper's arms, feeling refreshed and happy, ready for the future. But before she could fully move on, she needed to answer some of the lingering questions in her mind.

After coffee and a quick breakfast on the deck, which had an amazing view of the ocean, she and Cooper headed down to the LA field office.

Flynn and Damon met them in a conference room to give them an update. Although Damon didn't look too thrilled with Cooper's presence, he said he could stay, but some details would be discussed outside of his presence.

"Let's start with the basics," she said. "Who did you bring in last night? And do we know exactly who was running the operation? Was it Kim Lassiter?"

"There were three primaries," Flynn answered. "Kim Lassiter's travel agency was used to transport the pregnant women into the country. The realty company started by her husband, Steve, then taken over by her son, Will, used the staging warehouse to house the pregnant girls. They had plenty of beds and other items of furniture, and the location was private. Two nurse midwives took care of the women and the babies. Once the women gave birth, the babies were sold through Sergio Molina's adoption agency. The women were paid a flat fee. Some returned to their native countries. Others stayed and worked at the store."

"Kim said that her son TJ was not involved," Andi put in. "Is that true?"

"According to everyone we spoke to, TJ was not in on it. Apparently, they didn't think he could keep a secret," Flynn replied. "But we brought him and his girlfriend in this morning, and we'll be interviewing them extensively in the next few days."

She nodded. "Who else have you been talking to?"

"As I mentioned, there were three primaries. The second was Sergio Molina, who is Kim Lassiter's brother-in-law, by the way. He's married to Kim's sister, Joan."

"I didn't even know she had a sister," Cooper muttered.

"Neither did I," she said. "What does Joan do?"

"She works at an investment company that is a front for the money they were laundering," Damon interjected. "Joan and Kim both have roots in Eastern Europe. Their mother was from Poland, and their aunt was a midwife in Belarus when this started. She became the funnel from Europe to the US. We have our allies in Europe working to bring down that part of the operation."

"What about the baby boutique?" Cooper asked. "What's the tie-in there?"

"The store was owned by an LLC, but digging down we were able to tie it to Sergio Molina," Flynn said. "The manager, Veronica Kuchova, came over from Belarus twenty years ago as one of the pregnant girls. Unfortunately, she lost her baby and feeling sorry for her, Kim and Joan let her work at the store. Veronica is the one who took Hannah in when she was too sick to be adopted. When it was time to sell Hannah, Veronica put her foot down, and said she was keeping her. I guess they decided to go along with her, mostly because there wasn't as

much demand for two-year-old children. The family that originally wanted a toddler had gotten another child."

"Another *stolen* child?" she asked.

"We're looking into that," Flynn said grimly. "Getting back to
Veronica, she became an important part of the organization and
managed the store, which was also used to move money and to
provide supplies needed for the pregnant women and their
babies."

"What about Daniel Guerrero and Kristine Rozic?" Cooper
asked. "Was Daniel on the plane? Has Kristine woken up yet?"

"Daniel was on the plane and is talking," Flynn answered.
"He took Elisa out of the house and hid her in the home that was
for sale behind the Benedict's house as you suggested. He was
part of a crew of hired muscle, although he was lower level.
Daniel was driving the car that almost ran you down. His friend,
Tyler, panicked when he heard we were at the gym looking for
him. He was beaten to scare him into not talking."

"By Daniel?" she asked.

Flynn shook his head. "The organization had several hit men
on the payroll, the ones who attacked the safehouse and planted
the explosives at your townhouse and in the warehouse. They
were also on the plane and have lengthy criminal records."

"How long has this all been going on?" Cooper asked.

"More than twenty years," Damon replied. "And Agent
Burnett was a part of it. I had no idea that he was dirty when I
took the case away from him. I just didn't want a conflict with
him and Mr. Benedict. But he was a big part of their scheme.
Burnett helped them secure fake identities. He protected them
when they had to steal a child to fulfill a contract, as in the case
of Hannah Montgomery and Elisa Benedict." Damon turned to
Cooper. "That's why Agent Burnett focused on your brother, Mr.
Bradford. He needed a scapegoat to take the heat until the news
died down."

Andi looked at Cooper. He already knew that, but she

suspected it still felt good for him to hear someone from the FBI admit what he'd known all along.

"I'm sorry about that," Damon continued.

Cooper nodded. "Me, too."

"At any rate, Agent Burnett was planning to take over the investigation into Elisa's disappearance until I took him off it. That's when he got nervous and desperate. He must have figured if he could get rid of you, Andi, that I'd have no choice but to put someone from this office on the case. Then he'd have more access."

"Kim Lassiter told me he wanted to rescue Elisa and take the credit to allay what he thought were your suspicions," she told Damon. "That's why she killed him."

"Ms. Lassiter hasn't done any talking, but that makes sense," Damon said. "The group's biggest mistake was letting Hannah jump out of that van. If that hadn't happened, they'd be on the other side of the world by now and dispersed throughout Europe."

"How is Hannah doing?" she asked.

"We got her a few hours of sleep in a safehouse last night," Damon said. "We also checked her DNA. She's Hannah Montgomery."

Andi blew out a breath of relief. "I knew she was, but I'm glad the test came out that way. I would have felt horrible if I had convinced her she was kidnapped and adopted by a criminal family if it wasn't true."

"She wants to see her family today, but she'd like you to go with her."

"I would love to go with her. I don't know what her legal jeopardy is…"

"It will be minimal," Damon answered. "She's been very cooperative in providing us information and evidence. Because she was a victim of this operation, too, I think she'll be able to walk away and get her life back."

"What about her parents?" she asked. "Have you told them you found Hannah?"

"Not yet. But I'm happy to make the call now, if you're ready to take her home."

"I'm ready," she said, knowing she'd learn even more in the upcoming days. But getting Hannah back to her parents seemed like the only thing she needed to do right now.

―――――――

As Cooper drove her and Hannah back to their old neighborhood, Andi felt nervous, and she could feel the same tension coming from Cooper and Hannah. All three of them were going back in time, and she wasn't sure any of them were prepared.

She didn't know how the call had gone from Damon to the Montgomerys, because they'd left as soon as he'd told them that her parents were home and waiting to see her.

"Do you think they'll recognize me?" Hannah asked, breaking the taut silence. "I was only two years old when I was taken away. I'm sure I don't look like their baby."

She turned in her seat, to meet the uncertain look in Hannah's eyes. "They'll know you, and you'll know them."

"It's been a long time, almost my entire life," Hannah said worriedly. "I hope it's not too late to go back."

"I'm sure they've spent every minute of the last eighteen years dreaming of this moment, Hannah."

Hannah nodded, but there was still stress in her eyes. "They're good people, right?"

"Yes. Your father is a dentist, and your mom is a teacher. They volunteer in the community. They're wonderful people. They've just been really sad for a long time."

"Do they have other children?"

"No. They never had any other kids."

As Cooper pulled up in front of Hannah's house, she wasn't

surprised to see an FBI team at the Lassiter's house. They'd search every inch for potential evidence.

But as her gaze moved to the Montgomery's home, she was taken back in time, to the hot summer night Hannah had disappeared. This street had been filled with the lights of police vehicles. The neighbors had come out on their porches, afraid of what they were about to find out. And she and Cooper had spent the last few minutes of their friendship together, having no idea what was to come.

When they got out of the car, the front door of the house opened, and Ray and Shari Montgomery came walking out of the house hand in hand.

They were older now. Ray's hair was white, and Shari had put on a few pounds. Their expressions were a mix of hope, disbelief, and fear.

They met them halfway up the path to the porch. "Hannah?" her mother asked, her voice trembling. "Is it you? Is it my darling girl?"

"It's me," Hannah said, uncertainty in her voice.

"You're so beautiful," Shari whispered. Then she opened her arms.

Hannah hesitated, and Andi held her breath until Hannah walked into her mother's embrace.

Mother and daughter hugged tightly for a long minute, with Hannah's father finally joining in, putting his arms around both his wife and his daughter.

Then he looked at them and said, "Thank you for bringing her home. It's the miracle we prayed for every single night." Ray shook his head. "I couldn't believe it was the Lassiters. They were our friends. We thought they shared our pain, but they caused it."

"We're not talking about that now," Shari said. "We're just going to celebrate having our daughter back. Will you come inside, Hannah? We don't want to overwhelm you, so whatever you want."

"I'd like to come inside." Hannah turned back to Andi. "Thanks for telling me who I am."

"I'm so glad you're home," she said, tears gathering in her eyes.

Cooper put his arm around her as they watched the Montgomerys walk into their house.

When the door closed, they turned to each other.

"Eighteen years ago, we were right here," Cooper said. "We've come full circle."

"With far too much time in between," she said, looking into his eyes. "I was afraid to come back to LA. I didn't want to face the memories or see you or my father or anyone connected to my past. But I landed right in the middle of it all. I'm really glad now I made the move."

"Hannah might not be with her family if it wasn't for you."

"Or you. We solved this one together. What do you want to do now?"

"Whatever you want to do." He echoed a refrain from the past that made her smile.

They'd never be able to escape their memories, but she felt confident now that they could focus on the good ones, and they had had a lot of great times together.

"I have one idea," he continued.

"Does it involve us getting naked again?"

"Not right away. I think that might give my father a heart attack."

"You want to see your parents?" she asked in surprise.

"I want to tell them Hannah is home, that Kim and her family were responsible for Hannah's disappearance. My parents always believed in Kyle's innocence, but I think they deserve the truth before it hits the press."

She nodded in agreement. "Of course. But what do you want to say about us? We haven't talked about how we're going to make anything work. Personal past aside, our jobs could put us on opposite sides. You're not a fan of law enforcement, and I love my job."

Cooper took her hands in his. "I'm sure we're going to fight, because we're us," he said with a smile. "We're both stubborn and determined, but I know where your heart is and you're always on the side of right. That's the side I plan to be on, too. We'll figure out the rest."

"That could be a lot to figure out. Relationships can be difficult."

"I understand that love scares you, Andi. You've lived the dark side of love through your parents. But we are not them."

"I know. You are nothing like my father. You would never treat a woman you loved like he does."

"I would not."

"I'm not scared of anything when I'm with you, Cooper. You've always made me feel safe. I trust you completely."

"And I trust you, Andi."

Her heart soared with his words. She'd been afraid it was easier to win his love than his trust.

"As for what I'm going to say to my parents," he continued, "How about—I finally woke up and stopped hating the only girl I've ever loved, the woman I intend to be with now and forever. What do you think about that?"

"It's perfect. And by the way, we are definitely going to live at your house. I want that ocean view."

A smile curved his lips. "I have two bikes in the garage, so we can go exploring any time you want, just like the old days."

"I'd love that, but when we go for a ride, we are not going to look for mysteries or trouble."

He laughed. "There's no way either of us can make that promise. But I can promise that I'm going to love you for the rest of your life, Andi."

"And I'm going to love you, Cooper."

WHAT TO READ NEXT...

Want more thrilling romantic suspense?

Don't miss DEADLY TRAP, the next book in the OFF THE GRID:
FBI Series, featuring Agent Nick Caruso

Have you missed any of the books in this series?

Barbara Freethy is a #1 New York Times Bestselling Author of 85 novels ranging from mystery thrillers to romantic suspense, contemporary romance, and women's fiction. With over 15 million copies sold worldwide, thirty-six of Barbara's books have appeared on the New York Times and USA Today Bestseller Lists. She is a six-time finalist and two-time winner of the RITA for her single title contemporary novels. Her books are available in digital, print, and audio formats.

Barbara is known for her twisty thrillers and emotionally riveting romance where ordinary people end up having extraordinary adventures.

For more information on Barbara's books, visit her website at www.barbarafreethy.com

Ingram Content Group UK Ltd.
Milton Keynes UK
UKHW042337050523
421194UK00028B/164/J